DARSHAN

DARSHAN

A Collection of Short Stories

Massimo Abbruzzetti

VANTAGE PRESS
New York

The stories presented herein are works of fiction. Any similarity between the characters appearing in them and any real persons, living or dead, is purely coincidental.

FIRST EDITION

Published by Vantage Press, Inc.
516 West 34th Street, New York, New York 10001

Manufactured in the United States of America
ISBN: 0-533-13235-5

Library of Congress Catalog Card No.: 99-94959

0 9 8 7 6 5 4 3 2 1

To Stuart
(wherever he may be)

Contents

DARSHAN

Monkey in a Monkey Suit

South East Washington. Near the Old Navy Yard.
In the Early Days of August 1994.

Friday Morning, Around Four A.M.

"They're all in there, Frenchy," the uniformed officer promulgated with excited lassitude while he made an imaginary courtly path for the homicide detective of the District of Columbia's finest to pass through.

"What's going on, Walt?" the veteran of the force asked wearily as he strolled in nervous fatigue from too many late nights through the entranceway of the abandoned warehouse as he attempted to make visual contact with this familiar cop of the crime beat.

"You'd better see for yourself . . . it's quite gruesome," he explained awkwardly as he bowed his head in disgust, as though he was ashamed of what he had witnessed.

"It's a damn mess in there. A fucking horror show to be exact." The policeman continued to convey his thoughts blamelessly while he led Detective Nevile "Frenchy" Dupree into the apprehensive scene of his worst nightmares.

Yet these vistas of terror and insanity were unfortunately becoming quite customary and regular for this aged flatfoot. Ah, yes, for the past seven years (give or take a few weeks and misbegotten days) since the spring of 1987, he believed if memory served him well, was when all this lunacy seemed to have begun. This had become to him just a series of unwelcome surprises. But come to think of it, surprises wasn't exactly the correct word for it either.

Yet, what else could you call it?

Or how else should you describe such an inhuman phenomenon of events really?

Every time this case appeared to become—and please excuse me for this inadequate phrase—but *conversant* to him, something quite bizarre or strange would happen again, like some grotesque jack-in-a-box to test his skills at adapting or adjusting to, . . . if you will, to these new and peculiar ambuscades, like a dream gone maniacal. Because, in reality, these things couldn't actually exist, . . . could they?

"Hey, Zack, what's up?" Frenchy announced with casual informality to a member of his illustrious, yet unheralded, team, as if meeting one of his very own on a quiet gravel-laid path on some nice afternoon promenade in the park.

"Shit, Frenchy, I was hoping you could answer me that. Here, take a look at this," he replied with a hardened smirk that reeked of dismay and infelicitous regret.

Subsequently what this criminal investigator of twenty-odd years had pursued and saw was something that left him spellbound and in shocked awe for now and ever more while he was forced to view this antic and, he hoped, final display of some sick mind or minds.

He thought he had seen everything imaginable at this point, having tirelessly studied and delved into this demented case with its overwhelming, continuous dread that seemed to never end since the time he was first brought into this troublesome murder spree back in late December of '89, which spanned close to fifty-six, goddamn, grueling months of misleads and dead ends for him and his busy crew.

Yet, it was truly over now, wasn't it? he prayed wishfully to himself while he lurked cautiously over the corpses of these three, last victims. Moreover, it appeared to be some sick twist of fate that the ultimate conclusion to these murders had to be in the form of a trio of sacrificial lambs in order to save a couple of venerable souls (which will remain among the unmentionable for personal reasons, if nothing else) from the utmost blasphemy.

Yes, and lambs were exactly what they were as he glared over at the morbid manifestation that looked, in a sordid sort of way, like part of a makeshift Nativity scene minus most of the main characters including the focal point, the manger, with the newborn Savior swaddled warmly inside. But these miniature representatives of the Magi syndicate were definitely here though. Yet, wise men they were not, incidently, but maybe little lost shepherds or sheep instead, led astray by some sequestered powerful and fearful force while the forsaken trinity stared infinitely in their silent and calm agonizing poses into less than peaceful nothingness.

"Pretty fucking crazy, huh, Frenchy?" good old Zack remarked in total understatement while he searched the detective's missing and absent-minded daze for any sort of rational or otherwise confirmation.

"Hhhmmm? . . . Yeah, I should say so," he practically whispered while being summoned back from his darkest conceptions as they both, in a peculiar kind of way, admired the fiend's handywork, as if they were touring one of the many numerous grand museums that this fair capital of cities had to offer, or as a strange sort of scenario-one of the most prized pieces at the Smithsonian or the National Gallery of Art during one of their gala, seasonal exhibits that one traveled from miles around to catch a glimpse of, like an Edvard Munch masterpiece or something. But this particular gifted and dedicated macabre artist chose to use the living flesh of youth in place of canvas or marble to express his yearnings and inner desires instead.

Really, he was quite good, this one. Very talented indeed. Detective Dupree recognized his signature right off the bat, as though he was a devoted follower and specialized fan of this mad Michelangelo who dabbled in the fears of his poor, poor immolations.

Therefore, because he knew this artist so very well, he could also spot and differentiate a defect or flaw in this master's work. It was merely a slight mishap, mind you. A minor mistake that most amateur and nonexperts would possibly dismiss without a second thought. But it was his specific job, which he undoubtedly took quite seriously, to point out and to have these things made aware of if one was truly to figure out the mind of one's deranged subject in order to understand the true genius behind it.

"God! Now I'm referring to this psycho creep as a genius. Man! I really have been on this on this one way too long, much too long," Frenchy shook his head with dismal displeasure.

"Yeah, I certainly know what you mean, Frenchman. Looky here—" as his partner prematurely read his mind before grabbing the still bedazzled detective forward a bit in order for the both of them to examine the remains more thoroughly.

"Three adolescent bodies, somewhere between the ages of nine and twelve. Positive I.D. of the fatals still unconfirmed. Possibly runaways or orphans," Officer Zachery Halliday spieled out all of a sudden as though reading from a grocery list or a sheet of the day's daily events.

"A pair of Caucasian children, and, the other, Afro-American." (Afro-American huh! That particular phrase, no matter what context it was used in, still always seemed to hit me right at home pretty good. But why? No matter what color they might be, a murdered child is still a murdered child just the same.) "Two of them male and one female cadaver. Probably dragged here from another location by the looks of things," and then he lowered his voice a tad as if to stress something confidential. "Anyhow, the boys that work in the lab down at the precinct should be here in a jiffy to give us the complete scoop." Then he winked at his patient sidekick and went back into his official speech gab role once more to brief his fellow officer on the latest events.

"You see, from the lack of blood, it suggests that they were possibly partially dismembered at another place. . . . Could have been anywhere though.

"Dismembered! These kids. . . . Jesus H. Christ! These children were humiliatingly mutilated was more like it. Butchered in self-aggrandized mockery. And to think that I, me, mild mannered Officer Nevile 'Frenchy' Dupree, had spoken to this beast. Had polite, social conversation with this, this thing that enjoys killing babies—because, incidentally, they were still babies to me—babies forever, that is. Which currently brings to mind nostalgic feelings about my very own dear grandma. My very own grandmother, who would have been equally appalled, if not more so, to say the very least. The same as any other loving, caring soul would be by this unspeakable abhorrence. Stunned to death, even, by this inhuman travesty. I can still remember her calling me her 'baby,' even when I was about to become a father for the very first time myself."

"You're still little babies to me, Nevile. And don't you forget it, sonny boy."

"Are you still with me, Frenchy?" Zack asked nonchalantly while he watched him shiver in his boots.

"Yeah, Sure thing, Zack," he replied with a glazed look in his eyes.

Yet as he carried on with his briefing, Officer Frenchy Dupree began to drift off into another world. A more frightening universe, where everyone appeared to be vulnerable. He seemed to go deeper and deeper into the heart of the matter while he vigorously deliberated over these maimed angelic forms. What he saw was as follows:

Their immature soulless figures, crouched and huddled together in their own individual grief, cried in paralyzed frenzy. Yet you needed no real in-depth powers of imagination to view this. Their bland and raped features screamed their silent scream. Eternal it was . . . and extremely gut-wrenching. The fault he had spoken of beforehand was that this mad designer had placed them in single file, next to one another, with their tiny legs neatly tucked and crossed, Indian-style, beneath them so that the audience of treachery could view the placement with sordid delight. But Mother Nature had foiled this dreadful greedy schema and preordained plan when the bodies' internal structure had collapsed inward on itself. Rigor mortis had slowly started to set in. Therefore the young bodies had fallen almost on top of each other as if finding comfort and relief in this naked embrace. Like piles of dead sticks and twigs balanced by involuntary circumstance as they each met in a quiet clasp of mutual disrespect.

These three musketeers were helped and aided by this inveterate position from the upright, solid foundation behind them as if in one final stand, and even in death, they were going to fight to the last man, even while their backs were literally to the wall.

"They must have been drugged or something too in order for that sick bastard fuck to be able to do that to them. Look, that poor white kid has no damn *tongue!*" Officer Zack benightedly pointed out.

"Oh, yes! No damn tongue, . . . and that poor black child wedged between the poor white girl with no eyes has no ears either. And the very worst part of it is that it was all a crazy, fucking joke."

A demented farce true, . . . but a joke just the same, . . . and this particular lark was directly aimed at yours truly.

"You may have caught us sucker, but we got the last laughhhh! He-he he-he-he-he-he-he-he-hehhheeeeeee! Catch me if you can nnniiigggaaarrrrrrrrrrrrrrrrrrrr!"

"What was that, Frenchy. What did you say?"

"Oh! Nothing. Nothing at all. I was clearing my throat is all," and then he propelled an instant smile for appearance's sake, which fooled nobody really, not even that stupid traffic cop, Zack (whose-brain-is-constantly-on-vacation) Halliday.

"Yeah, kinda gets you right here, doesn't it?" Zack, the ticket enforcer, stated, gorilla-thumping his chest with his fist to emphasize again what he thought his buddy in blue (navy blue pinstripe suit, that is) was feeling.

Yet no one could possibly know what Nevile Frenchy Dupree was feeling, except for Frenchy, the Louisiana swamp rat Dupree, of course. Actually the closest thing to being a Cajun boy, to this outmoded, Southern kid, was Momma's secret family recipe of blackened catfish. Yes, sir! He really wished he was some simple country type now, leading some simple country life instead of being this big city, urban provider and protector of the law and order and peace.

"What in the hell am I doing this fuckin' job for? What am I doing here? Am I really serving the public's trust? And what in God's name was I thinking when I swore that silly, foolish oath crap anyway! My momma and grandma were right. I'm much too soft and kind to become some rough and tough cop—no mean shit Clint Eastwood. Or better yet, Shaft types here my main man—"

"You're still little babies to me, Nevile. And don't you forget it, sonny boy."

For a haunting split second, he thought he heard these immortal words coming from the open mouth of the poor white kid. (. . . that poor white kid has no damn *tongue*!) His hollow, blood-drenched void, like some ghastly hooked fish, echoed these sounds as if this juvenile carcass was sending a ghostly message from his dear departed grandmother. Then, as though in uncanny procession, the distaff child to the speechless boy's extreme left seemed to see his trepidation entirely. And her empty, dark ruby sockets wept tears of blood so rich that it appeared to gush in streams of torture onto her small bib overalls. Then last, but not least, the boy that lay dead center, who nearly resembled his very own son, listened vacantly with his one, noticeable, numb, clogged gap to his faintly haggard heart pumping in his ancient chest, while this immobile youth leaned writhingly, frozen-stiff, upon the young girl's rigid, fragile shoulder as the thick, cooled liquid oozed from that pitch-black crevice where his small ear once used to belong as this lethal poison dripped slowly down his shiny, pale, creamy brown cheek.

They knew, he thought earnestly. *They knew that someone had made a fool out of him. . . . They knew all right.*

"Hey, Frenchy, the crew's arrived. In here, boys!" he yelled as he motioned with a wave of his arm for them to move rapidly toward where he and Officer Dupree stood. Then the noisy group, who were unavoidably crashing their little private party, obeyed immediately as they quickly got down to work.

"So who discovered them anyway?" Frenchy sighed as he rubbed his wrinkled brow with his sweaty hand.

Consequently he was pulled aside as Zack allowed the boys from down at the magic workshop to do their brilliant legerdemain without any disruption.

"Oh, Christ! I almost forgot. There's these two white punks being detained outside who found them first. Wanna talk with them, Frenchy?"

"Sure, why not. Where out back?"

"That way. But you won't get much outta them. They're buzzed on 'ecstasy' or some shit like that. Real wiggers, let me tell you." And the jolly, snowflaked policeman chuckled as he expressed the "pathetic state" of these possibly once-nice, wholesome Anglo-Saxon suburbanites who had been seduced and corrupted by the jungle and ethnic, ghetto sounds of the evil, badass Negro.

Suddenly, Frenchy shot him a sharp, hard, piercing glance, which wasn't really what it was supposedly meant to be, namely a black man's bad reaction to an ugly, racial slur. It's just that he had never expected his own fellow officer to have him accept this as just some harmless joke among pals. He could have at least had the common courtesy to say this amongst his good ole' boy breed. This he could accept. Anyhow, he wasn't overly sensitive or high-strung about the racist color thing, as some of the white folks in his department were known to have contradictorily murmured and grumbled over among themselves about their "angry" fellow brothers-in-arms of a different and darker shade. It was and had been widely debated privately, and deemed and opined, down at the station house that the minorities (mainly the black officers and other "similar-minded crew members" no less) were unfair in their behavior and that their lack of a sense of humor was what made things what they were. And that it was some kind of clever, wicked, and discriminatory reversal plot that stirred the waters actually. That, to him, seemed a farce in itself.

Nevertheless, as a matter of fact, he felt he was liberal and mature enough so that he could take a decent, funny gag as well as anyone, whether it be prejudicially based or not. Hell, one of his most favorite tomfooleries of all time was the one told to him by that two-bit comedian who worked the local clubs around here. The one that made fun of one of his preordained heroes, Mr. Jessie Jackson himself.

What happened to that motherfucking jerk anyway? That loser was always showing up at the wrong time and at the wrong place. And then, one day he just, *poof*, disappeared. *Weird,* he thought pensively.

And come to think of it, so was he. Anyway, good riddance. That's all I have to say about it. Yet sometimes he could always come up with some excellent ones that made you giggle like some silly school girl, Frenchy thought with subtle amusement as he dismembered all former thoughts from his mind for a minute.

"Oh, sorry, Frenchy. I was just foolin' is all. I didn't mean anything by it," he apologized humbly as he precociously ascertained what Officer Dupree was thinking.

Consequently, Dupree, sly crocodile, beamed his absolution. No Uncle Tom passiveness here, Jack, just erudite tactfulness was all that was required, as his tame gesture suggested that this minor cop had his permission to resume his knowledgeable inquiries without the threat of punishment.

"Ah-hum," he began at once. *Clearing his throat of the phlegm of his Kiplingarian sins no doubt,* Officer Dupree surmised sardonically while letting his fellow crime fighter have the floor.

"Anyway, where was I . . . oh yes, they're what's is fashionably referred to these days as 'taggers,' . . . you know, graffiti artist—terrorists is more like it, though," he commented cynically, mostly to himself to express his talent at wisecracking, just in case it wasn't, as he feared, so obvious to the party in question.

"But these pint-sized punks eventually claimed, after I threatened to throw them in the can if they didn't own up—" he paused to smirk, indicating that he had no plausible intention of doing this. Yet the ruse unmistakenly and successfully had worked just the same, so what the hell, "that they were just cruising and roaming around after an all-night rave party near this area and vicinity. And decided from normal, teenage boredom to leave their vandalistic trademark and symbol on something and anything as a kinda nice memento, with the aid of a spray can, no less, on this derelict building over yonder, for some extra kicks, I guess. . . . That's when they discovered these unfortunate creatures.

"I questioned them for almost half an hour, trying to figure out whether they had scrawled that other obscene note also, but they seemed much too scared and confused after I showed it to them to have done it really. But shit, who knows. The youth these days are pretty slick at getting away with junk like this. Yet my personal belief suggests otherwise. They might be bad kids, but I don't think they could possibly be that bad," he surmised ruefully.

From this awkward consequence, Frenchy grinned in almost private joy. But it was not in satisfaction at receiving this tiny reward of humility from his fellow officer, which the initial and former biased comment had created, in order to get his immaculate blessing and subordinate respect and consideration by humbly filling him in on the current events with such thorough and refined aptitude. No not for that. Ironically though, he was imagining instead what those twin, pure, ivory snow kids really looked like; and he described them in his brain thus with ersatz, zany overestimation. He pictured one particular, premature individual with cornrows or piccaninny dreads as though he was an albino freak or something as outlandishly as such. He saw them doing their pimp-roll or standing in their clean neighborhoods chillin' so to speak. Meanwhile, the other "menacing" caricatured youth, with his probable protected (and maybe rich) background, might not be as drastic in his appearance as his pal was, but still, he would have to be wearing the latest gangsta rap gear and wardrobe, too, he assumed playfully.

First the baseball cap pulled as far as it will go in order to hide their violent visions and, maybe, with the Malcolm X emblem on it for extra good measure also. Then the customary baggy pants which should be hung way past their young butts for that perfect effect. And let us not forget those oversized shirts, which they would be evidently sportin' to their knees, where one would see their brand new Air Jordans while their blank features grimaced with grave intent as they talked the "street shit," with their imitation "yo!" and their "whassup" as they greeted their fellow brothers . . . Christ! My own thirteen-year-old was more conservative than them, he bet . . . shit! He even complained about being taunted and referred to as "a little Bryant Gumble" at his school by both black and white kids! Even had a white boy's name, come to think of it, . . . Gary . . . Gary Gumble now. No Dwaynes, Shorties, or Leroys here, my main man, he wondered deeply to himself without too much regret to muddle his sportsmanlike images.

If not in breed at least in creed. You dig 5.0?

My God! Who had said that? he questioned himself as he tried to recall this instantaneously. But the answer did not come as he rattled his brain feverishly for one.

Let's face it. Though my offspring was a square, yet what a perfectly in-shape angle he was. Honor role student. Straight As every glorious year. President of his class debate team. And school track star. This parent needn't worry about drugs or guns. Nooo, sir! My boy deplored both. Well-balanced friends too, of all backgrounds and races. Who could ask for anything more?

If not in breed, at least in creed, nigger! Monkey see, monkey do!

"Huh!" he cried out between pursed lips.

"Hey, Frenchy, what's up, dude. Is anything wrong?" a more welcome voice asked while Officer Dupree's mind was bought back into focus.

"What?" he hissed almost with a hush in his tone as he returned to Officer Zachary Halliday once more.

"You said something then. I heard yah," he mentioned as if imploring him to challenge his query.

"Monkey see, monkey do," he enunciated over gnashed teeth, as though he was retarded by his own pronunciation.

"Oh yeah, . . . that," Officer Halliday commented dryly, which seemed to be a yawn of boredom of sorts, while he glared in annoying remorse at the wall directly in front of him.

"Lord knows what the fuck that means, but that weirdo was a major prime-time cuckoo after all," the cop continued onward with his armchair analysis.

Meanwhile senile Officer Dupree, the renowned "Bogwoods" imposter, was simultaneously lost and baffled by what his companion was saying, as if he was speaking some ancient, cryptic language as he stared with utter bewilderment into this policeman's face.

"Are you okay, Frenchy? You look really pale. Are you sure you want to go through with this. You know, we could send for—"

"Nahh! I'm fine. Just a little sleepy is all," he remarked drowsily as if overwhelmed by his own personal troubles. And then he peeked into the concerned cop's eyes and added with a colorful smirk, "Woozy . . . you know, from too many nights out at the country club with the senator's wives," and then he laughed some crazy cackle, which only black men seem able to pull off cleverly.

Then while Zack, the cracker cop, attempted to jazz along with him with his own white-bread version, he stopped chuckling suddenly in order to point at the wall, this time in order to physically put his tangible punctuation across before speaking.

"Yeah, yeah, sure, sure. But you still haven't told me what you think of this."

"Hummm. What?"

"This, my main man, this!"

Subsequently crazy-legs Dupree followed the invisible line of his index finger until it metaphorically touched the wall in front of him, and what he saw sent his perspiration rolling again. Written in thick, red blood were the words, "Monkey See Monkey Do," in bold type, almost.

Was I imagining this? Did my delirious brain create this? I could've sworn I heard these familiar phrases in my head just a few seconds ago—

"Well, Frenchy, what do you think?"

No, this was no figment of my imagination. This was real. So goddamn real, in fact, that it was too frightening to be anything else. But why hadn't I seen it before? You dumb, colored bastard, the clues were written in ink-blood! Right in front of your black-assed complexion, and you still needed it whipped into you in order to see it.

"Man! I have no idea. It doesn't matter now anyway." He spoke solemnly as he tried, yet, couldn't, unglue his sedate eyes from foreboding scripture.

"Yeah, I guess you're right. Just crazy shit is all it is," Officer Halliday surmised, with a hint of disappointment.

There it's laughing at you again. Laughing at you even in death. It will never stop, will it?

You may have caught us, sucker, but we got the last laughhhhh! He-he-he-he-he-he-he-he-he-he-hhheeeeeeeeeee! Catch me if you—

Just at that dull, yet heightened moment, Officer Fred Goodman approached with creeping civility from behind them while the two officers seemed lost in a fathomless daze.

"Oh, excuse me, sirs, but we're just about finished now," he said in a smooth, heedful voice in order not to alarm them. Yet his attempt failed readily, as the pair of them were startled, without conscious remorse, back to the land of the living.

"Shit, Goodman! You scared the daylights out of me. What in hell do you think you're playing at?" Officer Zachary Halliday deplored in a deflated complaint that was partially fizzled from his lack of breath.

"Sorry, sir, but—"

"But nothing. Don't you ever do that again, you hear . . . Christ! I almost wet my pants."

Frenchy started to chuckle, in mild relief actually, when he heard this, and also when he saw the perplexed look on his partner's pallid and anemic features.

"Zack, don't be hard on the boy. He's only doing his job," he remarked between fits of laughter while the upset, young officer returned to some other pressing duties at hand.

"I don't care what he's doing, I just wish he'd do it somewheres else," he demanded in mock anger.

Then as they walked toward the small group of busy men, Frenchy Dupree detected a mild controversy and tame argument going on among two fellow officers that was in its climactic stage of progress. They delicately approached the officers without a sound so that this pair of hot, verbal combatants wouldn't be inclined to end what they were inadvertently free to express between peers, which evidently went something like this:

"It's supposed to be 'See no evil, hear no evil, speak no evil,' that's all I'm saying there, Ron. The one in the middle is fine, but the other pair on either side of that colored kid is all wrong. You see?"

"Man, you're loony tunes. What in God's name are you getting at," his pal quibbled and tiffed in dramatized fury.

"Look, you moron. Just because I said that it reminded me of that saying, doesn't mean you have to cut my head off. Oh, pardon me,

Dupree, I didn't see you standing there," the embarrassed policeman stated as he turned his head in a whiplike fashion when he suddenly glimpsed his presence there.

Officer Nevile Frenchy Dupree then shook his head lazily and grunted something inaudible as he glanced over at what had remained after the bodies had been removed, and his mind began to drift on a slow current of spurious perceptions.

Only a jagged, harsh chalk and taped outline and a few splashes of dried blood was all that was left of this human tragedy. Yet even though the horrid forms were gone, the shapes of what had happened to them were still there, weren't they? He was then instantly reminded of how perplexed he had been over the intelligence and skill that this diabolical, modern-day Attila the Hun seemed to have. It appeared to come in a variety of shapes, sizes, and disguises. Hence, he also remembered how he had suffered in his inadequacies to find a rapid formula to this interchangeable and transformable evil. Then he also remembered how he had punished himself at not being able to find a cure to this cancer fast enough. At one time, he believed it would never die. He thought with his faithless failure, how it would outsmart him, beat him . . . forever, in the initial end . . . his end, that is.

Then he walked away as though these two cops hadn't even been there and the voices he thought he distinctly heard from their mouths were merely in his head, after all.

Monkey see monkey do, indeed. What a sick, pathetic animal. I hope I never see the likes of him again.

A little later on, Officer Dupree finally left that derelict and forlorn disaster area for good and arrived back outside, where the air appeared unreasonably cool. Nevertheless, he knew for a fact though, from the recent weather reports, that the temperature all through the night and well into the wee hours of the next morning was going to stubbornly stay at a staggering level, in the upper eighties region, for quite some time, until it tapered off after dawn sometime the following day. Yet, it still felt reasonably less dank outside just the same.

Maybe the humidity, which this town was famous for in these dog days of summer, wasn't so bad tonight, he guessed to his lonely self as he searched the skies for an answer, like some out-of-season groundhog. Or maybe he hadn't realized how terribly warm it had been inside that den of desecration, owing to the towering presence of death that clung to such an appalling degree in all its own profane glory in there . . . in there! In that eerie, hot atmosphere and awful stench . . . in that damp, forewarning, converted butcher shop, which he entreated himself to attempt to forget with premature, urgent naivete. Yet it had not really been finally dismissed once and for all from his own aching mind after all, as he had hoped. And probably never will. There was no point in even trying to escape it.

Even if I was foolish enough to imagine it and attempt it by simply going outside, he thought, in welcome defeat, while he tossed his jacket over his shoulder and hooked his thumb into the inside part of the collar in order to carry this heavy fabric with more convenient ease.

But then again it sure was warmer in there than it had seemed, he pondered discouragingly to his liberated thoughts, which were evidently not so free after all. Because vital questions always appear to remain. But this case would be closed for good nonetheless . . . if he could possibly help it, he dreamed on as he studied the Indian summer of consternation with further consternation.

He was basically by himself now while most of the band of crime-solving gypsies had moved on, which included Officer Zachary whose-brain-is-constantly-still-on-vacation Halliday.

Thus, as he strolled the wooden police barricades and the familiar yellow line that warned against possible intruders, which was threaded around the contaminated environs to protect the not-so-innocent from their grazing greeds, he detected a sound from behind him that was no louder than a meek breeze lingering aimlessly in the rank and profuse atmosphere. He then forced himself to turn an about-face, like some mortal weathervane. What he saw was Trooper Fred Goodman heading his way, to ask him something urgent and profound no doubt.

"Oh, excuse me, sir. I didn't mean to disturb you again, but I thought you had left already. I've sent those two kids down to headquarters for further questioning, and to maybe try to contact their parents so that they will come and retrieve them if need be. If I'd known you were still here, I would have sent them over to you pronto. Sorry, sir," he commented regretfully, as if his life was one failure after another.

"That's all right son," and then he sighed with a deep mixture of relief and regret before slapping him on the back like some forgiving father while giving him the ultimate permit to break his profound thoughts of nothing in general.

"I have all the information I need anyway. I'll just leave the rest up to you. But if you find anything new, I mean anything whatsoever from them while they are down at the station house, let me know . . . all right?"

"I'll be sure to notify you on anything that happens to come up, sir."

"Good man. And I want a full report in the morning. Got it? So now what?" he mentioned with perfect diligence as he waited for further additional developments of guidance from this previously fresh cadet.

"Oh, yes, of course, sorry, sir. There's this foreign guy from some newspaper who says he knows you and who would desire very much to speak with you. Should I send him over, sir?"

Nah! Send him away—hey! Hold on a minute. What's his name, first?"

"Something like Peter Schelker. Here's his credentials."

"Peter Schliechner. Is that his name?" But before the young policeman could respond, Dupree asked him to get him this man on the double.

"So what a surprise to see you here, now that it is all over and done with," Officer Dupree remarked half-mockingly to his old friend and adversary.

"So you believe this is finished then?" he replied with familiarity and a crafty European accent.

"Well, don't you?"

"That depends, Inspector. One can never be so sure. Can one, Officer Dupree?" as he moved in a little closer, while he watched the other policeman disappear, with strange, avid interest before resuming with his statement "—regardless of what we really want."

Then Frenchy Dupree had to laugh, and for the first time in a long while he laughed like he had not honestly laughed before in days. Maybe in months, even.

"Oh, you're beautiful, Petey, my boy, you never stop playing the aristocratic baron, do you. Even now," as he chortled in nervous fits, which caused the darkened stained patches of sweat that was exuberant under his armpits to itch when rubbed up against his tight shoulder holster every time he moved.

"I don't know what you mean, Lieutenant?" he remarked without palpable violation.

"Oh, yes, you do. I've heard that you Aryan guys don't have much of a sense of humor, but I think you understand what I mean completely. You dig." And his amusement died before he said that last line to convey that he was in no mood to mess around anymore.

Just then the man from a distant land put forth a smile while he simultaneously brushed his strawberry-blond bangs away from his face to also convey that he knew when he had pushed his luck a little too far.

"Anyhow, I suppose you'll be going home to the fatherland now. I can't say that I'll be sorry to see you go, but I must admit you've been quite a treat. And your job is done and justice has prevailed after all."

"You always seem to forget, and I always seem to have to remind you, that I am Austrian, not German. And anyway if this is the form of justice you wish to conclude this case with, then let it be so."

Consequently Officer Dupree, who had never liked his smart-alec smugness to begin with, finally grew a bit indignant towards this frigid character, and he viciously parodied the latter part of his sentence with his own customized smart-ass reply.

"Let it be so, huh. Well, I believe you've developed a sense of humor after all. Congratulations, mister. And let me tell you something else, Herr Peter, I don't want you meddling into this business any further. You got it? This case is officially closed. And it will remain closed until I say otherwise. You speakider English, good buddy?"

"If this is your desire. But what happened to the American-what is it again—oh, yes, freedom of the press. The right to—"

He cut him off just before he lost his cool.

"I've always said that you were a gutsy fella. Hey, you're right, though. It's a free country, and you can do as you please. As long as you stay within the law. You know, it's going to be hard for you to go on alone this time around, though. And I'm afraid my department is going to be quite tied up from now on. So I hope you find what you're after. All I can say is good luck." And he turned his back on him as if he had already left.

"Don't worry about me, Lieutenant. I have my assignments."

He had to yell if he wanted to be heard further, because the object of his priceless information was moving away with quite a hint of rude swiftness in his gait before he was totally finished with him. Yet not rapidly enough, mind you, but getting just beyond this Teutonic gentleman's mild, vocal scope, and presence. Just enough distance between them, in fact, to be able to pretend to ignore him.

Nevertheless, this didn't deter this persistent foreign correspondent from expressing what needed to be said.

"What concerns me though, Officer Dupree, is what you intend to do next?"

Just then, the seasoned cop stopped and decided to confront and face his pressing questions after all.

"Is that really all you want to know, Peter, my friend?" Then he paused for a moment as if it required deep concentration and thinking, and consequently, he spoke at last; "Well, here's one for your own personal diary, Mr. Reporter—I'm going to go home is all, Mr. Schliechner, just go back home. . . ."

The Worst Things
To be in bed and sleep not
To want for one who comes not
To try to please and please not.
—*Egyptian proverb:* from F. Scott Fitzgerald's Notebook

Sweet Dreams

A bright, saffron glow burned silently on the tip of a dilapidated, chemically laced cigarette. The ash smoldered to life on its tiny crown every time the young girl inhaled on the opposite end of it, which brought great appreciation to her opiated, stained heart.

She was peacefully amused by its ember warmth. Tranquil in her thoughts to the point of physical insensibility.

"Hey, girl! Quit smoking my shit," an angry voice said suddenly from somewhere in the same room but still partially beyond the realm of the young female's conscious orbit.

The owner of this harsh voice had picked up on the strong scent and immediately grew hostile to its sweet aroma.

"What are you tryin' to do anyway, fry your fuckin' brains out?" he remarked in a bitter declamation as he came into sufficient focus.

"Miguel, why don't you just mind your own damn business . . . okay?" she replied finally. Her words coming out in a mess of slurs after taking a full drag from her magic wand of delusions.

Just her having to make the effort to talk made her enraged and furious with him: conversing with him through a gauntlet of heavy smoke, which rudely interrupted and robbed her of her small pleasures.

"Listen, bitch! Remember who looks after your sorry ass. So don't be jiving me and gettin' all smart with me. You got that?" he warned, showing his aggression more by tossing his jacket across the tiny room in a dramatic stunt of braggadocio.

Nevertheless, she paid very little attention to his phony extremes.

She knew from past experiences that if he really meant to hurt her, he could easily have accomplished it without a shadow of a doubt, instead of putting on this extravagant, convulsive display of macho strength to frighten her into submission.

He saw that he was getting nowhere with her. His dominating form of verbal menace and intimidation had worn thin on her. He again put on the jacket that he had furiously discarded in an empty corner, which was kind of a symbol of his unofficial surrender.

"What do you need that stuff for? I'm clean. You're just throwing away good shit," he acknowledged while disclosing an uncommon appearance of concern for her welfare.

Yet she was unappreciative of it, too obsessed in her own weak desires for the ultimate high to admire his rare charity.

"I bet you couldn't stop doin' that for one single day," he proposed, with a glint of challenge in his eye as he grabbed her forcibly by the shoulder by brute instinct, which she rejected with a simple nudge of her fragile body.

"You're crazy," she responded with brevity, stripping his allegation of all of its momentum by not elaborating on the recent concentrated discharge.

Nevertheless, regardless of her lack of enthusiasm, he suddenly felt in the mood to pursue it a bit further.

"I'm crazy? I'm crazy? Crazy, am I?" he fumed, repeated these adversive words until they were both sick of hearing them. "You're the one that's fuckin' crazy, bitch, not me!" he hissed.

She could feel his hot breath behind her pale neck, which made the microscopic hairs stand on end. She turned her back on him with an air of bored composure, which she attempted desperately to hide behind.

"Letting yourself be eaten alive by that crap," he rebuked her severely while he practically spit into her poor, scared face. "I'm surprised you can even stand up—"

"You're the one that sells it, not me!" she argued, lashing out at him in bold foolishness.

"Hey, babe . . . I have to make a damn livin' . . . someone has to. Who do you think looks after things around here and carries your sorry, sad, sassy ass 'bout?" he said while pointing an indicating finger into her pretty, sad features to stress his meaning.

"I can quit any time," she boasted with ineffectual vengeance. "But I like it," she admitted with a basic, lazy shrug of her upper limbs. "I just need a little pick-me-up every once in a while, . . . that's all," she concluded by dragging heavily on the ever-vanishing cigarette.

"Oh, yeah! Sure you can," he smirked malevolently. "If it wasn't for me, you'd be in some gutter somewhere or with that loser. And then gettin' high all day long and screwing that motherfucker all night. Or maybe worse. Like you'd be doin' tricks for that jerk-off again or somethin' like that," he conceded with self-proclamation.

"I don't need to put up with this! And I definitely don't need you! I'm sick of you always telling me how useless I am without you!" she cried out with absolute disgust and sorrow in her aching throat, and she threw the worthless butt away with deep resentment when she was done with it.

She rose to her feet to face up to him.

"I'll show you! I'll quit! I can make it on my own . . . and then . . . and then, I'll get outta this piss hole and away from you for good, too!" she exclaimed in shaky assertiveness.

"Oh, yeah! So where are you goin' to go?" he asked, mocking her empty threat.

"I don't know yet. But I'll do it, you'll see," she responded with uncertainty, which appeared to cripple her mental strut of novice independence.

As if a hefty mantle had inadvertently devolved, both intractable parties had become regrettably mute, which ironically made the "heavy" in this particular tragic scenario bulk to her flawed, but still quite potent, sirenlike will.

"Look, baby, I'm sorry for what was said. I'm just uptight right about now. Okay, sugar?" he apologized instantly as he had sympathy for her all of a sudden. He knew he had beaten her, and his shallow victory was quite sour on his tart tongue indeed, which was expressed very obviously in his street-savvy features.

She merely buried her face in her open displeasure, as she sensed that she was about to weep, and folded her narrow, bony arms up in nonverbal defiance.

"Listen, I've got to go. Don't fret over what I just said. Everything's cool. Are you going to be all right?" speaking softly to her wounded ego while he brushed her mousy hair from her sad face of discontent.

"I'll be back later. Okay?" he remarked cautiously while he kissed her gently on the forehead.

She merely nodded like a deaf mute in reply. Still too ashamed to look him in the eye as he opened the door of their apartment with grit, cocky perseverance that was a gesticulation which he prepared fanatically every day of his life. Like an automatic safety switch, that was his only weapon of permanence to combat this ugly, decadent, synthetic jungle that he attempted to survive in.

Later, she paced the floor for awhile, still heeding his afflicting sermon. She knew he was right—sort of. Yet what did he expect from her anyway? Her life was going nowhere. He knew that better than she. The drugs helped her cope with tomorrow and all the miserable days after, and also aided her in escaping from the painful present. And that was all she ever really asked for. And that's all she actually wanted from this unfair exchange. She could abandon it anytime. But why? To prove a point? Yes! Why not. Nevertheless she'd show him, that creep. She'd lived without him before. Right? Why not again?

When she felt more confident, she impulsively reached for another joint without a second thought, and as she put it to her solicitous lips, she realized what she was faultlessly doing. Before she had a chance to savor the delicate paper wrapping in her hungry mouth, she expelled it from her moist lips in disgruntled revolt. She then became quite upset by her own tottery intolerance.

"What's wrong with me!" she demanded. "I don't need this garbage!" She questioned herself through forced tears. Tossing the weed down on the coffee table in physical disgust.

At that moment, someone knocked at the door. She instinctively got up. And in a motion of sheer indolence, she reached for the door handle while simultaneously calling out "who is it?" But without waiting for a response, she opened it.

Standing in the dark hallway was a large, familiar person of her misspent past, which caused immediate fear to flame inside of her.

Her unexpected adversary grinned at her terror-stricken complexion with the utmost pleasure as he entered the apartment. She tried frivolously to resist him from entering, but she knew it was hopelessly too late.

"Hey, girl. It's me. Can I come in?" he commented with wicked complacency while grabbing hold of a closing door to invite himself in regardless of her impotent wishes.

After gaining the upper hand, he shut the door behind him with virile strength in his rude actions. A sign to her that he still held a grudge over retrospective, circumstantial calamities that had taken place between them in their dismal history; yesterday had become a hideous realism that was like a thunder clap in her frail heart.

She backed away spontaneously at the thought of such an evil reminder.

"What are you doing here, and what do you want?" she asked with uneasiness in her rough tone.

"Hey, that's no way to treat an old friend," he said finally while pursuing and stalking her to the center of the room, revealing her obvious fear of him.

As she walked backwards, her eyes were glued to his subtle, sly movements while she attempted to keep her awkward balance by seizing at unseen objects that seemed to be obstructing her failing retreat.

Thus, as she tried to put distance between them, as though he was some kind of contagious malady, she instead had backed herself into a tight corner with no formulated escape plan.

"Please, Anthony, you have to leave," she warned, trying unsuccessfully to sound firm.

"Why?" he asked ridiculing her strict exigency with mean and nasty joy.

"Miguel won't like it if he sees you here," she mentioned timidly while pressing herself to the cold, damp wall to avoid his touch as much, and as best, as she could under such intense conditions.

"Well, I don't think we have anything to worry about, . . . now, do we? I happen to know where Miguel is right about now," he confirmed as he smirked leeringly with an air of cunning smugness, which he brought forth straight into her defenseless features. And then, in a more vicious whisper, he said, "And if you don't mention our little reunion, then I won't."

She became tongue-tied, which in turn aroused her respiratory glands to a fever pitch, swelling up inside of her, which in the process suddenly gave her minor breathing problems.

"And I know another thing that you probably ain't aware of either. Your moron boyfriend's finished. He's on his way out. Do you dig?" he reported, with a mask of serious foredoom in his maniac expression of glee while making references to something that she didn't have a single clue about.

This bearer of bad news was so close to her that she could smell his liquor-tainted breath, which caused her to gag and blink from the poison he was exhaling.

She tried once more to flee from his swaddling and investing grasp, yet he had successfully caged her with his broad, powerful, sweaty arms, which extended to the wall as if he was there specifically to hold it up.

She didn't know what to say. His words sounded so strangely absurd but so certain and confident at the same time.

What could he be talking about? He's probably just trying to frighten me, that's all, she wondered frantically.

"What's wrong, babe, cat got your tongue?" he remarked with a grin, which stretched boastfully from ear to ear.

"I don't know what the fuck you're going on about! Just let me go!" she insisted, forcing herself by him with all her passionate strength.

"Hey, I'm not holding you back. You're as free as a bird," he teased and toyed, extending his arms out, gesturing to her to go anytime she pleased. "Though you're mistaken, girl, when it comes to who's made you a damn prisoner. It's him that's holding you back, not me," he declared, growing angry all of a sudden over her erratic behavior.

She jumped in her skin after this unexpected, yet not irregular, outburst of emotion. She had contused and bruised memories to prove it after all.

"Miguel is good to me. He takes good care of me," she exclaimed in an almost pathetic manner while she defended his good name, yet secretly wanting a fix real bad, which filled her brain more predominantly than any real concern she might have had to vouch for her main man's philanthropy.

"Look, baby," he retorted, softening up to her once again as he touched her with delicate, molesting fingers, "I can take care of you a whole lot better than that dick ever could," he purred while stroking the side of her flushed cheek with the tips of his brawny tentacles.

She was terrified to the bone, to say the least, when he did that. Frozen in panic-stricken emotion as his tangible presence became too much to bear.

Her immediate thoughts were of those horrible incidents of bygone days of abhorrence, which flashed back into her mind like piercing arrows, shattering her partially restored serenity, and, which by the way, had taken her many painful years to remedy.

"I don't want to hurt you. You know that. We'll be together again. But this time, I'll treat you better. You'll see," he promised while he attempted to get nearer to her as he ran a relaxed hand up the side of her skimpy shirt, her immobility only adding to the great delight that he already felt in his hardened loins.

"It's been a long time, huh? But you never forget a good thing," he mused contentedly to himself evidently, then seeing without seeing, how she was feeling nothing at all. Moreover, of how she was not particularly overjoyed by this trip down reminiscent lane like he was.

All her senses seemed lost to that one desire, though. The only important one actually. She would have died for merely one drag. Even a small taste of some bargain pot, anything to take away the urgency swelling up inside of her.

It wasn't that she was hooked! By no means! It was just that she couldn't deal with this bullshit with Tony right now. *Not right now!* her brain screamed in subdued agony.

"No, Anthony! I'm with Miguel now!" she blurted out, coming to her senses suddenly as she rubbed her temples with appropriate stress, banishing the lust for her true sensation from her impressionable mind before it was way too late to handle.

"What!" he yelled when hit with this direct rejection. "You goddamn *cunt!* You fuckin' whore!" sprayed at her his condemnation in rapid bullets of vocal punishment as he simultaneously slapped her face hard several times.

Alas, as the open cupped blows made contact, which cleverly would leave no noticeable or distinguishable marks for her ghetto Sir Lancelot to discover, she began to cry in response. Something she had wanted to do anyway, ever since he had arrived on the unwelcome scene. Then, as if by instinct, she bravely gained the formula to demonstrate her gut rancor toward his squalid retention by having a wild fit and tantrum, because, to be honest, unfortunately, she had been battered and beaten worse than this. It was merely the humiliation of it all and the choleric yearning to dull her lucidity with her favorite pastime that made her act in this exorcistic fashion.

Evidently, this only made him angrier still, and he savagely shook what little dignity she had left hoarded in the depths of her amnestic conformity.

"Shit, bitch!" he pulled and whined. "I haven't even started yet! I'll give you somethin' to bawl about in a minute! You'd be in your fuckin' coffin today if it wasn't for me. Do you understand!" he told her incessantly while he fervently and violently disposed of her onto the bed.

After a rough landing, she quickly attained command of the vibrant springs and shouted.

"I'd rather be dead than be back with you!" spurting forth her hatred of him by the mental cuts and scars, which she aligned herself with, finding the consolation of increased malice through them.

"And when Miguel is finished, who are you goin' to run to then, huh? Not me!" he pointed out, corroborating his own ominous question with a whiplash smile that appeared more like abashed pain than anything else.

"I don't want you! I never did! I hate you! You fuckin' bastard!" she shrieked at the top of her lungs amongst hot tears, which distorted her voice, making it sound as if it was a warped siren.

He began to chuckle at her affirmation, which mellowed his own tantrum considerably.

"We'll see. You'll be back," he predicted as he allowed himself the privilege of lighting up a fat, sufficiently packed blunt. A sedative for after such a brief, but severe, storm.

His words seemed to have taken some profound effect on her, and her crying fizzled to soft nervous hiccups that she forced back down her throat to settle among the other ancient injuries left over from previous age-old battles.

Yet what really put an end to her bawling, though, was the appearance of that slender smoke that he held carelessly in his bulky fingers.

Her pupils bulged and concentrated on its scent. Rising through the thin air, taking as its form, a misty, gray butterfly. And in her ruefully urgings, she wished she had had that special net, which she eagerly fantasized about using, to loop that evasive pletistic sprite. Then, as though by some amateur endeavor at telepathy, she'd claim it by her sheer willpower, wanton desires, and agonizing hunger. Maybe then, and only then, she would be able to truly embody it for herself, forever, if need be.

He spoke to her in abstruse riddles at this time. His lips and mouth were moving, but nothing appeared to reach her. All she could hear was her own saliva wetting her dry, cracked gums just from the mere thought of her previous lusts for mind-altering stupefication.

She wanted something to take away the thirst and greed. Anything at all at that desperate juncture.

Then like a miracle, her prayers were answered and granted, as she spied the half-smoked joint that lay beckoningly in the ashtray beside her, where he had conveniently discarded it.

She no longer cared about her urgent predicament. All she hankered for was that burnt stub buried in that field of ashes.

Suddenly, like some human turnstile, what she really badly wanted next was for him to leave. Yet, she was not quite daring enough to force this private bequest to move from the mattress of exhorting nails of excruciating exigencies to actually make this basic gesture a reality.

"I told you I don't need anyone. I can look after myself," she conceded. Yet, solicitous hesitation dwelled in her blood-filled pupils while waiting to see his reaction to her unproven confession.

"All right baby," he stated nonchalantly, noticing her invalid participation in their "challenging" discussion and conversation as he continued to drag passionately on the once-ditched roach that he had retrieved casually from the bottom of the tiny trash heap.

"But I'll be back. Count on it," he concluded, pointing a menacing finger at her as he opened the door, which had an obnoxious squeak to it; that was ultimately the indicative symbol to his impositional intrusion.

She, on the other hand, remained silent. Not wanting to say or do anything that might impede him from making his immediate exit.

Then without even a rapid glance, he walked into the vacant corridor, saying that simple cliche of cliches:

"Catch you later, babe." And he waltzed on down the hall, supporting an attitude, which he thrust a few a feet ahead of him to satisfy his enormous vanity.

She sat there listening to his footsteps grow distant for what seemed to be a long time. Yet she still was too comatosed to move an inch for fear of further retribution from her former catalyst.

After she heard no more of him, she smiled with a safe sense of luxurious deliverance in his absence, even though she was suffering from a mild aftershock from seeing him and from his having sworn to return. She was glad all the same that he had vanished from her sight for the time being, which was something to treasure very much in a temporary thrill of adducible consideration.

As a matter of truthful avowal though, she had never expected to hear from him ever again. Yet the opportunity wasn't what you would call an improbability either. In her carelessness, she had been ignorant of the price she might have to pay for running into him. And with the priceless interest it entailed, it amounted to a great cost, which she was now presently constrained to deal with.

Ever since she left him, she felt a relative ease in her life, which she hadn't the benefit of fully appreciating until this very hour. Then without another second to lose, she hastily fumbled among an assortment of objects that was littered in slothful disorder on the bureau beside her bed, with the aim of her craving her appetite for a hit of the previously banished opiate.

She then automatically put the filthy, scorched butt of a cigarette to her lips and relished the taste of the charred flavored outer foreskin in her parched mouth. But this heretic wasn't the least bit hindered by its repugnant aftertaste on her anhydrous palate while she searched ruefully for a match in order to ignite this simple prize.

She became quite impatient with her hunt. Becoming upset by the depleted results at trying to light this stupid morsel of reclamation.

An alerting thought entered her head like a bolt of lighting, and she immediately threw the pitifully small cigarette away.

"What wrong with me? I don't need this crap," she moaned miserably to herself. "I've got to get the hell outta here. I'm starting to climb the goddamn walls!" she yelled while feeling suddenly claustrophobic as she sought urgently for a coat.

She then darted around the room, randomly picking up articles that she believed she needed in order to make her celeritous abscondence. She was afraid that if she stayed here any longer, she would be tempted to take a drag from the repudiated stub. So she flew the coop, so to speak, and never looked back.

She strolled the dark, malicious streets with no thought of, or particular purpose to, where she was going. She still craved a quick dose of the potent stuff really bad but tried very had not to think too much about it.

She began to shiver intensely from a combination of the cold front hitting this unfair inner city and from the premeditated bout of withdrawal.

A chilling sweat showered her meek body, which made her humbly insecure while roaming the thoroughfares and back lanes of her eternally dying neighborhood, in a false quest of faith in herself no doubt.

She stopped suddenly and quickly scanned over toward a telephone booth on the other side of the road. And then she pondered over something while biting to the quick of her glossy, red, varnished nails. She then rapidly sprinted across the street to beat the surge of the oncoming traffic, as she had decided to make an urgent phone call. When she reached the plexiglass shelter, she rushed inside and immediately grabbed at the receiver as though it was a life preserver or something.

Yet, it seems that all this spontaneous effort took its toll on her, making her gasp for air, causing the transparent walls in that cramped space to fog up instantly around her like a natural mist or curtain.

She began to fish about in a hurried fashion in her purse for some loose change. And during this nervous frisk for available coins, she came up with the instant decision that she needed vehemently to communicate with someone quite different from her regular and customary domain. Someone very alien to her usual, social cesspool, which sadly festered around here these days. Someone that might understand her panicky situation more compassionately, now that she was seriously attempting to kick this horrible habit. Someone who would listen to her striving to willingly alter her dismal life. Someone who could hold her hand and lovingly console her while she tried to defeat this incommodious problem. And finally, someone to just talk to, so she could take her mind off of her weaknesses and vices. And so, she dialed a number of a person who, ironically, cared absolutely nothing for her at all. The one individual who had written her off as deceased and forgotten. A lost, sweet, innocent, little girl who had died a long time ago. Gone forever, as far as this other particular human was concerned, from this relative world.

Thus she waited skittishly on the line, growing impatient with the monotonous drone of the dull dial tone. Several times she almost decided to hang up before she eventually heard an answer to her distress call.

A voice of a lonely woman broke the tormenting spell of silence. And her heart skipped a beat as she recognized the female's voice in the distant location.

At first, she was unable to speak, leaving the poor woman in suspicious suspension on the other end repeating desperate pleas of hellos over and over again to this unknown phantom caller.

"Hello, Mom. Hi, it's me, . . . Jackie—Jacklyn," she replied in exasperation while she cuddled up to the impersonal mouthpiece in order to steady her trembling hand.

"Yes, Mom, it's really me. I'm fine, really, I'm doing all right," she stressed while trying not to sound annoyed and having second thoughts about calling her.

"No! I don't need any money! That's not why I've called! Yes! Yes! I'm fine. Listen, Mom . . . I was thinking—" stopping rather abruptly in her pattern of speech to let out a heart-wrenching sigh in order to gain some reacquired strength to carry on with this difficult ordeal, but which, on the other hand, gave her mother the perfect opportunity to intervene instead.

After being compelled to listen with mental blinders on to a mother's (unfortunately, by name only) long lecture on nothing of any relevancy, she eventually broke in in order to speak her mind once more.

"Mom, hold on a minute please! . . . Anyway, I was thinking—" repeating this line with less assurance this time around, while not too sure of how to say what she was thinking of saying to this stubborn woman, whom she barely knew anymore.

Nevertheless, her mother didn't even give her a chance to finish, interrupting her once again to stall what was so eagerly wished to be stated by yours truly.

"No! I'm not in any trouble! Just listen for once. Okay?" she begged, growing extremely agitated by her mother's deficiency in the craft of listening. However, her extrinsic method of parental devotion and regard was tossed at her disremembered offspring like so much spare pocket money, that was sort of comparable to bartering with a beggar to dismiss your own guilt and personal shame that you were coerced into revealing now. Things, to say the very least, were not exactly going very smoothly. And moreover, our forlorn urchin was presently regretting that she had even bothered to call at all and made her want to disappear into the annals of erstwhile "happy times" for good.

More realistically though, she wasn't too keen or accustomed to being outside for long periods of time either. Especially at night.

Usually, on a more regular basis, she would probably have been in her untidy loft of mediocrity toking on some special weed; that's what she usually would be doing right about now.

It kind of reminded her of the dismal, old days. The earlier days, when she was so much younger and very impressionable. When she was obliged to sell her once fine and clean body in order to survive. Struggling each precious minute, while working like a dog (a bitch is what she really meant) on the tough streets to "make it" with a john for her former pimp, Anthony. And it was at that insensate consummation when she was first introduced and hooked onto drugs of every conceivable kind in order to deal and suppress the reality of this inhuman skin trade.

This was all before she met Miguel, of course, who took her away from this truculent and barbarous business, and who, in the process, stole her away from the tyrannical hooks of big, bad Anthony, who she was at one time the sole and rightful property of, no less.

Yet her mother still refused to hear as poor Jackie leafed through this tome of nightmares returned, constantly being scolded by her dear, thoughtless mother at the moment for things that this confused girl couldn't even understand. Whereas, merely five minutes ago, this negligent progenitor had feigned a superb act at being full of joy over just being able to reacquaint herself with her baby's voice once more.

It forced her to recollect why she had left home in the first place. The false love and deceitful adoration that stank of regret about her accidental and inadmissable birth, which was that eventually led her, pressured her, into taking flight in the end.

"No, Mom! I don't want to talk to him. I mean Daddy!" she screamed, wanting very badly now to hang up on them but finding it difficult, all the same, to let go of someone who was required for most intense, emotional purposes to need her.

"Please, Mom, I'm trying to tell you something important," she whimpered hysterically while wanting to release her true feelings on this matter now, now that she felt she had the opportunity to do so.

"I'm straight, Mom! Please believe me! I'm not on anything for chrissakes!" she testified attempting to disguise her censurable tone by expressing feelings of shock and utter surprise at this reasonable accusation, yet knowing that her mother knew better, no matter whether she was a lousy parent or not. Mothers always knew, nonetheless.

"Mom! I'm finished with all that! I swear!" she lied in semitruth with passionate contemptible onus in her unreliable speech.

"I just wanted—no, Mom! It's over. All of it. I don't mess with those things anymore!" she yelled in her own fragile defense while grabbing at her chest from this severe interrogation that she was pressured into accepting.

"I just wanted to . . ." and then she trailed off again, mumbling in exhaustion over this verbal, strenuous exercise as she leaned her tired shoulder against the sturdy Plexiglas plate for added support.

"No, Mother! No! No! Don't call Dad! . . . Please!" she shouted while becoming instantly alarmed by this suggestion and unable to resist the flood of tears forming around her sore eyes. Subsequently, she decided at that urgent moment that she had had enough and rapidly stated, "Listen, Mom, I've got to go now. I'll call you again some other time. Good-bye." She quickly hung up the phone and proceeded to break down and weep as she had never wept before.

Later, after that demonstration of ultimate anguish, she literally fell to the floor and folded her body up to meet the tight requirements of the compact space, similar to some beaten porcupine in a failed interpretation of woe and affliction.

"Why doesn't she ever listen to me. No one ever listens to me," she complained in a pathetic whine as she slumped up against the wall of the telephone booth, sniffling away her blues and tears of pain.

She immediately sensed at that desperate moment that everything in her tiny universe was crumbling around her. Her own private Ides of March no less. Which, as a matter of official record, had come at an extremely tardy date for that seasonal oscillation to punish her. Yet it didn't seem to change the inconsequential fact that she was heavily doused by this curse, regardless of the discrepancies of time.

Then she braced herself beside the hardy glass and pulled and collected herself together in order to stand up straight once more to face another of her normal, miserable days.

She pushed open the doors of the transparent box. And when she entered the world of sin again, she was confronted with a discordant awakening in the form of a rain shower, which had started to descend right at that unlucky point when she began to crawl back outside of her available shelter.

She instantly hid herself from the damp and wet by buttoning up her flimsy coat while looking up with lost interest at the menacingly gray skies.

She wouldn't worry about it now, thinking it best to make a run for her apartment before she got completely soaked. So she raced the whole way, dodging large puddles and an increasing downpour with futile determination, wanting at this instant to be confined between four granite walls once more. The four familiar spaces of her preservative home.

Thus, as she made it back to the apartment, she paused, with grogginess for a moment, while standing in a sopping wet state at the front door. She felt she could breath properly once again if she stood motionless in the quiet, dark room of her very own favorite lodging (because she had no other to compare it with), glad to smell recognizable smells and happy to be safe in the safest place she knew.

Without turning on the main light, she rushed over toward the bed and searched with her acute touch for something on the floor.

She grew quite restive as she threw unknown articles across the room. She eventually, though, put on a nearby lamp for helpful assistance in order to resume without further hesitation or hindrance to aid her in her unattractive scrounging.

She suddenly expressed an upsetting frown at not finding this particular "it" while she sat in defeated, silent remorse, lamenting bereavement over her initial failure.

"I can quit this—I know I can." She spoke to the ceiling, as she contested her powerful dependency. But it was a hopeless and useless prevarication. And evidently she knew this to be the truth all along.

She wanted to cry, but the realization made her immune to such a meaningless paltriness. And alone in her nude gloom, she knew that she could never return to them (her quondam family, that is). And even if she could, she really wouldn't want to. She pictured them differently now. A wholesome, caring unit, based on superficial stability, that had no use for her, and which she was convinced, time had distorted for her, creating instead this novice vision of pure hideousness.

Consequently, she needed something to shatter this demented pain which was building up internally. The past seemed to be coming up fast, creeping back into her memory banks, poisoning her system, and clinging to her debilitated spirit like an invisible weight that was beyond description.

The pressure was too unbearable on her, and she desired to get rid of it before it brought a more objectionable collapse as she inched and crept on all fours around the dirty floor looking for it, this single thing that should repair the damage done and release her from these heavy chains that promoted her insurmountable troubles.

At that moment, someone entered the apartment while she was still on her hands and knees in the middle of the disrupted room.

Her first thought was that Anthony, the Harbinger of Doom, had returned to finish what he had promised to complete. But then she saw a pair of shoes, which ultimately belonged to her roommate.

She slowly rose to her feet, brushed off the incriminating disdain from her "fair" composure and then stood face to face with a very puzzled Miguel, wondering how she would explain this odd situation she had put herself in.

"What's going on here!" he exclaimed waving his arms wildly around in total disbelief after discovering whose body it was scurrying about on the floor like some cornered rodent or something.

"Oh! Hi, Miguel. What are you doing home so soon? You're early," she asked nonchalantly, trying to falsify her disgrace with cunning innocence.

"Don't bullshit me, woman. I heard that prick Anthony was around here!" he deplored while his twitchy eyes scouted the place for any signs of apparent danger, making doubly sure that this menace was truly gone for good. "Now, Jackie I know that punk was here, so don't try to lie to me!"

"Yes, he came here, and, and he threatened me. And he said horrible things about you, too," she blurted out while stumbling over indistinguishable objects in order to get to him.

Nevertheless, he stayed put, watching her with acidulate suspicion, not really sure whether he should believe her or not.

"How did he know you were here, huh?" he questioned her while still keeping his guard up.

"I don't know! It wouldn't be that hard to find out, you know," she answered spitefully, resenting the accusation right out.

"Yeah, sure," he responded, while already in opposition to her views and concessions. "You know what? I don't believe any fucking thing you tell me anymore," he remarked with cold-blooded defiance.

Just then, Jackie was hit with a slap of sober actuality, totally stunned by this sudden realization of their mistrustful relationship.

"If that's how you feel, then there's nothing really more I can say, is there?" she invoked with depressed bitterness.

"Yeah, that's how I feel," he replied, challenging her feeble integrity with sheer, unmerciful malice.

"Well, if that's the case, then I'm leaving. I don't need you or this shit. I can see you don't want me anymore, so I'll find my own goddamn way around from now on, instead!" she said rather pathetically as she looked away from him in complete regret.

"Oh, yeah! . . . And where are you going to go, and what are you going to do? . . . Go with that pig, Anthony, huh? You think that sonofabitch is goin' to put up with your shit like I do?" he rapped with pure anger.

"I told you and everybody else over and over again that I can look after myself!" she said offensively.

"And what about this small problem that you have, or have you forgotten about it, bein' all fucked up and all. I wouldn't be surprised really if you had, . . . but how you goin' to solve that!" he remarked harshly while producing a tiny bag of white powdery substance as his profound exhibit A.

Her eyes immediately lit up, similar in effect to a Roman candle, when she saw the beautiful stash, which she would have dearly loved to snatch from his outstretched claws; it was dangerously comparable to bait in one of those deadly steel hunting traps in order to lure her animal greed.

Then she quickly blew it off so that he wouldn't witness her fragile temptation and delicate reaction. Yet for all practical purposes, it was really quite preposterous and ridiculous anyhow, seeing how easily clear and unmistakable it was to anyone who knew the sad situation, of how powerful this regnant dependency had over her.

Anyway, her futile attempt didn't appear to work actually. He already caught a short glimpse of her hunger, which was more than satisfactory to convince a sharp dude like himself of her depraved necessities.

"I'll survive," she sneered indignantly at him. "I'll stop doin' that stuff. You'll see!" she shouted vehemently while wiping her dry nose in symbolic provocation and moved away from it so as not to be bothered by it further.

"That's it, huh? Just like that," questioning her false honesty, and then mocking her dare by tossing the cellophane bag at her in utter disgust. "Look, girl, don't be doin' me any favors. If you want it, just take it. Go ahead. There's plenty there. Jus' don't be tryin' to make a chump outta me."

She blinked with instinctive fidgetiness when the tiny package of goodies had hit her squarely in the chest, and she let it drop where it fell without deliberate action on her part.

"See! Look at you!" he pointed out viciously. "You're dead scared of it. Look! You can't even touch it!" egging her on while depriving her of any essence of respect, if she happened to have any left to begin with, that is.

"You're a fuckin' prick! You're doin' this on purpose!" she screamed as she was almost compelled to throw herself at him.

Then he struck her across the face in an enraged impulse, knocking her to the ground with the intended effectiveness. When he realized what he had done, though, he attempted to help her up with the utmost, absolute humility that he could muster at the moment with his own personal gesture of empathy.

Nonetheless, she was so furious, that it was beyond reproach. And when he reached for her, she threw her arms and legs insanely at him for protection against his willingness to show her pity, and during this fiasco of emotion, she scratched his cheek with her long nails, leaving behind her dented mark of revenge.

He immediately lost control of his senses again (which was a weakness that he had never been able to defeat), and he beat her some more with his demeaning fists.

She yelled and wailed in pain from every blow he inflicted upon her. And when he was finished, he jumped back in bewilderment, looking with innocuous surprise at his bloodied hands, as though he didn't recognize them as his own.

He dripped all over with shame as he felt a deep-seated disturbance swell within him over his perverse actions while he stared at her battered form in stunned innocence.

He loved her, that was true enough, which made it even more difficult to understand how he could have done such a terrible thing to the one, single person whom he cherished the most in all the world.

He wanted to say something to repair his ugly deed, but he choked on the insipidly invalid excuse that he attempted to create.

His next thought was to split, to get away rapidly, to erase the repulsive evidence from his tainted knuckles, as if to discard a smoking gun that was still warm in his uneasy grip.

Then without further hesitation, he took off out the door, leaving her unattended in the middle of the hardwood floor to lick her own injuries by herself.

She lay there in a disoriented heap, weeping for a long while. Crying more for her infirmity than for her superficial scars and wounds that blotched the once-attractive surface of this hurt female.

She then held onto the table leg like a crutch and tried to lift herself to her feet. She felt something soft and cushiony beneath her palm as she supported herself with the aid of the furniture top, which helped her stay erect until the strength returned to her to do it on her own.

Looking down now, she noticed that she was holding Miguel's surprise gift in her shaky hand. Holding it up to the light, all her aches suddenly became minor interests as she shook the contents of the bag into its proper place, which settled accordingly at the bottom of the plastic pouch.

She watched this organized procedure deliciously while the magic dust fell into perfect systematization.

After that, she held it to her bosom and scanned for a safe place to open it. She moved to the most private spot in the apartment that she could think of, the very corner of the room where she usually slept. Then, after making herself secure, she searched her grave environment to make certain that she was really alone.

After taking this preliminary precaution, she seemed convinced enough that she was safe in her own solitude. She then directed her full attention to what was deemed important, the small, yet bulky, packet of electric and delightful images and visions.

She sensed a cool sensation rush through her system from the mere contemplation of what it could do. Her lips began to desiccate, her mouth extremely parched over these wonderfully anticipative prospects that were bulldozing through her brain, and her pulse started to race a twenty-yard dash in her chest cavity, while she yearned for what was inside.

She then fondled it, as she intensively hunted for an easy opening. Then giving up, for lack of real effort, she decided to make her own, and she tore at the bag passionately. Consequently, the precious, white, flaky substance fell to the floor like an early, virgin dusting of snow.

She was able nonetheless to save most of it before it was sprinkled all over the place.

She felt the smooth, fine powder between her forefinger and thumb, and when she was satisfied with its nice texture, she licked the choice residue from her fingertips in curious glee.

An immediate kick and jolt shot into her veins like freezing ice contacting warm skin. Her pupils flashed in the fashion of high voltage lightbulbs in her head as she was awakened to the stirrings of angels' wings fluttering in her dull, lifeless mind. She appeared spellbound instantly by this, converging willingly toward a trancelike state, while the graphic art ballet was bringing its gorgeous patterns of fervor and commiseration to a sold-out performance.

She then relaxed her floppy body of deliciously imaginary flotation into a stable chair, immensely pleased with the initial results, while she continued to study the drug more inquisitively, as if she was some sort of professional chemist or something.

As she peeled back the tattered seal with eager grace, she felt the warmth that it seemed to disperse and which engulfed her senses with promises of hope and happiness. When this procedure was successfully complete, she stuck her dainty pinky into the slight, makeshift incision and yanked out a generous portion of the unequivocally clean, sparkling dust.

She stared at its chemical merit and excellence with careful admiration on the cliff of her lengthy fingernail. Then with a secluded smile, she snorted it up her nostril without losing one, single drop.

At first, she felt rather queasy and blunt in mind and thought. Therefore, in order to speed up the process, she took another helping, and that's when the exhilaration grabbed hold of her and she bathed in its splendid and marvelous current of libido that appeared to run its intoxicating and inspirational course through her accessible body.

Blinded by euphoria, she lay in a lazy stupor, letting the drug be the automatic pilot map and discover the ultimate desires that she sought. While "permitting" this luxurious potion to absorb freely within her, she wished to let go of this reality entirely so that she could enjoy this fantasy one better, seeing how the latter had outgrown its usefulness.

So she glared out from her little window and spied a bright neon light that flickered its glamorous attention device at her numbed condition from across the street. She visualized a reverie of Miguel (*Dear, sweet Miguel, who does not know what he does*), pondering over whether he still loved her.

Would he still allow me to stay? Or would he cast me out to the wolves instead, after all the trouble I have caused? She revolved and reflected this question without too much deep feeling, though, while her glazed eyes gaped at the pulse of the humming beam of electronic brightness.

"It doesn't matter anyway. I'll worry about that later," she responded verbally to her fuzzy thoughts and brushing this nuisance aside for future reference.

She then scooped her human pincers once more into the slowly diminishing pile that was lying scattered in a small heap on the table before her. She then decided, upon further, inadvertent investigation, that there was really nothing more to be concerned about and, consequently, considered it wise and proper not to worry about anything else tonight, seeing how it didn't agree with her tranquil specifications.

All the shame, remorse, and guilt could be simply eradicated and dismissed with a sufficient supply of this soft, chalky white powder, which seemed readily available to her whenever the situation called for its emergency assistance. Yet, every hour and minute of the day qualified as an emergency, as far as she was concerned.

So, as she stared out of the dirty glass pane, she could muse about a better existence somewhere else. One that appeared to be out of reach for her, yet so close, in fact, that if you wanted it bad enough, you could almost snatch it; the only thing you really needed was a change of heart. A bridge between you and paradise. But presently, she was too tired to carry forth such a strenuous adventure as that. It was easier to place it on a shelf and just admire and value its esteemed excellence and beauty from a comforting distance, to treating it similar to a precious artifact that was way too costly and inestimable to really own and hold. Better to save it for a rainy day—not waste or spoil its unique virtue and worth or destroy its sacred distinction and majesty, and more importantly, not to bend this fragile rainbow that was actually so very frail, like the rest of us.

After all, she was content for the present time. Glad for what she had, even if it was temporary, because she was no fool. She knew that when the colors disappeared, that their distinctive traces would still be out there somewhere, hidden momentarily by the gloomy shade of materiality. As long as she was in this current and contemporary stipulation, she could be patient, prolonging the inevitable for the length of this lasting, sympathetic chimera; that was more than she had ever anticipated or wished for.

Footsteps

A concept and story by Paolo Abbruzzetti

Adapted and scripted by Massimo Abbruzzetti

Cast of characters by order of appearance:

(In flashback sequence)	
Mr. and Mrs. Lardini	The parents
The two Lardini boys	Rich and Murray as kids
Elderly woman	The mystery landlady
Young girl	Probably Catherine as a child
Acts one through eight:	
Pete	Piano player
Richard Lardini	Advertising agent
Bill	Bartender
Catherine (Kate)	Mystery woman
Murray Lardini	Brother of Rick
Gwen Lardini	Wife of Murray
Ted Thornton	Lawyer and best friend of Rick's

Introduction

A car pulls slowly up to a curb and parks. The scene is very much comparable to a dream, very silent and eerie, and in some ways abstract and unnatural.

A man and woman, in what looks like slackish motion, climb out of the automobile. The man says something to his wife; yet we, the audience, do not hear what he says, as if the whole world has gone mute. The expression on her face hints of a smile, but this is uncertain. The husband then opens the passenger door of the vehicle, and two young boys (sons of these particular parents) emerge from the backseat.

The youngest of the two boys (a pudgy sort of kid) climbs out of the car without fuss, but the older boy seems reluctant to hurry as he is coaxed by his father to come completely out and be with the rest of his family on the empty pavement.

Finally the whole crew is joined together, as they, except the older child, walk contentedly up toward a house.

The boy is compelled to hold his mother's hand, and we get the impression that the boy is suspicious of something that he does not fully understand himself. His parents smile down at him, but their smile appears to be a mask of deceit to him, as we witness things through the boy's point of view presently.

Once they reach, what seems in the boy's mind, a grand home, the father rings the doorbell while they unconsciously await their mysterious fate. Yet, the boy, on the other hand, seems to dread something as he stands beside his mother, lingering in fear and unable to control the forces of his youthful destiny.

Almost as though a door was being pried open, the call is answered. When the entrance is fully exposed, a woman in her fifties or early sixties greets them. Friendly salutations are exchanged by both sides while the boy, with hidden consternation, stares up at these adults. After a short time, something is agreed upon as the kid continues to look on as though he's trying to fathom the "diabolical" deception taking place secretly before him.

Suddenly the whole family is allowed inside this house. Yet from the boy's disturbed imagination, this place is perceived as a gloomy dwelling of trepidation. Hence, while his parents and this (wicked) elderly matron have further discourse, the boy checks out his surroundings and envisions things which caused his hushed fear.

The conversation turns primarily toward him and his brother. He knows this, and we suspect, because all eyes are on this pair of boys currently. The two boys are introduced to the old lady. She first acquaints herself with the younger brother, who is ushered toward her, without too much concern on his part. Yet when she turns her attention towards the older brother, all the boy can do is back off, with a touch of skepticism. She attempts to smile at the boy in order to gain his trust, but the kid sees only evil in her approach.

Consequently, there is a period of awkward uncertainty by all involved. The parents then come to the women's rescue by making the boy shake her hand, like a proper gentleman. He does this with secret unwillingness, having no option available to avoid it. Everyone grins (except the kid of course), and everything appears settled, by these adults at least.

A conversation ensues once more, and the adults exchange handshakes of their own. Suddenly the boy panics inside as he senses something terribly wrong is about to happen.

Neglecting the boy's subtle fright, the adults walk toward the entrance once again, leaving the boys behind, as though they have been forgotten. Meanwhile, as this is going on, the boy spots a female figure almost gliding toward him as though blown his way like the wind. The form turns out to be that of a girl of approximately the same age as himself. She smiles warmly (yet shyly) at him. He is mesmerized by her instantly, as if seeing an angel for the first time. For a brief moment, they stand toe-to-toe with one another, and he finds comfort in her presence.

Then the older boy regains hold of himself when he realizes that his parents are momentarily missing. The boy then runs after them, fearing in his heart that they are leaving him and his little brother behind. As he rushes to catch up with them, followed closely behind by his brother, he eventually reaches his mother. He then forces her to embrace him. The adults laugh with slight embarrassment at his impulsive action as foolish childish behavior. Then the mother releases herself from his loving, desperate hug in order to be able to bend down and kiss her frightened son on the cheek. She tells him something, which we are not privileged to hear, and then wipes the lipstick stain from his chubby, sad, and confused face with a tongue-soiled handkerchief. She then rises as though all is well in the world, which it is not, unfortunately. Meanwhile, as the boy is puzzling over this strange (to him) situation, he barely notices the parental pat on his shoulder given by his father, while his mother has moved on to say good-bye to her younger offspring.

When this is all accomplished, the parents say farewell to the old lady and proceed to walk off the premises, leaving (abandoning, in the older kid's eyes) them in the care of this unfamiliar woman.

The child is stunned as he watches, in horror, his parents nonchalantly strolling toward their car; the boy is unaware or unconcerned for the time being of the old woman's grip on his shoulder, probably because of his strong preoccupation at witnessing his parents' flagrant oversight. Then with open, frantic despondency, the boy attempts to break free. At first, the old lady has a firm hold of him, but the kid soon struggles to freedom nonetheless. Yet, it is too late; as he sprints out into the street, he observes the automobile speeding away. Nevertheless, he continues to give chase, but finally stops short of his despairing advance and gives up only when he distinguishes his mother's faint figure waving carefreely back at him.

And there it all concludes for him as he stands alone in the middle of the road, watching his parents' car slip away into the distance.

A rainy midnight at Wild Bill's sports bar

Act One

The initial view is of a very sensationalistic television commercial blaring out at whoever was bothering to watch. Suddenly a hand reaches up and turns down the sound a tad. The next shot is of the proprietor of this particular drinking establishment returning to polish a glass. The next shot gives us a wider view of the place. We subsequently see a pianist playing a sad melody to an audience of one. Next, we move to the empty bar, where Richard Lardini sits on a barstool, drinking a gin and tonic. Behind the bar stands Bill, the owner, loitering around with nothing much else to do.

Rick: "Hey, Bill, how about another round . . ." (*without looking up in visual confirmation as he continues reading the financial section of his newspaper.*)

Bill: "Sure thing, Rick. (*Bill then moves with lazy intent as he pours Rick another.*)

Bill: (*while motioning towards the TV, which is situated on top of a shelf at the farthest end of the bar*) "Now that is what I call a work of art (*referring to a commercial currently being displayed on the twelve-inch screen*). That's probably the best spot yet. As a matter of fact (*turning to Rick, who seems unfazed by Bill's complimentary words and sly grin*), that's probably the greatest damn ad I've ever seen in a very long time. I guess the royalties from that one are just pouring in. You must be pretty loaded by now with all these strings of success. Huh, Rick?"

Rick: "Wha? Oh, yeah, just the same old dog-eat-eat game is all. . . . (*He folds up his paper with a mild expression of disgust in some sort of nonverbal conclusion, which Bill doesn't quite understand.*)

Bill: "I would think you of all people would be the happiest guy on the planet with all of that dough that you're making."

Rick: "Yeah, me too," (*with a sarcastic smirk*).

Bill: (*leaning in*) "So what's the problem?"

Rick: (*staring directly at Bill with tame suspicion*) "Is this the point when you start playing your role of amateur headshrink. (*He chuckles cynically to himself.*) How much is it gonna cost me, Bill? Will I be paying you by the hour or what . . . ? (*He swallows his drink in one single swoop.*) Spare me, Billy boy, I don't need it . . ." (*He pushes the now offending glass towards the ever pleasant barkeep.*)

Rick: "Hey, be a real pal . . . (*He motions to his empty glass.*) I think I need a double this evening."

Bill: (*pouring him a fresh drink while glaring at Rick with sympathetic concern*) "Come on, Richard, you can tell me. What's up? (grinning devilishly before finishing his statement in full) You haven't gone and wrecked that beautiful, brand new BMW have you?"

Rick: (*smiling at his small joke*) "All right, Wild Bill, you asked for it . But remember, I warned you" (*pointing a harmless finger in his direction and setting back to tell hs tale.*) "You see, it's like this. A few days ago, I inherited some property in a swanky part of the District that once belonged to some distant relatives of mine. It's prime time real estate. Yet, and this is going to sound nuts to you, now I don't want it."

Bill: (*looking all confused*) "I'm a little lost here, Rick. Come again . . . ?"

Rick: (*with an embarrassed smile*) "This is going to sound a bit crazy, Bill, but the place that was willed to me used to be a kinda boarding house for kids and orphans, which was run by some woman that was sort of a great aunt in my family. Yet, the strange part is that I had completely forgotten about how bad a place it was for me and my brother when the two of us were sent there as young boys while my parents were forced, unexpectedly, to go on some important trip out of the country. How's that for chronic denial? (*pausing for a second to check Bill's reaction but makes no genuine outward response, yet continues to look on with growing interest*) You see, we felt abandoned with no real explanation for why we were left behind—"

Bill: (*with more bewilderment, he suddenly interrupts Rick*) "I still don't follow you, Richard. So what's that got to do with you getting this building?"

Rick: (*pausing for a minute before speaking again*) "So what? I'll tell you so what. You don't understand. I happened to practically grow up in that damn house. I spent many years of my childhood in that place. That house gave me nightmares for years afterwards, and it took me a long time to rid my mind of the abuse I suffered in that hellhole."

Bill: (*attempting to express compassion and comprehension at the same time*) "Come on, Rick, are you yanking my chain or something?"

Rick: "I'm dead serious, Bill! (*feeling a bit ashamed of his former childish fear*) When I found out the very location of that property, I was slightly shocked. But when I ran it through my mind, I thought it wouldn't be a big deal, so I took it. Yet the other day, I went to look over it, and I swear to you, Bill, it scared me to death to actually see it first-hand again. It was so creepy to be standing on the sidewalk near that building once more. Hell, I couldn't even go inside, I was so shook up—"

Bill: "Rick, . . . Ricky (*sounding slightly cynical*) Listen to yourself (*while patting him on the back in order to cheer him up a little*) It's only a freaking house for godsakes! Besides, you can't let something that happened to you when you were a kid get to you like that. You have to face your demons head-on, Rick. Hiding, avoiding, and hedging away from them is only going to make it worse for you in the long run."

Rick: (*glancing over at Bill, as if he had just said enough to make himself seem looney*) "So you think I'm being foolish about this, huh?"

Bill: "Give me a break, Richard. You're not going to tell me that some ancient cobwebs are going to make you sell some, from how and what you described, goldmine of a house in some ritzy area and that was given to you for free, no less. You're not trying to convince me of that, are you, Rick . . . ? (*concluding with a half-raised eyebrow*)

Rick: (*with less confidence*) "I guess not."

Bill: "That's the spirit, my boy. (*happy as a clam now*) Now you go over there tomorrow and slay that damn dragon. You'll thank me later. So what do you say to that?"

Rick: (*with renewed hope in his voice*) "You're absolutely right, Bill. That's exactly what I'm going to do (*he reached into his fat wallet and pulled out a wad of cash.*) Keep the change." (*He lifts himself off the barstool and puts on his expensive raincoat.*)

Bill: (*watching him with concern*) "Hold on a minute, buddy. Are you all right to drive? It's still quite slick out from all the rain we've been having—"

Rick: "Yeah, I'm fine." (*heading for the door*)

Bill: "Are you sure I can't call you a cab or somethin'? (*beaming fiendishly*) You don't have to worry about leaving that gorgeous automobile with me. I'll watch it like a loving mother for you if you like."

Rick: "Thanks for the concern, Bill. Nah, I'm okay now," (*He yelled good night and stopped for a minute, as if in a semitrance.*) "Nice tune, Pete. Sad, but sweet. Here, this is for your retirement fund." (*handing him a large, crisp, new bill*)

Pete: "Rick, this is a hundred-dollar bill, man!"

Rick: (*grinning from ear to ear*) "So it is. Well, so long, fellas. . . . Don't work too hard." (*He was gone with the music still ringing in his ears in the distance, rushing from this joint in order to reach his car before he got too wet.*

Act Two

Bright and early Monday morning, around seven o'clock. It is a nice day after the thunderstorm of the night before.

Initial view is of Richard Lardini unlocking the door of his newly owned bachelor pad. As he enters the room he tries to hide his apprehension of entering this dreaded place. But he quickly discards this to the furthest part of his mind as he walks across the threshold.

As he blindly removes his coat and tosses it onto a bare chair, which he merely glimpses at as he randomly roams the room, he suddenly notices that all the furniture has been covered with white sheets. He starts to shiver slightly from a moderate chill.

Thus, while rubbing his shoulders in a brisk manner, he simultaneously surveys around for something while muttering out loud to himself about how cold it is in there. He then heads toward a bare wall and fiddles with the venerable thermostat, but it doesn't appear to be in working order, which he acknowledges with a minor huffing sound. Just at that moment, he thinks he hears an abrupt sound. But after not hearing it again, he assumes it is his mind playing tricks on him.

Suddenly his cell phone starts to buzz, which startles him a little. When he realizes that it is only a call, he quickly answers it.

Rick: (*His tone sounds mildly dismayed.*) "Yeah . . . hey, hi, Jack. . . . Yeah, I'm here now. . . . Sure, I'll be at the office in about . . . (*checking his watch*) fifteen minutes. . . . I know I have an important client to see at two. . . . No, I didn't forget . . . Sure thing, Jack . . . (*While speaking on the phone, he randomly lifts up some of the covers to see what is hidden beneath them—just for curiosity's sake, of course*) I suppose I can come back here on my lunch break, and I'll watch and check out the sample ad tape from here, while I try and sort out some domestic things around here. . . . Yeah (*chuckling a bit*), kill two birds with one stone. . . . Right. . . . Good, good . . . great idea, Jack . . . Yeah . . . and I'll see yah later at the nine o'clock conference . . . (*with a sardonic tone*) Yeah, yeah, yeah, . . . nine o'clock sharp . . . I cross my heart and hope to die. . . . All right . . . ? . . . bye . . ." (*He puts the contraption back into his coat pocket. But before he leaves, he looks about the place as though searching for something and is annoyed.*)

Rick: "There's no damn TV here. (*With impatient frustration, he speaks even clearer while staring heavenward.*) Wonderful. No central heating and no television set. Hell, what is this lemon gonna produce next . . . ?"

He casually shoves his hand into his coat pocket and retrieves his car keys. He looks around the place one last time and opens the door and leaves, but not for good, as we will shortly witness.

Act Three

Later that day. Richard returns. The initial view is of Rick struggling with the door. Suddenly the door is opened, and we see Richard picking a TV set off the ground and carrying it into the house. He places it on a table, then searches for an outlet. When he is able to plug it in, he removes his coat and places a tape into the VCR. Hence, he settles back to review the sample tape. Just as he is getting comfortable, he hears a noise, similar to one he had heard earlier.

Rick: (*with irritation in his speech*) "What the—" (*springing to his feet in an instant*)

He pauses for awhile, listening for any further commotion. He hears nothing. But he decides to investigate anyway. He believes the sound is coming from a room upstairs, so he goes to investigate. He cautiously walks up the staircase while keeping his ears and eyes open for any new disturbance.

Suddenly, he stops in the middle of the staircase when he spies something at the crack beneath the door. He knows something is not quite right, because he notices that a light is on in that particular room, which he deduces from the beam of light under the door.

He begins to walk up once more, with more care this time around. Yet, his weight gives him away on the creaky old boards, which causes him to make an imperative noise. Just then a shadow moves, which he barely makes out, from under the door. He now knows that someone or something is definitely there, so he moves more quickly, realizing that he has given himself away.

He rushes for the closed entrance with creeping swiftness, which he hopes gives him the element of surprise. Thus he opens the door and immediately comes face-to-face with a woman whom, he believes, he has never seen before.

While he glares over at this unknown female with mute shock, she equally stares back at him the same manner.

Rick: (*In a state of bewilderment, Rick proceeds to speak in a fashion that is difficult for him to convey at first, but he soon finds his voice.*) "Aahh,—hello. . . . Excuse me, but . . . but who are you and what are you doing here on my property?"

Catherine: (*clutching at her chest as if she is trying to stabilize her heartbeat, obviously stunned by what he has just stated*) "I'm sorry . . . ?"

Richard: (*more relaxed, but still a little perplexed by this odd predicament and with shaky confidence*)—"This property . . . I own this house. . . ."

Catherine: (*more confused than ever*) "*You* own this house . . . ?" (*backing away from him as though he is somehow physically confronting her without actually touching her*)

Rick: (*with stress in his tone now*); "Yes, that's right, but may I ask why you are here?"

Catherine: (*Looking startled by this statement, she thinks about this for a second.*) "I . . . but I live here."

Rick: (*his features all twisted and his brow heavy with disarray* "You what! Whoa. Wait a minute. Did you just say that you lived here . . . ? I don't understand. The people at the realty office never told me that someone was living here."

Catherine: (*fiddling with an embroidered lace handkerchief speaking meekly*) "Please, pardon me, but I don't quite understand what you are saying?"

Rick: (*growing impatient*) "The agency. . . . Did someone from the realtors send you over or something?"

Catherine is totally lost in thought and nervous as every reasonable question he asks seems to remain unanswered or is unanswerable, therefore making no positive progress for either one of them. She is at a loss for words now.

Rick: (*after a lengthy pause*) "Eeerrr . . . this is sort of confusing. Let me start over. (*pointing to himself as if this was an indication in order to aid her in comprehending him more clearly.*) I'm the new tenant here, (*pointing to her*) and you are . . . ?"

Catherine: (*still slightly startled but less shy*) "Did you just mention that you were the new tenant of this house?"

Rick: (*smiling mildly with inner satisfaction*) "Yes, I did."

Catherine: (*in a slightly distressed tone of voice*) "I'm terribly sorry, but I was unaware that this house had a new owner."

Rick: (*finding odd amusement in this*) "Then you have been living here all this time without knowing that this place has been bequeathed to my family? (*stressing every word as though attempting desperately to fathom her words and what she is suggesting to him*) Now I am beginning to understand what's going on here . . . (*hesitating for a while in order to quickly remedy and unravel this mix-up for both their sakes, he caresses his forehead, in deep thought.*) So I guess what you're trying to say is that you had no prior knowledge that the former, deceased possessor of this building had left this house to me? (*Feeling somewhat proud of himself, he continues on with his inquiry.*) Then I am correct in stating that I have come into a piece of property with someone else already in residence here?" (*sighing to himself as he finally realizes what a dilemma they both are in.*)

Catherine can only sheepishly nod her head in admittance as they both eventually make some headway over this awkward situation. Hence, he swiftly does an about-face and looks around immediately for something.

Rick: (*speaking more to himself, with a dramatic display of anger*) "All right then (*while rubbing his hands together*), I suppose the next step is to try and get to the bottom of this and figure out why this has happened. (*more directly at her now*) I'm calling that swindler down at that den of purloiners and finding out what's what. I do suppose living here, that you have a telephone around here someplace?" (*observing completely for the first time his surroundings and that her/his home is already comfortably and fully furnished*)

Catherine: "No, wait! (*getting his complete attention*) Please, there's no need for that . . ."

Rick: (*Pretending not to hear her, he still searches for the elusive phone.*) "I have to say though, you do have some classy stuff here.

Not really my style, but quaint just the same. (*Now gathering what she had just said, he turns toward her.*) Excuse me for my ignorance, but did you just tell me that there was no need . . . ?" (*having a little fun at her expense now*).

Catherine: "Yes. And I believe you when you say you own this house. (*She becomes inadequate in his presence all over again and speaks in a tone of intense eagerness.*) And you must also sincerely believe me when I say that I thought this house was vacant! For years it has been so—"

Rick: "Hold on a minute (as his mind starts to formulate a dirty trick here). Are you telling me that you are some kind of squatter or something?"

Catherine: (*completely ashamed now and, yet, in an odd sort of way, appearing attractive to him*) "Forgive me, but if I had known. Listen, oh, this is so difficult, maybe we can work something out."

Rick: (*His novice conspiracy theory builds more momentum with every passing moment the more she speaks.*) "Okay. Listen, lady, what's really going on? Do you have a right to be here or not?"

Catherine: (*For a brief period, she is at a loss for words, but then she quickly regains her speech.*) "Please, and try and understand that I truthfully wasn't told that someone had acquired this place. I had no idea, honestly! Miss Blanchard, who died so unexpectedly, has allowed me to live here for years merely out of kindness (*licking her lips in despondency*) These realtors of yours don't know of my existence because Miss Blanchard has allowed me to reside here without anyone else's knowledge. (*with downcast eyes that would eat into your soul*) Please, I have nowhere else to go."

Rick: (*For a moment, Rick is touched by her confession, but he forthwith recovers enough of his composure.*) "Look, lady—what's your name again, I didn't catch it earlier—?"

Catherine: "Catherine, but everyone calls me Kate."

Rick: "All right, . . . Kate . . . I'm sorry, but this just won't do—(*He is stalled from finishing his sentence when he notices that she might be starting to cry. Moving closer to her now*) Hey, there's no need for tears. I'm sure you can arrange it where you have some place else to go. Some distant family member perhaps, . . . Right?"

At first she just shakes her elegant head with a definite no: Also while being with her, he witnesses how refined and exquisite she is, both in character and in dress, as if she was taken directly from a different period somewhere in the past.

Catherine: (*distraught and pouting now*) "I have no one and nowhere else to go. This is all I have. Or had, at least—"

Rick: (*losing his poise and succumbing to pity*) "You mean you have no family or friends that you could stay with. No one. Nothing?"

Catherine: "No. This has been my only home for many years. . . . I have nothing else." (*looking so much like the melancholy orphan*)

Rick: "Hhhmmm . . ." (*having nothing else to say for the time being as he dwelt with sympathetic interest on this existent, personal crisis*)

Catherine: (*All excited now as an instant scheme pops into her beautiful mind*) "Listen! Why don't you let me stay for awhile, if it's not too much trouble. I can cook and clean. I'm good with pets and—"

Rick: (*with hands up in a gesture of surrender*) "Hey, hey! Hold on for a minute. Are you trying to suggest that you will be my housekeeper or something?"

Catherine: (*expressing a forlorn stature*) "Oh, you have a wife. That's it, isn't it? (*with passionate and emotional regret*) I knew it."

Rick: "A wife! (*a short laugh*) No, no, no. I never said anything about having a wife. Did I? As a matter of fact, I'm divorced. (*becoming irritated*) Anyway, that's not the point—"

Catherine: (*happy enough to interrupt*) "Well, that's splendid! I mean, . . . Well, I'm sorry to hear about that. Oh, please, I know you don't owe me any favor, but . . . please, just give me a chance. That's all I ask."

Her beauty was beginning to captivate him absolutely now. And yet, there's something more, as though he had experienced seeing her before.

Rick: (*totally astonished at what form of action to partake and lets this roll over him like a carpet.*) "Fine. All right. You win. You got a deal. (*his conduct more to do with frustration and defeat from bewilderment than by anything else*) Look, my name's Richard, Rick. If we are going to be housemates, you should at least know that much about me. But I have to run to my office now. (*checking his watch in anguish*). I have an important client to see and take care of . . . (*mumbling with dismay*) and I'm already late . . .

(*then under his breath in a sighing and huffy tone*) Lord knows how I got myself into this mess. (*glaring directly at her while gathering his briefcase and coat in a hurry.*) Listen, just . . . just don't worry about this too much for the time being, until we figure something out. And do whatever you've been doing, and, hell, I don't know. Do whatever you like. I'll be back at five so we can discuss this further and maybe sort this mess out . . . (*Something suddenly holds Richard in puzzled suspension, disrupting his train of thought effectively enough, it seems, for him to respond in this odd fashion by mumbling mostly to himself while gazing into space.*) Hey, sonofabitch. . . . (*now addressing her while cuddling himself from the affects of the abrupt change in temperature*) Did you just notice how warm it just got in here? (*then returning to discoursing with himself again*) The heat must be working in this place after all—"

Catherine: (*evidently surprised*) "What was that you were saying?"

Richard: (*perplexed by the "supernatural" forces doing a number on his mental rationale*) "Uh . . . nothing . . . Nevermind. (*while tossing his head from side to side in total disbelief*) Forget it. It's not important."

Then similar to the flustered White Rabbit in the tale of Alice in Wonderland, *he sought a way to leave that place in haste.*

Catherine: (*biting her bottom lip in a gesture to suppress what appears to be laughter at his ignorant expense*) "Uummm, Rick . . ."

Rick: (*still quite dizzy from the day's events*) "Huh, yes?"

Catherine: (*with a puppy dog expression*) "What would you like for dinner tonight?"

Rick: "Dinner? . . . What! . . ."

Catherine: "You know, a nighttime meal. A consuming of edibles that sometimes follows long after lunch. (*a private grin finally escaping, which had been successfully hidden beneath her pretty features.*) You know, supper."

Rick: (*still unenlightened by this subtle humor*) "Huh?"

Catherine: "Is borscht acceptable?"

Rick: "What! Wha's that?"

Catherine: (*all wide-eyed and bushy-tailed over his funny, chaotic behavior*) "It's a kind of thick soup or broth made with beets and other such things. It's a traditional Eastern European dish. It's really quite delicious."

Rick: "Huh! Oh, yeah! I knew that. (*smirking beyond the lying and showing it through his botheration*) Yeah, that's great. Whatever. I'll see you sometime this evening, but I really gotta go."

Then he was gone, as if he was the uncomfortable intruder after all.

Act Four

A man sits in a cozy restaurant in a secluded part so that he can have some privacy. He is munching anxiously on a breadstick as he waits for his wife to show up.

Subsequently, she arrives, escorted by a stuffy waiter. She glides into her seat as if she was a trashy beauty queen seeing her worst days. She acts as though she still feels quipped, while she lightly allows her uncouth, weasle-type husband the benefit of kissing her on her heavily painted cheek.

Murray: "Before you split, Gascon, I would like you to bring me another whisky sour. (*ogling at his wife*) And what would you like from the bar, my little sugarplum?"

Gwen: "Murray! (*sternly glaring over at him*) If I've told you once, I've told you a million times, never refer to me by that vulgar term. What, am I getting fat or something?"

Murray: (*meekly now*): "I'm sorry my little dove. I was only trying to—"

Gwen: "I know what you are trying to do, and I don't care to discuss it. Now be a good boy and behave yourself for once. (*turning to the dull waiter now*) Bring me a martini straight up. And don't come back with that awful green thing that you call an olive this time (*pretending that he already disappeared in order for him to perform this important task, she proceeds to attack her poor husband again*). And Murray, do you think it is wise to have another one of those? You, with your condition and all."

Murray: "Ah, Gwen! It's only my first one. Give me a break, will you."

Gwen: "Murray, dear, if you insist on embarrassing me in public, then

I am going to have to leave this instant (*simultaneously eyeing the bored waiter before speaking to him once more*). That will be all for now. You can take our orders when you return with our drinks. *(She brushes him aside, like he is a minor servant, with an arrogant wave of her hand, and he is given the fortunate permission to leave with a simple, very well, madam, while she continues nagging her battered husband without remission.)* Now, Murray, I know you can't help being the way you are. But you can at least try, for my sake, to act a little more civilized."

Murray: "What did I do now!" (*whining like a child*)

Gwen: "Well, first of all, it's not 'gascon.' It's *garçon.* Gar-çon, Murray. It's French. Not that that would mean anything to you" (*stating this with an air of a two-dollar harlot while she lit herself a cigarette*).

Murray: "Garçon, gascon. What's the difference—"

Gwen: "Forget it, Murray. It's hopeless. Why do I even bother. Anyway, I didn't come here to chat about your lack of social graces. (*exhaling her menthol-one hundred*). Besides, that would take decades to resolve . . . if even then. . . . It's your brother, Murray. That clever and filthy rich Harvard grad sibling of yours. Remember him? This is what we need to discuss—"

Murray: "Do we have to talk about him again. (*a sour expression planted firmly on his face*). I haven't even eaten yet, and I already have an upset stomach."

Gwen: (*glaring, with fire burning in her sockets*) "Murray (*her tone full of disappointment*), you're not listening to me. Hello, Murray! This is important. I'm only doing this for our, your benefit, you know. God! (*looking skyward now*) How I wish I had married him instead of you!"

Murray: (*with astonishment and hurt*) "What?"

Realizing her mishap, she begins to purr at her vulnerable husband in order to win him over with her usual and cunning influence.

Gwen: "Ooohh! I've hurt your feelings, haven't I? No matter, Murray, my darling. It's come to my attention through some very reliable contacts, namely myself, that your dear brother Richard seems to have found himself a little girlfriend."

Murray: (*with naive shock*) "Have you been spying on my brother or something? Gwen, I'm surprised—"

With an equal jolt of her own, she lashes out at her husband.

Gwen: "Murray, my love, someone has to look out for our interests (*with a scolding gaze*). Lord, knows I couldn't count on you to do it."

With bravery unbecoming of him, he turns serious.

Murray: "Still, Gwen, you shouldn't do such underhanded things. It's not dignified" (*ruining his point by burping afterwards*).

Gwen: "Murray, my loyal husband, don't you even start to pretend that you know the difference between what is *dignified* and what you appear to practice on a daily agonizing basis (*with her nose in the air now*). Besides, I wasn't *exactly* spying on your dear brother. I just happened to run by his office one day, during my daily rounds, to check on some things regarding that unfair family will of yours. (*with a look of innocence*) I just happened to be in the neighborhood, you know . . . anyway, I had a little pow-wow with your crafty sibling, and he seemed, while I was talking to him, to be very pleased with himself, . . . and this made me say out loud to him that it looks like a woman is in the picture and the cause of this unusual display of cheerfulness. And, Murray, I was right! Because he refused to discuss it with me while he sat there like a beaming executive Jack Horner with his hands caught in some pie. And, Murray, if it wasn't for my daring persistence and cleverness, you would have never discovered this outrageous surprise by yourself."

Murray: (*unfazed by this normal insult*) "Hey! Good for him. It's about time he found himself a nice piece of ass. Way to go bro!"

Gwen: (*her anger returned twofold*) "Murray sometimes you still amaze me."

Murray: (*feeling all proud inside from his wife's premature compliment*) "Oh, how so . . . ?"

Gwen: (*with deep dissatisfaction as she leers over at him*) "You know what, Murray, you're such a sad excuse for a donkey's rear end . . . (*his brief happiness vanishing now*) You know that?"

Murray: (*upset and sad*) "I know I'm not as smart as Rick, but there's no need—"

Gwen: "Murray! (*fiercely*) You're interrupting me again. (*calmer now*) Murray, try and understand this. If your brother Richard gets married and, God forbid, has children, I'll . . . we'll be ruined.

(*glaring directly at him*) Don't you see! (placing her hand upon his) The inheritance, Murray . . . the *money,* my dear . . . (*attempting to make it clearer for him*) your birthright from your dear departed father will be lost (*taking her hand away, having accomplished her deed of false compassion*). You do remember him don't you, Murray? If your dear brother gets hitched, he gets it all . . . and we'll be left with nothing—"

Murray: "Oh, Gwen! Don't worry about all that. (*he chuckles*) My brother's rich enough already. Plus he's a decent dude. He'll treat us right. He always has in the past. He'll see that we get what's coming to us. You'll see." (*glad all over, thinking that he has reassured her*)

Gwen: (*looking extremely wicked*) "That's what I'm afraid of."

Murray: (*puzzled, as usual*) "Huh, Gwen? . . . I don't understand what you mean?"

Gwen: "Listen, Murray. And listen good. If we don't take matters into our own hands, we are going to end up in the poorhouse. And how am I going to cope then on what you make, Murray, huh? (*with fear in her eyes*) Murray, we are entitled to more than what he might deem proper and appropriate. Besides, why should you always leave things up to him, hhmmm? You just don't see how he's been manipulating you all these years. He knows how kind and easy you are. That's why he's able to trick you and get away with it all this time (*glancing at him now as though reprimanding him for his virtues turned mysteriously into vices*). No matter how you may admire him, he was always your father's favorite. (*She holds her palm out as if to stall anything that Murray might possibly suggest in his own defense.*) Uh-uh-uh, Murray, you know this to be the truth. Therefore, he was always the one that got more than he deserved. (*Murray showing humiliation now.*) So now we have to try and find a way to turn things around in our favor for once."

Murray: (*forgetting about his shame for a second*) "How are we going to do that, Gwen?" (*while munching torpidly on a breadstick*)

Gwen: (*brooding over the situation, yet finding no reliable answers, she focuses back on the circumstances at hand with curt excitement.*) "That's what we have to try and figure out, darling, (*pensively now*) before it's too late."

Murray: (*his turn to brood*) "It seems too late already, Gwen. (*in a sulking voice*) It seems all but hopeless now, now that he's met this, this woman."

Gwen: (*all stern and eager*) "Look, Murray, we have to take the bull by the balls and grab them for all it's worth."

Murray: (*beaming with glee*) "Oh, that's pretty damn good, Gwen. I like that . . . (*giggling*) grab the bull by the privates . . . hah! I love it."

Gwen: (*returning to her former opinion of him*) "Oh, Murray, you're so lucky you have a wonderful and caring wife like me around. I don't know what you'd do without me sometimes. I really don't."

Murray: (*innocent since the day he was born*) "Me neither, Gwen. Me neither. And speaking of livestock, where's that damn waiter with our drinks anyway, . . . I'm so hungry, I could eat a herd of cattle."

Act Five

It has been almost a year now since that fatal day when Rick first met Catherine. They have basically worked things out and have learned to live conveniently with each other. As a matter of fact, through the course of many months, Richard has fallen deeply in love with this arcane female. Moreover, the fact that he still knows very little about her intrigues him. The secrets she appears to keep from him and the mystic life that seems to surround her only makes him want to be with her even more.

They do not venture out. Actually, they spend their time alone in that cozy building, seeing no one and desiring no other company, only that of each other. Only Rick has any kind of normal day-to-day existence. She, on the other hand, never leaves the house. And Richard learns to accept and deal with this strange behavior of hers . . . until . . . one ordinary day. . . .

We witness the lovebirds slowly dancing to a song that is being played over the radio. And from this image of affection, we can determine that they have grown quite accustomed to each other. Suddenly, the music ends, and Catherine gently pulls away from Rick with a smile of blessedness in her pretty features. She then kisses him softly on the lips and retires to bed. Richard looking delighted and confident, moves over to his work desk and resumes with some pressing business matters, which he was previously glad to have taken a break from to frolic with this incredible woman.

Catherine: "Oh, Richard, would you turn that radio down for me please."

Rick: "Sure honey, . . . is that better?" (*He is sitting at his desk that is located across the room from her.*) Hey, darling, I was thinking. We've been together almost a year now. (*disregarding his work now*) Well, I think we should celebrate, maybe have an anniversary party or something. What do say?"

Catherine: "Ooohhh! That would be wonderful, Rick. Just the two of us sharing a terrific and enchanting evening together. I'd like that" (*smiling at him with pure joy*).

Rick: (*with consternation on his brow*) "Actually, Kate, I was wondering if we could do something different, special, for change."

Catherine: "Oh?" (*with hopeless suspension as she stops what she is doing in order not to miss the full verdict*)

Rick: "Yeah (*while struggling to hide his anguish*). You see, Kate, there's this buddy of mine, an old college frat pal, who I got an unexpected buzz from the other day. Anyway, I'd like you two to meet. He's a really great guy, the best! I've already told him about you. And he'd love to meet you, Kate (*suddenly halting, noticing her discomfort*). What's the matter, Kate. Is something wrong?"

Catherine: (*upset now*) "Oh, Richard, I don't wish to spoil things, but—"

Rick: (*slightly irritated*) "But what?"

Catherine: "Please, Rick, we made a pact, remember?"

Rick: (*with a mordant chuckle*) "Well, yes, but I didn't think a social get-together would break or harm our little bargain. It's only my closest friend Ted from school, Kate, and maybe some of my relatives and a few of my coworkers, that's all . . ." (*trailing off as he sees how this is affecting her.*)

Catherine: (*heated by fury*) "A little bargain! Is that what you call it?"

Rick: (*perplexed with misconception*) "There's no need to take it like that. I was only trying to express to you how proud I am of you by showing you off to some people . . ."

Catherine: "Tell me, Rick, did you mean what you said? Did you mean to keep that promise, or were you just indulging and humoring me like some child?" (*her complexion all red and flushed in anticipation of his answer*)

Rick: (*his words coming out in uncertain terms*) "Of course I meant what I said, Kate. Why do you doubt me?"

Catherine: (*her features twisted in despair*) "I know you mean well, Rick, but . . . I just can't go through with it (*eyes blazing through to his dumbfounded ones*) especially with all those strange people to see all at once. It would be too overwhelming. Please understand my position, Richard . . . (*with a mellow demeanor*) You do understand, don't you, Rick?"

Rick: "It's only a party, Kate."

Catherine: (*sorrowful*) "Richard, I know this is hard for you to comprehend, but I'm not ready for all of that yet. In time, we will see, okay? But you must be patient for now. It's important to me for you to understand this."

Rick: (*confused but wanting to understand*) "All right Kate (*smiling*). Sure, no sweat. I understand. We'll just make it a night between the pair of us. Does that sound better?"

Catherine: (*looking a bit guilty and concerned*) "You really don't mind then. I didn't ruin any arrangements you made, did I?"

Rick: "Nah! No, Kate, nothing that can't be sorted out. (*then glancing at her*) You certainly are an oddball, Kate, but I love you anyway."

Catherine: (*running into his arms to embrace him*) "Oh, and I love you, too, (*kissing him passionately*) Richard?" (*she stares directly into his eyes*)

Rick: "Yes, Catherine?"

Catherine: (*loosening her grip on him in order to speak next with genuine intent*) "Your job, your commercial work, are you good at it?"

Rick: (*with a peculiar stare of his own*) "Do you mean good as in, am I the best in my field or something? Yes, I guess you could say that. Why do you ask?"

Catherine: (*shy about finding a way to say what is needed to be said*) "Well, what I mean is, being exceptional, like I know you are, does that mean that you are good at deceiving people?"

Rick: (*a bit stupefied and with a skittish chuckle*) "What are you driving at, Kate?"

Catherine: (*less bashful now*) "Just answer the question, please."

Rick: (*feeling slightly uncomfortable*) "If you put it like that . . . I suppose so, but one has to be a little crafty and sly in order to pull this off. There's a lot of money at stake, Kate, and it takes a cunning bastard like myself sometimes to do it right." *(And then he smiles at her to gesture to her that it is all part of the rat race sport.)*

Catherine: (*looking severely into his eyes*) "Promise me one thing, Richard."

Rick: (*with that grin still painted on his face*) "What, Kate?"

Catherine: "This is serious, Rick. Only swear this to me if you sincerely mean it."

Rick: (*his smirk gone now as he concentrates on being honest to her*). "All right, Catherine, I promise from the bottom of my heart. So what is it?"

Catherine: "Promise me that you will never treat me that way."

Rick: "What way, Kate? I don't get it."

Catherine: "Just swear, Rick . . ." (*touching his lips with her delicate fingertips*).

Rick: (*not really knowing what he is swearing to*) "I pledge never to do that to you. (*with a pleasant mood*) Are you satisfied now?"

Catherine merely grins warmly at him and then glares compassionately into his eyes as she moves in again in order to seal the oath with a simple kiss.

Act Six

The party that should never have been

We are back at Rick and Catherine's place once more. Yet Kate is not in the immediate picture. Actually she is upstairs in their loft bedroom waiting for, what she believes will be, a party for the pair of them being set up and prepared below by her lover.

In the living room, Rick is playing frantic, yet happy, host to his guests. There are about a dozen or more people at his place. But his try-

ing his best to keep them all silent while he sets up the surprise party for Catherine. Suddenly he is forced to answer the door.

Ted: (*all excited*) "Hey, old buddy! What's shaking?" (*flinging his arms around his pal, Rick*)

Rick: (*in a whisper*) "Hey, Ted! Good of you to come. Come on in."

Ted: (*still standing outside the entrance with a puzzled expression on face*) "What's all the whispering about? (*snickering a little*) You afraid of the cops busting up your little shindig or something? (*strolling into the house*) Hey, remember you have a very skillful attorney on the premises to take care of such things" (*while handing him a bottle of champagne*).

Rick: (*still keeping his tone below a normal level*) "Thanks, Ted. But you have to keep your voice down. This is a surprise party, remember?"

Ted: "Oh, yeah (*all wide-eyed*). Sure thing, Rick. I'm sorry."

Rick: (*leading him into the room in order to greet the other guests and with finger to his lips*), "Ssshhh . . . quiet, Ted. She's upstairs getting ready."

Consequently Ted is introduced to a few people, and they all shake hands and then intermingle with each other as they wait for the woman upstairs to appear.

Ted: (*moving over to where Rick is*) "So, Richy, my boy, when are you going to let me see your attractive new girlfriend so that I can steal her away from you."

Rick: (*smiling at him in jest*) "Tired of pinching little old, wealthy spinsters of their riches, are you, Ted?" (*And then he slaps, with a gesture of endearment, his buddy on the shoulder while enjoying making fun of his old friend for old times sake.*)

Ted: (*placing a cocktail sausage into his mouth before grinning*) "It's a living." (*They both stop themselves from laughing so as not to raise the dead.*)

Ted: (*Glimpsing around the room cautiously, he notices something which causes him to frown*) "I see you've invited the Wicked Witch of the East and her munchkin husband."

Rick: (*searching with purposeful eyes*) "Huh? . . . Oh, yeah, I had to. Hey, it's my brother, Ted. We need to make peace. (*glancing over at Ted again*) And I thought meeting Catherine and having a reunion at the same time was a good strategy."

Ted: (*chuckling to himself*) "Kill two birds with one stone. Fast thinking, young tycoon. (*glaring over at the odd couple once more*) I apologize for any rude comments I may have made about your brother Murray, but I'll be damn if I'll apologize for her."

Rick: "Don't mention it, Ted. She's one evil bitch that one . . . but hey, you can't pick your sisters-in-law, now, can you?"

Ted: (*staring at his friend with curious interest*) "You have changed, Richard. A new woman has softened you up, my friend."

Rick: (*grinning like a kid at Christmas*) "For the better, I hope."

Ted: "All right, Romeo, I can't hold in the suspense any longer. Bring down the beautiful prisoner."

Rick: "Relax, Ted. I will in just a minute. You'll get your chance to charm her off her feet in just a little while. (*becoming serious*) But first I have to level with you. You see, Ted, she's a bit nervous about all of this. Actually she's scared to death of meeting people I know. Don't ask me why, she just is. Even though I adore her, she's a bit eccentric. That's why I made this a surprise party. She doesn't feel comfortable around strangers. But I think once she sees the fun of it all, she'll calm down some and enjoy herself. And please, be a buddy, and try not to frighten her off, okay?"

Ted: (*with mock trauma*) "Who, me!"

Rick: "Yes, you. Now wait here. I'm going upstairs to see if she's ready. (*as he reaches the staircase, he turns around to address his guests and in a hushed voice*) All right, everyone. Listen up. Battle stations. Everyone be as silent as a mouse. I'm going up there to bring her down. Now, I'm going to go up, and I'm going to cut off the lights for a minute. And when you hear us come back down again, I want you, Peter, to start playing some music after the lights go back up. Is that clear with you, Pete?"

Peter does the old thumbs up as he readies himself beside his faithful piano.

Rick: "Good. Now, is everyone ready? All right then. I'll be back in a flash."

Richard creeps up the stairs and carefully enters the bedroom where Catherine is supposed to be expecting him.

We are now up in the bedroom loft of Catherine and Richard's house. It is dimly lit as Rick enters these surroundings. Only a single lamp on a dresser seems to be the only appliance illuminating this spot. Rick has a hard time seeing the inside of this room as he calls out to Catherine.

Rick: (*speaking softly*), "Kate . . . Catherine, are you there . . . ? (*Viewing her form at the opposite end of the room, he motions towards the center of the room.*) Hey, honey, it's time, you can come down now. Everything's set up."

Catherine: (*sitting stationary in a chair while staring at her own complexion through a dresser mirror*) "Oh, Rick, it's you." (*turning to face him now.*)

Rick: (*slightly edgy*) "Of course it is, Kate. Who else did you expect . . . ?"

Catherine: (*gazing at him for awhile with wide, doelike eyes*) "I guess everything is prepared downstairs . . . ?"

Rick: (*holding back his impatience, his hands firmly in his pockets*) "Yes, Catherine, everything is ready. Now all we need is you in order to get things started . . ." (*witnessing her discomfort*) "Is anything wrong, dear . . . ?"

Catherine: (*looking startled, but rapidly recovering*) "Richard, would you be terribly upset if I said that I wanted to stay up here instead?"

Richard: (*all bothered again*) "Kate, darling, what are you saying . . . I've spent all day—"

Catherine: (*breaking in instantly with a voice that almost sounded like she is pleading*) "I'm not feeling very well, Richard. I think I am becoming ill or something. Maybe I should rest for a bit" (*suggesting this absurd idea in a muddled stupor*).

Rick: (*anxious now*) "But, honey, you can't just cop-out now (*nearing her with tender concern*). Look, just come down for a minute. And if you still feel sick, you can go back up."

Catherine: (*with maniacal and distraught eyes darting around the room*) "I heard noises and voices downstairs . . ."

Rick: (*knowing how she is, speaks soothingly*) "That was just the cleaning lady and some caterers darling (*incommodious about lying to her*). They're gone now so there's nothing to worry about. (*ur-*

gently again) Listen, Kate, I've gone out of my way to make this day special. The least you can do is come down and try to enjoy it (*practically begging now*). Do it for me, Catherine (*pouting*), please . . ."

Catherine: (*staring at Richard with a sad, defeatist expression on her face*) "All right, Richard, If this is what you desire, then I will." (*She gets up from her seat and walks toward him.*)

Meeting her halfway, he hugs her compassionately and then kisses her on the cheek for good measure with pure happiness over getting her to see things his way.

Rick: "That's a good girl. You'll like what I have arranged for us this evening. You'll see."

Catherine: (*looking at him with eager hope, yet touched with a hint of despair while brushing his ch in with her dainty hand*) "Will I truly love it, Richard, Will I . . . ?"

Rick: (*studying her unreadable features*) "Don't be silly, honey. Of course you will. Come on, let's go before the mice start eating all of that delicious food" (*leading her to the door*).

Rick: (*turning to her with mild fervor at the top of the landing*) "Now, I want you to close your eyes, and no peeking. Then I want you to count to ten and then begin walking down the stairs. The lights are going to be all off, so don't fret about that. Hold onto the railing if it makes you feel better. Then when you reach the bottom, you can open them again. Can you do that for me, Catherine, my dear?"

Catherine: (*a little annoyed*) "Is that necessary, Richard" (*mocking his crude little game*).

Richard: "Just don't peek, Catherine. That's all I ask" (*playfully as he waits for her to shut her eyes before sneaking back down the stairs to join the others*).

We have returned once again to the living room, where the guests are still anxiously awaiting her formal arrival.

Richard, after silently descending the staircase in the dark, speaks to his patient audience.

Rick: (*whispering to them*) "Okay, everybody, get ready. Here she comes, ready or not . . ." (*and he stands next to the light switch ready to turn it on*).

Suddenly we hear her gracefully moving down the stairs, and everything is deathly quiet in that building at this climatic point.

one step . . . Two steps . . . Three steps . . . Etcetera . . . Etcetera . . . Etcetera.

A large clock is ticking in the background . . . then . . . finally . . . the lights go on, and everyone screams, "Surprise!"

But no one is there?

Only Richard is there, standing alone in the middle of the room.

Rick: (*happy as can be*) "Everyone! This is Catherine." (*With a sweep of his hand, the guests are directed to stare at a blank spot.*)

Everything is aberrantly silent, and everyone is confused for a moment. Muttering and mumbling of voices are heard over the sound of the piano as Peter plays a tune, obviously paying no attention to the embarrassing situation.

Rick: (*slightly disconcerted*) "What's the matter with everyone? (*then looking over at nothing*) Catherine, come over here. Don't be bashful. Introduce yourself to everyone."

Gwen: (*From her isolated corner, she secretly chats with her husband Murray.*) "What's this all about? Is this some kind of joke?"

Murray: (*Upon hearing this, he becomes alert instantly after stuffing his mouth with some food. He then gets up.*) "Some gag, Rick! (*raising his whiskey glass in a parody of a salute*) Come on, Richard, bring out the girl!"

Rick: (*looking lost and angry and sheepishly speaking into the void*) "Kate! What's the problem? Why are you just standing there? Say something."

Murray: (*sitting back down now, confounded by his brother's odd behavior, turns for support and aid by addressing his spouse*) "What's he playing at. Why is he talking to thin air. Has he gone nuts or something?"

With the party crowd still perplexed, Gwen, being her bad, conniving self, catches on to this strange episode immediately as she waltzes, comparable with a she-wolf with a plan or on the hunt, over to her brother-in-law.

Gwen: "Oh, Richard, what a funny trick you just pulled on us. You had us all going for a moment there" (*giggling out loud as if wanting everyone to hear her from some abhorrent reason*).

Rick: (*Still in a frantic and vulnerable daze, blinks into his sister-in-law's eyes as if she is speaking in an alien tongue*) "Huh? . . . What the hell is going on here? (*fretting and bewildered, then glaring at the invisible girl, which he is still convinced and believes is there*) Catherine, talk to me. Tell them this is for real. Kate, what's the matter with you . . . !"

Gwen (thinking that Richard had fortunately for her, lost his marbles, whether temporary or otherwise) secretly begins scheming a plot in her diabolical brain. A rapid, cruel strategy toward achieving an improvised objective in order to take advantage of the fragile situation before it slips swiftly away, and while she still has everyone's heedfulness, in order to benefit from the mob's rewarding and encouraging perplexed complexions of shock to bring her and to be used for, some sort of selfish added bonus. Even his good buddy Ted is at a loss for words at this juncture as he sadly watches with puzzlement this odd riddle and spectacle.

Ted: "Poor, poor Richard, of course we see your pretty girlfriend. (*turning to everyone*) Isn't she fabulous, everybody . . . ?"

Nobody submits or comments on this, probably afraid of their own feelings and thoughts during this disturbing vista.

Gwen: (*glaring directly into Rick's face*) "Don't worry about them, Richard, I believe you. Now come over here and sit down. I think you need to rest and relax a bit. (*searching for her husband*) Murray! . . . Get over here and help your brother find a seat. (*looking at Rick again with all the sympathy of a trained nurse*) Richard, come, sit. You'll feel much better once you get off your feet. (*calling for her husband once more as she leads a sick Richard to his designated seat*) Murray, hurry up, your brother needs your assistance."

Thus as Murray does his wife's bidding, while attempting to make this emergency rescue and at the same time successfully stuff more food down his greedy throat, Rick's pal Ted takes the eventual initiative to do some saving of his own.

Ted: (*Coming into the center of the culminated arena, he begins to address the whole motionless and numbed group of visitants.*) "Okay, everybody, the shows over. Everyone just get back into the party spirit and enjoy yourselves. I'm going to have a little chat with my buddy Rick over here and sort this mess out." (*Then when that was somewhat accomplished and sorted out, he nudges Murray aside before any more damage could be done, with a polite, but curt*) "Pardon me, Murray." (*He budges more rudely past the instigator Gwen, also in order to stand directly in front of his befuddled friend.*) "Beat it, Gwen, I think you've done enough for one evening. Thank you. But now, I think I'll take over from here, if that's all right with you" (*glancing at her with mild aversion*).

Gwen: (*With a flair for the dramatics, she parodies shock.*) "Well I never—"

Ted: (*Ignoring her now, being too concerned about his pal's welfare, he kneels down next to Rick, whose head is in his hands from this disturbing experience.*) "Hey, buddy, it's your old pal Ted. Remember me?"

Gwen: (*Not having the sense to give up, she attempts to cut in.* "Listen, Ted, I think you should let us, his family, handle—"

Ted: (*rudely interrupting her*) "Give it a rest, would you, Gwen."

Gwen: (*once more acting out a role of being insulted as she grabs at her chest as though she is having a mild heart attack*) "How dare you speak to me that way . . . (*searching out Murray now to come to her relief*). Murray! Where are you? (*startled to see him right behind her*) Oh! There you are. Good heavens, Murray! You frightened me half to death. Do you have to stand there breathing down my neck like some slobbering idiot."

Murray: "I'm sorry, my little peach, I—"

Gwen: "Never mind all that, Murray. Are you going to allow *this man* to get away with addressing me in that fashion?"

Murray: (*being used to this behavior*) "Well, maybe you should let Ted help Rick. After all, he is his best friend."

Ted: (*confronting Gwen once more*) "Listen to your husband for once, Gwen, and make yourself scarce. He's actually making some sense for the first time in his life." (*Neglecting her, he turns his full attention back to the real problem and appeals to his friend again.*) "Richard, hey, Richy . . . (*shaking him a bit to gain a hold of his feeble concentration*). Why don't you tell me exactly what the hell is going on here. Huh, can you manage that?"

Rick: (*Gaping up at his buddy with a new sense of awareness, he jumps up and cries out as if trying to control some semblance of his sanity and regain some needed order.*) "*Stop this!* Everyone, just back the fuck off. *Then returns to his former miserable and sober state after receiving the customary effect from the jolted few that surround him, he falls into a chair and places his aching head firmly in his caring hands once more as though to suppress some ethereal pain)* . . . Just leave me alone."

Gwen: (*playing the willing part of victim in some farcical drama, and with fake empathy*). "You surely don't mean me (*moving in for the kill*), Richard, my dear—"

Rick: (*in a rage*) "This is ridiculous! Why can't any of you understand this (*flapping his arms about in random hysteria*) Just leave me alone . . . and quit bothering me—*a feeling of urgency comes over him all of a sudden as though something treated currently derelict dawns on him with monumental importance*) Oh, my God, Catherine . . . ! (*appearing to be lost in a mad daze*) I have to talk to her. She'll straighten this out . . ." (He starts to wander about as if in a hurry.)

Ted: (*grabbing hold of Rick*) "Easy, Richard. (*holding him more firmly now*) Richard! Rick, this has gone far enough (*catching his attention now*). Richard, listen to me, damn it. She's not here, Rick. There's no Catherine here, Richard. Can you understand that?"

Rick: (*staring at his pal now as if Ted was the one with a mental issue*) "Ted, you don't understand. She's right over there. (*and then with pleading eyes*) What's the matter with everybody? (*in a tone as though he has a hard time believing it himself*) I'm not crazy, if that's what you're all thinking. (*Pushing everyone aside, he gains some much needed breathing space.*) Listen to me. Give me a chance to talk to her! She's *right over* . . . there . . ." (*his words trailing off as he points in that general direction and begins to see what everyone else of the faithless sees . . . and mesmerized by what he doesn't see, then sounding all lost and forlorn*) "She's gone . . . Catherine . . ." (*Struggling to control him, Ted turns him around to face him, but before he can mention anything, Rick frantically breaks in*) "Where'd she go? She was right here."

Ted: (*with a soothing approach*) "Richard, look at me. Yes, she's gone." (*even though it distresses him to hurt him so by saying this*)

"Richard, you have to get a grip on this. Please, Richard . . ."

(*More bewildered and confused than ever before, Rick looks at his buddy with the composure of a beggar*)

Rick: "What? . . . (*then desperately scanning the room in a frenzy with his hopeless vision*) Catherine . . .? (*then partially and almost mostly to himself*) She's . . . gone."

Ted: (*Feeling like the worst person in the world right about now, he turns to the crowd once more.*) "All right, everybody, I'm sorry, but the party's over. Rick's not feeling very well. So I think it's best if everyone left. I'm terribly sorry to announce this, people . . ." (*while herding the disgruntled bodies quickly out of the place*).

Gwen: (*heading over towards Ted with a bitchy attitude and a false display of bravery*) "Well, Murray and I are going, and not because you have taken it upon yourself to kick everyone out. (*turning toward Murray*) Let's go, Murray. (*back at Ted before making her triumphant departure and with a tone gleaming of a warning*) You'll be hearing from us, mark my words. (*smug now*) Don't think you're going to get away with this either. (*guiding Murray toward the front door with the rest of the befuddled horde*). Come on, Murray, the air around here is starting to smell stale" (*with that, she was gone*).

Ted: (*watching her with regrettable relief he mumbles under his seething breath*) "Good riddance to bad rubbish."

Act Seven

It is months later, and we find ourselves viewing the scene of a doctor's office, a therapist's office to be more exact. Ted is there, nervously smoking a cigarette, as he constantly checks his watch as if in a rush to keep things moving along. A minute or two after, the door is opened and in walks our main character, Richard, looking the worse for wear.

Immediately recognizing his friend after a long absence, Ted gazes at him with initial scandalized regard as he realizes what he has been through during the past few months.

Ted: "Hello, Rick. You look like total crap."

Rick: (*feeling all awkward and slightly angry*) "And seasons greetings to you, too, Ted. (*finding himself a seat, he slumps down into it lazily as if he was snugly in his very own private pad*) If you came here to admire my state of health or gape at me like some side-show freak, then you're wasting your time" (*avoiding his gaze as best he could*).

Ted: "Listen, Rick, old buddy, I came here today to save your ass (*grabbing a seat for himself before resuming with the conversation*). It took a lot of handshakes and brown-nosing with the right people under-the-table deals and trade-offs in order to have this golden opportunity to have this private interview with you so that we can discuss a plot to spring you outta here. (*then while casually surveying the doctor's impressive office*) I had to pull some strings, do some sooth, fast talking and shifty schoomzing with that weird doc of yours that your sister-in-law has looking after you in order to grant you this delicate proposal."

Rick: "Don't take this the wrong way, Ted, but I'm not in the mood these days for social chitchat or guessing games, if you don't mind" (*his aura and posture all dark and despondent at this unhappy time*).

Ted: (*Leaning hard on the desk now while peering directly into Rick's bloodshot sockets which he continually rubs with his hands, Ted mentions the harsh reality forthwith.*) "Listen, Rick, you've got to snap out of this bottomless pit, moody bullshit that you have been under the spell of lately (*pointing a reprimanding finger at him*). Because I am here on an important mission to set your sorry self free, whether you agree with it or not. (*He twists the stiff-backed chair around in a theatrical flash so that he can lean his elbows against it, for possibly moral support, in order for this parley to be even more secretive in case prying ears were mysteriously listening in. Meanwhile, Rick is monitoring this procedure with a queer look now that is, ironically, brightening his gloomy expression, as Ted continues with his important and excitable dialogue*) Yeah, my main man, this is a jailbreak" (*emphasizing his point at the grand finale by striking his index finger against the tabletop, while being all pleased and proud of himself at introducing this wild idea to his doubtful friend.*)

Rick: (*all annoyed and tiredlike*) "Ted, what the hell are you talking about?"

Ted: (*pulling up his chair fast as if attempting to straddle it in a vague comparison to taming a rebellious colt, he focuses in on his half-asleep and ungrateful friend.*) "Listen to reason, Rick, and check these facts out, pal (*licking his lips suspiciously as though the weight of them were holding him back somewhat*). That damn sister-in-law of yours is trying to swindle you out of all your money. She's taken complete control of your life for christsakes! Look Rick, I don't care if this girlfriend of yours is a fictional character of sexual repression . . . or, or . . . a goddamn blow-up doll, or whatever! You're my best friend, basket-weaving material or not, and it pains me to see you wasting away in this loony hospital while Gwen and your naive brother rob you blind of, not only your birthright, but of your very own riches. She's taking legal grounds to have all your personal financial holdings and assets transferred over to her and your brother . . . meaning—and I can't stress this any clearer than this, Rick—that she will have sole control and guardianship of, your estate. Don't you see, she's treating you as if you are too crazy to take responsibility for yourself. She's using this fucked-up situation of unprepared circumstance that, I might add, you have brilliantly gotten yourself into, to fleece you of everything you have built and own in order to pocket it for herself."

(*After Ted's conversing with his stubborn buddy with exhausting stress and eagerness, Rick looks on as if he is trying to avoid the truth of the matter as it stands. Yet he remains speechless as he tosses this diabolical, yet smart, set-up around in his troubled head for good measure.*)

Ted: "I don't know if you care about this or not, but I do, and I won't sit back like some rubber-necker and watch them slowly destroy you. (*leaning in ever nearer now to speak confidentially with him as though the walls may have ears*) Listen up, Rick. I've arranged things so that you can get released really soon. You see, Rick, I know a fellow lawyer who owes me a great big favor, and he has information about that quack doctor of yours that will boil him in oil for all eternity and bring ruin to his . . . (*pausing to gesture with his fingers the universal sign of quote/unquote*) so-called prestigious reputation that should make Jack Kevorkian seem by resemblance to be the unmistakable equivalent of Florence Nightingale (*almost too glad to admit it, even though it was such a catastrophic tragedy for the individual in question*).

"It seems that are cardigan-wearing Freudian was involved in a malpractice suit a couple of years ago. And I know from moseying through his untidy closet and from lurking around the grapevine that he wants this to remain strictly behind closed doors at any cost. He's even willing to do just about anything to keep this entirely under wraps. Owing and due to his respectable position in the community and all, of course. Anyway, I also have an expert of my own, as a backup if the good doctor chooses to play hardball with us, which should make a nice addition to his once 'meticulous' résumé . . . (*vacillating for a brief second or two to express an unscrupulous sneer*). We'll paint him so colorfully black that he will emerge as an exiled charlatan. And the only employment opportunities he'll ever be able to accept in the future will be as a permanent member of the darkest regions of fucking Africa as a freakin' witch doctor.

"Yet luckily for him though (*winking at his buddy*), he's willing, on further review, to evaluate your condition once more and set the record straight. (*Finally, fully softening up and becoming matter-of-fact*). It's all been previously contrived if we keep that noose carefully tightened around his neck merely a tad bit longer; that is, he is going to give you that precious visa outta this fruit and nut shack (*lifting an eyebrow as if to hint*), a clean bill of health, Richard. Now, all you have to do is play along. Let's say, for argument's sake, that this girlfriend of yours in genuine, who's to say what that is (*raising his arms in a manner of unconditional surrender*). Don't you want to be with her again . . . huh? Now, speaking hypothetically, if I was you, this would be on the forefront of my mind right about now. I don't give a rat's ass if this Catherine chick of yours is a figment or fantasy of the imagination. Let's not put too much consideration on this at this present stage—we'll take care of those particulars on another date—at any rate, first on the agenda is for you to have to at least pretend, for the public at large, that this was all a big and horrible mistake (*with wide-eyed innocence*). A misunderstood, honest prank which just got a little out of hand, that's all! Just silly make-believe stuff. End of story. (*eyeing him with stern determination, he sums up*)

"Richard, don't make me beg like a dog. Just say you made the whole thing up. If you prefer, say it was due to stress or something, I don't care. The important issue here is to get yourself out of this jam in one, solid piece, and with flying colors. Do you understand what I'm saying, Richard? This is very significant that this sinks in. Or you're going to be stuck in this stinking hole for a thousand eons for all we know (*staring at his buddy now with an ardent desire to know what he thinks of his dazzling pet project*). So what's it gonna be, huh, partner . . . ?"

Rick merely stares at his friend as though craving to tell him something. But on second thought, he covertly shrugs it off as pointless as he scratches his lower lip from the affects of a phantom itch while in deep contemplation and heedfully reviews the situation over and over in his cluttered and medically prescriptive mind.

Scene finishes with the ever-brooding, tormented image of Richard.

Act Eight

It is some time later, and we are led to view a scene from a former existence. We have returned once again to the building where this whole madness began, outside the residence of Rick and Catherine's. We then spot Ted walking toward this property, coming to pay his old buddy a visit.

Ted rings the doorbell a dozen or so times, yet for all his efforts, he receives no answer. He presses on, eager and curious to see his pal again. He tries to peep through the shutters, but they are curtained inside and sealed to the outside world. He doesn't give up, though, and decides to check the mail slot. He sees stacks of letters and junk-type postage stuffed into it and surmises that no one has been home for quite awhile. Then he steps back into the street to maybe try to spy through an upstairs window before finally calling it quits for good. Then he detects the sound of faint music coming from an open gap on the second floor.

Ted: (*Looking up while shading his eyes from the sun*) "Hey! Is anyone up there?"

Ted: (*Getting no response he decides to shout louder with cupped hands over his mouth in order to be heard over the sound of the soft song.*) "Yo, hello up there! . . . Is that you, Rick . . . ?" It's me, your buddy, Ted. Can you hear me?"

Just then the window is pulled up further, and the face of someone appears. It is not Richard, but somebody else vaguely familiar instead.

Peter: (*sounding all irritated from this interruption*) "Yeah, whadaya want?"

Ted: (*realizing who it is*) ". . . Oh, hey, it's Pete, right?"

Peter: "Yeah, it's me (*still bothered*). What do you want man? I'm trying to work up here, dude."

Ted: "Sorry, Pete, but I'm looking for Rick. Have you seen him about?"

Peter: (*unconcerned and bored*) "Nah, can't say that I have. (*then his mood changes to a more pleasant and excited one*) Heeyy, I remember you now. You're Rick's friend. You were at the party, right?"

Ted: (*happy now that he is recognized*) "One and the same. Listen, Pete, this is important. I haven't been able to contact Rick for several days now. He doesn't even answer his phone anymore, either here or at work. All I want to know is where he is and if everything's all right."

Peter: (*Apparently and appearing all serious and distressed somewhat, thinks for a minute or two before responding*) "Sorry, man, I haven't seen him myself either since he was released from that crazy asylum. He just phoned me up one day about a week ago or so, outta the blue, and asked me if I would care to watch his place for him for awhile, cause he was going splitsville or somethin'. Anyhow, he told me I could use this pad next door for as long as I wanted. And if I cared to practice here or whatever, that was cool and fine with him, too. Also he pays me pretty well with a monthly check, which I go and pick up from the P.O. box. Gave me enough cash that I couldn't refuse the offer really. Beats tinkling the ivory keys for tips, you know."

Ted: "I'm glad to hear it, Pete. But I don't suppose he has a forwarding address by any chance . . . ?"

Pete: "Nada, Ted, just somehow finds a way to leave the loot at the local post office."

Ted: (*frowning a bit*) "Are you certain that there's no possible way to touch base with him, Pete?"

Pete: "Sure as everlasting love, Ted (*sending these prophetic phrases courtesy of a smile*). Seriously, though, Ted, I've no reason to steer you wrong. I'm sorry man, that's all I know."

Ted: (*straining to think of something quick as he ponders this odd scenario*) "Just one more thing, Pete, if you don't mind."

Pete: "Shoot" (*leaning onto the sill now as he waits for him to speak*).

Ted: "I don't suppose you've seen any unusual woman around either, huh?"

Pete: (*finding comedy in his serious interrogation*) "Unusual, you say? Natural and unnatural is what you mean. Gee, Ted, I wish I knew what the difference between the two were. Ahhh! The facts of life. Anyhow, like I said, Ted, he just left me these simple instructions and the money, and said I could stay as long as I wanted. No questions asked and none taken. (*A bit more serious now, he shrugs indifferently*) That was it."

Ted: (*staring up at Pete for what seemed a lengthy time, permissible in measured terms and not be taken impolitely as though reading more into his words*) "All right, Pete, you've been a big help. Thanks anyway."

Pete: "Don't mention it, Ted. Hey! If I get word from him, I'll be sure to tell him you tried to reach him. But look, dude, I've got some rehearsing to do, so I got to split."

Ted: "No problem buddy. I'll be seeing yah." (*Then, with an idle wave by both parties, Pete shut the window and returned to his playing.*)

Ted didn't budge for a long time. He merely surveyed his surroundings with a sense of nostalgic melancholy. He then turned to stroll away . . . and then he was gone . . . and he never looked back.

Well, we've been lucky devils both.
And there's no need of pledge or oath
To bind our lovely friendship fast, by firmer
stuff close bound enough.

—*Robert Graves,* Two Fusiliers

Face the Music

A young man strolled briskly along a path with a step measured with determination. The birds sang him a sweet melody, and the trees released their blossoms like soft rain upon the earth to celebrate the height of the virgin spring, while Rogar welcomed it all gratefully with open arms.

Later, as he entered a cafeteria of the local university, his cheery mood changed immediately to a less pleasing one, patterned after the dull, torpid atmosphere which colored his senses. He looked about the place for signs of activity, but most of the tables and chairs were deserted of students. It made him feel a little lonely and depressed all of a sudden. He made sketchy headcount of the depleted number while he quickly maneuvered his body around the pendantic property that was scattered throughout the room like forlorn orphans about the scholastic complex.

He hurried in motion in order to escape the destitution rotting wastefully before his very eyes. He then came to an even more abandoned area, which had the audacity to call itself a corridor: A so-called avenue of higher learning, of all things.

Its white, uncontaminated walls gave him the impression that he was possibly the first person to ever have set foot in there. Then without much clemency than just deserved, he moved on down the hallway, scanning the identical rooms that decorated the walls opposite him. Because, after all, he was in too much of a hurry to dwell on the mundane. He marched by their blurred entrances, throwing brief glances into each of them. Yet, he already knew where he needed to be as he shot rapidly around a sharp corner.

At the end of this particular hallway, he could hear the distinct sound of music vibrating warmly from every angle. He immediately recognized it like an old friend coming into his life to accessibly greet him. It was as if the music had been beckoning, calling for him, drawing him from afar, sort of in the fashion of a snake charmer, to finally gather him here, at this very spot, for some needed respite and consolation.

He poked his head shyly into the room that he assumed the playing was coming from. There he spied the performer sitting in stoutly elegance on a stool for disciplined support behind an impressively huge piano. As he crept into the arena of creative ambition, he could see from where he was, the figure of his best friend deeply involved in the composition he was anxiously projecting from the grand, musical instrument.

As he came closer, he could feel the energy rising up through the air and beyond the confines of the rafters in a kind of phonic inferno; he was drawn to its harmonious heat like a moth to the compulsive sound. It was the type of cogent vibration that would soothe the savage beast in us all, like most successful beliefs and superstitions should convey, no doubt. But to our itinerant friend, this spoke to him in realistic form.

It seemed to echo and bounce off of the sturdy beams, which evidently steadied the ceiling, to emboss everything throughout the hollow building. Changing its direction and constitution at an escalating speed and level that marveled the meek below it as it ascended to the heavens, gave it that certain eminent flair about it while it continued to climb effortlessly higher still.

Rogar stood in a sensual fidget, watching his friend run his delicate fingers across the enamel keys with such skillful pouncing that every stroke injected from his studied desire appeared to produce an emotional electricity that shot back into his system, regenerating his performance twofold.

He dared not interrupt his friend's pious concentration, so he quietly moved toward an undisturbing place to rest his legs a bit and wait his turn.

At that moment, the youthful pianist looked up, sensing a sudden presence.

"Rogar, I didn't hear you come in," he said, with detached surprise in his voice as he read over his composed material.

"I heard you playing. I knew you'd be here," he replied, nodding his head unwittingly as he appropriated his human outline to meet the required structure of his seat in order to find the best quality for relaxation.

The proud artist spared a whimsical smile aligned with an ounce of bashful modesty.

"What was that you were playing?" he asked directly.

"Oh! That! It's just something I wrote a while back," he shrugged as he packed the sheets of paper he had into perfect order by hitting them with kid gloves onto the pampered wood.

"Did you like it?" he inquired with a liberal grin on his chops as he slipped from his bench so that he could stand beside his accompaniment with unassumingly modest confidence.

"I liked it very much. Really, it was good," he understated in honest shyness while adjusting his frame in his chair in order to be in a more alert position.

"A bit moody for my taste, but good just the same," as he elaborated on a fundamental stumbling block. "I've been working on it for a long time. I just finished it today, as a matter of fact," he responded, with downcast eyes as he ran his fingertips along the surface of the piano like an ambivalent masseur.

"What are you going to call it?" Rogar asked, following his buddy's movements with foreseeable suspicion.

"I'm going to call it 'Song of Cassandra.' What do you think?" he mentioned while staring up a with an ostentatious faculty and flair of showmanship as he addressed his friend for his wide-open, no-holds-barred criticism.

"Yeah! It's fine," he answered with semigenuine excitement, which he used as a decoy, not really paying much attention anymore because of a burning question, which he, all of sudden, had flaying inside of him and seemed to need his immediate consideration. "I heard about your scholarship. Congratulations," Rogar muttered, trying not to sound brusque in his manner as he changed the subject on him.

"Oh, yeah, I almost forgot about that," he gasped, forging an odd smile to suit himself.

"Well! Aren't you excited about going to New York," Rogar exclaimed in happy irritation.

The boy then beamed his features of mediocrity, being slightly amused by his pal's behavior and concern.

"Yes, of course," he answered, trying to forage for a polite stimulant to show his own excitement over the fortunate circumstances.

"What's wrong, Bobby, you look a little upset?" asked Rogar, sensing his buddies intricate margin of grief, like a misty halo above his sophisticated crown.

"Nothing. Why would I be upset. I'm fine. Why do you ask?" he responded, shrugging it off as a nuisance to his protected dignity.

"Is something going on between you and Denise?" Rogar inquired, knowing the precarious conditions behind the shaky relationship.

Bob appeared unperturbed at face value, yet underneath he shivered in his fragile skin, releasing creepy vibes, which you could almost smell, with a strong, sweet odor.

"No, everything is fine," Bob reported with meek cheer. "I think everything is all right. She's just going through a phase, that's all."

Rogar studied his friend's facile volition, attempting to read into it. Nevertheless, his acute intuition told him something entirely different, as he twisted this problem over in his aching brain. He wanted to push it further but decided it was none of his business, after all. So he let it pass for the time being.

"So how are things with you?" Bobby asked turning the tables on his friend to avoid any more disturbing questions.

"Great! I guess. The kid has been sick though for about a week. Yet Anna is okay," he replied with a smudge of worry in his facial expression, which revealed more than it should have.

"You know what?" Bob began, looking straight into his friend's face, as if something needed to be directly approached. "I envy you," he said ambiguously while he stepped down from the stage platform.

"What! Why on earth would you envy me?" Rogar remarked in humorous shock.

"Being married and all, I mean. I wish I had someone that loved me that way," he mentioned with rueful frankness. Yet, speaking more to his own heart, which seemed to his pal, Rogar, to have this constant requirement of always needing to be mended these days, rather than an actual preening of his buddy's social status of conjugality and wedlock, which Rogar knew he couldn't be really covetous of.

"Hey, man, you're going to be going to one of the top colleges in the country, and on a full scholarship, too. You've got so much to look forward to. How can you possibly be jealous of me," he acknowledged abruptly, feeling a little guilty about what he was insinuating all of a sudden.

Bobby picked up on it right away like radar, having noticed his friend's deep-seated resentment and incited dilemma for quite some time.

"No, Rogar, you're totally wrong. You just don't understand what you've got," he blurted out in mild rebuttal. You think that I'm lucky because I have no chains to tie me down, but I do, just like everybody else does."

"Please, Bobby, give me a break," Rogar exclaimed.

"Now wait a minute, Rogar. I know what you're thinking." And then he grinned, yet this particular smile was lightly dimpled with sadness and grief. "You're thinking that maybe you did the wrong thing in your choice of life. That you're too young and ambitious to be married and starting a family," he presumed with faith in his personal judgment.

"Bobby, what the hell are you going on about. What brought this crazy subject up anyway. And anyhow, what makes you think you know what I'm thinking about, huh?" Rogar chimed in, feeling a bit of animosity toward his closest friend over his baseless assumption as he propelled himself from his chair in flared-up emotion.

However, once he was on his feet, he felt slightly embarrassed by his tone of voice and his erratic actions and quirky conduct. And worse still, he wasn't even sure why he was acting so defensive in the first place. Was his buddy right after all? Was the burning truth, which brought such a flame into his soul, causing this? Or was it the jealousy dominating his brain after hearing this lecture that spread thick with a precocious imputation and incriminating the real culprit? Yet, in all honesty, he didn't even know for sure. But one thing he did know was that this fortunate brood had it completely and entirely backwards.

He had had plans—big plans. Major plans to go to school and

maybe be somebody, be someone important—but now, those dreams had been sidetracked or possibly destroyed forever. Wherever the road turned though, he was definitely screwed over about his once promising career and future. Not to say that he regretted his choice. He loved his family very dearly, but he felt he couldn't support and care for them the way he could have if he'd had his chance. And if he had the opportunity to do it all over again, he probably would have done the same thing but the way he would have liked. Because that was the point really. The fact that his decision was made for him, and that he had made a huge sacrifice in the process.

It was too bad, he reflected, *that you couldn't have all the things that you ever wanted and which you took for granted. All the options so easily laid out before you. Because honestly, you could only hang onto so much, like having all the sand on the beach in the full palm of your hand, and then to watch it slip through your fingers until you are left with nothing.*

"I didn't mean to be so judgmental," he apologized sincerely, seeing the fumes of discord distorting his pal's vision.

"It's all right, Bobby. It's no big deal," Rogar claimed understandingly.

"I've always considered you a very good friend, the best. And Rogar, . . . I hate to see anger come between us."

Rogar felt strangely emotional after having this confession brought forth so. They rarely ever got mad at each other. And when they did, it was usually a great misunderstanding anyway. Similar to the one they were having presently. That was usually the real instigator behind all of their troubles anyhow. Because they could never actually find anything justifiable enough to demolish and ruin what they had.

Moreover, they had this certain knack for deeply understanding one another in the end. Sort of like second sight or nature, which no words could account for. So when a confrontation would occur, it was usually so unnatural really, that they immediately felt compelled to resolve it and restore a peaceful equilibrium.

"Hey, man, don't get all soft on me," Rogar responded, playfully tossing a used notebook at him in affable offense.

Bob then caught it with the same confidence of good will, as though it was a cordial offering of appeasement for bridging the gap between them, to come to common terms with one another in a style that only they knew how to personally express.

"I just want you to know that I'll always be your friend, no matter what. And whatever happens from now on will not effect that," he announced with bold conviction.

"There you go again. God! I wish I knew what the hell you were going on about sometimes. Christ! Sometimes you say the craziest things. Anyhow, there was no need to say that. Nothing is going to charge our relationship. And I'm really glad for you, though. And I really mean that. And maybe someday I'll be able to get my act together, too," Rogar remarked soberly, yet with a hint of sad humor in his speech.

"Yes, Rogar, you have to not give up. You'll get your break soon also. You'll see."

"Well, I don't know about soon. And not the way I'm going about it, anyway. Look, I'm relatively pretty happy though, I guess," Rogar insisted while he clenched his fist, then hit his thigh with it in some kind of nervous show of grit. Subsequently, he paused for a second, as if he had blacked out, or if he was in some sort of nonverbal phase that he couldn't totally control or delete for some reason.

"I'm probably just a bit green-eyed of you, after all, I don't know. But don't worry about me, I'll be fine. Anyhow, it's you that should be worried. You have so much to think about now. Yet, it must be thrilling just the same."

"Yeah, I suppose I do. But it's not going to be the same without my good buddy around. You've helped me out a lot. I still don't know sometimes how I would have managed if you hadn't been there for me all those years," Bobby admitted bashfully.

"You see. I told you not to get all mushy with me. We're both starting to sound like a damn couple about to split up or something. Come on, Bobby, let's get outta here. I think the atmosphere in here is getting to you," Rogar replied jokingly, as a substitute remedy for the awkward situation, feeling slightly embarrassed for the both of them over this abundant display of affection while he waved to him to follow.

Bob hesitated for a moment to smirk, surprised by his buddy's funny weakness. He then mimicked his friend's attitude by shaking his head before making his own exit.

Once they were both in the isolated hallway, Rogar spoke again to his long-time pal.

"Listen, Bobby, let's grab a cup of coffee somewhere. I have something to tell you that I heard today and that will interest you, I think."

"I'm sorry, but I can't go with you. I have to run. I've got something very important to take care of," he explained, with gut-wrenched sorrow and deep regret on his brow.

"Oh, come on, Bobby, I don't see much of you these days anymore. Just one cup of coffee. Come on. What's so important that you can't spend time with your former academic chum?" he asked in partial witticism.

"No, really, I have to leave," he repeated in earnest as he collected his stuff together in his arms.

Rogar was spellbound momentarily, distracted by his friend's serious ambiguity, which stifled him for awhile from any further attempt at challenging his buddy's more unattractive side for conformity.

Just as Bob was about to flee though, Rogar was hit with a sense of rejection that he had never felt before. It made him distressed with worry all of a sudden, as if his friend was trying to avoid him for some reason.

He was always aware of his buddy's extraneous behavior, and he was usually used to it. It was probably one of the reasons why he liked this mysterious person so much to begin with. Yet this time, it hit a chord in him that made him feel a bit disturbed right about now.

His ideas and plans, which he kept locked up inside until he felt it was safe or appropriate enough to let him in on it. This was the unique, eccentric quality that appealed to this conservative person. But you usually have to take the good with the bad. That was usually the case and how the deal was cut between this pair of individuals.

Sometimes it was irrepressible and irrational what they had. But he knew the score and his friend's ways very well; that was the major basis of them staying and being together really anyway. And that, after all, was reasonable enough for him to cope with more or less.

Most people couldn't keep a secret or keep something private to save their lives, but Bob was an exception to that rule. You could tell him just about anything, and he wouldn't tell a soul. And that kind of guarantee was as good as gold in Rogar's book.

"Hey, wait a minute. At least let me walk you to your car," Rogar requested, catching up with his swift friend, who appeared to want to slip away for some odd reason.

"Sure, why not," Bob answered with searching eyes.

Together they left the building, chatting about old times and laughing about them all. They were happy again like the kids that they once were. And yet, it felt new and refreshing speaking of these former glories, which only made the company ever more rewarding.

It was late afternoon now, and when they were outside, the sun could be seen descending in the distance. And as it sank lower in the darkening sky, a bright, orange headdress seemed to be trailing behind it, which was sort of a reminder that she would be back tomorrow, to bring the world an even more extolling sumptuousness than she had given us unworthy beings today.

However, they appeared to miss this marvelous spectacle, being too involved in their elaborate conversation. It was as though they were teenaged boys once more, enjoying the fruits of their smattering youth without actually comprehending the significance of these fleeting moments which could never last.

"What was it you wanted to tell me about before?" Bob mentioned casually as he leaned against this car door.

"Oh that! I almost forgot. Thanks for remembering though. It's nothing really, now that you brought it up," he remarked with a fazed flush on his cheeks.

"Well, tell me anyway," Bob responded, dying to know what the information was, after seeing the affect it was having on his chagrined pal.

"Anyhow, do you recollect hearing about that rock star who killed himself by tying himself to a rope in his basement? And how the authorities couldn't figure out how he did it because there wasn't a chair or anything around to prop him up. Remember that, huh?"

"Yes, go on."

"Well, you know that pool of water they discovered beneath his feet? Anyway, that turned out to be a big block of ice which melted or something while he was standing upon it, or he slipped on, I assume.

But anyway, isn't it kinda wicked how he planned the whole thing, huh? How he took the time to elaborate his own death?"

"How did they figure that out anyway?" Bob asked, being totally enthralled by the whole, weird concept.

"I knew you'd be interested in this. You see, he made this video of himself. As if he was making a performance out of his own hanging. Crazy, huh?"

"Shit! I'd never do anything stupid like that," Bob remarked.

"Yeah! Well, who would? He was obviously very sick and demented."

"No. I mean, I would never have filmed it. I would have let them guess," Bobby mentioned in speculative thought.

"Ah, Bobby! You're so fucking kooky sometimes. I should have known you'd say something screwy like that," and Rogar laughed at the prospect of it as he punched his buddy playfully in the arm.

"Look, Rogar, I really have to go."

"All right, Bobby. Anyway, call sometime, okay? Don't be a stranger."

"Yeah, right. I sure will." And he jumped into his car, waving at his best friend while he sped off.

Thus, while Rogar watched him leave, he felt suddenly woeful, which he couldn't quite explain. Probably suspecting, that it would possibly be a long time before they would hear from each other again.

It was a few hours later when Rogar found himself entering his home. He was completely exhausted from the day's hard events, and he was looking forward to relaxing quietly with his young family once more in the pleasures of domestic life.

"Hi, darling, how was work?" the woman who had recently become his wife called from the kitchen.

He felt a certain regularity in her voice, which struck him rather glumly as he answered her in the same pattern of concord.

"Oh, fine. How was your day?" he replied, staying within the resigned routine.

"I made dinner. Are you hungry?" she asked, showing herself now from behind the kitchen door.

He didn't respond to her, but instead, sat down on the first thing that resembled a seat and proceeded to remove his shoes, symbolizing an end to his work day.

She then returned to her own chores with the instinctive knowledge that he was ready to eat his supper.

He was always hungry, as a matter of fact, at about this time. Therefore, why bother making the effort in answering her, he thought, it was utterly pointless really.

All in all, he had grown accustomed to this daily procedure and schedule of coming home: eating his victuals, and then digesting his bountiful lassitude with great relish while falling into inactivity by watching the evening tube.

He would have eaten it anyhow, whether he was hungry or not. It was there to be consumed. So be it.

"You had a phone call today," she told him, yelling gently from inside the refrigerator as she assembled his food into a sufficient meal.

He sat up with his back pressed against the cushions, which he had propped up for comfort. He had a stern expression on his face while he waited for his wife to finish her vague statement. But she was done, regardless of his avarice to know more, which angered him a little as he accepted this morsel of information.

He was growing tired of her inability to complete a sentence and of her being unable to communicate with him in person. Yet, that was the trials and tribulations of marriage, after all.

"Who was it?" he shouted to her fragmentation. Not really feeling up to raising his voice but making the exertion anyway.

"Oh! I don't know who it was, dear. She didn't leave her name or anything," his spouse explained. "She said she might call back later, though," she concluded while standing in the same room with him presently with contingency in her mind. "You look tired," she mentioned endearingly, sitting on the arm of the soft chair in order to stroke his weary mane.

"Oh, I'm fine," he remarked, coming back to earth briefly as he shrank away from her affectionate approaches.

"She didn't leave her name?" he inquired in echo from the out-of-the-blue newsflash, which only made him even more confused over who it might be.

"No, why? Were you expecting a call today or something?" she asked harmlessly while rubbing the arch of his back with that extra female touch, which he usually loved.

"No, I don't think so," he replied, scanning his memory banks to make doubly sure.

"Where's Michael?" he asked, suddenly dropping the topic like a hot potato.

"He's asleep. He's still not feeling very well," she confirmed somberly while kissing her husband gently on the head.

"Have you taken him to see a doctor?" he asked, with deeper interest as he turned to face her.

"Yes, yesterday. He'll be all right in a couple of days. He just has a mild fever now, that's all," she reassured the both of them with honest suggestion as she warmed him up with her distaff touch. "I better get dinner ready," she announced all of a sudden, giving him one last peck on the cheek before departing his side once again.

He watched her leave the living room and thought about what Bob had said. Was he really a lucky person after all? And was all this love and family stuff ultimately the answer to everyone's banes? This was worth more than a thousand college degrees, wasn't it? If it was, it was still a mystery to him, quite frankly. Nevertheless, he'd have to wait awhile longer and let it bear fruit before drawing any definite conclusions. Moreover, that's all he had, actually, time to allow it to develop into something that he could positively feel secure about.

He tossed this slippery, mental orb around in his troubled brain, weighing its durability against the forces of doubt that impatiently haunted him. Yet, he couldn't come up with the type of convincing answer to his silly argument that he immediately desired. *I guess it was all irrelevant anyway,* he consummated, not wishing to think of it anymore. But he couldn't help or stop himself from wondering who might be calling him. For some odd reason, this thing really bothered him, even though most of the time it was usually no big deal.

It was the not knowing that disturbed him the most.

"I guess if it was important, this particular person, whoever it was, would call back. Jesus! what is wrong with me these days? Why am I so worried about some stupid phone call, which probably will amount to nothing in the end anyway," he exclaimed out loud to his aching mind.

"Honey, is there anything bothering you? It's this woman who phoned today, isn't it?" his wife responded suddenly, assuming that he was talking and addressing these questions directly to her.

He then turned to her after witnessing her materialize into the living room.

"What? Oh, I don't know," he pondered in a quandary while rubbing his cropped hair with sheer intensity from his brief spell of mad singularity. "I can't seem to be able to get it outta my mind. It's just that something very strange happened the other afternoon, which I've only started to realize," he mentioned immediately as he turned to his spouse for some sort of hopeless relief.

"What do you mean, Rogar?"

"Hell, I'm not really certain actually. But I saw my friend Bobby yesterday while I was on my break, and it's left me with this creepy feeling ever since," he acknowledged.

"What's that got to do with this woman calling you, though?"

"Man! That's it. I don't know. This is gonna sound kinda silly, but I have this funny sensation that there's something wrong, but for the life of me, I can't figure out what it is," he replied in open anguish.

"Look, all you need is some food inside of you, and I think you'll feel a lot better, huh? What do you say?"

"Actually, honey, to tell you the truth, I've lost my appetite. I'm sorry, Anna, maybe I'll eat it later. Okay?"

"All right, darling, whatever you want. I'll just leave it in the oven for when you're ready."

"Thanks, dear, I appreciate it," he responded with rueful guilt.

Nonetheless, she was lost for words and adequate assistance, standing rooted to the floor as if nailed to it.

And then, as though set free from her psychological bonds, she returned to the safety of the kitchen in a flash, having found nothing to aid in the support of his overzealous demeanor.

At that moment, he lay down on the couch, wanting to forget about the monkey on his back, feeling the vibes of sleep run through his nervous system.

He hadn't realized how tired he was until right now. Yet he foolishly attempted to fight off this powerful drowsiness by pretending to browsingly flip through the pages of a magazine.

But this formula wasn't enough to stall the process as he drifted off into the depths of sleep.

When he was completely unconscious, all he thought about was that stranger calling him, as though he wasn't even safe in the sanctuary of slumber. And what was worse was that he was scared to death of this consistent and persistent boogeyman, which obsessively tormented the confines of his brain. But why? This was a question which he couldn't answer as he struggled in the doldrums of his disquieted dreams.

Then he awoke, which in an odd way, rescued him from his emotional bog. Drenched in sweat and unknown fears, he was startled by the sound of the telephone ringing in his naked head.

He heard it beckoning him in his subconscious thoughts and was totally surprised to hear it when he was roused from his distasteful nap.

For a timeless moment, he just stared at it, amazed by its nervous vibrating noise. And then his wife entered the scene ready to put an end to the persistent repetition that he was unable to fathom at this point.

In order to be the first to answer, and being nearer to it, Rogar took the honors by picking up the phone with lightning speed, before his wife had a chance to deal with the unavoidable responsibility.

Seeing this eager action, she stopped abruptly in her tracks and watched him with spontaneous turmoil while he spoke through the receiver.

"Hello," he whispered, coated with danger and somnolency in his weak tone.

"Hello, Rogar, it's, it's Mrs. Lynn," a voice replied on the other end of the line.

At first, the name just blew straight over his poor, absentminded head as he attempted to recollect who it was. And not only that, but the woman's voice seemed to have the same effect as a shot from a tranquilizer on him while he stood with gaping jaws over the plastic mouthpiece trying to unmuddle his brain into working order.

Then it immediately came back to him who it was, bouncing back from the farthest part of his dormant mind, to then strike him hard on the cerebral cortex like a sledgehammer.

"Oh! Hi! Mrs. Lynn! . . . What can I do for you?" he asked in polite discomfort and apprehension while clearing his throat and straightening himself up as if she was right there in the room beside him to inspect his slack composure.

For a short while, all he heard was silence on the other end. And then he thought he heard remote crying. Soft crying, similar to a groan or a meek moan coming through the cords of distortion. He almost spoke again before he was cut short by louder more distinct weeping.

"I'd thought you'd want to know first, being his closest friend and all . . . Bobby was found—Bobby's . . . Bobby's dead—he died late last night," forcing out and spilling out these grief-stricken words, breaking the dam that held her sorrow inside as she bled wholeheartedly her guts out over the phone as though she was crying on his shoulder. After that difficult task, she could no longer speak. And when she did make a further attempt, the sentences came out all mumbled and incoherent while Rogar, on the opposite end, went totally blank.

His head swirled with images, but he said nothing—produced nothing of any relevance to speak of. And finally, thought nothing. Because, in truth, there wasn't anything he could say that made any sense to him at this juncture while he tried to comprehend what she had just stated.

Then he noticed that a male voice had taken her place, relieving her of her remorseful duty.

Consequently, Rogar overheard this man attempting to console and soothe Bobby's mother as she was led away by some other family member.

"Hi, Rogar, it's Mr. Lynn. My wife can't talk to you at this moment. I'm sorry to call you at such an hour—"

"Oh, it's quite all right," Rogar burst in instantly as he felt the sad irony of this person's unwarranted apology at notifying him at such a late hour of his best friend's death.

"But the other reason we contacted you at this time is because we wanted to know if you had spoken to Bobby at all today or some time earlier?" he stressed from under the extreme pressure that the accidental circumstances had put upon him.

For a brief minute, Rogar couldn't even accomplish this simple chore as he raced to find a feasible answer.

"Yes, I did. Tuesday afternoon, but he appeared fine to me," Rogar explained, with chaotic nervousness in his guilty speech.

"I'm sorry to bring this up, but are you sure nothing out of the ordinary happened?"

"No! I don't think so."

Yet, what did he mean by "out of the ordinary" anyway?

"It's okay, Rogar, I'm just trying to sort this out, this ugly mess and make certain that we haven't left any stones unturned."

"Please, Mr. Lynn, sir, you don't need to worry about upsetting me about that. If I really knew something that could help, I wouldn't hesitate to tell you, believe me."

"I know, I know. . . . It's a horrible situation, and I wish I wasn't the one to bother you with it," he noted, with pain in his voice, which it seemed he was attempting to hide for some strange reason.

From then on, he carried on a conversation of sorts with Bobby's dad. But what he said from that period forward, he wouldn't be able to remember, and would never be able to recollect. In fact, he felt as if his voice was acting on his own behalf, a substitute filling in for him where he could not while he drifted off into never-never land, as he attempted to retrace his steps in order to find something there that might aid him in his quest to figure out this "ugly mess," as Mr. Lynn had so salubriously put it.

He tried to envision what his friend looked like that day or what he might have looked like during that expurgated tragedy, even what he might look like now. He pictured him all cold and lifeless. A mass of heavy flesh. Useless anatomy, all stiff and frangible, speaking to him in private of these secret clues. And resolving for him personally this dark mystery which he suspected his pal would have so much enjoyed to have revealed and done.

Yet this idea was utterly sick, and all these disgusting visions swarmed into his brain suddenly, like an uninvited plague of locusts. Moreover, he couldn't hold them back, no matter how immoral they may be. It was plain as day, and that was that.

The pure force of it was too overwhelming for his deteriorated mind to handle. Especially now that his guard was down.

Where did it happen?—How did it happen?—Why did it happen? he thought in rapid, but somber, irregularity as these *protests* raced and intermingled through his brain. Nonetheless, all these significant questions went unanswered, because, in all honesty, he didn't have the courage to ask them.

Furthermore, none of this made any sense to him, even after speaking with his poor family. Just the other day, twenty-four hours ago, to be exact, give or take a few minutes of course, in that span of a few hours, they had been talking and laughing about what they had done and should have done, as if it was all an inadvertent fling.

Why would someone leave all those precious moments behind? Tossed to the wind like useless garbage. Why did he leave me in the dark so that I would one day have to hear the bad news from someone else instead of from the proper source? Why not discuss this with the one single person who knew better than anyone else the true nature of things between them? Why, then, didn't he tell me!

Evidently, none of this crap made any sense to him at all . . . and it probably never would, as far as he was concerned. He fought hard to listen to Bobby's father, who spoke nervously between bouts of grief as Rogar answered him, whenever it was deemed appropriate, in equal meaninglessness. He wanted to say something to ease and comfort and comply with what had happened, but he couldn't.

What was he supposed to do? He couldn't interrogate this unfortunate, bereaved man anymore in order to satisfy his own selfish needs with more worthless stuff. He wanted just to go. Yet this man kept him on the line for a length of time that was more than he could bear at this moment.

Rogar desperately reached out with his eager emotions for someone to rescue him. And then, suddenly, he saw his own wife poised in the corner of his blurry view, waiting for him to let her in on the terrible details behind this gruesome ordeal, having only grasped bits and parts of it from her husband's morsel of audible, broken words. Finally, it was all over, and he bid farewell to Mr. Lynn.

"Yes, sir. I sure will. Thank you for everything. Yes, good night to you, too," he stated while he pressed the hot piece of plastic to his tender ear as if it was solely to blame as the deliverer of dark messages, . . . and then he hung up the receiver with delicate conformance onto its cradle and fell back in his chair in weary frustration, left with the aftershock of the whole, traumatic experience, which echoed in his mind like a nightmare.

Yet with all this anger and discontent, he hadn't shed one, solitary tear for his lost friend. And to tell the truth, he felt his buddy had somehow copped out and given up too easily on him and himself. Therefore, he felt as if his old pal had done a cowardly thing by quitting on life like that. Deep down, he couldn't help but believe Bobby really didn't deserve too much sympathy from his perplexed friend.

Even if this were the ultimate truth in some weird way, which he struggled to decipher, your closest companions were exempted from normal rules and regulations, so why not release a few tears, or two dozen, for that matter, for a dead buddy. It was the only right thing to do at this point, . . . wasn't it?

All these problems buzzed and droned with a heavy humming sound in his head and eardrums as he rubbed his burning temples.

He felt completely depleted and drained of energy, like some drunk wino spiked to the gills with booze.

After placing the telephone in its proper place, he attempted to recollect what was said to him, having forgotten most of the conversation, except for the part about his friend's demise of course. He seemed to show no outward signs of loss or sorrow at all. That really disturbed him a lot. Even his poor wife didn't know what to say, seeing him in this queer shape. So she stayed quiet until something more plausible came along.

He tried to conjure up the right emotions, but he couldn't fake a thing such as that.

He thought stressfully about his inability to feel hurt and of his insensitivity toward the situation, leaving a sore knot in his stomach, which he nurtured with his profound guilt-ridden conception of the past, which once upon a time was so pure and intimately secure.

Maybe things had changed between them after all. The evidence was obviously there if one desired to seek it, ultimately being reproduced from this realistic crisis. He questioned himself intensively as he fell back into his chair, which seemed always ready to welcome him whenever he needed some kind of artificial solace.

Yet, he still held fond memories of their strong relationship regardless of the consequences. Snapshots yellowed and withered from the unexplained prospective.

He subsequently glanced over at his wife, who returned his unclad gaze with her own silent, stunned expression from the untold particulars.

He then had an ugly vision: Maybe his wife had something to do with the loss of his best friend, like some trade with the devil, he supposed, while he gazed into her sullen features.

He started to conceive a deficient image of his buddy's death being caused by their loss of brotherly love, which he forthwith felt very strongly about. And that it had been taken away ruthlessly and given to her. Or was this just a last resort regret to relay or broadcast some unseen condemnation towards someone else, like his infelicitous Anna, for example.

No! That was ridiculous! How could I think such a disgusting thing! he exploded and berated himself from the inside of his tormented skull, which appeared to mentally split in two from this cerebral decision.

I must be just upset, that's all. . . . This stuff is driving me crazy or something, he stressed internally as he applied pressure to the soft section of his palms by attempting to absorb them into the sockets of his red eyes, trying vehemently to expel the awful idea from his mind.

"Darling, what's the matter? Can I help?" Anna eventually said as she saw him punishing himself so.

"He's dead," spoke Rogar, imitating the sound of pain through his emotionless tone, which he wanted, but really didn't have, relating it to being upset over this huge, personal misplacement, instead of by the actual sense of treachery and betrayal that he carried.

Consequently, his wife dropped into the next available seat, like a falling from grace, and mullishly stirred this instant announcement around in her mind for awhile, until it settled down deep within her like a precipitated attack or infection.

He watched this performance with complete indifference, thinking how easy it would be to pick up the telephone and dial his buddy's number. And then when he heard his familiar voice, all clear and sharp on the other end, that's when everything would be all right once more. It seemed just a sick, practical joke after all. A big, stupid, terrible misunderstanding which could be simply resolved and cured by this basic act.

Anna then rubbed her legs skittishly as if to gain some needed fortitude before being able to speak her mind.

"You mean your friend Bobby? How did all of this happen?" she asked carefully while clearing her lungs of all her shy indignities as her submissively glazed eyes peered at him with inconvenient uncertainty.

"It was some kind of accident, I think. I don't know for sure. Nobody knows. They don't have the whole story yet," he sputtered out in sensitive disarray, getting up to circle his space while suddenly dying to get some fresh air.

Anna sensed his irritation and avoidance and fell silent again and proceeded to distract herself from his patent attempt to not involve her further by picking nervously at her fingernails, wondering what she should do.

"I'm going out," he proclaimed rather spontaneously as he scurried around in one place for the unknown.

"Where are you going?" she demanded pathetically, popping from her seat with the force of a compressed spring.

"I don't know . . . I need some air," he answered her uniformly, throwing this petty excuse at her while he paced anxiously around the small room like a chicken with its head cut off.

"It's pretty late, Rogar . . . would you like some company?" she practically pleaded timidly.

"No, thanks, I'd rather be alone," he replied, putting on a smile for her when he noticed her concern, which touched a nerve in him as he kissed her lightly on the forehead.

After that, he rushed out the front door, leaving his wife standing by herself in the doorway to ponder over what was going on.

In less than an hour from sunrise (because, for the reader's information, he had been out most of that erstwhile night), a car pulled into a spacious parking lot. And a little while later, a person slowly stepped out onto the black asphalt, still warm, surprisingly, from the previous afternoon's heat. He stood gaping at his surroundings as the dawn began to make its presence felt.

He looked over at the school buildings, their dark, majestic shadows casting Gothic beauty, and he thought of the last time he had seen his friend alive.

He didn't know what he was doing here, but a strange possessive energy had seized his free will and had drawn him blindly, for some unexposed reason, back to this spot.

Besides all that, it was peaceful and relaxing here. He could think openly and expand his troubles on endless boundaries of nothingness, where recently he could not, so that they would be able to amplify and, maybe, have answers, which he desperately sought.

He walked toward an array of large structures that dotted the scene like giant, stone redwoods on a man-made hill of blood, sweat, and toil, carrying with him a sense of alienation never felt before, which was characteristic of a suspicious, undesirable entering of an undesirable land.

It was six o'clock in the morning by his surprised and discovered account. Just in the nick of time to witness the changing of the guard and the faculty earlier-risers and those who had the burden of being scheduled to be taught at th is ungodly hour.

When he entered the municipal building, he duplicated his movements in the strictest form of that of the minor masses who simultaneously tagged along with him. He had the funny feeling that if he followed the normal procedure of the day, no one would question why he was here to begin with. If anyone cared to inquire, that is.

He came to a room, the very same one that he had heard the spiritual music being beautifully played not long ago.

He pricked up his ears as though expecting to hear a ghost's rendition of it, but instead all he heard was the empty vastness of stillness drowning in his head.

It was so quiet, in fact, that it was comparable to being in a vacuum. It sucked the life out of his pores with such skill, that you would have no knowledge of such a thoroughly evil deceit, unless you were rendered extremely sensitized to your recognizable environment as he was, which, moreover, was similar in enhanced quality to a human radar device that he had lately developed during the recent couple of hours.

He strolled about the place until he registered something familiar, that gave him the instinctive suggestion of uneasy snugness, which was the only thing he was provided with to make him feel easy in his present surroundings.

Subsequently, he took his favorable, regular seat in the front row of the tiny amphitheater, staring straight ahead at the grand piano, which was still evident in its usual magnificent position as before. Except, of course, for one major, important, adjustment, or flaw, as you will; the brilliantly talented and gifted prodigy was unmistakably missing from his rightful stool. Like witnessing a tragic vacancy. As though surveying an abandoned vessel with no one left to take charge at the controls of a pilotless ship of creative magic: And this left a disturbing impression on Rogar as he sank into astonishment over this incommodious dilemma.

He felt uncomfortably warm all of a sudden. The air seemed thick and displeasing, yet he wanted to stay and punish himself for his ignorance and lack of compassion. And that's when he heard dainty footsteps in the hall. He impulsively swirled in his chair to see who dared to intrude on his private lamentation.

Positioned in the doorframe, in innocent reluctance, was a small child in the shape of a girl of maybe nine years of age.

Rogar then had a shocked expression on his face, which made the young female ill at ease suddenly, and who, consequently, became too frightened by this particular grown-up's peculiar visage to budge from her safe spot at the entrance.

He was lost in his own thoughts no doubt, not realizing what intangibly influential damage he might be having on such a delicate creature such as she.

The reason behind his odd behavior can be summoned up like this: she was the last person he had expected to see in the whole, living world. Actually, in a strange way, he was hoping that he might be having another form of visitor, preferably someone from a very divergent and disparate existence.

Having show up so was a great disappointment to him that could only be taken as a forlorn consideration for his extravagantly overzealous actions of ardent conduct to see the unseen, which was quite unbecoming of someone who would be regarded as normal under average circumstances.

When he regained control of his composure, he noticed the disturbing impression that he was probably making on this poor child. Therefore, he tried to make up for it by putting on a feeble display and gesture of calm and innocuousness for her special benefit.

The result from the experiment seemed to shed no light on an optimistically mutual linkage. Actually, his change of temperament and manner appeared to temporarily backfire on him, a bit as she seemed to oppose him by reversing the effects of his semipositive approach by backing off timidly into the hallway.

So he began to speak, aspiring to correct the bad intuition that seemed to be spreading rapidly inside of her.

"Hi, what's your name?" he asked in the most friendly tone that he could possibly muster at the moment, attempting to break the social ice barrier that had just been created between them.

"My name's Emma. What's yours?" she shot back with quick boldness. Then she regretted what she had said after thinking it over while she clutched her lower lip with her young, teeth.

"I'm Rogar . . . Emma, huh? What a pretty name you have," he responded, finding utter amusement in her puerile demeanor.

She peeked at him and smiled innocently after seeing how his reaction had become more inoffensive and harmless, and losing almost all of her shyness in the process.

"I'm waiting for my brother. He goes to school here," she announced with uncorruptible pride as she stared at something behind him, in the background, which he was blocking from her with his bulky form.

He saw her baby blues shift and he followed their direction. The general location of the object of her view, like an independent vivacity on an honorable throne of respectful reverence, was the baby organ.

He was slightly bewildered at beholding it through her interested vision. He had almost forgotten about its enormous presence, for some odd reason. Even though it had clearly been in the room the whole time, it appeared to have suddenly manifested from nowhere to attract his attention once more.

"I can play," she claimed, pointing toward it. "My mom says I'm good," she declared proudly, forgetting her fear of him entirely as she made another attempt to enter the place again.

"Oh, yeah! Why don't you show me then?" Rogar said in bland encouragement, positioning himself at a secure distance to give her ample space to slip by him safely so she would be inclined to test her practiced skill.

She looked at him, not sure whether to trust this stranger or not. But her desire to play was much greater than her apprehension, so she came forward.

He then reclined into his comfortable chair and waited patiently for her to situate herself properly. Once she was ready, her tiny frame appeared to be subdued by the massive, symphonic apparatus. Then she began to play, cautiously at first, but eventually gaining confidence and harmonious dominion over her natural aptitude to perform.

Her capacity grew every second as her exquisite fingers danced across the black and white pegs. He monitored her closely while her cute features transformed into a serious complexion of an expert musician and as they both became engrossed in the pulchritudinous sound, which brought bright color into the damp, humid chamber.

Yet his mind was driven by a different passion, as the music seemed to add something to his puzzled and melancholic mood—feeding him false hope—while her own commiseration was drawn by the true love of music.

His eyes flashed with an innovative spark, as if someone had prodded him with an electric rod.

"What is that you're playing?" he exclaimed with blind demand.

She stopped instantly what she was doing after hearing the harshness in his tone. She once again became the scared little girl of before, unable to move or say anything. Frozen to her seat in terror of retribution.

Rogar saw the discomforting blemish he had left on her yet was unremitting in his determination to have his will enforced.

"I-I found this . . . this lying here. Someone must've left it," she admitted in a benighted, regretful, quivering explanation.

"Play it again," he cried as he was still in an unpremeditated rage while manipulatively almost reaching for her throat to have his way from the confines of an audience's boundaries.

She sat shivering in ambivalence. Her only thought at that intensely suspenseful moment was to cry over her precarious situation from which she felt she had no hope of escaping.

Her suffering and lack of understanding was the sedative that brought back his solemn composure, as he fully comprehended that he had inadvertently spooked her.

In order to reassure her that he meant no harm he told her to continue again, in the softest and kindest speech he could feign, which was bordering on the most superfluous etiquette he could mobilize at such pressing a time, that he believed was acquainted with a true gentleman. He pleaded beningningly to her, wishing with all his might that she not flee from him so soon, being unable under the circumstances to come up with anything better as a solution to keep her around longer.

"Please play it again. . . . I'm terribly sorry for my rudeness. But please, play some more, . . . please."

The youthful lady wasn't too sure of what to do either. She wanted to run real bad, but yet found that she could not move for the life of her.

"I won't interrupt you anymore. I promise. Please go on," trying to show her his good intentions by folding his hands in his lap and sitting appeasingly with his shoulders back for extra good measure. Yet, inside, he uncoiled like a hungry serpent with a burning lust to listen to more.

She trembled a little as her fingers started to touch the smooth keys once more. And from where he sat, he could see her small pupils darting randomly in search of encouragement and reinforcement while her tiny mouth chapped from diffident quavering.

Rogar felt sorry for her, because he knew he had spoiled the moment for them both. That poor, vulnerable child, who he erroneously treated like the whipping post for his mental inquiry. Yet, he couldn't help himself. *I have to hear it again. I just have to!* reproving himself as he concentrated more this time over the significant notes she was conveying to him.

She doesn't understand how important this is to me. Maybe I should let her be. Let her free from this chastisement. Why torment others with my problems. Especially defenseless creatures like this one. It's best that I suffer alone than involve others in my own private hell.

At that juncture, the music seemed to really return in full force. Richer than ever. Strong and vibrant, as though his outburst had brought the genuinely real, masterful strokes out of her former, withdrawn, juvenile sentiments, common in most small children her age.

Rogar listened intently, following the vibrations, like he had some special searchlight watching her every move with restrained gusto equal to that of a paramour.

It was as though it was an actual form of communication, which, in an abstract way, was what music really was anyhow.

But more than that; it was something that couldn't be transcribed with mere words. Something much more meaningful and personal that was too brutal and severe for dialect alone, yet delicate and refined for melodious language only.

The lush sound carried him away, taking his soul on a joy ride on a chariot of sonority. Embracing the tender part of him with an angel's soft kiss.

It's a love song, he guessed as he whispered sacredly in a private rumor.

A song of lost love probably . . . Yes! That must be it he envisioned with cozy helplessness: enlightened at last through painful tears, which began to fill his bloodshot eyes.

But his heraldic proclamation refused to go beyond his own hearing as his novel enunciation was being swallowed up whole by the current of a sad sonata while he wept for something he couldn't bring back. Something he could no longer embody and contain as he sank into his own oblivion.

Because the truth, in conclusion, can be more hurtful than a grieving heart. And sometimes it is easier to forgive than it is to forget. Therefore, leaving it to the bruised pathos to mend itself in the end.

Rebus and Rabble

Written by Eric Helton and Massimo Abbruzzetti

The longer I live my life, the less I understand it. And the less I understand about my screwed-up existence, the less I understand about other people. It's kinda silly and stupid really, to constantly dwell on it, I mean. Nevertheless, no exactness was ever better spoken or dearly departed from these tainted, but sincere, lips.

I've just got this one-way ticket to Paradise via a short cut through Purgatory. No shortcuts or return trips. Nonrefundable and nonnegotiable. So I've got to do something quick, real fast like. And don't ask me what, because I have no idea. Driving blind among the incessant stench of a road kill, or something prevalently wise like that, . . . quote unquote.

Have you ever just sat by the ocean closed your eyes, and just listened to the great big, blue mass of water? No, really, it's no joke. It's really fucking amazing! It really is. Picture this for a second. First, there are these unbelievable crashing and repetitious waves—crash, boom, bang—really overwhelming shit. It's sorta scary, and at the same time, . . . I don't know, there's this mesmerizing silence in the air, too, . . . You know what I mean? Well, maybe not. But it's far fucking out stuff just the same.

Anyway, when you listen closer, . . . no, closer than that, your mind takes you past the waves. Way past the current and everything . . . until you're way past the place where you are sitting or standing or whatever. And get this; you end up at this spot, which is composed of equally intriguing lightness and darkness, where the whole harmony thing disarms and consumes you somehow while simultaneously beckoning you closer and closer. It's really something, something out of this world. Anyhow, where was I? Oh, yeah, I was discussing something about not knowing where I'm going, right . . . ? Yet, I've still got to go somewhere. Somewhere where everything has to be kinda hushed. Somewhere mollifying and calm so that I can submerge in peace. Can you comprehend what I'm getting at? Can you? Hey, the hell with it. No sweat, it's just another day in the life of a social castaway.

Rise of the Rebus

Hi, teenage America! Welcome to this year's biggest theme park. The one of makeover and make-believe. And ultimately, it is billed (to you) as the granddaddy of all swindles in a nutshell, I daresay and add shamelessly. Keep your eyes on the tiny, magic pea . . . round and round she goes, where she stops, nobody knows.

So without further ado, I will demonstrate by calling out to all you righteous dudes and dudettes. Don't attempt to adjust the picture because there's nothing else on.

Tune in and don't try to resist, because this thing is bigger than the both of us, the macdaddy of macdaddies.

Rise! And gather around the campfire, all you anxious pyromaniacs, and witness this sad, diabological spectacle unfold, while it smolders before your very eyes and burns to the very core of your tender retina. Burn, baby, burn and enjoy.

Don't be shy. Didn't your mother ever teach you not to play with fire? It's a serious vocation after all, nothing to toy with, you know.

Meanwhile, here I sit, twiddling my thumbs with my mentor, while I act out my role of the grin-and-bear-it-honey deaf mute. He is death in all its gory glory. A fatality on two legs, this one. The hidden assassin who slays social conversation and small talk at will with a wink of an eye. Because, if the truth be told, this jerk really kills me. Jesus H. Christ! God help me, if I have to hear any more of his five-and-dime philosophy, I will, with no-holds-barred certainty, rub this punk out. Just like that, . . . I swear I will! . . . Scout's honor. And that's the way the Girl Scout cookie crumbles, I'm afraid. Yet, who am I kidding, . . . right? And I can, and am, big enough to admit with incomplete honesty that I feed off of this two-bit hustler/pariah and cracker-faced parakeet, from the moldy tidbits which he tosses at me from time to time.

Polly want a cracker?

Hi, my name's Polly, and I am a recovering simple errand boy.

Hi, Polly, welcome to the rest of your life.

Oh, brother, what fine mess have I gotten myself into ollie . . . ollie, ollie, oxen free. And free me from this dumbass of an ox, pleeez!

I am a pretty little errand girl, as pretty, as pretty stupid as they come and can be. And there's no hope of going dutch with this one. For there is no dutch treat for the likes of me. So I say, fare-thee-well for now until the day comes when the tide will turn in my favor to finally rid myself of this drugstore pimp! This, this two-bit Scarlet Pimpernel. Because it would take the strength and courage of a very butch dyke to plug up and finger that particular hole, . . . with wooden clogs and all. Furthermore, in order to avoid sounding a tad trite and trivial, I shall reiterate one more time only that I am all thumbs and tied-up in knots by a self-inflicted bondage, one of my own making. So let's cut to the chase and cut out all this Mickey Mouse shit and try to think about building the perfect mousetrap instead in order to catch ourselves a very juicy, big, fat cat, which should tide me over for a very long, long time to come. There, now there's a plan in the works, and a pleasant thought to chew on.

A catnip kidnap.

We seek him here, we seek him there, we'd French kiss a garlic, foul-mouthed dog to seek him anywhere. Is he in Heaven, or is he in Hell, that damned elusive Pimpernneelll.

Curious as it seems, it's the dainty prick you feel from a razor-sharp daisy that causes the most excruciating pain, you know. Funny, a sudden thought just occurred to me when I just said that. I shall commence to paraphrase it correctly . . . if I can. Thus, from the innermost profundities of my bleeding heart, I give you this, . . . so here goes everything, minus the kitchen sink, as we speak and began to sink and sink deeper and deeper and deeper, et cetera, et cetera, et cetera.

I dreamt I saw a butterfly as it flew in through the open window of my fatigued brain. Yet, what I really witnessed was the sweet smell of pollen from the endless scent of an eternal daisy chain. Alas, it was a daisy chain that I saw. A daisy chain saw that hewed and masticated me to the very depths of my soul. So there I was, without a choice or a proper focus. But I was here to stay. Hence, there was only one logical thing left to do—set my mind free by blowing it away.

Yet I fail to see the significance or meaning (as I imagine you feeling the same, being on an equal wavelength as moi) behind all this private screening of the matinee shenanigans. So without waiting around for the credits to begin rolling, I rapidly made a beeline through a secret passage that was located conveniently in the backstairs of my skull. And then, and only then, did I proceed to shut my eyes, thinking that I was worthy of a second chance lest I open them back up again and burst into flames. Ditto, like birds of a rare feather in a flight of fancy from being so footloose and fancy-free after all. Henceforth, I made like Tom and cruised down that handy fire escape toward a freedom masquerading as reality.

And yet, I can't help pondering still, what if it had only been a simple dandelion instead. A delicate weed are we that blows my mind with the slight touch of one's breath. Speaking to me between puckered lips with the temptation of a tiny kiss. Putting us in a condition of being one. Or of being the same. Or of being the very one. So this girl, having no living will of her own, crying out in lonely soliloquy for all for one and one for all, promptly puts her index finger to her head and metaphorically kill herself.

Thus poisoning the mind with the lethal antidote that saves, as they debatably say. Because death deceitfully comes in degrees, like a masochistic paramour with envious tidings and with fringes on top.

So here we are once more in the womb of wombs, all dead calm on the shores of slumber as I spiral downward into everlasting sleep . . . sleep, sleep . . . sssshhhh . . . zzzzzz. Shut your eyes now, . . . and remember, no peeking.

Peanut Butter Preference

All good girls do certain bad things sometimes. And all bad girls do certain things that may be construed and considered proper every so often. But I, ironically, fit into neither category. In other words, you might say that I have this special sort of immunity status that prevents me from being singled out for such a perverse and anal system of selection.

Hence, being unfortunate enough to be a well-intentioned female trapped inside the body of an extremely bad-assed wench that ends up ruining and corrupting all my inner salutary purposes. We all, as it turns out, are our own unguarded mirror images, passport ugly and all, which most people, we think, don't see. But in fact, they see with great clarity and in very fine detail. Right down to the scabs on our pretentious complexions.

Mirror, mirror on the wall who's the biggest fool of them all. The answer cuts like glass, because we all refuse to play fair, even to ourselves.

After annihilating myself in the morning, I then expose myself to the outside world like a reluctant vamp. I set my sights greedily onto this not so innocent city with the brutal task of raping and pillaging it of all its potential suckers by doing my dutiful, respected rounds. In a jif, I start pounding the pavement with my delicious bag of goodies by my side.

Hurrying along with chain-smoking determination, I pass the time by enjoying some righteous tunes, which my walkman provides me with as amenable company on my routine route. Meanwhile, I navigate with homing pigeon finesse toward important uptown deliveries, while being the perfect and dutiful courier all along the yellow brick road by passing and distributing these curious and cursory envelopes to prestigious businesses and other eager customers of merit and clout, while continuing to receive (and always reviving old habits) similar envelopes in return.

Lying and tight dress and bare feet . . . oh, my!

Meanwhile back at the ranch, while returning back to our regularly scheduled programming, yours truly has decided to take a much-needed break from the rough-and-tumble laundromat world of consumer hysteria. So what better way to relax from such a habit-forming capitalist monstrosity than by reclining the rest of the afternoon away in my typical (yet unpredictable conscious) fashion in the booth of an unappetizing 24–7 cheap eatery on the lowest of East-meets-West side of town. In a place beyond malice and forgotten by most civilized civilians.

There I sit, taking an upside down view of the confined spaces around me, which to some, on a full stomach, is a little bit hard to swallow before or after breakfast. Yet, unlike little Miss Muffet, I gnaw at my discount lunch while deeply enthralled by a groovy magazine while simultaneously shooing away the creepy crawlies and other curds of a sick and frightened society. So take a tip from me: never accept a doggy bag when the cat's already been let outta the bag.

Hhhmmm . . . food for thought and all that other nonsense.

Subsequently, a friend/acquaintance of mine makes an entrance into this diva of dives, interloping on my midday snack and private reading session, and begins blabbing away at me like nobody's business. I feign acknowledgment of this annoying presence at first, never once glancing up from my glossy page. Yet a woman's work is never done, and as if put under a spell with ladylike mannerisms, I sit upright and uptight once more and nonchalantly pull out one of my many envelopes from my backpack of year-round holiday gift-giving and hand this secret message over to this individualized customer. It is quickly snatched, comparable to a snake in the grass, from my uncompromising fingers. And then bread is broken between us because dough is ultimately needed on such occasions. In other words, cash is exchanged as it is discreetly crumpled into my hungry fist, which then smoothly slides into one of the hidden compartments of my numerous pockets. The person of unknown origin then proceeds to leave momentarily on some undeniable quest, only to return a few minutes later with the same purpose in mind, repeating this sordidly fair transaction once more with true emphasis on the money taking top billing once again.

Blah! Blah! Blah! Blah! Blah! Putting all controversy aside—it all means crap anyway—life, as we know it, is all relative. No choice, pal. Those are the cards we are dealt with, with no aces handy up our sleeveless shirts to rely on. No one can choose their relatives, only choose how to deal with them. It is all a big gamble, and it is a kin that we are forced to wean to. Reared and suckled from day zero until we are totally brainwashed and left out to dry. Forced upon us all from our undemocratic youth. A baby formula which has become sour and contaminated from too many shelf-life years, which I have no nourishment left for any longer anyway.

So lift your noble glasses of our favored, favorite ale, the one which ails you best, and drink a hearty toast to your new-found straitjacket freedom! Three cheers to all that. Word to your surrogate mother. Yet save one word of caution to all you would-be guzzlers rotting in a gutter somewhere. Remember, don't spread it on too thick, because it may ultimately stick to the roof of your bloody gums, which definitely will cause you to gag on these valuable bodily fluids that in turn will leak and seep all over your brand-new morning rush, and then, where will you be, huh, Skippy?

Skip to my loo, my darlin', and take a piss and relieve yourself of some more of your perpetual suffering is my advice to you. Because there will be no mercy or use in begging to the porcelain god whose forgiveness is bottomless and shallow anyway.

After all is said and done, this busy girl then walks down a crowded street, skirting, curbing, and bustling by faceless people in my path, when all of a sudden, and seemingly out of nowhere, I diligently put on the brakes in my daily stroll and my jaw does a vertical drop with my cigarette still desperately dangling and clinging from my neglectful lower lip, while fighting a superhuman battle to hang on for dear life to my gaping mouth. Thus I begin to swivel my head around, and I instantly see this beautiful vision of maleness in a perfectly rough angelic form. The guy, gliding in all his detached brilliance down the sidewalk (like he was some kind of out-of-practice *GQ* model waltzing on an unending red carpet) on the other side of the street doesn't even notice his number-one fan silently yearning out to him.

Jesus, have I just died and gone straight to Heaven or what! Just hold on tight, girlfriend, and don't get your panties in an uproar. So loosen up and let the music begin. Let it pump freely through my veins from the top of my head to the tips of my toes until it joyfully drives me quite insane.

Crack open your mind and let me step inside. Lay your weary head next to mine and let the heart surrender. It's so *eeaasssy* when you bend the rules. It's so *eeaasssy,* all you have to do is fall on your knees . . . play the game. Everybody play the game.

Then like a huge *flash* chimes could be distinctly heard all around in every luscious and delectable nook and cranny. It was a miracle to be sure. King of the impossible. Queen of all the fates. So in order to honor this royal occasion, the cherubs are in full swing and the mighty trumpets are blaring for this, this . . . dare I suggest . . . mere man. Just a man with incredible sex appeal packaged firmly in a pair of skin-hugging jeans. And it would take all my female courage and cunning to steal this modern-day, rock and roll Prometheus from the mighty gods themselves. Because the fire burns way too hot not to handle;

therefore, it is up to me to warm my lips and bosom against his. Intertwine us in cool passionate embrace, . . . even if it kills me, or, better still, the both of us if need be.

For there art the Archangel Gabriel before me in all his luscious glory.

So pay attention and listen, all you fake princes and phony pretenders of lust and adoration, I descend upon you and stand before you naked from the skies. I command your very souls, you nonbelievers, to lay before me what is rightfully mine. And I will destroy anyone that abuses my trust. I swear that you will be mine, do or die . . . forever and forever . . . I will get you, and when I do, I will take you upon the ride of your life.

We will, we will rock you, because we are the champions, my friends.

In any event, I decide to follow and pursue him. So in the most debonair fashion possible, I start to track down and snare this wonderful stranger.

To make sure that he wouldn't catch on to my little game, I keep at a safe and fair distance while I lock in on his frequency, when he goes into a dingy coffee shop. Then as though in a trance-type state, I make my next move by entering the place a short time afterwards.

Now once in this lair I position myself in a seat directly across from my desirable adversary in other booth, while I enchantingly and hungrily target and monitor his every move, as if it was poetry in motion. I lustfully ogle his supposed Greek, masculine merit, dotingly studying even how he holds and lights his cigarette, even down to how he sips his mug of coffee.

How he tortures me with such casual delight. And how I would love to be healed by those very vibrations that he cleverly and covertly sends me.

Now this is when the gratuitous masturbation scene should commence as we all lay back (after finishing our cigarette of course) and slowly begin touching and caressing ourselves.

"Okay, pay attention class and start to shut your eyelids.

First step: He leans into her and in slow motion, she begins to kiss him. She lies in bed unattained, stares at the ceiling and takes a long passionate gasp and simultaneously closes her eyelids and slowly and playfully starts sliding her hand down her own face and across her own neck.

Second step: She seductively grazes *her* delicate fingers over *her* ripe breasts and nipples while, with the other, she navigates this hand down her own smooth stomach until she reaches the belly button area.

Third step: We begin to frolic among our thighs while slightly pulling ourselves upright. . . .

That's it . . . aahhh! That's the spot . . . right there . . . mmmmm, that's ggooooddd . . . with a cherry on top.

A-hem! All right, class, that was fine. Very first rate for the early initial try. Now let's proceed onward, shall we?

Fourth step: He then sits up with our back to him as he carries on smothering us, and especially our neck, with soft kisses while we close our eyes even more tightly as we lay grasping the ruffled sheets with our head buried in ecstasy and overwhelming rapture in the now-wet pillow. Meanwhile, as nature professionally takes its course, we then remind ourselves to reach for something hidden beneath the pillow. Our smart girl, having found the thing that she seeks under the pillow, our girl then arches her back in order to allow him to have his way with her before the final countdown and payoff.

Fifth step: The girl then turns over and leans into him for the great reward. Even nearer to him in order to permit him the luxury of performing the act of suckling her hot, erect tits. (We're not finished yet!)

Sixth step: Slowly . . . ever so slowly, he makes his way down to her slightly parted, yet inviting, golden trove, which stimulates her enormously into panting warmly. Hhh-hhh-hhh, to herself while with intense and blind blissfulness, she caarreeefully grabs for a shiny, sharp blade.

(For your information, this is an apparent punctilio and important item in this picture at this time, so bear with me for a few more seconds. Thank you.)

Seventh step: (Don't slip now) She raises the object above her head as she is thrust upward by him, gasping mouth open and exhilarating. Climaxing to the hard downward, symbolic, sexual thrashing of the knife. All this comes to an instant and screeching halt though, when she opens her visionary sockets once more. She is alone again.

We pause as she disgustedly looks down briefly. And then she proceeds to wipe the evident blood-soaked hands across the front of her pure white shirt, as if this article of clothing was like some sort of disposable napkin.

Now, children, we have come to the end of our exercise. I hope you have enjoyed this experience as much as we have. So this concludes our first lesson for the day. And remember, my dear children, you are not a failure if you have only tried this once. Twice is for luck. And on the third, God created woman. Well, even if He, or She, didn't, She/He should have. So that's one below the belt, all you gender benders. And to the ribs, too, which comes straight from the hip.

If I didn't know you better, honey child, I wouldn't know you from Adam.

Rebel, rebel, you've torn your dress. Rebel, rebel, your face is a mess.

Rebel, rebel, without a cause.

We're not sure if you're a boy or a girl. How could they know?

They can look, guess, and pause.

Why won't you dance with me!

After that final and conclusive climax of the sexcapade (sic), this hot tramp flips back and forth like a fish out of water, as though suffering from morning sickness or in a state of frantic delirium. A fountain is represented during this dramatic frenzy as it produces an immense gush of spray strictly for the purpose of theatrical effect, though a mushroom cloud is more like it, on further review. Wow! This could become contagious if we are not careful. Yet I always get my man without a fight in the end, now that I feel that I am ready for any test pilot, . . . because the joys of flying has made me indifferent to heights, and, more important, to the lows.

Going doowwwwnnnn!

So while we cascade downward at a speed of death-defying, horrific proportion, at a zillion miles an hour, mind you, we shall relax a while, on our ride to certain doom, with some soothing elevator sounds, which should help glide us merrily on our merry, merry way.

Ready? (she says with such sugary sweetness)

(then with not so much sugary sweetness)

Okay, Charlie! Let her rip . . . Roll the tape!

Renegade soundwave is a nightmare.

This is the guns for boothill. You can shove it. He hasn't got the time. He hasn't got the time. So he fax-off like a suck-sess. Buckles his holsers . . . keepa trouble in mind.

Slide with the gutter.

Make your heart flutter.

Whistles when he walks. Drolls when he talks.

Just one of the gang. Number one with his fans.

He fought hard he was winning through, he's pistol-whipping his way to yooouuu.

Bang!

Now you're dead, pilgrim, and I'm not.

So there, . . . Quickdraw McGraw.

Time to saddle up and head off into the sunset.

Hi-ho, Silver . . . a wwwaaayyy!

Hunka Hunka Burnin' Luv

Hey! Fuck you all. And damn all you male torpedoes to boot. I don't need to apologize or make excuses for my wanton, libidinal behavior. It's all in a day's work, my fair-weathered cock. The girls' gotta have it, and girls just want to have fun.

Scavengers in the matrix, baby. Fuck it!

I liked mine creamy. He liked his chunky. So what's not to like when you don't have to choose.

Yet, the ultimately delicious thing though is that we are all naive like pure spring water. A senseless and expensive commodity that was once considered a cheap thrill, which is the paradise of sin, where nothing but ourselves shall come between us. Thus no sandwich was ever prepared better, my evil twin.

Then again, on second thought, there's a lot to be said and learned from one's own appetitive partialities.

Ah! Big sigh.

Yeeaahhh, lunch-box style. . . . Way too cool . . . Dig it with a ding-a-lang-ding-dong.

No more of my dear mother's plain-jane cucumber-slapped-between-wonderbread concoctions for me, my little crumb.

Let them eat cake, and off with their heads. Don't you dare try and make an ass outta me by humping me with that shriveled pathetic excuse for a carrot on a stick.

Yeah! Stick it where the sun don't shine, why don't yah, . . . you scared little shadow boy!

From dusk to dawn—oh, wait a minute—that's wrong. Oh, silly little ole me. Gosh! How I do carry on . . . I do de-clare. Yet Scarlet as my face may be, I still don't give a damn.

Gone with the wind and all that blow hard epic blow job stuff. . . . Let's put that in reverse and make it vice versa.

Sunnyside up and then another sun down for the count.

. . . Thank you . . . that will do nicely. Now I can proceed as improvised and planned.

Next slide, please!

Bluesy true and totally disturbed by the gray areas in my ambition, this cowgirl barks at the moon while reflecting over a gushing fountain, with the dark springs playing with my heart strings with their eternal prancing. Prancing like a herd of Bambies (who'd ever heard of such a thing!) through my aching noodle while I walk out of an art supply store.

Impulsively, I immediately set the can of paint thinner, which I have just purchased, down on the sidewalk with violent insignificance and import as I thrust my skinny, bare knee to the acquiescent level of the dirty pavement in order to rigorously submit to the demands of my disobedient shoelaces, which seem to constantly come undone at such climatic opportunities such as these, as if a conspiracy was afoot.

Hhmmm, better watch my step from now on. One never knows whose sneakers might be sneaking around at this hour.

Hence, as I pick myself up by my bootstraps once again, I presently notice that my laces are now imperfectly intact once more.

Home sweet home.

Meanwhile, back in Candyland, little Miss Sweet Tooth pours the contents, the thinner, into a bucket. I then, with sheer sloppiness on my part, leave a nice-sized puddle from my inadvertent neglect. I pick the pail up, leaving a forgotten trail in its wake, which I then absentmindedly step into, bequeathing another fine mess, and leave a neat set of wet footprints as my rebellious signature of disregard;

which curiously, are supposed to be some kind of guide back to somewhere else, while I toss my misused brushes into the misused bucket.

Thus time marches on.

Tick tock. Tick tock.

Close up of me posturing at a bare table.

Next shot in the dark of me is of me staring aimlessly at an incense burner while the scented smoke sprouts and curls upward in an exquisite and exotic dance, which conjures up in my brain visions of angels and demons swirling about in a tempo of lost time.

Boredom makes for bad company. A strange bedfellow that steals all the covers during the night. a deserter who never gets its just deserts, being too much of a coward to sleep without proper dreams. Yet wait. . . .

Just wait one second, bud. In the crossfire, my insensible attention is diverted and drawn away from it as my eyes dart quickly to my left in a devilish sweep.

Next shot. Pan left. The clock! Is this the demonic contraption that torments me to the point of undue distraction . . . ?

In a matter of nanoseconds, this fiendish thing is seized and lifted by me, the slayer of wasted eons, as I clasp it in passionate strangulation. Ringing its bland face until all hands are on deck.

Hells bells, for the bell tolls for thee.

Jackhammer Jill went over the hill to fetch a pail for slaughter.

Jackhammer Jill came down hard, and then the thrill came tumbling after.

Smash! Pow! Crash! Ka-bbooommmm!

Finally, we witness the end of time, as we know it, after I forcefully pitch, coercively, the mechanical piece of Swiss excellence across the room.

The damn swine! . . . That should show 'em whose boss.

After all, nothing is neutral in this cruel world. Everything must suffer. No matter how small and innocuous it may pretend to be.

Then all is calm, all is bright once again, as I nonchalantly mosey back to my unoriginal, sedate position, with my chinny-chin-chin resting firmly on my delicate hands, while I resume watching the performing cloud of spirits as if nothing, and everything had just happened.

Thus like a thief in the night, I steal away any ideas or schemes that the night drowsily dangles in front of me, like whetting the lips of a chronic, bed-wetting pickpocket.

A wide spherical, circumferential image takes hold of me, slowly revolving around my cracked nut, comparable, in exploiting effect, to a small satellite mooning me with crude delight.

Because she don't dance to techno or trance-out to house or jungle anymore, ever since the day she let go.

Taking a long sabbatical from that bad trip, temptation being the mainline drug and the sweet salvation from all that shit, while I play a game of hide and seek and tag with these lustful vices eating away at my dreams, while I loiter behind a propped-up canvas.

Later, I furiously and feverishly try vehemently and intensely to taxi back and forth like a dope fiend as I start to sketch something on the once-blank canvas.

We eventually spy the voluptuous outlines of a woman taking shape from my dripping-with-blood brush as I stab at the paper-type foundation with fast, agitating strokes, while I carry on slashing hysterically with Van Gogh meets Jack the Ripper genius and inspiration.

After a short period, we see the trappings of a recognizable picture beginning to take substantial form in the guise of a selfish self-portrait. Then as febrile as when I had started, I suddenly halt cold in my skid-mark tracks, once the thunder and brainstorm taper off to nothing more than a slight drizzle.

Frustratingly I struggle with my hidden inhibitions while I renew my work, only to end it all incessantly once more in angry defeat.

Thus, I step away and back in disgust to survey my crime. I then wipe the evidence of paint from my thick, laden, soaked brush onto my nervous hands, which I then proceed to streak in symbolic punishment across my chest and stomach. Unable to actually put paint brush to canvas anymore, in some kind of handicapped, blind guilt complex, I verify my protest further by clutching my aching head of straw in my viselike fists after throwing down the tarnished brush. Subsequently I fling myself with apparent force onto my bed in a frantic temper tantrum, which I illustrate without shame.

There are no fair fights as we surrender to death. I honestly didn't know that things could be so one-dimensional and sketchy . . . yet without being able to reach the fundamental bottom of things. But still, no one has been able to peg me.

Congratulations, you have won. But if you remember one thing, and one thing only, remember this, that you were all wrong about me all along . . . because there are things that one should never see.

Now it's time to cut to the flames, as we draw back to witness our girl lighting and setting our painting to the destruction of a single flame, like some sort of baptism by fire, and then, as if on a remote cliff-hanger edge, I watch this with fortuitous inquisitiveness momentarily, and we (similar to a sort of out-of-body experience . . . chalk one up for experience) then view me walking away as the painting is engulfed by a tiny inferno of my own making.

Hence, let it be said that I leave no bridges unburned.

Bridging the huge gap between quality and quantity with brightness and warmth.

Masque of the Rabble

. . . Brightness and warmth . . . Brightness and warmth . . .

All of sudden my hallucination burns away quicker and easier than . . . than a fragile frailty, while leaving this choked with smoke, scorchingly black-to-the-point-of-ugliness reality in its place.

Leaving the demolished painting behind, and furthermore, actually denying ownership of this obvious catastrophe, I found myself glaring down a lonely dirt and gravel-laid road. (at least something has gotten laid around here . . . phuh! . . .)

Well, anyhow, seems the more I accept it, the more endless it becomes. . . . Made in the shade while the sun bakes my bare back.

Nothing in my vulture sights. . . . Damn! . . . And nothing to write home about either.

Hi, folks, wish you were here instead of poor little ole me.

You know, there's nothing in the whole goddamn world . . . except for sex, and peanut butter of course. . . . Oh! Hold the phones. I should also add . . . and not necessarily together or in that order either. . . . Anywwaaayyy . . . there's nothing in the whole goddamn world more special, even the blue plate special of the day, than to be on a secluded, tranquil, rural road with the natural heat machine shining in a clear blue sky up above, and with time on your side, for once, which ticks peacefully and marches in all its stormtrooper drag excellence to your selfish beat . . . preferably your own special heartbeat, no less. Because time is such a terribly wonderful thing to waste . . . especially when you're wasted. Don't you agree? Psyche! Fooled yah, didn't I . . . ha ha hhhaaaaa! Actually I was just kidding. . . . Well, with all kidding aside now, I have to say that this has to be the most boring of days of my entire life. And that reminds me of something else, now that I'm on the subject, now that I have so much time on my hands to pick at my scabs with, that I should mark this down on my mental calendar and stress importantly to myself, never to have such an appalling day like this ever again.

Oh, yes, and please forgive me and allow me to apologize to you all for my recent, unladylike, crass behavior. Because, you see, I'm not quite myself this sickly morning, the reason being that most of me is still back in some bed somewhere where it should be, sleeping, slumlording, and attempting to snooze this nightmare off . . . and yet, come to think of it, there still remains something to say about this quaint, pastel, and novice scene after all, as I continue to breath in and breath out while patiently scanning the distant horizon with X-ray specs, discount sunglasses. Looking down one road to my left and then down the other on my right, waiting and pondering endlessly for my ship to never dock or come in. How gloriously lonely everything looks when viewed through such a wide-angled lense though.

Ho-hum. . . . Oh, fuck it. Fuck all this bullshit to hell also! . . . Forget everything I just said. Just erase that last memory. And forget that I even mentioned any of this pointless drivel and dribble. Because I'm merely just a girl in the world chewing the fat and cud of my Bubble Yum, so very bubblecious bubble gum, while tooting a semidry, double-barreled water pistol on the verge of a major crisis.

You know, though, retaining water like this, while at the same period having a dry spell, is like constantly being on the rag. . . . What a royal pain in the ass that is, let me tell you, fellas. For I am woman, hear me roar. The lionized drag queen compelled to peel out down a lengthy, bloody drag strip.

So just grin and bear with me for a minute as I attempt to bare all, . . . you know, the naked truth and all. Because this is a two-for-one offer, which the world as we know it will never see the likes of again.

Don't you dare blink now, because things are bound to get a lot worse before they get better, . . . so here's cum in your eye.

Just a minute . . . I think I hear something.

I believe I finally have a visitor! Gosh, and me being in this completely and purposely disheveled state, too. Dear, oh, dear me, what will the neighbors think? . . . Huh! Oh, piss on that! . . . Down with those suburbanites anyhow, and all those other dark knights slaying damsels like me in distress.

I then lift up my shades and twist and stretch my neck in superhuman opportunism. Hence while I wait for ambition to fail me, I pretend that my fingers are magic binoculars, making a pair of goggles out of inventive hands as I place them around my massacred by mascara eyes. So peep with me, won't you, as we identify these wicked hubcaps blaring and blazing to my rescue.

Incidently the jalopy of past bad experiences skids to a crippled halt next to yours truly instead. Then the window is rolled down, and we see little Miss Cheesy Wheat Thins smiling back at me while she pokes her head out of the open space like a cute little turtle.

Presently, me-the hitch-hiking parasite is hijacked by these sky high terrorists. The cheese puff female that I spoke of way too earlier on, sits *bitch* on the right side of God's rejection. This cheesy girl resides on the passenger seat to those not in the know. Yet there are other characterless characters in this tragic comedy inside this funny sidecar, also unfortunately.

First and foremost (but not first for me and never ever on most occasions) on the a list (a for assholes) is a wanna be *it* girl who sits center stage. Then there's this laid back Guido guy, who lounges somewhere in the back somewhere left of center, whose presence I would prefer exit stage left.

Then the holier than unholy swiss cheese scank, who we've already met, is next. Then her lapdog, who is driving this rust bucket, pants beside her. Probably waiting for a treat from his leash-tugging mistress, who happens to always be in heat, whether she's in a cold-turkey or cold-fish condition.

Thus, as we drive along, I start having this tiny seizure, in a particularly unique shape known as annoyance, which is directed mainly at the pilot and a minor tiff toward his female co of this runaway train of no thought, as we weave in and out of traffic, which materializes out of everywhere.

Hence as we rollercoast at the incredible speed of one single,

American mile a minute—in reverse, believe it or not, Ripley—in order to get to where we need to be, each personality defective person in attendance (including myself currently) holds a domestically nasty beer in one hand and the pursuit of happiness in the other. Meanwhile the sloppy, jalopy, jolly green-without-envy-pint-sized giant does this circus act of carrying a brew in one paw, with the other clinging to a buff joint as he loosely grips the steering wheel like a dual patched Captain Hook.

So that's the whole kismet and kielbasa, folks. . . . So what do you think? . . . Humph! . . . Thought so.

Everyone places, please, for the orgy even a horny Roman wouldn't dare shed his toga for! The showoffs must go on, naturally, as we heed to Nature's barbaric mating call. Hollywooding this as the late, great, gangbang theory, which with fingers double crossed, is all it will turn out to be.

So what do you think of when giving head while doing your duty in bed?

Therefore give me head room while the mindless mob rules as individuals lose their faces in the crowd as they are crushed by the feet of shoeless joes and by the who's who of unsportsmanlike, unconducted hooligans.

Later, but never soon enough, everyone is totally fucked up, partially from the dizzy acceleration and car fumes and, mainly, from the weed killer scent engulfing our minds and that of the sorry vehicle. Within this century, I might get excited enough, out of general curiosity, at actually reaching a pointless point-of-interest destination. In this modern scientific world, anything is reasonably possible I suppose.

Phase two and phasers on stun, the wanna be it chick keeps sniffing and wiping at her nose, which really bothers me, the ultimate protagonist, to no end. And on top of all that, cheesy girl seems to be even cheesier by the second as her cheesy smile grows bigger and bigger after every hit of the communal joint as the delicate smoke rolls succulently from her mouth. Guido, in the Greenwich mean time, just sits silently for once, wasted as he scratches arrogantly at his balls. The whorish joint continues to be passed around to all the passed out, and this girl gets even more irritated with every passing moment, while this savage powwow begins to be played out to a packing-it-up, dying-from-boredom audience of one.

Furthermore, to make matters worse still, Guido accidentally loses his grip of his brewski as it goes flying fast forwardlike, when the car comes to a screeching, banshee abrupt halt when we reach our only and final destination. Then I practically get avalanched and squashed by the flaying and wild arms of this motley crew of subhuman losers. Guess who is the only one to get drenched and gets to take a swill bath from that runaway beer can? Yeah, fucking A . . . fucking A+ . . . actually, if you happened to have picked correctly. . . . Dare I say more.

Have you ever had one of those days when everything appears to go haywire? . . . I'm sure you have. Well, if you haven't, then you have been very fucking fortunate. Because right at this very instant, I'm having the hayride from hell. No kidding, Jack. And if it wasn't for the weed being circulated around, I'd probably waste these motherfuckers right now. Yet I have to keep my wits about me and my head in check, owing to the fact that this could turn out to be the ride down easy street that finally pays off for me. No, no, I mean it this time. This could be the pot (no pun intended) at the end of the freaking rainbow for me, if my lucky charms happen to hold out and don't happen to get wet and soggy from some bogus bullshit pouring down upon me . . . a possible shit storm to ruin my ticker tape parade so to speak. Yet this unpromising flaunt is starting to show signs of becoming a funeral procession to me, and I wish that this chauffeuring dickhead driving the imitation hearse would speed things up a little and get this traveling sideshow on the road.

Easy now, girl, don't blow your top. Things can't get any worse than this. Can they? But now that I'm on the subject, while on this joyless jaunt full of freaks and zombies from central casting, let me introduce you to problem number one thousand and one:

See there's the real fake wanna-be "it" girl, whom I've already discussed in more horrible detail than I would normally give a person of her stature the gratification, who keeps yapping into my aching, please pass the Advil, goddamn ear. Squawking away, like a chick with its head cut off, about girlish trash, which she assumes I'm interested in. Dahhhh! Like let's be for real here. Like I would seriously desire to spend the rest of my life exiled on a deserted island with that trippy, radio commentary-mouthed bitched. Oh, brother, this slut of chitchat is more like the *shit* girl than the *it* girl, actually . . . full of "it," I mean.

And then there's contestant number less-than-zero. Exhibit G for Guido, from the out-of-style section of the junior department at K-mart. A class act moron who has to be the biggest greaseball jerk I've ever mistakenly slipped over and encountered in my whole, twisted sister life. Close-in encounter of the Velveeta kind is more like it though. And if you look up feebleminded in the local dictionary (no joke, Sherlock homey) a moron, equal to this pin brain, would be described with an IQ a notch higher than an imbecile and two tiny notches higher than a complete idiot, which is a reward reserved and tailor-made and catered to the driven-to-tears motorist. Now, that's a scary thought. Hey, and that's a charitable person like me giving these guys compliments. Gosh, what next . . . handjobs maybe?

Hence, three down, one to go. Now we turn our attention to the last but not least important member of this illustrious team, lest we forget, which we couldn't even manage even if we tried our damnest, by golly, unless our damnest meant giving ourselves a lobotomy, with a tire iron, no less. Even if we happened by some odd circumstance to enjoy giving ourselves lobos with temptingly hard, solid, and manly objects, then the pretty, little, cute urchin says tee hee with an extra sweetened helping of shits and giggles in an attempt to add comic relief to this sad drama; which is not even worthy enough to be televised during pathetic soap opera hours.

Yet all fun and frolic aside, owing to her ghastly presence, the very idea of slicing and dicing one's own noggin (while pushing to one side even the pleasure or pain factor) this mooing cow, who can't stop spurting and milking me with her saccharine-coated bull session crap while beaming and grinning her stupid head off, is going to drive me to suicidal tendencies. Or to less drastic measures, by compelling me to blow chow and puke my brains out any minute now if we don't stop this bus ride to nowhere soon. And this affliction is not from the effects of motion sickness either. The reason being that even my senile, ancient grandma couldn't get ill from riding in this slow barge to bumfuck China. The vomit hypothesis though is strictly dedicated and awarded to having to schmooze up to these grotesque monstrosities of uncoolness. Boy! Never let it be said part II that I've never made any great sacrifices for my fellow man . . . or to the beasts of burden for that matter. For God be my witness, I promise never, ever, to be this starved for attention again.

Meanwhile in a not-so-distant part of the city . . .

Close up and time to focus in on a box being wrapped by an anxious girl, whom you and I know all too well, as if it were an unusual Christmas setting at sometime not considered festive . . . like sometime in late July for example.

Anyhow and anyway, girl wraps up her parcel like it's some kind of gift to herself, in an average, brown paper wrapping. In the background, quite out of view and out of mind, former joyriders and mobile party members and "fun-loving" crowd persons lounge, resembling, by my acute imagination, like spectators at a dull croquet match. These fiends from a town called sterile, smoke yet another joint. We then shift our attention, owing to a lack of activity on their part, to a set of scales lying next to the "mysterious" time bomb. All right! . . . It's the box, damn it! . . . Quit ruining my mood. Okay?

Subsequently, the box goes out of the picture as the background jealously is put back into focus, where it feels it belongs. The limelight is currently on the happy (but you wouldn't know it) faces.

Incidentally, P.L.C.U. girl synchronizes her watch for no purpose but to synchronize—?—Yet the timepiece refuses to yield while it happens to still say 11:45 P.M.

Well, that figures. The watch is P M Siinnngggg . . . hardy har har har. Get it?

Whatever.

Next, there is a close-up of good old useful himself, Armand Hammer Baking Soda, and we see our golden girl get up and walk toward the camera's fish-eyed lens and set the scales beside the good old Mister Armed and Hammered package.

Girl then exits to her left instead of right, for luck, possibly.

So this is where we start to get into extreme focus once again. And like the legendary fountain of youth, an infantile idealist squats and ponders the day away, searching for that false aspire. Waiting and endlessly waiting, which endures and captivates my indifferent, eager thoughts . . . 'til it 'urts. Then again, I've heard it said that if you linger around long enough for something, you'll probably get something in return. Well, I did get something all right. I got nothing. a whole lot of nuthin' honey. a big, solid nothing at that. a major, fat zero in spades.

Aces high for my measly trade. Nothing begets nothing. Nothing gained, nothing lost, as they always say. What I really mean is that nothing remains the same, yet nothing changes either really. Does that make much sense? It certainly would if you were in my shoes. A size or two too large for my own good, if you really want to fucking well know.

Consequently here I am waiting once more, waiting for yet another one of "my man's" court jesters and buffoons to escort me to him, His majestic Majesty. The royal *Boogieloo*. His eminent pain-in-the-badass self. My main man no doubt. No doubt about it. And no joke either. The main attraction to this significant, dreary existence, if you damn well dare call it one. Thus like some cursed angel of death, he will appear in all his pretense and distinction to wrap me up warmly in his thoughtful wing. Nevertheless, and yet, like the goody-two-unlaced-shoes servant that I am, I get up and begin strolling down the naked pier. Walking past the forlorn sundial, whose shadow annoyingly reminds me of my own eternal snug calamity. Subsequently I find myself a good place to wait some more, succumbing to the forces that wilt.

May the forces be with you Skywalker . . .

So she plops down with her hands on her chin and seconds later, comparable to some obedient clockwork, a car pulls up and idles momentarily like some obedient ghoul. And then it leaves and then our girl has mysteriously vanished in its wake.

The female, lush and soft like a mink coat, is muffled and embraced by the powers mightier than her.

Therefore minky pretty, so minky must die. Must die! You can't change the system, because it is bottomless like the sea, even if your heart is as big as the ocean bed. Hence, you can't change the tide. Your hope is too small for such things.

Then a remote voice announces in the vacuum, Does she have a hook in her throat? Why can't we hear her anymore?

Maybe cash carries with it the price of silence. No point for a reason when there is nothing that money can't buy. After all, she only needed one swift boot when she had only one leg to stand on. A seagull too big to fly, thus, it's sink or swim from this time forward.

Thus the urgent voice asks some of its many difficult questions:

Where does she go? what does she do? . . . and will she be tossed back into the sea?

Then the answer arrives, this time more rapidly with the whispering wind: Sweet little lady knows she looks good. But she doesn't get the joke because it really isn't meant to be funny.

Meanwhile the fairytale continues. Once upon a time, lurking by a stone in the mud, two beady eyes looked to see where I was, and then I spoke, and this is what it said to me.

Alas, we find ourselves carousing in the back of his infamous sedan like a pack of wild sardines. A mob of laughing hyenas, if you will. Yet it only leaves me with this single, subliminal flash card.

It kills one's taste for switchblades, is one cynical thought.

And yes! Lest we forget. Guess who's decided to accompany this pitiful, merry crew down that yellow-stained, brick road? None other than our cunning hitchhiker in the imperfect guise of Little Red Riding Hood, namely, little ole me! Bearing goodwill and joy to all who defy to welcome it while on my eager way to Grandmother's cozy, unidentifiable, ambiguous cottage.

Lost in space with the Boyz from the Hood while heading to Grandma's cozy, unidentifiable, ambiguous cottage.

My, Grandma, what big teeth you have?

Better for those who are gullible enough to see your sharp as jaded glass eyes sparkle in them, my dear.

Because he was one smart, tasty cookie that one (and just as greedy as hell also), who never cried wolf when it was so much easier to just constantly hound you into submission instead.

As far as I was amusingly concerned though, these comic-book symbols were all suckers of the basement variety. Twenty times below the norm of ordinary separation. And hungry poseurized and vampirish bloodsuckers at that. Deprived and impaled of any kind of dignity whatsoever when the stakes were high. Yet anemic to their discord when the blood count level was at its lowest. Just the same, they were consummately designed in order to be made fun of. Yet this was becoming a major drag to me on the one hand, but business was still business, and a general drag on the other. My hands were full and fit to be tied. But fate had made me their official and unofficial dragon priestess. The trixie of all known trickers to these phony, acid speed racers.

Go speed . . . goooo! was their unauthorized motto and checkered flag.

Hey, this was the story of my goddamn life, after all. No sanctioned regrets, says I. And none intended. So shit, what else was new. Man! At this very moment, none of this garbage made much sense to me. But sense has never been my forte. Or had ever been anything my crowd took much stock, lock, and load in anyway, while imaginary and otherwise traffic whizzed by with their own individual, humorous quirks to add some added humdrum confusion to the already humdrum confusion.

"Amusing, ain't it, while dying to stand tall, while living on a skinned knee?" Bozo said to the clown.

"Diagnosis is attributed as 'Untied shoelaces syndrome,' Herr Doktor," remarked the little old lady that lived in a shoe to the house spider and the fly.

And dippy doppy doo and ditto to you. That reminds me of something else that should amuse you and bring a smile to your upside down frown, which I picked up from the soles of my ruby slippers, like gum along the way. And it goes something like this. But for godsakes, don't fuckin' misquote me, mister, . . . All right?

"It's Jesus's sly grin that keeps us going, isn't it?"

I think I hit the nail right on the head on that one. Don't you think?

Contacts renewed and deals cut and transacted during this successful powertrip. Because it was better to be a hired assassin than a victim of circumstance. She was one mean sister toting a machine gun L.A.-style while cars swirled by aimlessly in the high noon spark of low-heeled boys. Endless twisting and turning between reality and semblance among this unconscious ship of fools. Who, as the case in point blank, drifted in and out of combustible slow motion, as if riderless and by themselves, which was in some ways a resemblance of the whole and broken segments of her superficial existence.

In broad daylight arrogance, the crew walked the walk toward the bungalow with wicked intent in their besmirched veins, yet with less than actual deed in their calculated thoughts.

Close up of call box outside of a ransacked building as numbers are pressed. Then a hand leaves the initial picture and girl leans directly into intercom to speak the speak. Words are unrecognizably exchanged as girl is buzzed in along with the others. Girl attempts to enter the slightly opened derelict, hallway barricade. But she is then forced to give it an extra nudge, and then it swings to life in order for it to be wide enough for her to make her grandiose entrance. The silent as a mouse mob enter after her, like rats leaving a sinking ship. Gliding by her presently, she follows their usual scent and strolls the naked hall with that sinking feeling drowning in her gut.

They come to a door marked accordingly and then actually bother to knock before going through it. As they are welcomed into these new, but familiar, surroundings, they are showered by a beaded, curtain as though passing through a metal detector or immunized by some invisible plague before they are allowed to move forward. This trinket distracts her from her serious objectives for a second or two, reminding her of a crystallized waterfall, as if the mute environment was made to look like some kind of Hollywood-designed Moroccan harem, which continued to amuse her slightly in an offbeat sort of fashion as she passed beyond it.

Thus as she peeks through the beaded strands and into the other side, she witnesses a trio of human waste products loafing around a coffee table, minus this particular caffeine stimulant no less. She surmises that they are waiting for something more rewarding to perk themselves up with, rather than that common fare that can be bought from any local yokel. Something that certainly would be good to the last drop.

Yes, indeedy, I conjectured with smug evilness while diverted by my own personal form of entertainment. Then Mr. Reliable—from the faded heydays of a disco crystal ball, my acute (and B, sexy) instincts, which is just another term for a female's mythical intuition, after all—started to kick in and picked up a novice smell. Furthermore, if my little feelers were correct and accurate, which four out of five times they were, I was going to hit easy Monet pretty freaking soon.

Once inside this den of thieves, shaded and darkened with the right proportion and affects to give it that significant, natural feel and panache of a Tarantino home grown movie to it, I head towards the threesome, who were busy having a casual orgy.

Oh dear, oh dear, I shan't look. The prudent virgin, quite dated and dried up, pruned prude narrates between gloveless fingers.

Orgy porgy pudding and pie, kiss the girls and make them cry.

Take one! Crying out in ecstasy . . . Slap!

. . . All right, all right, take two if you like.

Agony to ecstasy leads one with an appetite à la fricassee.

Voila! In other words (sic for sick again), divorced and irreconcilably ex-tasty.

Tasty, tasty, oh, you're so hasty. Tasty, tasty, do it clean and don't make it messy and pasty.

Thus this was the prime time moment to showcase my wares and barter for better days. We then all fade out in order to leave them with some pretense of privacy. Because tricks are for kids. And because of the adult content pertaining to this series of events, viewer discretion is advised. And honestly, we are not stupid, only mildly backward, enough to leave any eyewitnesses at the scene of this misdeed.

It is yesterday once more. Hence the precious loot is then bandied together for my wealthy dowry. Think of it as a security deposit for future vacations in the sun. Delivered in a fortuitous secret process that gives me the golden prized goose in the form of grade-A green bills for my costly efforts.

Oh, shucks, it was my pleasure . . . really.

Subsequently, I smirk proudly to myself beneath lipstick traces of black market, cosmetic surgery.

And the colored girls on the wild side sing, Do de do de do de do de do . . . and so on . . . because of the wonderful things she does.

We'rreee jerking off to see the wizard. The wonderful wizard of Oz.

Because tao and zen, it is better to be one oz them than to be with the singular utz.

Get it, you wascally wabbit.

Now, enough about me. Let's discuss things that are only a kindred spirit to me. So let's see what is behind curtain number . . . whatever . . . shall we?

Drum roll, please, maestro!

Be-dum-bum bum. Because I know that I am going to pull off the greatest fraud and caper of the Gatorade decade by enriching myself fatly (with capital P and H) by skimming the crème de la, delicious and delightfully and delectable and de-gorgeous, crème by stealing from the evil imperial forces with my Jedi mind warp in order to make the entrepreneurial sale of the century. Thus with my mind-altering and -bending merchandise of top quality shit, this should be a snap, crackle, and pop easy peezy procedure.

You see, it's all about percentages. You need a mark to make a yen if you wanna make mulla. Hence when no one's watching, I'll be licking from the foamy top of the rich cup in order to, in a perfect, private enterprise manner, recycle this kickback so that I will be able to fill my very own lengthy pockets further with more of the addictive cash. And the surprise filling in this cupcake is that, as long as I don't get caught with my hand in the cookie jar while nibbling at the edges of each chocolate chip, no one should or will be the wiser. At least not wiser than me, the wise ass sugarbuns herself. Yet this was no fluke, and I was far from being a flake during a snow job. No cream puff here either, my mutual wise compadres. I intended to have my cake and eat the whole thing, including the covert ingredient icing too, without choking on the measly crumbs that I was so used to getting.

Meanwhile, though, I had to try and avoid having my head hacked off on the commissional chopping block by keeping my nose to the grindstone and my neck above water. Yet the fierce, unpredictable currents have a way of changing on you. Therefore, you better be a good navigator or you might end up drowning in your own sweat, blood, and toil. Ah, yes, let's not forget tears . . . forget to shed them, I mean.

Okay, enough said. Let's resume with our story, shall we?

Hey, check this out. All right, on your mark . . . ready . . . steady . . . go! One, count them with me, why won't you. One, two, free little wise asshole men sitting in a tree. No, no, no, that's all wrong. Shit! Let me start again. All right, there's these stoned dead, trippy triplets, see, sitting motionless (whoa, big surprise) in their unmanageable hypocrisy. Yet, it is their subtle shadows that silently rollick to an erotic dance that they display for their own enjoyment upon the blank wall behind them, from the candlelight, which the trio of forms appear to worship, that also seems in a far-out crazy way to intrigue me too, almost to the point that I have forgotten the impossibility of the mission.

I shall self-destruct in five seconds. Beep beep bbbbeeeepppp!

Wham, goddamn, thank you, mama. And all that other loud and hysterical mumbo jumbo that makes for the best Armageddon, welcome-to-our-holocaust-crash-type parties.

Phew! That wore me out. Anyway, where was I? Oh, yes, now I recall. Something about some kind of chaotic images doing the hokey-pokey on the center stage, while avaricious in their own performance more or less. So much, in fact, that they attempt with refined brilliance to cover their carrier's features in a parasitic boast of self-confidence from the poker playing would-be hustlers. Poker-faced and all from bowing and worshiping in devout concentration to the low transparent table, which they have gathered ceremoniously around. But it is a craze that will die once the pet treats are handed out. A reward for their patient obedience or disobedience, no less.

Our Avon lady of alternative and inordinate consumerism then greets the guy to her extreme far right. Straight from the hip, or better yet, directly from the torso viewpoint, I spy with my little eye the main man among the big boys loitering around the sandbox. The crown prince of this tiny tributary, which he rules with a heavy, rusty ruler. So it is highly recommended, by those in the know, to make sure one has had his or her latest tetanus shot before proceeding onward. Because, after all, we are involved in a vicious guerilla war, which, I might add, was quite uncivil at the moment. Yet a gorilla war in my midst may sound more appropriate, on second thought, owing to the simian company that I am forced to deal with at this immediate juncture. And this particular Tet offensive was far from being a Vietnam national holiday. No Sunday outing was this, to say the very least.

She liked to think of him though, this big cheese (moldy and aged and smelly and fusty, at that), as the reprehensible fist fucker of the first order. A confidential lark and prank, which she preferred to be kept from most, and which included the celebrated trio back by popular demand, the three wise Stoogies, namely, better known as Me, Myself and I. And the best way to describe this unfortunate enema on the other cheek (the left-handed one preferably) was that he was such a fucking asshole, who was known to screw certain, selected individuals up so badly that they couldn't shit for a week. A hardass who took no quarter bags or prisoners with equal injustice.

This sharp well-dressed sand shark sits with his legs crossed with the biggest man-eating smirk on his kisser, which would usually scare a school of uneducated fish, fair means or foul. Yet, I had earned by degree from the elementary study program of hard knocks. And I was wise in the ways of predators, whether residing below or above ground. Nevertheless, I had to watch my back regardless, having known certain persons to be taken in, hook, line, and sinker, by his initial, unappetizing bait. And no matter how crafty, clever, or smart he believed himself to be, I still had a couple of tricks left up my sleeve. Anyway, to be or not to be, if that be the question, he gestures to me for the bag while holding out his greasy, manicured, tentacled claws for the treasured and consumer-tagged loot, like it was some kind of handout.

This girl waits and gestures like a puritan with annoyed anticipation for the promise of payment. The king of the heap therefore turns his royal self around in order to address one of his many lackeys for the dough, as if it was a mere afterthought. The middleman hands it to him like the decent slave that he is and then his highness likewise gives it to me in snobby disgust, as though the whole idea of this natural bargain nauseates him for some absurd reason.

I take this bundle of joy from him with the opposite regard to his superficial composure and leave my own. Then putting it, the prized tash, securely into my front pocket of my baggy jeans, I begin to feel all warm and snug, all over, which symbolized for me a done deal. At that very moment though, the big man begins to smoothly reach into the inside of his jacket, which instinctively sets off a dozen or so alarms in my pretty little head. The message read: Danger, Will Robinson! Danger, danger. Thus with fair warning, I concluded that danger was afoot, or at least a few inches away from me.

Hence, there were only two plausible explanations for this that one would put their sly, underhanded hand directly to their heart like that, and you didn't have to be fucking Inspector Clouseau, or Jack Clouseau, for that matter, to figure this one out. One plausible clue for his abnormal behavior was that he was struck with this desire to pay allegiance to the goddamn national flag or something idiotically patriotic like that. And this creature of the Black Lagoon didn't lightning strike me, or give me that nice homegrown sensation, of someone with a taste for baseball, Chevys, and apple pie. No, sir, he wasn't exactly a major candidate for the red, white, and blue-eyed poster boy type. He was more like the red, black, and blue garden variety to me. He was way too far off in left field for such an honor.

The reason that I came up with next, the one that frightened me the most, having had near experiences, like the assumed one that I was Sanka instantly imagining currently, before. And it was the kind that killed or, even worse, maimed you for life, that injured you much more mentally than it did physically, mind you. This kind of thing could make a hard working, ambitious gal like me change career and profession real quick and soon like.

What was a poor gal like me to do?

Choose your poison, gentlemen, and get ready to drop your dirty linen and start grinning your salutations in order to meet your Maker.

Stand and deliver, your money or your life, because it is, like what Ole Blue Eyes once pronounced many many years ago in a galaxy very far far away, my way or the highway.

Simultaneously and in dramatic slow motion, the perilously innocent girl begins to freak out. So what does she do, kiddies, in order to counteract this serious threat to her well being? Well, she does what any other decorous gal would do under the strained circumstances. She challenges him to a duel in the sun of course.

What? Huh! For crying out loud. Sure, sure, sure, technicalities. Always fucking technicalities! All right, scratch the sun bit. A duel then under a sun lamp. Is that better? Good! Now can I go on, or is there anything else bothering you or something I should know?

A-hum . . . therefore, in a perfect rendition of Annie Oakley, she produces her own weapon of choice and randomly fires at her slower opponent, squirting him with deadly accuracy with her potent water pistol. Thus the victim of her wet wrath plays the role, which was made only for him, as that of the dumbfounded corpse, while he nonchalantly stands like a person very much alive, as he proceeds to vigorously brush what should have been blood but, instead, water stains, from his stylish threads. Ironically the only violation committed and the only agony he felt from the liquid bullet was his feeling slightly perturbed by having to live with witnessing a permanent soiled spot on his expensive jacket, which he accepts only after rubbing his precious vest down with his so-very-refined silk handkerchief.

And when she blew away the conceptual smoke from the conceptual smoking gun, all she could say without a hint of regret was:

No name, no slogan.

After that hank-panky, helter skelterish, ambush, which would have done any fiendish murderess proud, he petitions with no false modesty for an expedient peace treaty and truce with me in the form of his very own brand of cigarettes, which he uses shamelessly, and without too much hesitation, as a token and white flag between twin, battle-scared warriors. Henceforth, so that it can be properly documented, whereas he happened to have taken the worse for wear part in the skirmish, he proved, in afterthought (even though I still thought of him in afterthought as scum), to be quite a good sport about the whole, mistakened accident. Moreover, to prove he had no hard feelings and could take a joke (even if it was literally on him) as well as anyone, and because of no real harm done to his indirect person (which besides any hidden ill feeling, a decent cleaner could fix in a jiffy anyhow), as an act of his good intentions and esteem, he offers me once more one of his brand of smokes; it oddly enough was his (our!) previous action that caused the whole misunderstanding in the first place, was meant to be in the first place.

Yet, like the stubborn Calamity Jane that I was customarily cursed and bred to be, this particular Jane Doe declines the gift with no option of regret on her part, while I grab my own characteristic pack instead. And with ultimate coolness frozen to my steady chops, I pop one unfiltered, feminine designed, and slender trademarked cancer stick between my less than rosy, rough lips with suspicious content. It was at this period and full stop that I partake to add insult to injury with my very own glamorized bitch-mode attitude by touching it all off by lighting my own stiletto with my very own blue butane flame with my very own monogrammed and personalized Zippo instead of allowing him this tiny appreciation. Hence, there was a very logical purpose to this prefab prejudice after all. I had to send out the profound message that I wasn't the sorta fatal epicene that was about to take any shit from anybody, even if I had been the one to dump the motherload on others first.

Match point made and no love taken.

The End of the Beginning of the End

Now it's time to say good-bye to all our friends, fans, and families.

Aaaahhhh!

I know, I know. It's come to a complete, electric chair shock to me also. And I feel your pain right down to the seat of my pants, gosh darn it.

Anyway, folks, we wouldn't leave you hanging like a pair of your father's boxers without singing you our famous clubhouse song. It goes something like this. . . .

M-I-C . . . from sea to shining sea . . . K-E-Y . . . Why? Why ask why . . . M-O-U-S-E.

Eeekkkk! Not more of that Mickey Mouse bullshit again! Please, somebody, put me out of my misery and kill it before it's too late!

No? No applicants today? No pitchforking types with fire and brimstone in their riotous follow-the-rest-of-the-mindless-masses-artificial-bravehearts-about-to-storm-and-torch-Doktor-Frankenstein's-monster on the menu this gorgeous morning? All right, then, be that way. How about someone for that crazy jig from the golden oldies fifties, called the Monster Mash? No takers either? Seriously? This is your last chance? Going, going, gone.

I thought not. Oh well and gee whiz and shucks to the rest of that tearing jerking sort of stuff. Then I guess it is up to me to destroy the beast all by my lonesome.

Alas, Little Bow Peep has lost her sheep and doesn't know where to find them.

And the Vegas cheeseburger with bacon and peanut butter (mmmm . . . , did someone just mention peanut butter?) icon eulogizes this tearful requiem straight from his rotund gut; Are you lonesome tonight . . . exchanging rubbers, this one is too tight, I need another.

Ah, fuck! So I forgot the damn words. Hey, sue me if you don't like it. Okay?

Too bad my name ain't Sue . . . Yak, yak, yak.

Well, you know as well as I know (well, you should, damn it) that there is no way out of this without giving ourselves a decent burial. So let me finally close the chapter and verse on this one.

Are you ready boys and girls?

. . . Five . . . four . . . three . . . two . . . one.

We have ignition. Blast off!

Ground control to Major Tom, this is Houston speaking. Don't forget to take your pills, and put your damn helmet on!

Anyway, come with me, and I shall lead you to the big finale. Hold hands, children, because we don't want to lose anyone, especially me the irate narrate.

So the story unfolds thus, with me being victorious over the latter-day Goliath. You know, that fat load of shit that I sprayed with my hydro-powered ray gun. Remember?

Anyhow, once I had him submitted to my will, (you will submit to my will, motherfucker!), he was nothing more than a vulnerable, beached whale after that . . . or so I thought.

Alas, the party was just beginning . . . or ending, if you choose to look at it with negative waves. That's totally up to you. Be my guest.

Bastard!

All right, moving right along at warp speed, . . . uummm . . . one kaxillion light years a kaxillion second (wow!), we find ourselves slap dab right where we started for chrissakes!

In other words, not yet used up, I stood my ground like the tough and hard-as-glued-on-nails wench that I was thorny crowned to be.

Thus, I stayed in this position until this Mexican standoff started to bore me to my short-attention-span tears. Yet I was still itching and trigger-happy enough to give him another dose of my watered-down pain from my ever present, rusty water pistol.

Holy wet dreams Batman! I wish I had filled my trusty ten-gallon shooter this mornin' with bleach instead.

Wouldn't that have been a jumping jack flash is a gas, gas, gas type thrill. Must be growing soft around the middle, though. Gosh darn it.

Anyhow, it was getting late early, and I was in no mood for nap time. I needed to split while the going was good. Take my booty, while shaking my booty without breaking my stride, and head for the hills or, better still, the border.

Yes, I could go for a couple of tacos for a job well done right about now. It's funny how violence and excitement leave this empty feeling in your stomach, don'tcha think?

Yet, before I had a chance to say adios amigos, the icicle of flubber then proceeded to make me a proposition that I couldn't, being the genteel lady that I was, refuse.

Yet, on shoulda coulda woulda reflection, I shoulda taken the money and ran. Cash and carry while leaving no receipt and no trail in order for them not to have an excuse for a refund.

What made me stick around like a buzzing bee to honey, though, was the appearance of that fart-faced Guido guy. Yet something was oddly funny about this particular, fuzzy picture. What I was compelled to view was him being dragged in the style of look-what-the-fat-cat-just-dragged-in from some other room.

My radar was in full swing when I noticed the not-so-happy-to-see-anyone expression on his face. Yet no matter how repulsive I found this guy, I couldn't keep my eyes off him for the next ten or so minutes, until his ugly mug was, contrary to the laws of dermatology, made more perfectly disgusting by its being mashed into pulp fiction. I remember even feeling slightly sorry for him . . . or think I do remember.

Oh, yes, let me explain why this particular individual was chosen to take a beating. You see this was all politely unraveled for me as I fantasized about spending my small riches, my nest egg, for an insignificant magpie.

Anyhow, between floggings and such, the sad history 101 of this minor actor was foretold. You see, they had been monitoring certain suspicious persons for some time. And for their efforts they had found a fall guy in the guise of this Guido fella. a perfect rendition of a scapegoat, no doubt. Plus they had further proof, if they wanted excuses for their special kind of fun, by displaying to all in the shotgun jury, an incriminating pager that had been swiped from his belongings with certain numbers of known enemy, competitive types discovered on it.

In more sampled other words, they had found a spy in their camp. So to make and shake and bake an example of him, he was virtually put through the wringer without the benefit of an adequate spin cycle. And when I thought he had seen the worst part of the day, he was forced to his grubby knees to beg for his meaningless life. I believed this (at the time) to be a ruse in order to see him sweat. But I was wrong. The next thing I witnessed was a gun being pulled out from someone's belt and a shot fired. Yet because of the unbelievability of the whole thing, all I remember was their devilish shadows playing and up to their usual tricks by dancing in a macabre beatitude on the blank wall behind me.

Nonetheless, even my inventive denial couldn't remove the splatter of blood which was the conclusive realism to this sordid drama.

Girl Wonder then wipes a single teardrop of crimson blood from her pale cheek before deciding to flee for her life.

Run, girlfriend, run! The voice in my head yelled as I picked up my heels (and anything else that I needed) and rushed toward the exit.

Pant, pant, pant went my poor lungs as they attempted to keep strict tempo with the accelerated beat box booming in my chest.

Just when I thought for sure that I had escaped hell, I found out that it was actually designed deceptively like a layered cake with devil's frosting, and the whole nine lives, instead. Or maybe Satan had more than one pad in his many times at leisure, after all. Anyway, I had basically jumped from the frying pan into the fire as I fled into the unknown mist and heavy fog of a chaotic and very, never mind the eardrums, party, which was in full progress; that was also conveniently obstructing my sudden plans of flight. Thus, while I coughed and pushed my way through the wall-to-wall plebeians of drunks and spaced-out cadets, I fought desperately, mainly with myself, to find a way out of there.

Yet, before I would breath the clean air of liberty once again, I remember in my splintered mind's eye, if memory serves me well, faces of people. But it was as though these random faces had features that were imitations of what they really were. Do you catch my drift?

No, hang on a sec. I know what you're thinking. This girl has smoked way too much harsh weed or something. But no, really, I could have sworn to never curse again that these persons were wearing masks made to look like themselves. Hey, it's just as weird to me as it might appear to you. Anyway, what can I say. That's what I imagined I saw, so kiss my ass and screw off if you don't believe me. That ain't my freaking problemo but yours, truly.

Besides, it doesn't really matter now in the grand scheme of things. The important thing was that I got away scot-free. You see, sometimes when you are born under a bad sign, or the only luck you ever seem to catch, like the goddamn flu, is of the common cold persuasion. Colder even than an eskimo's hard prick. You know, the badder than bad kind (and when I mean bad, I don't mean, hey dude that's too cool and righteous, I just mean in plain olde English . . . bad) Or even when you seem to be the only one to get wet by wanton puddles of water when crossing their path during busy traffic hours. Or the victim of faulty condoms when you happen to be beneath one. And if you always choose the death card when playing go fish with the fortune tellers.

Sometimes, but not always, the number thirteen can become a fortunate number for you. Therefore, so too, for example, can borrowed pagers that you were sure, on a Bible stack of pancakes and on your living mother's grave, was stolen, and therefore, you had foolishly forgotten, like the foolish brain-dead girl that you are, to erase incriminating numbers from it. Oh, well, what do you expect from a girl who has never learned to tie her shoelaces properly.

So this girl, having no living will of her own, crying out in lonely soliloquy for all-for-one and one-for-all, promptly puts her index finger to her head and metaphorically kills herself.

Kiss, kiss . . . bang, bang.

Dame Hickory, Dame Hickory, here's a wolf at your door.
His teeth grinning white. And his tongue wagging sore!
"Nay!" said Dame Hickory, "ye false Faerie!" But a wolf
t'was indeed, and famished was he!

—*Walter de la Mare*

First Cut is the Deepest

Matthew stood with intense concentration, glaring out of a motel window, watching the vacation traffic breeze by his bemused vision with their onanistic indifference from above.

He had been in that volatized daze for much of the morning, ever since his new bride had left to do some express grocery shopping.

She was expected back anytime soon, but he still had plenty of time left to kill . . . and kill it, he did.

Yet, he couldn't help envying this holiday species, like a leaf begrudges leaving a tree, while he remotely played and fidgeted in emotional abstraction with an article of deliverance, which he had securely in his pants pocket.

He ended his catatonic immunity and reverted to staring over at the cheap floral design that was pasted throughout the low-cost room. But even this mild display of impassivity could not take him away from his crude molestation. He had to touch the lengthy cold and solid object in his hidden, possessive clutch and eager clasp at all times. A helpful and sincere keepsake to give him strength.

Did he really need this reassurance?

Not really. But it couldn't hurt to caress and fondle it just the same.

Could it?

Yet, he didn't want to jinx it either. After all, even though it was his custodian and aid to brighter and better things, it was still a constantly agonizing reminder of what he needed to do. His most thought-out plan to date, that is. And he was ready, more ready than ready, really, to see it through to the end. Even a bitter one, at that.

Suddenly, as if that last thought had caused his private party to be pooped slightly, he decided then to try and discard his grand plan for a few hours by relocating the article far from his person. He scanned around rapidly in a calm fuss for a place to put this most important of objects.

There! his mind rejoiced as he spied his light windbreaker beckoning to him from a nearby chair to give it the ultimate pleasure of claiming such a treasure.

Just as he finished shoving this special weight into one of the jacket's loose compartments, the door was opened instantly, and his freshman wife waltzed in, as if this was the best day of her life (which it was!) Or as though to cleverly catch him in some deviously cunning mischief, which he, as a matter of fact, had been in the act of doing.

"Hello, honey," she said, in a pleasant mood, while she closed the door behind her.

He released a nervous smile as he turned around to face her. She detected his skittish behavior but quickly swept it aside as nothing.

"I'm sorry I took so long. Seems as if every high-school-aged kid on the East Coast was in that damn little supermarket today." Then after that alleviatingly satisfactory excuse, she carried her goods over to where the kitchen was located. "Would you like me to make you a sandwich or something?" she asked as she removed the item from the bags.

He hesitated for a few seconds before answering, as though this was the most difficult question in the universe to answer.

"Yes, that would be nice. Thanks," and he fastened another grin to his edgy chops before reclining onto a huge sofa-type seat in order to regain his natural composure.

After emptying the last articles from the bottom of the sack, she focused her attention back onto her husband of a few days.

"Is everything all right darling? Is something bothering you?"

Once more, he was brought back to the realm of reality to answer this new, pressing subject.

"I'm fine. Why do you ask?" he remarked while trying to contain his overpowering guilt, which he was forced to bracket behind a false sense of mild equanimity in order to avoid dubiety on her part.

She stood motionless for a short, puzzling moment.

"No reason really," she mentioned shyly before being compelled to stock this novice sense of insecurity into the darkest archives of her mind. Yet, even stored way back there, it had this tendency to drift to the center of things. But even if she couldn't totally deprive herself of relieving herself of such negative ideas, she could at least deny them in a less painful jurisdiction.

"What are we going to do today?" she asked as she walked calmly into the living room, partially recovered from her scattered perceptions of adversity.

"Huh?" he commented in an absent daydream as he was jostled back to her as though a theft had just taken place. "Oh, I thought we might take a walk on the beach later this evening . . . if you are up to it."

She scurried over to him and flew into his lackless arms.

"That would be great," and she attempted to smother him with kisses.

After she ceased this outward show of affection, she pulled back her thick brunette mane and glared into his darting eyes.

"This was a wonderful thing we did, you know," she stated as if in self-defense while she scanned his blank features for an open channel to his embargoed heart, whose cargo seemed depleted of sentiment. "And we are going to be happy, you'll see." Then she touched his unshaven cheek with a concealed desire to understand the inner workings of his soul. "No regrets, Matt, I swear." Hence she bombarded him with urgent warmth, hugging him hard, as though to feel him was to know him.

He gently pulled her away and stared at her as if seeing her for the first time.

"There was no need for you to doubt, Jen . . ." Then he paused as if carefully crafting his sentences, and continued. "There's no need to worry, Jenny. Everything's going to be all right, you'll see." And he patched on another grin from an endless supply of false emotions before she allowed him to get up.

"I better prepare something to eat before we both starve to death."

She hopped over into the tiny kitchen area once more, satisfied with what she heard.

He monitored her feminine movements and wondered suddenly how he was going to pull his plan off without too much incident. For some reason he felt a tinge of ambivalent infirmity in what he needed to accomplish. He then looked away and rubbed his brow roughly with emergency relief in order to restore the former puissance and purity of his strategy. Once he sensed his acquiescence and willingness return, he calmed down once again.

"Matt," his wife urgently inquired in an uneasy voice when she saw her husband in such private, mental agony, "are you sick or something?" Then she urgently came to his aid by comforting him with her touch.

He attempted to avoid it as best he could without upsetting her or giving her reason to suspect him of something immoral.

"I'm okay," he quickly responded as he got up from his seat not a moment too soon. "I just have a slight headache, that's all," staring at her while trying to appear good as new. "I'll be all right after I've eaten and gone for a walk." Then he was forced to look away after being beaten finally for his prevaricating.

"Are you sure, Matthew. Maybe you need to rest today. We can always do this tomorrow, you know," she replied gently as she glared up at his skittish form.

"No," he erupted as the unthinkable horror of his plan being sheared and shattered entered his paranoid imagination. "A little walk on the beach will do me a world of good, I think. I'm fine, Jen. There's no need to worry." And with all the strength he could muster on short notice, he roamed over toward her and softly caressed and cuddled her until he sensed that her feelings had become somewhat settled once more.

After such difficult intimacy on his part, they both were released from further duty, and Jennifer once again resumed her work of fixing lunch. Yet, before she completely left his side, she paused for a few seconds in the compact living room and glanced down at his light windbreaker lying innocently on the chair. She quickly seized this article in her immediate grasp and then turned to face her spouse.

"Matthew, you know, you haven't changed a bit," she joked with serious undertones before tossing this item of outer clothing straight at him. "You're still the same sloppy and messy person you always were. It seems that married life hasn't changed you one bit." After he caught it with a look of shock in his eyes (which initially she didn't comprehend fully, because she did not know what was secretly hidden in the pocket), she proceeded to giggle and announce to him that she was merely kidding. Hence, she cut the cord on her fit of laughter when she saw the stunned expression on his face. "What's the matter with you now?" she inquired while still trying to suppress her tittering.

Matthew, once the crisis has passed without any damaging occurrence, displayed a new expression of normal placidity.

"Nothing, honey. Just lost in thought for a moment." Then he turned away, unable to handle the strain of fooling her further, and he pretended to be occupied with something else.

Yet Jennifer knew something was up. But she could only guess at what it could be, having no known resources to call upon to gather clues. Call it woman's intuition if you like, and nothing more. She also let this slide, hoping it was nothing more than something usual and less harmful than what her imagination was starting to dream up. She turned back to her task at preparing a meal for them both. Aspiring to a thought that this too would pass after a solid meal.

Later that evening, a loving couple could be seen strolling along the beach, hand in hand, in fists of adoration and devotion. In the background, far away in the distance, one could hear the sound of happy noises of a ruction coming from a carnival fairground at the farthest end of the lengthy boardwalk. But these twin lost souls were heading in the opposite direction, finding comfort and joy in their own dual solitude.

While their footprints left faint marks of where they were, the waves advanced, comparable to an army of amenable butlers, and ended this delicate memento by quickly washing away the unassuming reminder.

From viewing this as an innocent bystander, one would rationally make the wild presumption (possibly a jealous one) that these two were deeply and contentedly matched by the strict articles of love. Yet one would be terribly mistaken to jump to such a random conclusion (but with only a margin of subtle error). There was definitely adoration of the first degree, to be sure; yet, it was a distorted confidence on much closer inspection, which would be difficult and hard to explain, being on the outside peering in. Yet, if one was able to climb, crawl, and enter the inside of this pair of complex emotions, one then might understand something of what was taking place, what was (more importantly) going to take place not so far in the near future.

Jennifer, one could argue the assumption, was merely a bit player in this confusing petty drama, albeit, an important one. Her naive role (not of her choosing or fault, no less) was without a doubt the most important part in this hidden scenario. And it was up to Matthew to fill her in on the responsible details. This task he would eventually oblige with eager, but grievous, satisfaction.

So while they teased the ocean's menacing tide with their unprotected and minor forms, Matthew used this special time wisely to conjure up and cleverly improvise a private and impersonal and calculating formula, which should not fail him, if done with the utmost care and proper respect that it justly deserved and which was required. Meanwhile, Jennifer was content enough with what the night brought, for the time being at least. Simply, she was appreciative and cherished the fragile period to embrace the man she desired, without any outward hint of what was in store.

After a short while, she paused to scan the enchanting surroundings (her very own enchanting surroundings), as if hearing the sound of the siren's song merging and intermingling with the mighty current. As she pulled her luscious hair from her pretty features (which the wind was fighting to obscure her vision with), she spied something up ahead.

"Oh look, Matt," she cried out with glee while she suddenly tugged her husband's loose arm. "Let's go over there," she added as she pointed over toward some dinosaur of a structure, beached like some gigantic dead whale in the wet sand.

Matthew merely stood poised as though stunned by her typical English.

"The pier, Matthew," she pleaded, like a child. "Come on, let's stroll along it," and then she sprinted over toward it as if this was the real carnival artifact, while leaving Matthew alone to make up his own mind whether he wished to follow or not.

Matt would follow, but not yet. He took this precious respite to search for his significant instrument, which he had conveniently brought along. He didn't want his mind's persistently neutral side to think that he had forgotten about the substantial job that needed to be accomplished. Therefore, he rubbed the instrument of courage and allegiance between his sweaty fingers, gratifying the object with his blind touch.

"Matthew come here!" Jenny called from the path leading to the ancient pier. "What are you waiting for, honey? Hurry, darling! . . ."

Yet, he didn't know what her hurry was. But alas, he would hurry to her anyhow. As for him, he had all the time in the world to complete his specific mission. And all the ripples in the great water were no match for his carefully designed persistence. Thus, he knew he would be greatly rewarded for his resignation. Greatly rewarded. And so he indulged her female whim nonetheless and ran quickly to her.

"Isn't it terrific!" she exclaimed with glee over the masterful volume of the dark, wide sea. Thus turning to him, after hearing his telltale footsteps, she remarked, "It's wonderful, darling (smiling with innocent shyness), and it's all ours . . ."

She then seized his cheeks gently in both hands and kissed him. He returned a rewarding smile to compliment the act and spoke while turning slightly away.

"It looks like we are all alone, too."

Her expression shone with agreement.

"It's like it was prepared especially for us . . . private and nice like—"

She searched his unmarked expression for a sign of something positive. Then settling for what it was, she decided to walk along the planks in a dreamy state of bliss.

Matt followed close behind, like a faithful mutt.

Without looking at him, she asked for his hand.

And obediently he gave it.

They roamed in the refreshing chilled night, similar to ghosts browsing the deck of a shipwreck.

They walked for awhile in silence, each enjoying their own sacred thoughts. And while the incorrigible wind howled them a replica of a haunting song, their naked toes sacrificed by a few splinters along the jaggedly coarsed, weather-beaten board without either asking for mercy.

Matt's thought swam with drowning images of infraction while he spied the water below, whipping and splashing itself into a magnificent frenzy of white foam against the defiant sodden beams, which held up rather gallantly under such punishment, and which he was able to see with all its majestical brilliance between the decrepit wood. It gave him a perverted vision, comparable to an open wound pleading with him to act fast before it was much too late.

Yet, Matt wouldn't be rushed. He had been planning for this very day for a long time, and he felt he should have the luxury to relish in its prolegomenon before the die would be cast for good.

Then while he was picking at his fantasies and desires, like extracting the petals from a flower, she had found herself a place to sit, a bench at the far end of the pier.

"Matthew, come over here and sit with me," she beckoned mildly as she patted the empty space next to her that she had reserved for him.

Suddenly his bubble was burst, and he was compelled to the realization of the moment. Then without a word he inched and sauntered his way over to her.

"Listen to that roar. Doesn't it fill you with exhilaration?"

After a brief moment, she turned to him, still waiting for his answer.

Actually it exhausted him somewhat, as if it was in competition with him to see who was the most stirred up.

"Yes, . . . it's wonderful," he remarked pensively as he stared into the robust hollowness and desolation.

Afterward, they both grew quiet once more, as though the quarrelsome tempest had a halcyon and sedative affect on them both.

Yet, Jenny was merely being mute in order to find the proper words to correctly express directly from her confident mind and tell her devoted husband of a hundred and some hours what her mouth and lips, with no assurance, were currently having a difficult time formulating.

"I guess by now everyone back home has discovered that we have eloped . . . (then a mixture of laughter and chuckles distorts her voice) I'd love to see our parents' features when they get our postcard." And then she flopped over in a fit of giggles onto Matt's solid shoulder as if these delicious pictures were a comedy for her. Thus, while her face was submerged deep into the rough cloth of his windbreaker, she said, "I bet they think we've gone totally mad . . . (then glaring up while still declining to become vertical again) What do you think, Matt . . . are we nuts or what?"

"Huh! No . . . of course not. (then staring into her endearing complexion, he finished his sentence) . . . I don't think so, anyway," and he laughed with slight effort at the absurdity of it all.

And at the absurdity of everything.

"I wonder what everyone is doing right at this moment," she remarked in a remote tone as she continued to curl up in serpent style comfort beside his warm form, while Matthew stroked her extended hip with a free hand.

"Who do you mean?" Matt commented with fake indifference that coated his true emotions.

"Well, . . . everyone. I guess, Larry, for example," she replied, with no guilt in her voice.

"Why do you single him out?" Matt cross-examined in a subtly coquettish mode of questioning.

She then lifted her tired lazy head just enough to traverse his immediate expression before it might disappear.

"No particular reason, my dear . . . she paused for a split-second to reach some impersonal conclusion). Well, he is, after all, your best friend, Matthew. Haven't you even thought about what he might be—"

"*Was* my best friend, Jen, . . . *was,*" he broke in harshly, and got up instantly from the bench in order not to be coaxed any further by her female qualities.

Jen then sat up and glared over at him, as he appeared to be interested in something far off and deep in the massive ocean.

"You're still angry at him, . . . aren't you?" she remarked in a careful, ominous manner, which wasn't meant to offend him outright.

Yet, Matt would not answer her—with words, at least—and continued to stare ahead into nothing.

"You still blame him for what happened, don't you?" she added in depressed undertones of weariness as she braced herself with rigid responsibility against the bench seat, the shackles of the embarrassing past coming back to weigh on her conscience once more.

Matt leaned against the railing, with his arms acting as buttresses, as though he no longer trusted his legs to hold him up straight.

"Forget about it, Jen," then he sighed once before lowering his head until his chin almost touched his sunken chest, "in any event . . . it's all over now."

Jennifer grew instantly inimical when hearing the frozen apathy in his tone.

"What the hell do you mean by that . . . forget what?"

Matt turned around swiftly and confronted her at last.

"Jennifer, just drop it, all right."

Jennifer studied him with quick, puzzled, searching eyes while her bottom lip began to tremble because of here almost perfect, but now ruined, evening.

"Matthew . . . I don't understand what's going on (wiping away a single tear, which could have been a solitary spray of water from the ocean and not a weakness toward further tears). Why are you so suddenly hostile, when I'm only just trying to make simple conversation?"

This attempt at innocence (genuine or not) made his blood boil, which was something he had taken an oath to himself that that would not happen.

"Let's not play games with each other anymore, okay, Jen. I'm not an absolute idiot, you know."

This only caused further consternation to build up inside her, as she desired to weep out loud, but didn't.

"Why are you being so cruel to me? What have I said to make you act this way? Tell me, please. . . ."

Matthew felt as though he was losing control of the situation, and instead of trying to remedy it, he made it worse by becoming more upset and angry.

"Look, Jennifer, it's too late for trying to correct the situation." Then he turned back around avoided her presence as much as possible under the strained circumstances. "I don't wish to discuss or talk about it anymore. Just let it go."

Suddenly, like a fast slap in the face, she knew something of what he was referring to; the shock of it stunned her more than any hand striking her ever could.

"You know, . . . don't you?" she murmured through shocked and hushed lips before adding, ". . . the whole thing . . . everything. Don't you?"

Matt didn't even pretend to be surprised or bewildered by what she was ambiguously suggesting as he glared over at her, with the harsh gale hitting him squarely in the face, as if all the enemies of the world were upon him now. To mock him and debilitate his spirit. Now, in this hour of need. Now, that the time was ripe.

"I know enough (twisting away again). If that's what you mean."

She was paralyzed with silence as she let this sudden realization bleed into her pores like some icy liquid, which made her shiver slightly now as she attempted to rearrange her muddled mind. Matt seemed to be totally insensitive, as he relapsed into muteness himself.

She finally found the courage (or maybe the rash desperation) to speak suddenly, albeit with strained weakness.

"We never did it. (choking back some concealed tears). You know that, . . . don't you?"

Matt neglected to respond and continued to stare down the storm, which swirled around him like manic seagulls.

Then she rose as if to testify further. Or as though standing would add further believability to her statement.

"You believe me, don't you, Matthew? (the volume of her voice pitched to a slightly more pleading level) You do believe me, . . . Matt, you must believe me!"

Matt merely ignored this, too.

Consequently, this nonverbal approach had the same effect on her, or worse, as if he had said no, I don't believe one single phrase of it. . . . Thus, Jennifer felt this stab to her heart like a rusty, brutal saber, and she fell back onto her seat.

"Matt, please answer me! . . . (sobbing openly now) Say something, anything! . . . Tell me you believe me!"

Through her immediate suffering, she got her wish, but wish that was cursed with a heavy price. A penalty that always accompanies such false, short-cut yearnings.

"That's, that's really wonderful, Jennifer . . . really terrific. Expressing regret now. Well, I have news for you, my dear, it's way past that deadline for such grief now," Matthew complied with malicious, subversive, and nasty fury while aching inside still more by an endless supply of bountiful lust for additional revenge. Yet, Matthew no longer had the energy or the strength to shower her any further with inauspicious congratulations. Because for this simple reason, that he felt way too sick. So ill indeed, that he was unable to bring this menace forth from the current and abortive sting of the actuality. This bitter truth was one tough act to follow and one very difficult pill to swallow in one absolute gulp.

Nonetheless, even he could tell even from his lack of putting his prey out of its misery, that this brought him no cogent rewards that he felt he had deserved and what he thought he would be promised. No valid gift of enthusiasm or joy, which reeked of shame and which battled presently with his cruelly perfervid emotions for the pinnacle notch of what was truly genuine.

Even though she was emotionally torn, she picked up on this instantly, not fooled for one solitary second by his semifabricated anger; she knew that he took some delight in hurting her. Yet, for the life of her, she remained uncertain of why in the fullest sense. Then she dried her eyes with an available sleeve.

"What's wrong with you all of a sudden, Matthew? I thought you were happy . . . glad for both of us. Aren't you the one that said everything was going to be all right, . . . huh . . .? Isn't this what you . . ." She then drifted off, losing her thought pattern in a mass of precipitated confusion, as if she was bushwhacked by a herd of elephants. "Oh, I see . . . I should have known," she suddenly confirmed confidentially to herself in a partial whisper while glaring up at the night sky for some kind of foolhardy salvation.

"Look, Jennifer!" he protested, yet without really knowing what he was remonstrating.

"Don't 'look Jennifer' me, Matthew, don't!" gesturing to him to stay back and, more important, to stay away. "Just tell me what you really wish to say without putting me through this pointless agony . . . all right!" while she began moving in the opposite direction of where he was located, moving in slow-motion reverse toward the very edge of the pier.

And when she felt he might make a sudden move, she ordered him to stay where he was.

For the first time in what seemed a lifetime of never having taken commands from her but only giving them, he now took these dire instructions from her and remained where he was, unable to control the circumstances unraveling right before his very eyes in a matter of seconds.

During this brief, endless pause, Matt was able to gather in his clotted brain a back-up, emergency plan. This time around, he decided to use a more clever and soothing calm approach in order to regain the upper hand.

"Listen, Jenny, . . . just relax for a minute (moving with crablike finesse towards her). I admit I was being a little bit too harsh with you, honey. I'm sorry. Please, Jenny . . . Let me explain—"

"Don't!" Jennifer exclaimed as she swiftly removed herself from his immediate reach until the heels of her bare feet were practically over the side of the pier. "Stay away . . . I don't want you to explain anything. I already understand enough of why you're so angry with me . . . so don't try and trick me into thinking I don't," she lamented with bitter weeping.

In despondency, he pleaded his case again.

"Look, baby, I said I was sorry . . . so don't do anything foolish . . . all right."

Jenny glared over at him, as to a threatening foe or enemy.

"In all honesty, Matthew, I don't give a shit whether you're truly sorry or not. I really don't. I don't think you or I have any other major surprises left to hurt each other with, so stop this bullshit right now," she reprimanded and stressed viciously.

"All right, Jenny, all right, . . . just chill out for a second. That's all I'm asking," he remarked with arms and hands open in symbolic surrender.

Thus, after seeing that she was not going to do anything rash for the moment, he judged it prudent to speak once more.

"Okay, so you know why I'm so upset . . . all right. But how did you expect me to act? What did you want me to do, huh? Jump up and down with joy or something after what I had heard," he argued profusely as he attempted to project his anger towards something less sinister.

"Yes, I do. Sure I expected something like that, at the very least. Sure, if you really ever trusted me," and her indignation crept to the surface once again, like the thunderous tide smashing everything, guilty or not, in its wake. Then after that short but effective harangue, she softened the blow somewhat by stating, "I guess what I am saying to you is hard for you to comprehend . . . huh?" she moaned in disgruntlement, feeling extremely miserable, while she watched with folded arms the crashing waves slam into the jetty with such furious brilliance as she waited, but not really expecting, to receive a favorable, or otherwise, response from him. She twisted back around and dared to look at him in all his pathetic glory. "Just as I thought . . ."

Subsequently, Matt leaped to the forefront with these burning words.

"I can't!" he shouted out his complaint that was heavily sprinkled with a soft dusting of sorrow, then he hid his face from her, trying his best to avoid her powerful stare, which was deadlier than the sharpest of sharp objects. Thus with his features well obscured from her passionate gaze, he was able to add, "Well, I just can't answer you that easily. It's much more complex than that, don't you see?" pleading with her better judgment in order for her to quickly comprehend (for his personal sake) the fathomless intelligence of his annoying dubiety, with the equivalent, intense behavior of a criminal seeking justice at last after having no hope left for a possible and clear-cut acquittal. Yet, on second thought, he had revealed too much already from his paranoid tergiversation, bequeathing her an option for further inquiry, and foolishly falling into checkmate himself as he attempted desperately now to switch gears once again, grasping at the loose straws of his randomly uncontrolled emotions toward something much more stable. But all he could manage to do was to become more impulsively reserved while he braced himself to confront her rage that was building up slowly from the inner sanctums of her gut, no less.

"No, Matt, I don't see, . . . and don't take me for such a foolish moron either. Just answer me with a simple explanation for once, why can't you, Matthew?" she requested wholeheartedly and with no quarter, as she was momentarily ignorant of his alternation of temperament. Hence, it then suddenly hit her like a ton of bricks, causing her to stop in midsentence. From a ceaseless supply of postponed and incomplete sentences with ugly gaping jaws, she simultaneously and rapidly reviewed what he had just stated, realizing at once that she already could guess what the answer to her question could sadly be all along.

"Now I get it. You think . . ." she paused and fought and tried to contain the overpowering grief, which was as profuse as mucous in her raw throat and was ultimately the cause of her hesitating to produce the necessary words, not wanting to consider and suggest what she could no longer deny to be the genuine article and true faith.

"This is all about Larry again . . . isn't it? (then screening her pretty, mournful eyes with the palm of her hand, she completed her dire proposal) . . . the person that you once treated like a brother . . . your goddamn buddy, Larry," she vaguely responded in disgusting mockery.

She wanted to laugh and scream in this insane exigency. He stared at the gloomy floor around him, unable to look her squarely in the eyes any longer. Moreover, the hateful phrases she spoke were too heavy on his brow to sustain any more tormenting facts such as these, and such as they were.

"So you do know, then, the whole sordid story between us after all?" she acknowledged bluntly while she whined, which helped, but did not succeed, in conquering the sick humor of it all with slow, painful ease. "And you never said a fucking word all this time," she testified, partially to herself and in remote and distant care and regard to her beloved, while she collapsed onto the bench in order to regain and restore some much needed relief.

For an eternal moment, both were struck with the virus of silence once more; And the only prevailing sound around them, locking their incontrovertible ears, was the legitimacy of the great water's current, which played an active supporting role in this sad drama. And if you paid even enough closer attention, you would, and could, possibly ascertain the festive noise of the carnival fairgrounds and the hysterical, happy yells from the massive Ferris wheel on a faraway corner of the vast boardwalk, where the numerous, cheerful people dwelled and still enjoyed themselves and their simple lives with pleasant blessededness and bliss.

"If you knew, why did you marry me?" she commented, with an incertitude filled with remorse, while she still continued to peer and gaze out at the yearning emptiness: the only companion she had, being the immortal, rolling surf breaking against the sturdy banks and its vulnerable sister shoreline.

He tried to comply with her request quickly, but the sentences failed him in the end.

"I suppose you found out later . . . right?" she verbalized again while attempting, for her own benefit, to fill in the disturbing gaps for him, choking sorrowfully on a huge tear of distrust and disappointment, which she wiped off her cheek. She let the remaining stains stay on her tortured features, sensing that she couldn't bear so much grief any longer with so little time left.

Thus, she proceeded to talk off the top of her head as dejection descended upon her rationality. She was no longer in a proper frame of mind, which was similar in effect to the mighty waves in all the known oceans knocking over something smaller and weaker in its hankered path in order to arrive at a comfortable location on the peaceful coastline.

"And you probably knew about the baby beforehand also?" as she continued her sorry query while glaring over at his mute form for comprehensible ratification.

Yet he put forth nothing, vocal or otherwise, as he still monitored the pathetic ground around him for possible guidance and despairing support, kicking out a loose sliver of dilapidated wood with the tip of his sandal as a useless distraction.

She almost asked twice, until. . . .

"Yes, I know about it," he confessed sharply and curtly, not wanting her to repeat the dreaded and damned locutions again.

"Who told you, Matthew?" she asked, speaking carefully this time, while suddenly feeling betrayed even more.

"Does it matter? I know, I know it all. That's all . . . and that's all that really counts," he replied spitefully, yet his tone failing slightly with regret, which he soon dispelled and banished with a fueled gesture of bravery.

"It's yours, you know" she remarked, sounding dejected because of the obligation to explain.

"I never did it with him . . . I wanted to . . . at the time (*sniff*) . . . but I couldn't go through with it in the end (*sniff*), . . ." all the while beginning to shake with dilatory anguish from the pointless admission.

"I don't want to hear anymore!" he shouted, in a fit of disgust, while compressing his agony in his pressure cooker of a skull with his nervous, ineffectual hands.

"Matthew," she cried back at him, "You have to understand first why I did it," holding back the tears in an attempt to resume her indigestible avowal.

"It's because of what he told me, . . . your best pal, Matt. It's all because of what he told me, . . ." she prematurely emphasized without truly emphasizing, in harrowing stress, before carrying on with her tragic tale. "He said . . . he said that you were fooling around with that Patty whatshername," she verified, without truly verifying with faithful conviction, by making mention of this girl's identity sound so blasphemously evil.

"So you had to go to bed with Larry. Is that it?" he responded in a depreciative volume.

"Yes! Yes! That's right. That was the idea. Yes!" she exclaimed offensively. "But I-I-I didn't . . . Funny, but I can't think of a reason why I didn't do it in the end though. . . ." Then turning to him again for an improvidently scorpion strike at him, she added, "Can't you see, I knew what he was doing. He was using me too, Matthew, in some sordid, sick game . . . by lying!" she begged with utter motivation in her smart deliberation.

"So I told him, no, no! I wouldn't do it . . . so I left," she said, yet still reacting to the situation with living passion as if she was in a time warp or something.

"Just like that, huh?" he remarked with hideous sarcasm, knowing full well that he had made a major blunder and had also been utterly defeated and wrong somehow.

"Yeah! Just like that. Don't you believe me?" she ejaculated in hopelessness, hating him for his lack of trust in her.

"Why didn't you tell me before?" he mentioned, scolding her dubious behavior with a guilty person's choler.

"What!" she yelled, while almost wanting to laugh at the absurdity of his denouncement. Yet the hurt inside was too great for such an impossible effort.

"Tell you what, Matt. That I almost slept with your best buddy, we didn't really do anything, so dumb me presumed everything to be okay. Peachy! Fine and dandy," she stated, returning the irony in full swing while answering his silly comment with the ache of a thousand cuts.

"I wanted to . . . really, I did," she noted pensively, this time around lowering her chin to her sunken bosom and hanging her head in a demeaning and humiliating manner, where it lay in foul repentance. "But I was too ashamed of myself . . . and too afraid to go through with it. I figured you'd hate me forever, . . . and that was more than I could bear. I wanted you to find out on your own anyway. That way I would be punished somehow. Christ, I don't know. It's all so stupid now . . ." she distressed in full blame while she began to feel the worthlessness of the whole, pointless conversation and excuse.

She then lay back on the bench once more, feeling mentally and physically exhausted, drained of all hope and resolution. It seemed to have taken its toll on her completely. But after all this time, she could suffer openly in peace for once.

"I guess you regret everything now," she said, in a remote voice, listening patiently for an eager reply. Well, maybe not such an eager one at that, yet, something to aid her in dealing with the pain. Nevertheless, anything was better than nothing to quell the stillness engulfing her at that moment. Anything was better than this placidity. She had to lean on something, soft or hard, so that she wouldn't have to endure this unfavorable and equitable quiet. This maddening discipline from him, much more than what was required for merciful clemency.

Matt, meanwhile, refused to contribute to this insultingly crazy farce, hence, rejecting outright to grant her a speedy reprieve. Thus, returning to his natural habit of putting his hands into his deep pockets, he smothered his soreness by embracing the only ally and sense of security he had left, and of which he knew contemporarily.

"I know you wished you had never married me, huh, Matt?" She addressed him with a vacant tone. "I screwed up your chances to have a normal, decent life, didn't I? Go on, say it. I know you want to," she moped while character-bashing herself vocally and hoping for some compassionate redemption at the same time, which she actually imagined she didn't rightly deserve.

"Anyhow, now I've made a mess of everything you've ever wanted, right? Shattered fantasies and aspirations," she remarked in an unusual, rambling calmness, which made her feel like her whole world was crumbling right around her.

"Well, me, too! I also needed to be somebody, too. Don't you think I had dreams!" she wailed among a shower of heated, sodden, and wet stains which appeared in abundance. Shouting out her grievances to the unsympathetic ocean, she was absolutely lost in her own wretchedness to the point that she didn't even bother to notice anything else, finding substitute contentment from the gale's mean, cold breath. And as she was mesmerized by the tempest's gusty force, she seemed to summon its majesty by proclaiming in a defeatist tongue, "I wish I could make it all disappear . . . yet, I can't."

Albeit the words she spoke appeared to only injure her more, her pessimism reigning supreme was kind of comparable to a spike that was being driven severely further and further into her decaying ambitions, that was diminishing in its brightness with such a fast pace, that she couldn't seem to deal with it much longer.

"I thought having this baby, this child, would make everything turn out all right," she mumbled on while attempting to compete with the magnificent elements in order to be heard (shattered fantasies and illusions revisited).

"Why did you marry me then, Matt, . . . Why?" she implored as if he was merely an image in her mind, while she swiped away the washed-up smudges from her tainted features, sniffing uncontrollably from the leftover defection, no longer having the strength to release her meaningless agony anymore.

"Maybe you were trying to punish me?" she pondered out loud between breaks in the overpowering hush and equally overbearing background commotion. "Or maybe Larry instead . . . to get back at him," she questioned herself analytically before resuming. "Huh, was that it? . . . Yes! . . . That was probably it." And she practically sounded pleased with this personal and clever deduction when another wild concept entered her sickened brain like a secret murmur from the chilly and busy breeze.

"Then you must have been probably punishing yourself also. Maybe . . . because you loved me so . . . and I hurt you . . . so . . . so you thought it was something that you might have done." Then she drew in a deep and covert breath before adding, "That must be it," concluding this paramount statement in an atoning daze.

Hence, she paused for a long time, which knew no bounds in an accurate measure of length, with a lost and puzzled expression of gloom mixed with desire that was quilted in clusters of confused patchwork, as if searching and digging to find a path to an impossible solution.

"A new beginning is all we need, Matt . . . a brand new start. Don't you see," she resonated with vigor while spinning around by the seat of her pants in order to petition this to him directly and properly.

"Matthew," she called out shallowly as she peeked at the very spot where he once stood.

"Matthew!" she repeated louder this time while she scanned the vast blackness before her for any sign of visible existence.

But he was gone. And only her shadow lingered about as a companion to remind her of her own sour solitude.

Therefore, she immediately picked herself up while frantic thoughts drilled, suffocated, and stormed her mind. She wandered about in awe as she tried to remember if he had ever been there at all.

She yearned to yell out once more for him, but knew that he had vanished from the scene for good. She then wanted to burst out crying again, yet knew that that wouldn't do any good either. Besides, there just wasn't anyone there to care anymore. And besides that, she was weary of all the grief and just wanted to quit and bury it forever.

She then proceeded to walk in circles, aimlessly for awhile, her only thoughts were of what to do next. Then her toe instantly struck something hard and cogent. It felt icy cold on her nude foot, which forced her to jump back in imperative impulse from the minor fright. Thus with her heart pounding perfectly in her head and chest, she pushed back her loose hair in order to view what it was that had startled her so.

Yet because of the inadequate lighting, she had trouble seeing it with her average, at best, 20/20 vision. Instead, she was compelled to kneel down to take a closer look at the blurred object. Thus, as she tore away the last strands of her glossy locks, which had become in common practice to always inconveniently get stuck and glued to her truthful, moist guise, she nearly had to bend over completely in order to retrieve the tiny, rectangular-shaped, metallic mystery. Once in her grasp though, she began to study it curiously as if deeply fascinated by its beautiful gleam.

She then held it up for excoriated screening and for a closer inspection, and that's when she caught the resolute blade's amazing reflection, shining with absolute star quality in the tantamountly dazzling moonlight. Thus, just like magic, she forgot herself and all about her worries and problems while she watched the dwarfed and beauteous spark do its dance silently on the edge of darkness.

All I know even more, more I can tell. Once, by his violent hand, a dragon fell. He bathed in blood grew hard and can't be skein. And may have seen this again, and yet again.

—*Das Nibeleingenlied*

See Emily Play

In the dead of night, he awoke from a disturbing dream and stood face-to-face and erect in order to confront the darkness that surrounded and lay before him. In his somnolence, he heard a faint cry of an infant. Or, at least, that's what he believed it was. He was puzzled somewhat by the fact that it could still be audible when he was semiawake, while he listened with deliberate intensity in his vigilance to the distant weeping.

He then glanced over at his sleeping wife to make sure that what he was experiencing was genuine. He thought of waking her but declined the temptation, deciding instead to ease his trouble mind with an investigation of the immediate source of the odd vociferation.

Thus he then carefully slipped out from beneath the covers, the whole time keeping one eye evenly on the dormant form next to him, whose back was luckily to him, so he wouldn't be afraid to take action for further enquiry, which he would not have been able to do if she had been turned his way, evidently.

When he felt it was safe, he removed himself slowly from the edge of the bed, moving with such proficient grace, it would have put a cold-blooded reptile to shame while it left its den to feast. He then vanished from her sphere of influence.

By some strange, amazing unknown force, he seemed to be drawn in the direction of his daughter's bedroom. He walked the straight and narrow, half of him in this dimension, and the other, floating through a hallucinogenic-type purgatory. The corridor walls appeared to breathe heavily as though in a deep trance, giving the surroundings and atmosphere a futuristic Boschian texture to them. Yet, even that hefty glum absorption could not drown out the pale moans coming from afar.

It was like being in a sordid funhouse of some kind, slanted and distorted. But that's where the similarity ended. It was far from being amusing, in any shape or form, but he felt compelled to go on regardless, to see it through to the finish, no matter what.

His dark, comic performance came to a conclusion when he made his exit from the maze of the conceptual river Styx and onto the shores of his daughter's room, which put the finishing touches to this mock-drunkard binging on the verge of disaster.

Or so he thought.

He opened the door as if he was expected, while in pursuit of the mysterious sound which became a foregone conclusion of sorts when it was discovered that it belonged solely to his little girl. He was struck dumb by the sight of a frightened young child whose wide, terrified stare gleamed and dazzled the senses from the tears that she'd shed, which were underscored in a black, dull setting.

She was propped up in her bed with her legs tucked beneath her with her doll at her bosom screaming her lungs out hysterically into space. He turned abruptly around, instinctively. What he should have logically seen was a bedroom wall, yet standing there in full color was a huge, hideous creature that appeared from out of nowhere. A prenatal birth it was (or ghastly abortion) originating from the fears of a nightmare.

He stood his ground, more from incredible wonderment than from trepidation. Because after all, he was not frightened (even though under normal circumstances he should have been), just stunned motionless, having waited for this day all his life. The monster informally informed of the premonitory calling, approaching him, knowing full well the significance of this encounter. Our man then lifted his arm and discovered to his initial surprise that he was holding a gun. Without much contemplation over how he had possessed this thing without his conscious knowledge, he gripped it firmly as if destiny had bequeathed this engagement. Pointing the piece at the beast now, and without a tingle of hesitation, he set his sights on it, knowing the extent of his prearranged *fait accompli.*

His daughter then screeched.

"Kill it, Daddy! Kill it !"

"Don't worry, darling, everything's going to be all right," he reassured her with explicit composure, without taking his eyes off the offensive target. Thus he began the process of pulling back the trigger to commence firing the weapon, which he did by the release of the hammer.

Jeff, in a fit of frenzy, shook himself awake, with the echo of a shot still drumming in his brain. He quickly rose from his mattress of nails to catch his fugitive breath, noticing at once that he had returned once again to where he started. He glared with aimless forthrightness around at everything familiar for the unfamiliar, but all he saw was a mesh of ebony and silver, the faded shades of a prelude to dawn.

Nothing has changed . . . Everything exactly the same as before. . . . Thank God, he thought in a barrel full of relief. And thus he sighed with twinge of discouragement to conclude his early fears. Turning to his sweet wife, he could tell that his internal cyclone hadn't disturbed her slumber at all or in the least. She was as fast asleep as ever, like an immobilized rock during a guffawing fusillade of abhorrence. She hadn't moved an inch, in technical fact, oblivious to the chaos circling his mind's schizoid eye.

He then exhaled deeply with oppressive exhaustion, feeling his heart pouring directly into his chest like some eerie, thick batter. He sat straight up, no longer able to bear the panic of being horizontal for too long, while covered from head to foot in a sheet of sweat as he tried his best to excavate his former composure.

Later he shifted to the side of the bed and placed his naked heel and toes onto the fake lamb's wool rug. He then let himself drink in this small accomplishment by sucking in the stale air, which the remaining night still was beholden to. Holding his head in magniloquent despair, he produced an immediate thought that seemed to drown out all other possible impediments.

And this is what he imagined:

He awoke in the morning to the sight of a brilliant ray of sunlight pouring in discreetly through his bedroom curtains like a flood of golden hue. Looking around the room in a languid daze, he adjusted his tired eyes to the pristine daylight.

After a short spell, he noticed that his wife, Elaine, was already up and about and probably downstairs fixing the family breakfast.

Then flexing his nostrils, he caught a whiff of freshly brewed coffee and homemade Belgian waffles that his gracious wife was probably superbly preparing. This was a sure indication to his dormant brain that this was no ordinary day. Actually, it was quite the contrary. It was, after all, late Saturday morning, which meant that he was in no particular hurry to do anything whatsoever this weekend but rest or do light recreation. And believe you me, he was very happy about it too, which incidently suited him just fine. Just think of it, to actually be able to lie there in a free sense, manumit for the time being from the shackles of society's ritualistic duties and demands. Ah! What a bountiful idea that was for one to inveiglingly endure and behold.

So he lay back for slothful moment, resting his weary head on a soft, fluffy pillow, reveling in all its glory, exposing his body from beneath the covers while basking in the fervor of pure light that saturated his anatomy from head to toe.

Suddenly the titanic, precious period was broken when he heard the voice of his spouse calling his name from somewhere at the bottom of the staircase.

"Honey, are you awake yet?" she cried, with her usual tenderness.

"Yes, dear, I'm up!" he responded while straining his yet untrained, today utterances in order to be heard as he jumped into an upright position to make it so. Thus, rubbing the drowsiness from his droopy sockets, he rose from the disheveled bed and yawned all the way to the bathroom.

He stood in the four-walled enclosure, fumbling around in an equally tiny medicine cabinet, searching for the vital items that should make him feel whole and much like himself again.

While shaving in the mirror, he spied his daughter's reflection staring timidly straight back at him from behind her favorite teddy bear that looked the worse for wear from years of loving intimacy and devoted affection.

"Hello, muffin," he said awkwardly from behind a delicate mask of foam, which prevented him from twisting his neck around in order to face her.

"Whatcha doing here, huh, kitten?" he asked with gentleness in his tone. But the shy, bashful, little, female urchin made no reply whatsoever and only glared up sheepishly at his towering frame, which loomed above here dainty crown like a divinity.

However, before he had a chance to divert his attention away from his toilette and then be able to address his primary heedfulness onto and toward his beloved daughter, she suddenly disappeared from sight with not so much as a word as a kind, polite calling card.

Jeff, after a brief interlude, stared at the empty space once occupied by his tiny treasure, making him remember something that he hadn't dared think of for quite some time, which caused his heart to ache and flutter in the extremity. And because of the unbearable pain he was feeling, he quickly dismissed it from his mind's scrapbook in a flash, returning instead to his daily chore of scraping his face with a cold piece of stainless steel.

"Emily," Jeff whispered under his breath, as though this name was something paramount or sacred, as he returned once more to the dark universe of his bedroom.

Thus he had another earnest thought which made him reach in a mild seizure for the dresser draw located beside his bed.

He then scrounged and rummaged around in the blackness, still careful not to wake his spouse, for something lost in the attic of his dusty mind. When he found what he was searching for, after an intense exploration, he yanked out a solid piece of metallic steel which shone brilliantly in his pale hand as he held it up to his face. He felt the cool, bulky, nickel-plated object between the warm skin of his own fingers, astonished by its cogent beauty. He couldn't quite believe that such a marvelous tool of craftsmanship could have been made with mortal skills. Moreover, that it was used, whether for wrongful purposes or otherwise, uniquely to exterminate life. This powerful pistol was still referred to in his personal manuel as "bad" in colloquial language, be it ghetto slang or posh British. Bad was bad. Yet, unfortunately, sadly necessary in drastic circumstances to do verbatim bad things . . . very bad things.

Yet, come to think of it, there were many things that man alone could do just as damaging without the aid of any kind of instrument. Oh, yes, one solitary person, male or female, could destroy anything pure and decent if he put his or her mind to it. But worse of all, sometimes they were deeds done by accident that left the most bitter wounds. Yes, indeed. It was the careless and casual actions of a person in day-to-day operation that were the most destructive.

Hence his memory began to drift again. Meandering to a world lost inevitably in the past . . . to a distant dream that refused to be forgotten or taken lightly. So he succumbed to its will, because he had no choice in the matter really. Thus he returned once more to events long lost and erstwhile. . . .

Later that day, the whole family, father, mother, and, oh yes, let us not forget, and the child, Emily, prepared themselves for a trip in which none of the above were particularly looking forward to. But for which none of them could with any plausible verification back out of either.

They each felt in their own amber ways that it was their moral responsibility to go through with this deed. So this dismal, motley crew of oblation gathered together to set out on their trek (because, after all, as we all know, misery loves a lot of company when it can get it. In this case, it came in a family dose, and reluctantly, they all knew that in the fissures of their doomed hearts) while they climbed into the station wagon and, with silent regularity, pulled out of the driveway of their quiet street of their picturesque neighborhood and were on their less than merrily way lickety-split.

As it happened, it turned out to be quite a gorgeous afternoon to perceive, yet from the individual perspective viewpoints of these sad players, it went virtually unnoticed. These occupants of this dark crusade (self-imposed of course) were totally ignorant of nature's gift of warmth and transposed splendor. And if they had bothered to appreciate it, it might have made the miles more bearable. But as it were, their selfish (justified as it may be) tribulation dulled every one of their senses completely.

During the early part of the journey, Elaine sat nervously beside her husband, trying her best to conceal her anxiety while she constantly peered over her shoulder to check on their daughter Emily, reassuring herself by smiling at the placid nymph, whose only reaction was to gaze through the passenger window of the car while still cradling that ever-present stuffed companion of hers in her thin arms.

They were only on the road a couple of minutes when Elaine felt she had to break the icy silence.

"I feel a bit edgy about going through with this, Jeff," she confessed, finishing her threadbare statement with a slight, tense laugh. Jeff, in a strange state of suspended latency, didn't appear to hear or comprehend her at first, as if he was attempting to absorb what was being said to him.

But when breaching this flimsy momentary quiescence, he spoke up for the first time since leaving his home.

"Elaine, everything's going to be all right," saying this without so much as moving a single muscle of his granite expression, his vision barely animated, while his living Mount Rushmore bust was permanently glued to the beltway ahead. And then assuming he had to end his trite statement with something tracery, he leaned toward his beloved wife and, with his physical touch, sales-pitched her a wealthy condolence by patting her knee with a half-hearted effort at mitigation.

Elaine, in the process, grinned back at him rather meekly while still conspicuously vexed over her true emotions as she turned once again to deliver her desecrated proffer to her darling daughter, hoping to find a far more encouraging sign of concern from her.

However, sweet, innocent, timid Emily wasn't going to remedy this situation for her either, as she unintentionally (or otherwise) ignored her mother's visual embrace while she sat there, a bump on a log, in unyielding repose, gazing with blind awareness out of the dirty glass pane at the passing blurry objects that whizzed by her, which left their smeary traces in her tiny mind in the form of easily forgotten fragments, facsimiles of what they used to be.

"Are you okay, pumpkin?" her mother asked gingerly while almost frightened by her own question.

"She's fine, Elaine," Jeff burst in with his own two-cent bid, answering by exemptible proxy for his little, tart sugar cube. "Everything is going to be fine. Now just relax," he stated further with gentle persuasion. "We're going to be there soon, all right? Everything is gonna be fine. You'll see," he concluded with a cheap, nickled smile, while swaddled to the fact that he was being monotonously redundant, as a limpid smudge of irritation became creepingly crystal clear on his transparent features, revealing to his wise mate the more truthful passion if there ever was one.

Up to this point he had tried to disguise it beneath a veil and shawl of mild composure, producing in the end though, an artificial smirk as an unworthy substitute, which he nevertheless was unable to fully expose anyway to her.

He turned away instead, hiding his guilt-ridden lineaments as best he could without arousing too much suspicion on her part while they continued on their jovial way that was destined for them.

After awhile, everybody seemed to drift off into their own private, shaded thoughts where they all verily felt the safest. Seeing the distinctiveness between each individual characteristic, it would be appropriate to say that the assembly on this fateful day of days was not a joyous one.

Eventually though, the spell was smashed into tiny fragments when they came nearer to that all-so-familiar place of their bluest lachrymations. Ensuingly, Jeff quietly parked their mode of transportation beside the curb, and then, uniformly, the solemn group removed themselves from the comfort of their seats, making as little noise as was humanly possible, not wanting to disturb the peaceful sanctity of the eternal abode.

After they all obediently stood on the pavement, exactly parallel to the large aperture, in a condition of unconscious synchronicity while looking out at the . . . Pleasant Valley Cemetery . . . with perfect assiduity.

Jeff, being the head of the family, was the first to enter. Elaine, tightly clasping her daughter's frail hand as if the mere touch of it was a necessary precaution, followed closely behind the chief of this small clan.

As they walked beyond the threshold of mortality, they paused briefly in obsequious silence to survey the field of blessed sepulcher.

"Well, . . . we're here," Jeff announced rather temperately while signaling to mother and child nonchalantly to follow as he led this minimum entourage through the sacred maze of consecrated mementoes and discarded pariahs.

Thus, as they strolled among the hallowed stones that littered the beautifully rich, green grass, these relics to the dead produced in all of them an effect of inebriated narcosis. Elaine, pursuing her husband in unquestionable accordance with her role as faithful wife, carelessly tugged her baby girl along her side while being hypnotized by the ponderousity that softly vibrated from the grounds of the plush lawn.

Hence, like grave robbers in the figurative night, these spectral impressions mysteriously began seeping into Elaine's veins to contaminate her bloodstream, which then caused her to shiver in the virgin sun.

"Come on, sweetie. Let's go with Daddy," she whispered, trying to coax the six-year-old Emily into moving a little faster in order for them to keep pace with her impermanent husband, who somehow was able to slip from her sight momentarily and position himself a great distance from the rest of the pack without his or their knowledge of it happening.

Jeff wandered through the graveyard in a delirious search, possessed by some strong, secured desire to find this one particular headstone, which seemed to have eluded him for some reason in that endless enigmatic conundrum, which by the way happened to be his only primary concern at that present time, while he callously forgot all about the living, loved ones who had accompanied him.

When his kin did finally catch up with him, he was already standing over the object of his fervent and eventual quest. His woman, seeing this act of good grace, crept up carefully next to him, trying her hardest not to interrupt him and having the discretion of a monk to keep silent while he read the inscription etched in the smooth, marble finish.

He stayed in that pose for quite some time perusing his son's name over and over again like he was trying to understand the meaning behind the words inscribed in the rock and also in his troubled brain. But all of them, adult and infant alike, knew the engraving by heart. As a matter of fact, it left its ugly reminder in them every day in the form of a deep, irreversible scar on their souls, which they knew they would have to carry around with them always, growing heavier and heavier with the passage of infinity.

While standing there together in absent grief and endless suspension, they all, in an ironic paradoxical convolution, were very much alone. Then all of a sudden, to overcome the desolate void, Elaine, in a typical style all her own, produced a bunch of freshly cut flowers that she had been carrying around unobtrusively on her person and delicately put onto her son's marker.

This offering to the deceased was, in her eyes, a panacea to ease her suffering for all those lost years. Well, maybe not. Yet, it didn't really matter now. Except that it made her feel that she still needed him even today, that her baby boy was gone but not forgotten. This was in a way somewhat superficially pathetic. At least that's what Jeff's image of her was all about at that particular moment (even though he had the better judgment to keep it to himself).

When this unforeseen performance was played out in front of him, which appeared to shatter his concentration (or lack of it), her traditional partner could only see a degrading farce in her single, simple ceremony. Then to add to the discomfort, he discovered to his amazement that he was perspiring rather profusely, even though the weather had been kind to them on this morbid reunion in sending them a cool breeze. Yet Jeff knew better. It had nothing to do with the temperature. No! . . . Not likely. It was the fire inside that burned so very very bright that caused this inferno in him as he proceeded swiftly to wipe the evidence from his sweaty brow before anyone else happened to discover it.

Elaine rose to her feet, unaware of her husband's nonverbal diatribe over the way she purposely express her affection for her major, personal loss. However, and maybe, just maybe, unknown to the trio at large, the waters were running much deeper than even they truly fathomed and expected. And just maybe, it was more than just her pretty, cute, petty, feminine behavior that he was secretly scoffing at, which was the ultimate cause . . . perhaps.

Actually it might be something else entirely. Something concealed underneath that masculine performance of deception that he had to display, which really only covered up his natural feelings that we are all unavoidably born with and which he was stupidly and enviably insensible to.

Elaine called to her daughter to come over to her. Emily, who during the whole scenario had kept a smart, respectable distance, cowered behind her very own innocuousness now after hearing this request from her mother. She hesitated for a moment when her name was called, before proceeding to her elder's parental demand.

"Here, honey, place this over there," her mom ordered in sufferance while speaking just above a murmur and just loud enough for Emily to understand before handing her the lone, red rose. The sensitive little girl stared at the solitary, scarlet, velvet petals clutched gently in her mother's outstretched fist, while she, the young lady, shifted her gaze from one parent to the other, searching their "mature" features, which were forcibly portrayed before her, for some sort of visual confirmation.

She was outright ambivalent about what to do next (yet closer to the truth, she wanted to run and hide) as she glared profoundly down at the polished slab, duplicating its form wonderfully by standing perfectly erect on that small segment of perfectly, if you could describe it like that, mown knoll. Thus from the required span of a lack of activity from any of the other party affiliates at the scene of the crime, she did what she believed was the correct thing and which she presumed was her unconditional duty. Because if she was to refuse, she would be blamed for neglecting her progenitor's strict wishes.

So in order to safeguard herself from a lot of untold trouble, she timidly took the dainty blossom into her equally dainty fingers and dropped it carefully onto the sacred spot. Just near enough in fact so as not to bother or disturb her younger brother's eternal slumber.

When this act of bravery was fulfilled, her father then took the initiative to speak up.

"Come on, everyone, let's go. It's time we left," announcing intrusively in a remote voice to no one in particular. Reason being that all his thoughts were still obviously gripped by the dwarfish obelisk. And he hoped that maybe, somehow, somewhere, his son would be listening from a not-so-distant place.

Consequently Elaine immediately grabbed hold of Emily's frail, limp hand and in quiet dignity hurried from the cemetery with the child in tow.

Jeff, during the rapid exodus, couldn't bring himself to leave or release himself just yet. His sorrowful look was adamantly fixed onto the solid, hard structure that held his namesake. This alone made him a prisoner.

This painful reminder that was encised in stone was likewise scratched even more severely into his bleeding heart. Yet when he could take it no longer, he turned and fled from the acrimonious precursor of his worst fears. Yet no matter how far he attempted to run, the words that he had memorized constantly wailed out to him, ringing incessantly into his ears as he futilely tried to escape their cries.

Once again it was tranquil there, there in that burial area. Thus the absence of the living brought back the subtle wind of late noon, which blessed the earth with peace and stability once more.

Meanwhile Mother Nature (whose job, as we very well know, is never done) took this occasion to take care of her own by diligently cleaning up after herself when her unexpected, early guests had left. Hence she swept away the organic and other forms of waste and debris from her presence, blowing it from the fertile soil in her usual housekeeping fashion. She then in its place disclosed to the nude world more clearly the lurid message that had caused so much grief and attention for a certain group of people already mentioned, leaving behind instead this simple epitaph for all of mankind to witness. And this is what was written:

Adam Jefferson Christian
Born 1986—Died 1988

Rest in Peace

Yes there was no rest for the wicked. Only the dead could enjoy such a luxury, if even then.

These were the kinds of problems swimming in Jeff's brain as he petted the old .38-caliber handgun with its cylinders fully loaded and ready for business while he sat in his pajama bottoms and stockinged feet.

The reason for this deep curiosity over a simple piece of hardware is easy to remedy; he had not literally touched the pistol in eons, by his forgotten account. Nevertheless, it felt new to him, the same as if it was some relished archive item that had never been tested or used properly. And then again, it was like a long, lost buddy coming back into his grievously nasty documentary to bail him out.

He stopped and faltered for an extended period, dismissing the cheap sentiment from his foggy, emotional photograph with relative ease, like sawing in half the roots of a giant redwood with little more than the tip of a pin.

Thus he stared into space and became abstractedly tense while he listened for a vestige of familiarity. Hearing nothing to his liking except the ticking of his busy alarm clock, which was rivaling his respiratory system for the vacant lack of noise (or any wishfully visible sound for that matter) in the blank environment, he turned to his life-mate again to see if she had noticed the so-called tranquility. But she only rolled over in some impulsive desire for comfort as he positioned his body above hers, using his arms like a brace in order not to accidentally tumble on top of her while he meagerly hovered over her, trying to snatch a glimpse of her shrouded features.

He studied her thoroughly with a grim expression, almost with utter disappointment, actually in forethought. Yet he couldn't quite put his tiny pinky-sized finger on why. He didn't want to think about it right now. He lifted himself from the bedspread silently, as if he was moving in slow reverse motion peculiarly comparable to a character in a vintage 1920s movie reel rewinding its own tape just for the fun of it, in order to know for certain if he was disturbing her deep nap or not, as the case may be.

Back on his feet, he felt alone and confused, suddenly not knowing what to do while rubbing his bristled chin nervously as he attempted to quietly pace the floor, deterring himself with this own gloomy ambivalence.

The bedroom seemed to him to be closing in on him. This cloistered wedge only added to his increasing and developing fear that he was experiencing now, and he wanted desperately to hear something. The sound of anything, so long as it broke the tension building up inside of him in escalating proportion.

Thus he was determined to grant himself a recess from his current delinquency and put is faith in former deliquiescences instead. And this is what they were, to be exact:

It was round the prefix and introduction of the period known as lunchtime, when Elaine decided to fix a special brunch for her hungry kinfolk.

She felt most comfortable in the kitchen. It was the one place where she felt she could get away from it all, where she had complete, totalitarian immunity and control. And she ruled her domain with an iron will.

She stood behind the kitchen sink, preparing some fresh vegetables for a meal she was cooking while periodically peeking out of a tiny window to check on her spouse, who was tinkering with a very ancient lawnmower. She leaned over the countertop and prudently pulled aside the curtain which had obscured her view. A private grin crept across her delicate, thin lips as she found amusement in her husband's attempt at playing mechanic.

Meanwhile, not too far away was the saccharine darling, Emily, playing a game by herself, of her own making, preoccupying this procrastinator's afternoon with an imaginary conversation with her favorite doll.

Her father meanwhile practiced his own form of make-believe by way of ignorance at his own task, blocking out his daughter's inculpable dialogue while he struggled with his tools to find the right ones to repair his personal, big toy. And like all proud dilettantes, he bore false witness on the manual implements that he had picked to take full responsibility for his human mishaps.

Between all of this banging and clanking and so forth over bits and pieces of metal, his daughter's tiny voice could barely bc heard as she complied with her mandate in a crude imitation of a maternal role while she scolded a pretend child of its natural blunders.

Ultimately though, Jeff completed his herculean chore, tightening one last bolt to put the finishing touches to his masterpiece. He then sat back admiring his accomplishment and privately congratulated himself on his achievement, which appeared to change his whole attitude and mood somewhat toward a more pleasing one.

Later he got up to stretch his aching legs, catching a glimpse of his daughter at last, who still was conversing with her artificial endearment while lost behind an imaginary shield of innocence. His heart warmed instantly as he beamed a smile at her earnestness. But she didn't seem to notice that she had an audience now, being clearly too involved in her sequestered reverie to notice.

For awhile, Jeff studied and watched her intently, unconsciously caught up in her childish fantasy. He listened carefully to her serious diversion with the female-shaped plastic, which is better referred to by a kid's very own personal label rather than by the brand name merchandised from a huge, advertised conglomerate. . . . Sarah was its favored title. A doll similar in design to any factory-line kind, yet one that can never be replaced if it is sincerely cared for and protected by an imported impedance.

This reminded him of the times when she would perform this exact, same, model-parent sketch to her baby brother. That's when

Jeff's soul began to sizzle in his body at the terrible thought of those absent days never returning.

Up in the sky the erstwhile high-noon sun sank into the western side of the globe, radiating its last agitation that caused Jeff to squint in its swaggering brilliance as the dirt, grease, and sweat from his labor amalgamated, entering his sensitive eyes and obstructing his vision somewhat, giving him a limited view of his relatively distant young lass. And because of his temporary blindness, he decided to move out of the way of its potent glare, and he walked over in the direction of where Emily was.

"What are you doing, sweetheart?" he asked in a rather unprovoked manner, while expressing curious affection, something he hadn't really shown her in a long time. Yet his daughter didn't appear to be impressed by this instant, dramatic change of character and behavior, or whatever it was. The reason being simply that she was still so involved with her game, and also from her not actually having seen his official presence really. He then knelt down beside her while removing the sticky perspiration and sultry grime from his forehead and then directly smearing it onto his tattered workpants. He then made the extra effort of speaking to her once more.

"Emily, darling, I'm talking to you," he said with soothing firmness. Suddenly she looked up at him as though he had just materialized, appeared from out of nowhere right before her very eyes.

"Honey, what's the matter? Didn't you hear me?" he asked while his tone took on connotations of worry as he heedfully brushed aside the loose strands of her golden hair from her fragile features, which seemed to be annoying him more than it was annoying her, for some odd reason.

Right then, at that moment, she released herself from her isolated spell and let him become a part of her reality, which, in the process, made her suddenly grow reserved and apprehensive. Her eyes then took on that familiar downcast demeanor, especially when she felt threatened, which often happened in his attendance.

After realizing her precarious predicament and with nowhere else to run, she, with no other recourse, finally replied meagerly to him.

"Nuthin'," hoping that this straightforward approach would suffice for now and therefore save her the trouble of communicating with him further.

He sensed in a flash the nippy coldness that she was projecting in her slick reaction and was a little startled by it.

"Emily," he began again, "if something is bothering you, I wish you would please tell me," he pleaded, placing his big, beefy palm on her soft, frangible shoulder.

But she only became more reticent. As a matter of fact, you could say that she was making a weak effort (yet an effort all the same) to remove his claw from her person, as if it carried the damn plague or something, nudging it away as diplomatically as she could without creating too much of a great scene with the slight, subtle movement of her delicate form.

While all this was taking place in a distant corner of the yard, back inside the house, Elaine had momentarily forgotten about the events outside, satisfied with what she had previously observed, while she put the table settings in place in order to start the family feast.

After she was done, she decided to take a peek through the kitchen porthole again to call them in for lunch. The first thing she saw though was that her husband was no longer working on his cumbersome device (the so-called lawnmower), which, by the way, spent most if its sorry existence being repaired or in some hardware store somewhere for constant maintenance purposes more than for actually being in use. That was her basic assumption anyway. According to Mrs. Jeffery Christian, that is, the one, individual person who was in charge of their budget and private finances no less.

Elaine started to worry a bit at first when she was unable to spot the pair of them. And then she grinned to herself with relief once she detected her husband's figure crouching over that of their Emily's diminutive form while under the shade of a large oak tree, which made viewing those two extremely difficult for her in the beginning. However, it was what she witnessed next that gave her spirit an awful fright and sent her rushing quickly from the house.

By the time she reached the outside, what she imagined she saw had become a horrible truth. Jeff, as far as she could tell, was struggling frantically with his daughter, trying for some absurd, weird reason to contain and detain her.

"My God, Jeff, what's going on?" Elaine screamed hysterically while attempting simultaneously to catch her breath from that hundred-yard dash from the kitchen to where she was located now. And also from empathically being caught up in the furor taking place right before her eyes.

Jeff, the ultimate culprit, was undisputably and prematurely stumped for finding a logical explanation for his brash conduct and was volatilely tongue-tied from the whirlwind incident. This gave the little girl the opportunity to break free from her father's heavy-handed grip and to run into her mother's protect arms.

For a second, everyone was silent. Jeff looked the most confused of all, holding out his hands as if he still possessed some sort of semblance of his emancipated daughter. His wife, likewise, stared at him in a state of utter perplexity trying to comprehend some aspect of clear understanding from all this. Jeff looked at her, feeling a modicum of disbelief which was fertilizing like a cancer toward nefarious boundaries. Alas, he instinctively seized upon the desperate situation, which in his mind was being taken way out of proportion.

"Elaine, I know what you're thinking . . ." he blurted out, already rejuvenated with a twinge of guilt by association, while his wife's frozen glare filtered passed his feeble defenses. "Listen, Elaine she went crazy. I tried to stop her, calm her down!" he exclaimed, in a perfect display of innocence, yet hating himself for having any doubt about his real intentions, whatever they were.

Elaine just glared at him with even more bewilderment, reinforced by listening to this babbling man explain his apparent abnormal behavior. And no matter how hard he tried, none of it seemed to be getting through to her. It was as if she had come upon a total stranger disguised as her husband, whom she couldn't quite make out or even determine what he was ranting and raving about, like he was speaking in a foreign language or something.

Jeff, in the meantime, grew frustrated with each passing moment, but kept it securely hidden, as much as humanly possible, behind a pretense of composure, not wanting to cause any more strife to an already damaged condition.

Despite valiant efforts, Elaine still wasn't convinced. Hence turning to her daughter, she sought her incongruous explanation instead.

"What happened, honey? Tell Mommy, dear."

Yet Emily's only reaction was to bite her upper lip. Anything more than that was suppressed by her own fear as she clung to her mother's apron while her old man looked on.

Elaine then knelt down to Emily's level, hoping that maybe using a different approach would render more positive results. Jeff, meanwhile, felt completely ignored. And to be honest with you, he was exactly right on the button and on cue on that point. Thus, as he voluntarily stood at a safe distance, just out of harm's way, that is, while under the umbrella of the huge, aged oak tree, like a preordained, condemned man, he waited in vain for his sentence to be proclaimed and delivered.

Emily, during this grand ordeal, was suddenly thrust into the precarious limelight, which ironically she had attempted to avoid putting herself into. Thus with all eyes focused upon her, she felt extremely ambivalent about what steps to take next. So she stood there as though in an endless dream, yet closer to a coma really. Feeling the pressure of saying the proper thing, which unfortunately fell onto her with the added weight of her mother's stare, she who was supposed to be there for guidance.

Funny, it didn't feel that way was what she probably thought to herself, as she cowed from her responsibility.

In the end, Emily didn't budge from her skill at holding onto her special trait of tacking on the silent treatment. And not because she was remotely stubborn or anything comparable to that . . . no way. It was ultimately linked more to the fact that she didn't know which course to choose. Not desiring to upset either camp, friend or foe alike. And like the smart child that she was, she waited until one of them would answer for her in her mental absence.

No such luck of that happening though . . . right.

Consequently it was her father that eventually brought her around.

"Emily! Tell Mommy what happened . . . please!" he practically begged. He still held a powerful influence over her, even at this dubious stage. Therefore, finally, she turned to him, looking toward him for the first time since that queer, bizarre circumstance had occurred a millennium ago, with an expression of hallowed vacuity, and with that articulate introduction, she spoke these fateful words:

"Daddy, I'm sorry. I didn't mean it," and then quickly, but assuredly, lowered her pretty head, hiding that cute face once again from view, protected now by her mother's warm embodiment.

Jeff held his ground for a minute, unable to believe what he had just heard while studying his daughter's young, impressionable conduct for hints of an ulterior motive. He had to admit, it was kind of equivocal, to say the least, and left him with sensations of skeptical infirmity, which he didn't really want to think about.

"It's okay, darling. Daddy forgives you," he answered while finalizing his statement with a guise of impulsive amnesty and cheeky absolution. It was a weird twist of fate really, seeing how only a split-second before, the circumstances were entirely against him, not in his favor, as though he was a free man once more when he almost imagined himself swinging from the proverbial gallows merely a few minutes earlier.

His wife, standing on the fringe of cognizance, an innocent and commiserative bystander, watched him with an almost mirror-image of his own, trying in her own way to figure out what was going on.

Consequently, though, Elaine rose to her feet.

"Emily, darling, go inside now, please, and wash up for lunch, okay? Now, go quickly," she ordered tenderly while patting her small rump for good measure as an indication for her to leave right away.

Yet, Emily stood fast, eyeing her father, who was too engrossed by his own guarded reflections to be much concerned about anyone or anything else at this juncture. Or so it seemed, while he kicked a patch of dirt about beneath the toe of his boot while awaiting his own dismissal.

"Emily, go on. Daddy and I are going to have a talk. Now be a good girl and go inside. We'll be in shortly. Go on . . . quickly, now," she promised sternly.

After hearing this proposal with no room for any discussion and being the smallest member of the family, the little girl almost jumped out of her skin, heeding her elder's words. She obeyed this new command instantly, without hesitation this time around, sensing in her mother's manner a growing persistence.

As Emily disappeared into the house, she never once looked back, afraid of what she might see.

"Elaine, I know what you're thinking—" Jeff began in a mild frenzy.

"Jeff, don't tell me what I'm thinking!" she retorted, stopping him in midsentence while unsure about whether to pardon him fully or not, yet keeping her voice down and her options open until she was sure that Emily was safely out of earshot.

"I hope you don't think I was really trying to hurt her . . . do you?" he disputed, as that disgusting thought started to materialize in his brain, while he precluded, in the direction of a minor rage, that he was beginning to lose control, of being incapable of sustaining it any longer, as her frontal accusation was the straw that finally broke this camel's back . . . as far as he was concerned.

"I don't know what to think, Jeff. I really don't," she anguished, sounding a little dejected by the experience while shaking her head from side to side in total disbelief.

"I thought all of this . . . this crap . . . was behind us, over and done with!" she added, almost driven to a shower of tears.

Jeff became speechless after gathering this and was unable to move except for a constant fidgeting with his hands in the privacy of the inside of his pocket, as if he had some trinket in there or something, which was starting to irritate and get on his wife's nerves very much.

Then to distract herself from it and concentrate onto more important matters, she lowered her head and then crossed her arms in order to have the will to say what needed to be said.

"Jeff, . . . I know you would never deliberately harm Emily, . . . but I want to know what's going on, huh, Jeff? What's happening to us?" she demanded with the utmost compassion while shuffling her feet back and forth in the same spot of ground, causing a dirty hole to appear where there was once only green grass, and which she continued to aggravate as it expanded in an endless sea of verdure.

Jeff walked up to his spouse, feeling her mental remorse, which gave him the initial boldness to come to her aid. Then placing one hand on her trembling shoulder and, with the other, he lifted her chin to face hm.

"Elaine," he repeated softly, ". . . don't worry about a thing. I won't let anything else happen to this family ever again, . . . I swear," whispering these reassuring words while inserting a smile to make, at least, the appearance of faith in his own judgment.

Elaine saw this and accepted it at face value, feeling pity for treating him so harshly. And more than anything else, for jumping to conclusions without giving her husband of thirteen-odd years the benefit of the doubt.

"Look, Jeff, I'm sorry too for the way I've acted. I just lost my head, that's all," she confessed while trying to appease the situation as she softly pounded her hips with the palms of her hands, which she often did when in a mild state of unconscious neurosis. "I just . . . I just, I don't know what's happening to us. I thought our problems were finished. I'm scared, Jeff. I really am!" she exerted, wiping away the telltale tears from her eyes as she fell vulnerably into his waiting, strong, powerful arms.

"I know Elaine. Sshhh, I know," he crooned soothingly while cradling her gently to comfort her as best he could in this hour of need.

"I just don't want to go back to the way it was," she sobbed openly, in a voice cracked and muffled, being smothered by his tear-stained shirt and by her head being literally embedded into his chest.

"I understand. Please, Elaine, don't cry. We're all under a lot of pressure right now," he consoled, kissing her gently on the top of the exposed part of her crown because the rest of it remained buried in his large torso.

She then stared up at him and smiled gratefully, extenuatingly convinced at last of his innocence. Now that her loving, devoted hubby (that she knew and adored so well) had returned, she felt helpless and rewarded in the same peculiar cortex once more and, therefore, gave herself into a weaned realm of guardianship vouchered by her mate, Jeff.

"Come on, honey, let's go inside," he proposed satisfactorily, becoming rather cheerful all of a sudden, now that all was forgiven and settled between them as they strolled arm-in-arm toward the back door.

Yet things were far from satisfactory. So far from that aspiration that it was unforgivable enough to be pardoned as a matter of fact. Alas, we'll move on, because there's more.

Somewhere in a tiny, dim room, an ambitious, fair-haired young man was busy finishing up an important business report, which he hoped and prayed would turn his life around.

He sat studiously before a flimsy, wooden desk, furiously punching at the keys of an ancient, beaten-up, manual typewriter.

The deeply captive, youthful man was totally absorbed in his vocation and operation. It was very close and very near to midnight, and he was the only person awake (or so he thought at the time) in his comfortable, but modestly humble, apartment where he lived with his postnewlywed wife and two children.

The chiming and resonating echoing from the desecrated device filled a mental vacuum in his bustled mind, in which he found great complacency in acquainting himself with, that consoled him through his stress, tension, and compulsion. Yet time was against him while the seconds grew ever so shorter. And still he had a lot of work ahead of him to complete before he could call it quits.

Hence because of his frantic intensity toward his work, he hadn't noticed or recognized the screams of an infant child coming from a distant room. Ultimately, though, he was forced to address it when the noise escalated to such a fever pitch, that even his zealous concentration was perpetrated and permanently destroyed.

He then picked himself up in a frustrated frenzy and proceeded to march blindly in the direction of the source of the pandemonium, which happened to be in the adjoining room next to his, leaving behind his once and only peaceful sanctuary.

When he entered the other place, he searched the darkness for a tiny crib that belonged to his baby son, which he suspected was the cause of all the ruckus. But before he had a chance to make another move, he detected another familiar sound—that of the voice of an older child behind him. He quickly twisted around in the direction of the female intonation, and standing in the bright light of an open entranceway was the silhouette of his daughter Emily.

"Daddy, Adam's crying. I can't sleep," the toddler moaned while still under the influence of drowsiness as she tried to rub it from her eyes.

"I know, dear. I'll take care of it. You, young lady, though, go back to bed!" Jeff advised her with parental sovereignty while simultaneously rushing to the aid of the sobbing cub.

"Please, Emily, go back to your room. It's okay, Dad's taking care of it!" he exclaimed, shouting above the cries of a very sick baby while he clutched him awkwardly at arm's length. But he was far from being restrained or the circumstances resolved as he held his little boy away from him, as if he was afraid of catching whatever was ailing the poor thing.

Emily just stood her ground in utter disbelief, coupled with curious bewilderment, refusing any external requests at that moment.

"Emily, . . . Emily! Are you listening to me?" he yelled, becoming considerably irate and wound-up at attempting to juggle and balance control of a one-and-a-half-year-old son and a disobedient daughter of four, going on five, all at the same time.

And then, all of a sudden, it dawned on him why his little girl was acting so peculiar as she continued to glare in his general direction. Thus as he turned his head without another thought, his mind became repressed by the stark prospects while he focused his attention on the infant that he currently had a hold of before him.

What he saw caused a horrendous shiver to creep up and down his spine, which, hereafter, would be an indignant trademark that he would have to bear and deal with and would taunt him for the remainder of his born days.

The child left in his care, to Jeff's amazement, had stopped crying. As a matter of fact, for the record, it had stopped doing anything at all. Jeff's body froze instantly but his brain was aflame with terror. His immediate reaction caused him to perspire profusely, adding even more tension to his distressfully ballooned plight.

In the background, like an obliquely abstract insignificance, he could make out his daughter bawling from the developed, ratified trauma that she was now forced to experience. And yet the words that she spoke went unheard by her father, which were incomprehensible to him because of his total absorption into this unexpected, unwarranted tragedy.

Meanwhile Adam's complexion had mysteriously changed to the consistency of a dull, bluish white cast that had an uncanny glow about it, and the child had become quite limp in his arms and felt almost as twice as heavy as before, which intoned the disturbingly spontaneous, perverse doctrine that proved something was seriously wrong.

It felt like a lifetime had stingily been depleted, as Jeff was halted by this irreverent prank, which alas was no putative sham or fluke. This unholy oath was so unreal to him that he felt, in intense irrationality, that it should be exchanged and converted for something much more fair. Regrettably the wicked imprint, with no possibility for an exculpated reversal, was something that he was compelled to accept.

He had no clue to what to do next while he urgently tried to bring the life back into his precious offspring. Obviously stunned, without calm reason, by the strange consequences while lost in a mesh of his own confusion.

His beautiful, angelic boy was gone, taken from the amenities of this existence right from under his very nose and was replaced instead by this grotesque, alien thing. His little Adam, who had disappeared forever in a horrible daydream, was exchanged for this bogus legacy. And try as he must, he knew that he couldn't deny it and solve the impossible. Therefore, to attempt a rescue of the youngest of his brood and bring him back to life was basically futile. And the reality that he just now was obliged to document was defying all other speedy acquisitions. Hence he had to accept this dreadful calamity like a fallen seraph, which hurt him so bad in confiscated opposition, as if he had had a scar scraped across and on the naked spirit itself.

After a while, he was distracted again by the sudden movement of his daughter, whom he had understandably totally forgotten about, while she stormed from the room, screaming uncontrollably at the top of her juvenile, banshee lungs, toward her own bedroom. Her voice shrilled in his ears like that of a repeating, loud siren, vibrating in his head, which ultimately dominated his whole consciousness.

And then all of a sudden, everything went completely black, followed by a smooth, soothing obfuscation, which was taking predominance in the lonely, empty abyss, until—

"Jeff! Jeff! Wake up!" Elaine cried softly in his deaf eardrum, shaking her husband's ebullient body back to revival.

Jeff, in a trancelike catalepsy, was slowly drawn (mostly with his wife's help) from the throes of a stupor, guided in turn by Elaine's remote voice to a state of consciousness. And once he identified her utterance from the insulated shoals, he jumped up immediately to advertence and glared dumbfoundedly into the veritable darkness.

He sat straight up in his bed, collecting himself, and immediately urged his lungs to regain and recycle his missing, misplaced breath. Thus, for a brief moment, his mind seemed stalled temporarily in his dreaded nightmare while he grappled with its thorns in an effort to set himself free.

"Jeff, honey! . . . Are you all right?" Elaine asked apprehensively as she timorously stroked his back while moving her fingers tenderly from his heated nape to his wet, matted mane of hair. For a second, he couldn't say a thing. He turned to her with a sharp spin of his head, but as far as communication was concerned, not one, single syllable could he muster. He had a thousand and one things to say, yet his brain was too jam-packed with distorted images that was giving him great difficulty in sorting out into distinguishably precise, clear thoughts.

"I'm fine, I'm fine," he exerted, finally breathing in heavily from the ordeal. Then he glanced at her adamantly, masquerading his real emotions behind a face of serenity; it was a relief to Elaine to find his expression favorable, as he likewise searched hers for the realization of his existence.

"Did you have a nightmare again?" she inquired with profound concern, talking to him with motherly charm as if he was a frightened child.

"It's okay. Really, I'm fine," he replied, being mildly insistent as he displayed a grin to ease her mind.

She didn't believe him. However, she kept this tidbit to herself, not wanting to press him further in his condition for unanswerable answers to questionable questions. So instead, she let it slide for now, returning his simple expression with one of her own, and then suspiciously watched as he rearranged himself for sleep once more.

When this was accomplished (in absolute, strict silence, of course) he ejected a plain good night. And with his back facing her, he shut his lids and went back to the world of slumber without even acknowledging whether she had done the same. And what might have been expected, Elaine lay poised over him, not knowing how to take this new perplexity. Moreover, not knowing whether to care anymore either, as she pondered this fiat and idea while letting herself fall into her own abnegation, symbolized in the form of a soft, fluffy pillow. Renouncing all that she knew or what she didn't wish to remember.

Henceforth, with the pull of the linen covers, she surrounded herself with the false warmth and security while putting to rest these repulsive thoughts that started to make some sense to her in a kooky sort of way, and that she almost wanted to suffocate and banish. These dreadful prevailing symptoms, presently in her own custody, that she hoped would never be disclosed to anyone, including and especially herself, ever again.

Back to the dreadful, present state once again, Jeff hung his head in depthless sorrow as he ran his hands through his messy hair, hoping for the outcome of pitiful relief. Yet, there was still more to tell . . . much, much more . . . and it was Jeff's ultimate burden and curse to reveal this open injury, no matter what pus was let loose . . . so we continue on.

A man sat basking in the hot sun beside a swimming pool, wasting his afternoon away by relaxing in a garden lawnchair, when suddenly his serenity was interrupted by a spray of water, which made him sit up attentively and search for the source of the minor hindrance. Splashing around in the shallow end was the tiny figure known to everyone as his daughter Emily playing contentedly a game with the water's ripples and soft waves.

"Emily, please, you're getting me all wet!" he yelled, while gesturing with his hands at the assessed damage made by the light moisture already beading on his tanned skin, which glistened in the sunlight like tiny jewels. The little girl stopped what she was doing instantly and became ashamed of her natural, childish revelry. Her father, oblivious to it all, seemed more interested in his personal self than in the humiliation that he had just branded his Emily with while he casually wiped the harmless drops away. Now closing his eyes once again, he resumed his worship of the mighty Sol as Emily floated silently on the pliable current, trying her best not to move her body too excessively for fear of reprisals.

The situation remained that way for quite awhile. But it felt more like an eternity for Emily as she punished herself by pouting with culpability around the large pool's perimeter. Then, like a smack of lightning, the stagnant calm was fractured when her father, with a sudden change of heart, rose from his horizontal position and decided to take a plunge into the blue aqua to moderate his overheated form. When he landed in the undrinkable drink with a clobbering, applauding clap made by his body smashing the mammoth, liquid volume, he surfaced to prove that no lumps had been disastrously acquiesce from the primitive, Olympic dive as he waddled near chest-high in the chlorinated, giant bowl.

He hesitated momentarily before he let his whole frame be absorbed by the tepid fluids while tarrying in the four-foot depths as he gradually became accustomed to the different temperature. After settling in, he called to his daughter, who, with abandoned repose, watched him from the other end with faint suspicion.

"Emily, come here for a sec. Daddy wants to show you a neat trick," he shouted out while wading through the water in order to reach her. Emily appeared stunned at the suggestion, positioning herself as far away as possible.

"Emily, what's the matter with you?" he remarked sensing her fear as he approached her innovatively.

Finally, though, he was able to corner the staid fawn, which wasn't very difficult, seeing that she had done most of the work herself. The fissile creature looked so frightened that you would think that it was awaiting its ultimate fate, which wasn't too far from the postponed validity actually.

"Honey, what's wrong?

"Are you all right?" he repeated with greater exhortation, as the tone in his voice had aspects of anguish in it, which was very apparent to his dejected daughter, who remained incredibly motionless while hugging the pool's edge with her back literally to the wall.

Staring at her, he felt as if he was a stranger trespassing on her, which only flared his temper even more. As he came closer, he touched her shoulder gently to exhibit his good intentions. But t his openly physical contact just made his little girl cringe in psychological pain as she attempted to wriggle free like a captured fish on a line.

"Emily, please, say something!" he cried unintentionally while raising his lungs to a fever pitch.

At that moment, she began to scream wildly into his menacing face, flinging her body at him by using it as a weapon of deterrence while her father tried to control her as best he could by clasping her frail structure in his massive arms.

"Please, Emily, stop this! What the hell's the matter with you!" he blasted from his blistering spleen at his disarrayed, frantic daughter.

Thus from the fringes of chaos, a voice was heard.

"My God, Jeff, what are you doing?" a female voice shrilled from the side of the pool, which then caused Jeff to glare up immediately. What he saw was a confused and angry woman's expression belonging ultimately to his wife Elaine, who stared down on him like an avenging guardian from heaven itself. He then let go of his daughter, who went shivering into a safe corner, evidently overcome by shock. Unable to stabilize her trembling, she gripped the inner lining of the wall for support.

"Elaine, let me explain!" he protested outright while grappling his way toward her through the intruding water.

"You've done enough already," she seethed while helping her daughter out of the water.

"Please, Elaine, I must have frightened her or something," he explained, in a quandary while isolated presently in the middle of pool. But his spouse ignored him completely, her only concern being the protection of her baby as she cradled the child at her warm breast.

Suddenly Elaine faced him.

"I don't want you to touch my baby . . . *ever*! Do you hear me! Never again. *Understand!*"

Then, without further ado, she stormed into the house, hustling the little waif along beside her. Jeff stood where he was, soaked to the bone, sopping wet in total and utter disarray, wondering what he was supposed to do now as he listened, in a condition of stupefaction, to the substance dripping torpidly from his body, . . . a stupefaction that was racking and smiting him to this very day.

What went wrong? his mind protested to the uncaring blightness, which reined supreme in his lonely room that night. . . . *was it still night even?* his head sparked to find an answer to this easy question. *One . . . two . . . three . . . four! . . . What time was it now anyway?*

Then he glared at his clock like it was an enemy to blame.

"Four thirty-eight . . . almost five o'clock. Was it that late . . . or that early, for that matter . . ." as he conversed with the semblance of his foredoomed insistence.

But there was time enough left to still tell more, which he did. So we carry on, shouldering his weight along with our own.

Later that evening, a slam was heard at the front door. Elaine, sitting at the kitchen table, was frozen in motion as she held a mug of coffee to her lips. Standing in the darkened hallway was the figure of a man. Elaine automatically rose to her feet, pressing both her hands on the steady table as though it was an immense strain on her. Walking into the kitchen light, the form of the male became recognizable as her husband, Jeff, which wasn't necessarily an encouraging sight to behold at the moment while she stood across from him in a retrenched period of silence.

"Where have you been?" she questioned him, indifferently, trying to sound as calm and collected as mortally possible.

At first, he just released a dynamite sigh while gaping guiltily at the linoleum floor beneath his heavy feet, as if he was hauling a grueling burden that he couldn't quite shake loose. He stopped in midstep.

"Elaine, we have to talk," releasing these words in a quivering voice while still glaring at the same pattern on the pantry tiles.

"Jeff—" she began, moistening her lips as she emerged from the shadows, while moving ever so slowly toward him.

"Elaine, please let me finish," he interrupted, raising his tone and his head while gesturing with his hands for her to stay where she was.

She obeyed indubitably as she nervously fondled the wedding band on her finger, twisting it this way and that as if it irritated her for some queer reason. Then, while she waited patiently for him to continue, he frustratedly searched his mind for some rational thoughts for her to examine.

"Elaine, I love you . . . and I love Emily, and I wouldn't do anything to jeopardize that," he blurted out, almost choking on his statement as he started to weep. Simultaneously, Elaine began to cry also, trying to hold it back as best she could, which was to no avail really, while covering up her agony with the palm of her hand.

"I don't know what's happening to us, but something definitely has to be done," he stated, sobbing openly, while struggling to control his ignoble, emotional outburst.

Elaine was speechless. Lost in agonizing limbo. Trembling uncontrollably in the soft, incandescent light above her, she could smell the alcohol reeking from his mouth. Something she had never come across before the accident of their son. Since those many anniversaries of their "successful" marriage, which was now a part of the dismissed, pink-slipped section of the social archives. But that was the least of her worries right at his time, while straining her ears to listen as she attempted to bear with him in this moment of exigency.

"That day . . . ," he commenced again while clearing his throat of his own private sorrow and emphasizing his vocabulary with great difficulty as he sorted it out in his foggy brain. . . . "that day we went to see Adam—" pausing in half-sentence in order to make sure she was still with hm. "Remember, Elaine . . . ?" looking up with sunken eyes while reaching out to her for understanding that he desperately needed.

She nodded her reply silently while swiping away at her new batch of tears with passionate strokes of her hands.

"And then later, with Emily, when she was playing," mentioning her name with the slight movement of his barely parted lips, as if even to speak of it was taboo of some kind, while he walked from side to side, staying within the confines of his bisection of the table.

"And I went over to her," he went on, with an instant look on his face that was becoming distorted by the complexity of it all, while moving to wider spaces in the tiny kitchen, as though he was reenacting a scene that deserved a larger audience actually.

Elaine watched him with patient inquisitiveness while he strolled from one end to the other.

"She just went mad for some strange reason," he said, and raised his arms. "And, and I tried to help her. I didn't know what else to do. But I did my best. God, Elaine, I did what I thought was right!" he exclaimed apologetically.

She monitored him with a glimmer of bewilderment while grabbing at the lapel of her detached, terrycloth robe like she was clutching a security blanket, holding it firmly to her neck for anchorage.

"Don't you understand. I was trying to help her, for godssake! You know I would never harm her. You know that!" he argued with himself. Yet sounding more as a plea for sanity while leaning over the table pressing into the treated wood, which caused his knuckles to turn a sickly white as he attempted to make her comprehend.

Elaine, still in a trance-type position, was slightly girdled and frazzled by his unusual, dramatic display. Yet she remained professionally composed. At least on the surface anyway. His features became quite distinct to her in the limelight, as he focused in on her, making her feel as though he was putting her in a situation to address his pardon and answer it forthwith.

This unorthodox behavior, plus the public confession, was almost too much to handle all at once. After all, it was her husband saying all this, not an abstract character who had no special relationship with her. It was a person whom she still believed with all her faith and trust. Who she believed loved her in devoted equality, therefore, more than everything or anything else on this earth, except for Emily of course. Because Emily was without a doubt a part and an important component of these geometric, dual hemispheres that had no match. Until, of course, when this current, immoral conduct had gone and screwed everything and everyone up that is.

Nevertheless, no matter the outcome, they were both going to be taught an important lesson. Because she was just as much a part of this as he, whether she admitted it to herself or not . . . so how could she deny him now?

At that moment she came over to him.

"Jeff, I'm sorry. I didn't know what to think. I was confused also, that's all," she confessed while capturing him in her arms as she tried to smother the fire burning within him with emollient forgiveness.

Subsequently though, he pushed her away gently, not wanting to be influenced, so it seemed, by her kindness, needing to think clearly and needing more breathing space, too.

Elaine stared at him with astonishment. Obviously puzzled by his reaction, she was forced and dared herself to state:

"It's back, isn't it? Those . . . feelings have returned . . . haven't they . . . ?" she remarked ambiguously while following his eyes adamantly.

"It's all my fault, isn't it?" he lamented to her conspicuous allegation as he probed her features for redemption. But then giving up too quickly and lowering his vision to elude the plain, ugly truth.

"Our daughter, to this day, still blames me for what happened to Adam. You know that?"

"No! Don't say that, . . . please. Jeff, stop torturing yourself," she hushed and begged in and for his frail defense while placing her fingers to his parted lips while she fought the urge not to turn her back to him now with some unconscious shun. She then let go, placing her bothersome hair behind her ears which was becoming a regular, nervous staple for her. Fixing her attractive face, she started thinking impulsively that maybe it had been premature of her to have given him amnesty so rapidly, while attempting to fight a personal battle of logic verses emotion.

"I can't help it, Elaine. It's how I feel," he grieved while thumping his chest hard, unaware of the impetus second thoughts surfacing to the top in his "faithful" wife's mind.

"Stop crucifying yourself, Jeff!" she demanded. "If anyone deserves to be blacklisted, it's me! Blame me!" she screeched, shoving her fist up above her rib cage to achieve the strong, maximum amount of melodrama that was required to punish herself. "Don't you remember? I'm the one that left my baby when it needed its mother most. Adam was very ill . . . sick . . . my innocent Adam, whom I abandoned while he was suffering," she mumbled while fixed to an invincible memory. And then springing back to life she hollered, "*Don't you know!* . . . It's my fault, too!" at a decibel loud enough in the beginning to chip through her bull-headed husband's iron skull, and tapered off to a more mealy tone, which ironically appeared to have a more substantial, iridescent result on him, still, not quite high-pitched enough to alert a dozing Emily to this grown-up quarrel.

"I should never have gone on that damn trip, but I did, and see what price I paid for it," she retorted, howling like a she-wolf over her lost cub. And then, regaining her stature to release this thermal bulletin: "I think we better see someone, someone professional, Jeff," suggesting this with serious resolution in her sad ballad as she glared at him from the corner of her eye.

"No way, sweetheart, no way," he barked, knowing full well what she meant without even letting her elaborate on the proposal. Waving his hands excitedly in the air as if he was swatting mosquitoes while gesturing profoundly his objection by clearing the atmosphere of the fumes of obsolete ideas of the past that were clouding his troubled, censored brain.

"Jeff, this is way too serious for us to handle alone," she replied, with grave concern.

"Please, Elaine. Not now, okay!" he growled, detesting this new and reincarnated thorn in his side.

"Jesus! I can't think properly anymore," he added while moving away from her to avert her womanly spell before it was too late.

Elaine said nothing, but watched him instead with an oval, pathetic forlornness. Jeff then molested his temples with such brutality that Elaine thought he might be drilling a hole to his brain. But in actuality he was just proofreading what he wanted to say to her next.

"Elaine, those shrinks and quack therapists said everything was all right and peachy. And that everything was back to normal—solved. Don't you recall them saying that garbage, huh? And now you wish to go through all that again!" he explained in a tone filled with bland irony.

Elaine, who had a problem looking her husband in the face after that verbal lashing, finally spoke up, having listened carefully to what he had to publish. Mulling over his jaunty, jeering reasoning while this characteristic liberal held onto her mindfulness.

"Okay, Jeff, you win," she responded with a deep sigh as she put the brakes on this troubling discussion for good and washed her hands completely of the whole controversy, having been taught a valuable lesson about family commerce.

Jeff, after receiving this rapid news, was surprised by how easily she had been convinced, as he expected more of a fight from this iron-willed mate of his. Especially when it came to the topic of their unexpendable, juvenile Emily. As a result, he didn't feel like a winner after all. Instead, he had a sneaking impression of having been betrayed somewhat by these paltry actions of hers, which worried him immensely, like the buzzing of an unpredictable wasp zooming over the crest of his head.

Hence Jeff couldn't at this stage of the game treat this as a minuscule nonevent after thinking that maybe now he had lost her for good and reveled in the fruitless rewards of this stale settlement, while secluded in his own, lonely solitude.

"Look, honey, I'm not against any help from anyone, whatsoever. But we tried that angle, and look where it got us?" he rationalized with earnestness. Elaine didn't exactly follow his example with an agreement. As a matter of fact, she did the opposite by hiding her penitential view from him while pretending to be busy cleaning up after herself on the spur of the moment. Yet, in all honesty, she wasn't sure of what to approve of at this time, glutted and rattled by the flux of choice.

Jeff's first thought when seeing her mute revulsion was how much alike mother and daughter really were. Especially when they both put up that stubborn resistance of theirs.

"Elaine, we can work this out ourselves," he proposed, with an annoying whine while grabbing her affectionately by the wrist to provoke her from continuing on with her tidying up routine. She tried to break free, yet put up a very weak exertion in the end. "And quit making that mistake. Your mistake. And putting it as your own personal fault. You didn't realize he was in that bad of a shape and condition. No one did. . . . That, that damn pediatrician told us he had a mild case of the measles, remember?"

Right then, Elaine dropped her head over the aluminum basin to cough up this:

"Please, Jeff," she sobbed with palliated, crocodile tears (because she lacked any more real ones), while docking her compassion with his as she merged toward him. "Let's both end this self-incrimination. It's demolishing and killing what's left of this family. We've only got this tiny thread left to keep us together. Don't snap it, Jeff, please don't, not now," and she pinched her thumb and forefinger together to enhance the drastic report.

"Elaine," Jeff gasped, "if I-I only could, hell, don't you think that I haven't fought this? Every, fucking hour, week, and month every single day. I've busted my balls to make things right!"

"Jeff, that's the problem. Don't you see. That's the very thing that I'm getting at. You don't have to feel this sin forever, you know. Isn't it enough that we hurt inside from the death of our only son? Our little baby boy. We've suffered. That's proof enough that we loved him with all our hearts. And there's nothing on this earth we can do to bring him back, Jeff. I'd give up and risk losing my own life, anything, in exchange for my children. You know that. Let it go, honey." Elaine preached while rubbing his cheek punctiliously to gain his favor.

"Let's bury the dead and move on as best we can. It's all we can do really, not only for Emily's sake, but we owe it to Adam, too," she urged, while fusing both their hands as one. Praying that he would be convinced to comprehend her philosophy.

Thus, when Elaine realized she had him under her wing, she took it upon herself to discontinue the message, resolving that she had brought him around to her practical convictions at this crowning apodosis and she went back to her assigned kitchen drudgeries. Jeff, on the other end of the spectrum, when seeing the outcome of his own pickled, passe-triumph over his female counterpart, took the opportunity (if you dared call it so) to change the precarious subject to a less scandalous one.

"Where's Emily?" he asked rather mildly. This question seemed to hit a nerve in Elaine for some apparent reason, to the point where she almost forgot what the previous conversation was all about.

"Oh! She's asleep," she answered, wondering without contemplative intent what was up his sleeve now to bring up such prickly material for intercourse.

"Where'd you imagine she'd be? It's late you know, almost one-thirty," Elaine subsumed in superfluous credulity, which she intelligently didn't let perforate too much.

"She's had a rough day, so don't bother her right now, okay, Jeff?" she stated in as friendly a way as she could, transmitting this proposal without rocking the waterlogged boat any further in an effort to stop, but not kibitz him, for what the sloshed situation called for. Apparently she had read his mind before he did. And she cut him off at the pass in an attempt to avoid any more rowdy confrontations with him.

"All right then. Tomorrow . . . I'll have a chat with her tomorrow then," he commented flatly while staring in the direction of his daughter's bedroom with streaks of wreathed woe.

He nodded his approval with a sort of sad, heavy, grin into solid rationality. Meanwhile, Jeff headed for their master bedroom.

"Are you coming . . . ?" Jeff called, stopping halfway down the hall.

"Yeah, . . . in a few minutes. Go on without me. I'll be there soon, darling," she responded indifferently as her attention was distracted by her own green thoughts. So much removed was she from the ugliness of reality, in fact, that she was able to preoccupy herself with the relentless gnawing of a hangnail that refused to yield to her wishes while she stood under the warm, electric glow of the overhead kitchen light.

The next morning the family of three were gathered together around the kitchen table. All of them suspecting something monumental was about to take place.

Jeff, representing authority here, felt it to be his place to put everything into its proper prospective and regularity once and for all, as he lay his allegorical cards on the table. In order to pull this off though, he felt he needed to stand up for some particular reason. Maybe to boost his confidence possibly. He bided his time by idling about the kitchen cabinets while slowly drinking his caffeine-enriched, billionth serving of black coffee while privately rehearsing a script under his breath.

His wife stood across from him, acting as if she was busy with a mountain of dirty, breakfast dishes piled up in front of her. Yet Elaine was fully aware of the format about to unfold before her as she occasionally peeked over at him. Their daughter, the object of contention, couldn't help but realize more. And then that was all that his facial pallor would give away and tell for the time being.

Elaine glared at him, trying to decipher the words between the lines, that she plucked from his brain. But the fact remained she really didn't have any special gift of a grifter for it. Having to be satisfied with what her intuitions had given her, she forced a smile onto her face to veil the mixture of plaid quibble that she was unable to pronounce or transfer as all eyes were upon Emily while she submissively ate from her bowl of cereal.

"Emily, Daddy would like a word with you if you don't mind before you go on your field trip," he announced while positioning himself in a chair next to her.

Emily just carried on munching and chewing, feeling like she would prefer to be anywhere but here.

"I know you don't want to chat with me, but I think it would help clear things up if we opened up to one another, huh, what do you say to that?" Jeff sweet-talked her while his eager wife hovered in the background.

"Kitten, I know something is bothering you," he said while removing a strand of her hair from her bashful face, which made her flinch a bit from his immediate touch.

"You must know that I would never ever hurt you, even though it looks sometimes that I'm not acting like the way a daddy should. You know what I mean?" he explained in an almost inaudible tone while he shot brief and rapid glances over at Elaine, which he may have deliberately done—directing the comment really more to her rather than to his baby girl.

"Do you understand, Emily?" he asked her while waiting for a prompt response. She then stared up at him timorously and then shook her head in silence. Her father, pleased with the initial results and infinitesimal reply, grinned approvingly and felt completely glad inside for the first time in a long while.

Then all of a sudden, a usually introverted Emily burst to life:

"I know you don't mean it, Daddy. I'm sorry, Daddy. It's all my fault. I'm sorry, too . . . I love you," and with that, she ran into his unprepared arms. Her father, on the other hand, reacting perfectly in accord with his own reflexes with killer instinct, held her tightly in gratification.

"I love you also, baby," he chuckled now, finding humor in her precocious accusation and action. Thus he was also happily relieved in finally bridging the wide moat between them as he stroked her golden and soft pigtails affectionately while Elaine watched from the near-distance with a heavily supportive endorsement. Therefore she stayed clear of those reattached twins in order not to disturb this fragile reconciliation already in progress.

Ultimately though, they did part from each other with a sense of renewed discernment. They were relieved, in part, by the preconceived notions of paranoia while acknowledging their new-found feelings of optimism by simultaneously disclosing an intimately warm smirk to one another with the total absence of any reservations whatsoever.

"All right, sugarplum, you'd better be off now, or you're going to be late for your bus." Jeff warned while slapping her rear tenderly to send his child out the door and on her way.

"Come on, Emily, Mommy will walk you to your stop. Got your knapsack and things?" Elaine asked while escorting her child out the door to meet the other Girl Scouts at the corner for their holiday field trip.

"Yes, Mommy, I've got all my stuff. I'm ready," Emily proclaimed while springing from her chair to join her mother waiting at the exit.

"Bye, Daddy," Emily said while giving her father one, last, big smooch on the cheek before leaving.

"Yeah, bye, babycakes. Have a nice day," Jeff returned while a less than cheerful overcast crept onto his features, which wasn't made public. Because with a slam of the screen door, he was left with only the echo of their feminine, chirping gaiety in its swan song entering his sensitive ears, that exclusively he was banished to solely hear in his solitude presently.

"Light!" Jeff envisioned to its opposite, darkness as he slipped out of this series of recollections. Thus we come to the inevitable conclusion.

"Light at the end of the tunnel . . ." Jeff added as he stared deeper into the profundities of his troubled soul.

Thus we must resume with our story and search for a final climax to these complex circumstances as follows.

So that's how things stood at this baroque period. That simple act of congeniality, proliferated by the happiness expressed from a normal preadolescent, was enough to make an ordinary person forget their darkest phantoms for at least an eternity. And yet, forever might still not be adequate, or seem on a scale a wee bit too short, for compensation. But all in all, when you calculated it, however, things appear justified on the surface, and no one would ever really be the wiser.

Yet Jeff knew better than anyone alive that justice comes to those who wait—waiting for it in the hereafter, that is, and not in Heaven, but in Hell!

He then imagined that he was hearing a distorted angelic voice (because at this point, he couldn't comprehend what was real anymore), but he couldn't be a hundred percent sure.

A weak, distant siren no less. The parallelism being uncannily close to his former dream, which caused goose bumps the size of golf balls to fertilize across his bare skin. He looked inward and became lenitive, knowing that he wasn't sleeping anymore, dispelling all the useless muck from his mind and all the traces of temporary paranoia.

A little later on, the noise repeated itself as if to keep him in the game, so-to-speak, which startled our player even more than before, thinking that maybe it was just restored retention haunting his brain after all. Yet he knew that to be strictly a lie. It was far too clear and precise this time. Too real to be a figment of idealism really.

Then he felt a great dread dangling on the outlook, as though he knew beforehand something of what was about to happen. Something he wasn't brave enough even to admit or inform himself completely of. A dream within a dream which was out of control.

Without another thought, and with intense urgency, he took off down the saturnine hall. Then throwing open his daughter's bedroom door, which naturally caused her to awake instantly, if she wasn't already up, that is thereby, he, Jeff, hadn't had time to formulate a clue or lead as to why she was stirred; there was bigger fish to fry at the moment, as he was sustained in a deaf mute pose of locomotion and was barely mindful of what he had just done as he gaped at her. But to his benighted surprise, she wasn't acting the way she was supposed to. Or in any need of being rescued from any dragons on further examination.

"Daddy, daddy, what's the matter?" she whined sluggishly while still not quite alert. Yet as she scrubbed the quiescence from her sockets while trying to adjust them to the Manchurian affect of the forces and elements of darkness, which was conflicting with those of light at that duration.

He said nothing, bewildered by the anticipating chimera, which wasn't available. When her father came into full focus though, she immediately noticed the shiny object in his hanging arm, and that's when she impulsively sensed something was critically wrong.

He followed the invisible line of her eyes and was just as ambuscaded to find the mysterious weapon there. And at that moment, she let out a bloodcurdling shriek. His next reaction was to drop it. Letting the amputated article of destruction fall as it will.

"Emily! No! Don't be frightened . . . Daddy doesn't want to hurt you," Jeff cried nervously, unsure of what his intentions at this point were.

However, Emily wasn't listening. Her high velocity squeal took excellent care of any external resonance, drowning out his own pleas of misinterpretation.

"Pleeaasse, Emily, stop it! Listen to meee!" he shouted while approaching her at a rush with an open and mad embrace. Coming in fast to salvage her from the imputed, false demons (so-to-speak), he went to the foot of the bed, where he halted and abided momentarily and then crept slowly toward her, displaying his empty palms while affirming his reassurances, which only upset her more.

Unexpectedly, like some wild animal, she lunged forward, kicking and yelling the whole time. He witnessed this physically and tried preventing it by grasping the swirling whirlwind, yet ended up having very little success at handling those preadolescent limbs and delicate, spindly legs of hers for his efforts.

Above the cries of his daughter, another less climactic voice could be heard from behind him. But he virtually ignored it, being too involved, and much more concerned, with the trouble at hand. If he had bothered to pay attention though, he would have discovered that his wife was the dispatcher arriving on the scene.

Shocked beyond belief at what she was forced to watch like some perverted spectator, she became emotionally frantic with motherly proclivity, joining in the furor by hollering, at the top of her vocal chords until they were raw, for this insanity to cease at once. She didn't know what else to do, being late on the scene, while helpless in her own grief. Too scared to intervene, yet too scared not to.

Just then she spotted the revolver on the carpeted floor, and without much strenuous thought behind it, she picked it up in an instant. When she had possession of the robust, compact firearm, Elaine felt a surge of power and energy flow through her nerves and blood vessels that she had never speculated she had ever had before, before this climactic moment, that is.

And even though she wasn't fully aware of this potential strength growing inside of her at the time, she clasped the pistol in her strong grip, nonetheless, as if she did. Yet if her features had been allowed to speak of firm oratory, they would have purviewed a polarized diagram altogether. So instead, she pleaded with her husband to leave her daughter alone.

"Please, Jeff, what are you doing?"

"Let her go, for godssakes. Let here go!" Elaine rambled on and on in a fit of frenzy, fit, in fact, for an overprotective lioness, while making herself delirious with her own hysterical words.

Then she started to cry profusely, knowing full well what she desperately didn't want to do, but had to. And what she was about to gamble away. Through anger and agony, she raised the treasured "Saturday night special" while Jeff, unbeknown to this exculpated execution, continued to suppress his daughter's mania.

Thus, after Elaine stopped shaking, she set her sights on her difficult target. Hence, just when Jeff finally had a hold of Emily, he became aware of someone else's presence in the insane asylum referred to once as his home. He then looked up, like a jungle cougar sniffing the air for the ostensible danger.

Also throughout this disorder, he recognized his own erratic behavior and felt paramountly enkindled by it. He instantly let Emily loose and was about to turn his head when he heard a very loud bang, followed closely by a sharp pain piercing his shoulder blade. He winced as the hard, severe sting entered his system, forcing him to twist around in an awry collapse. Then, before he had a chance to complete his descent, he was caught with another bullet on the way down. This second slug hitting him directly in the abdomen.

He then lost regulation of his lower body as he stumbled to the floor with a heavy thump. Thus as the lay there, he grew extremely light-headed and his sight became quite dim. Yet he fought and struggled to get up, but his legs refused to cooperate.

In his diminishing mind, he detected their voices keening and wailing out to him. But he was too far gone to say anything audible in response that they could hope to possibly understand.

". . . Don't worry, Elaine, I'll protect her. I won't let anyone hurt you or my baby," he groaned in a speculative daze as he crawled across the bloody bedroom floor.

In his subconscious, he could see the monster profoundly now, and he knew exactly what it wanted, being on the same level as this conundrum and horrible mystery. Therefore, he knew it was attempting to take his dear family away from him. And if he had one last, single breath left in him, he was going to prohibit and prevent that from happening at all costs no matter what the price.

"I'll save you . . . I won't let it harm you. I won't let anyone hurt you ever ag-aggaaiinnn . . ." he mumbled while his voice was obstructed by his mouth being so near to the fabric of the carpet as he reached blindly, and at a snail's speed for his absent daughter Emily, who was mentally injured with paralysis as she crouched in a trembling posture in a dark, safe corner.

Before he was able to get to her, though, a final and conclusive shot and blow brought the curtain down on his encore. Thus lying in a pool of his own blood and filth, he felt his potency and vigor abandoning him at last. So he decided to rest his tired head for awhile. He felt at ease for the first time in millennia and wanted to stay this way forever if it was at all possible. And so, with his fingers stretching perpetually out in front of him, he gave himself permission to die.

How doth the little crocodile
Improve his shining tail,
And pour the waters of the Nile
On every golden scale!
How careful he seems to grin,
How neatly spreads his claws,
And welcome little fishes in,
With gently smiling jaws!

Black Dog

The only sound heard for miles, it seemed, was the distant roar from an engine of a powerful, shiny, red, convertible sportscar of European design as it raced down a lonely country road.

The driver of this impressive vehicle sat perfectly erect in relaxed coordination with imperative protuberance in his faithful machine, while the chilly air soothingly caressed his boastfully weary face like a pair of soft, gentle hands running its transparent fingers through his wavy, salon-gelled hair.

The stern-featured young gentleman, sitting pretty in his sleek chariot of insurmountable horsepower, handsomely dressed in a custom-made suit, refused to be distracted by his own impeccable integrity. His composed expression, which lacked any fear or conviction, was the epitome of his youthful efficiency.

Meanwhile, as he eased and slid forward, in the night sky above, a full moon shone brightly between an opening in the dark, gray clouds while they moved discreetly across the brilliant horizon to blot out this laconic orb, bringing with them the threat of a storm with possible inklings of duress at their hemorrhaging rakes.

Yet the passive young man appeared oblivious to the would-be menace around his restricted world. He would not allow himself to be hamstrung by this sprightly fuss and funk as he drove past endless fields of tall grass swaying mollifyingly in the nippy autumn breeze, as though they hadn't existed at all.

It was approaching midnight when the eager young fellow came within sight of familiar surroundings. In the near distance he could see an old, narrow, wooden bridge, and beneath it flowed a calm, shallow stream that happened to run indirectly close to where his final destination would be, which happened to be only a few miles away now.

After hubristically crossing over its serene waters with the integumentary assistance of the anile causeway, the young tepidopentist felt a little relieved knowing that his journey's end was almost near.

At that moment it began to pour with rain, which suddenly altered the moon's present, dominant position by its being engulfed in a total eclipse by an omnipresent, overcasting firmament. Furthermore, the temperamental winds began to stir wildly and to howl angrily through the trees, causing the extant rampikes to sway violently in an increasingly frantic fusillade of naturopathic bedizenment.

While the events outside his sphere of maven comfort grew worse with each passing moment, the young pilot's perception of the open road became considerably impaired by this Pantagruelian nuisance.

Unable to ignore anymore the irritating obscurities that surrounded him, he started to feel slightly frustrated with the whole, pantheonic situation. When, with a tap of his manicured finger, a fabric awning unfurled and electronically sprung up and was then latched into place with the simplest of robotic efficacy in order to overlay the crown of our flecked yuppie Prince Charming.

However, the shower continued to augment, beating repeatedly upon his mobile tent in a parvenued arraignment without a cruet of clemency on his part.

The belligerent spanking endured to the point of intensification, literally hurling his fragile machine from side to side with ease. And then with the added bout of collateral hacking, it showed him that there was no sign of its bruteness letting up anytime soon.

Our suave equestrian, passionately gripping the steering wheel, started to have the feeling that the weather outside had some kind of personal vendetta directed toward him. And now that his anxiety was developing at fever pitch under this sort of pressure, he was provoked into increasing his acceleration further. Moreover, he began to race quite recklessly with a stubborn persistence, flying like a bat out of hell along the wet and winding roads.

Eventually though, he came to an intersection, which forced him to decrease his speed to a crawl. Incidentally, at that particular moment, he knew exactly where he was. That very place having reminded him of the indelible memories of his childhood, his rubrical childhood, that is.

He then intuitively turned to his right, which placed him onto a crude, gravel pathway, evidently sheltered on both sides by an endless row of towering trees with lofty drooping branches dangling lazily from their heights.

Subsequently he entered that gloomy alcove of dreary despair just as the rain began to slowly dissipate, until it no longer was inclined to dispense the earth with its pulverizing rile altogether.

Once he was inside the naturally made tunnel though, the only sign of apparent life left (besides his own) was the whispering wind, which teasingly seeped through to him from a gap he had made in the window of his stuffy automobile, which consequently became his sole companion at that present time.

The young gentleman felt completely alone all of a sudden as an unexpected, cool sensation came over him. He sat there, hopelessly, confined to his seat, listening profusely to the sound of his car's tires grinding along the turbulent path while he cautiously made his way through the labyrinth.

He was almost at the end of the passage when he felt the urge to make a rapid, immediate egress. Suddenly, he was confronted by a dark, shadowy figure standing directly ahead of him. Appearing from nowhere, the immobile form was apparently in a state of utter bewilderment. Blinded by his powerful headlights, the strange apparition stood there, vulnerable, like a sacrificial lamb at the altar.

The mysterious creature's eyes instantly came into primary contact with his, glowing erratically in the dimness from a reflection of his car's bright lights. For a brief moment, the confused young man was distracted by their hypnotic affect. Then realizing his desperate plight as he plowed onward toward a conclusion with disaster, he quickly took control of the probable calamity at hand. In order to avoid a catastrophe with the so-called wraith, he was forced to make a pretty sharp turn, which resulted in causing a rather violent skid.

Then slamming on his brakes hard, with sheer, frightful force, he averted another possibly tragic confrontation with the encompassing trees. After jolting his helpless body around like a rag doll for a few seconds, the car finally came to an abrupt halt.

He sat in shock for awhile, cursing to himself. He was completely numb for a long time, in a sort of atrophied tranquility while trying to recovered from the ordeal.

Slowly though, he regained his normal equanimity, running a sweaty hand down the front of his face as if such a basic gesture was enough to erase away the whole, traumatic experience.

Later it dawned on him what had just happened as he gazed with emptiness through the rain-smeared windshield, while the stupefaction of the nigh accident began to take its toll on his imagination.

He sat quietly in his plush seat, comfortably lost in his own unsettled thoughts while listening to his obedient machine purr contently to itself.

Eventually his curiosity got the better of him, and he decided to take a closer look around outside. Letting his engine die, he emerged from his hiding place and was immediately struck by the wind's biting breath as it quickly embraced him like an invisible blanket.

He stood in the unimpeded air rigid. Every bone and nerve in his body alert for any conceivable suggestion of danger, but standing unaccompanied in that eerie remoteness, convinced him that the creature, or whatever it was, must have vanished as rapidly as it had appeared.

His effortless search proved futile, only the silence prevailed that evening while he suspiciously spied into the infinite darkness one last time.

Finally, drawing in a sigh of relief, he decided to give up on this silly charade and return to his cozy, waiting vehicle, coming to the ultimate consummation that the odd episode was all a complete trick of a tired, worn-out mind, after all.

Next he then opened the car door, hesitating for a minute, as though he was giving the *umbra* one last chance to redeem itself. Yet the night, it appeared, wasn't giving away any secrets at that aftermath of twilight, not to him, or for anyone else's benefit, for that matter.

Our gentleman friend then pulled up the collar of his expensive, camel-haired coat and, in the process, practically covered his ears in an obvious act of defiance to the weather's harshness towards him.

After that, he sedulously slipped back inside his welcomingly warm cockpit and once again shut the fiercely unsympathetic wilderness outside, where he stoutly believed it belonged.

When he was securely fastened, he sat staunchly still, contemplating the strange irrelevancy that had just taken place. Nevertheless, with a raspy smirk that flunked all statues of rectitude, he promptly dismissed it from his semitroubled conscience as he started his ignition. *It's getting late,* he thought to himself while the engine came back to life. Then grinning privately over his foolish behavior, he shifted into first gear and impetuously continued homeward.

After eventually leaving the enclosure behind him, he felt a sense of deliverance, simultaneously resumed with the moon's triumphant return, followed closely behind by the rekindled stars which paid their special homage to the celestial globe while deploying their appanage to shimmer eternally together in the clear, mauve heavens.

Meanwhile, far off from beyond a distant hill, he noticed a large, white building suddenly coming into view. Drawing nearer, the edifice became recognizable as his former home, which seemed to be sprouting from the very depths which supported it, similar in effect to a subtly foreboding phoenix ascending from the verdant ashes.

However, the actual, initial thing that came forthwith to his attention was the huge, ivory pillars that stood rooted to the front porch. The massive columns, which endured with proud strength, reached perpetually upward to the skies. It was quite sight for his sore eyes to see while he was drawn ever closer to them.

When he arrived at the main gate of the structure, the pillars stood fast, wide apart as though expecting his untimely recurrence. Passing through the rusty, ancient, ironclad jaws, he was unpremeditatedly overcome by a flood of mixed memories and emotions while entering this once-forgotten domain.

He quickly found a convenient spot to park his wheels, and then, for the last time that night, he left his stylish conveyance.

As he stared up at the ominously apathetic mansion, (because it really was one, after all), he felt an uncontrollable hostility toward it. Yet for some reason or another, he couldn't exactly define why as he casually sauntered up the lavish mound in order to reach the gridiron-type veranda.

Searching his pockets for his keys and finding them, he blindly sought the keyhole. When he finally was able to unlock the front door, he was immediately vanquished with alleviation.

Once inside, all his anxieties seemed to disappear into thin air, somewhat, as he entered the grand foyer of the elegant house.

It was deathly quiet in there while he walked about the vacant vestibule before imposing a tribulation to probe every other room in the bosky palace. Switching on disregarded lights and fixtures accordingly, he tried hard to familiarize himself with everything in sight.

Nonetheless, he soon grew bored of this, even though he was keen to make a thorough investigation of the oversized abode. In the end, he retreated upstairs to the master chambers, where his parents had once slept. And once there, he braced himself over the kingsize, inviting substratum, recollecting how things used to be. It brought great warmth and sadness at the same instance into his torn soul, especially because of how the "castle" had changed since he had been gone.

He then silently removed his clothes, putting them neatly upon a small, lounge settee, which was probably used for that purpose anyhow, he surmised exhaustedly, and our royal patron slothfully crept between the satin covers of the large, canopied bed. Instantly, he fell fast asleep, permitting himself the luxury of dreaming of pleasant things, such as how he was going to itemize and evaluate all of the rich inventory in his antecedent's personal, wholesale gallery that they had gracefully left in his expert care.

In the days that followed, he would forget about that incident on the road that fateful night. However, what he didn't realize at that particular moment was that even though his journey homeward was over, a more important one was about to begin.

* * *

It was on one, ordinary morning that the young squire rose to greet the day with his unsullied presence, without busying himself right away with setting his inherited property in systematic organization. As a matter of fact, there were merely a few loose ends that remained to be ironed out, which gave him the worthless extravagance to kick-back and spend the rest of the cockcrowing phase with pointless leisure.

Anyway, it wouldn't be long before it was time for him to go back to work in the big city. But he didn't really have to worry about that presently because he could easily take care of business affairs from where he was located with the use of a cellular phone system and the magic of a portable fax machine.

To constitute his early rise, he innocuously sipped his first of many cups of coffee while glaring impassively out of his tiny, kitchen window. He preoccupied this period of repose by watching the numerous trees in his backyard remorselessly shed their remaining leaves of burgundy and gold which randomly cascaded to the ground, creating an ocean of discarded foliage in their wake.

Yet his mind was elsewhere, on more pressing matters at the moment. Far more important than engaging his spare time with such trivialities as the passage of rites of the changing seasons.

His only main concern, actually, was returning to his swank penthouse and job in town, which frankly, he was very much looking forward to seeing again as the perturbation of being in an unruffled and placid environment began to take root inside of him.

He had only been in that magnificent cottage a couple of days. But it seemed that the serene, rural, arcadian lifestyle really hadn't agreed with him at all.

It was at that juncture, while gaping out at the panorama, when he observed someone strolling toward his back door, carefully carrying an unrecognizable bundle in his arms. The stalwart figure then stopped briefly and looked inquisitively about.

He seems to know his way around perfectly, the young spectator deduced from the person's precocious actions as he loitered idly back and forth outside in the neat garden, deciding whether or not to cross into this private dwelling.

Just then, the puzzled young man heard a piquant rap at his kitchen door. He automatically put down his mug and proceeded to answer it. Standing at the entrance, was a silver-haired, old gentleman, shabbily dressed in a plaid shirt and worn-out pair of trousers, greeting him with a friendly, cheerful smile.

"Hello!" he announced, "My name's Mr. Thownsend," as he extended his single, free hand. The young man received it graciously, wondering the whole time who this person was.

"Hello, Mr. Thownsend, how can I help you?" he responded with a hint of dubiety.

"I'm sorry to disturb you like this," he replied shyly as they shook each other's hands. "I live down the street a piece—" gesturing with his head in the general direction of his own home.

"Would you like to come inside, sir?" the young man asked, interrupting his visitor while moving aside as an indication to his guest to enter.

"Why, thank you, young man. How kind of you," he commented, accepting the offer congenially.

After shutting the door behind him the host turned to his unexpected visitor.

"My name's Frank. How can I help you, Mr. Thownsend?" while his eyes were unmistakably distracted by the living package cradled gently in the old man's arms which happened to be the form of an awkwardly large, puppy dog.

"Well," the older man began, feeling the weight of it in his aging limbs as he shifted the dormant canine to a less burdened side, "I see you've noticed the dog here," he mentioned while intimately stroking the animal's soft, infantile fur in an attempt to pacify the suddenly restless creature, which was growing a little fidgety from being held so long.

"Yes, I did," Frank replied, finally taking his eyes off of it and back onto the old man's.

"Do you mind?" Mr. Thownsend asked, politely making the suggestion of wanting to release the animal onto his nice, clean floor.

"Oh! Sure Go ahead," Frank responded, yet not particularly thrilled about the idea, but, nevertheless feeling sorry for the old guy's encumbrance.

"Thank you, my boy." Mr. Thownsend sighed gratefully while he dropped the pooch to the immaculately waxed tiles. The mutt, once relinquished to the ground, had a difficult time staying on its spindly legs, struggling clumsily for a short while to stay on its oversized paws, which quaintly resembled a child's mittens.

Any lover of small, mammal-type things would have found the display innocently cute. But not Frank. He was more concerned about the creature's naturally inquisitive habits than about its playfully youthful disposition. However, on the contrary, the apprehensive pup refused to budge from its stooped and hunched position, contentedly satisfied with where it was appropriately placed.

Its sole, true demonstration of interest was its feeble endeavor at sniffing the alien atmosphere around it.

"What's its name?" Frank inquired, making niggling conversation, when, in actuality, he really didn't give a rat's ass to the pet's christening as he skeptically monitored the poor, neonate mongrel while equally keeping any kind of social separation intact.

"You see, son," the old fellow began rubbing his bristled chin as if stalling for time while he shaded an embarrassed grin, which started to form around the corners of his mouth. "I thought maybe you would be able to tell me." The young man was instantly dumbstruck when hearing this odd accusation. "I thought . . . maybe it was yours, Frank," he continued as he delicately chuckled open now over the queer scenario which fate had passed to them both simultaneously searching and checking his host's youthful eyes for any kind of confirmation, in case he had misjudged the receiver's stunned expression.

"No! I mean, I'm sorry, Mr. Thownsend . . . it's not my pet," he refuted with great emphasis, shaking his head passionately at the absurdity of the question. The puppy meanwhile, stared up at the twin, predominantly superior, figures, pricking up its floppy ears, trying to comprehend what was being stated.

"What made you think it was mine?" he asked in a disconcerted tone of voice while attempting to discover some unique humor in all of this, and he glanced misgivingly down at the orphan, who likewise gaped straight back at him.

The old gent then bent down on one knee beside the animal and proceeded to stroke it affectionately again.

"It's like this, Frank," Mr. Thownsend confessed. "A couple of nights ago, my wife, Martha (uttering her name with a thoughtful smirk) and I found this dog here wandering around in the rain, poor thing. It was barking up a storm of its own, right fella!" he added, supplementing his empathy upon the creature in a sorrowful expression as he patted it on its pudgy rump. "So we rescued it . . . so . . . to speak," he concluded while looking up at the young man, who could only muster a pretentious grin from this very sad, former spectacle while expressing no real vestige of compassion whatsoever, in actual truth.

"Then we found out that someone, you, that is, had moved into the Harding residence. Anyhow, well, we figured . . ." and then he shrugged his venerable shoulders to complete his statement by trailing off into a useless mumble of ambiguity, as though he was lost for words when he considered it irrelevant to go on, comprehending that he had been innocently mistaken.

After listening to his neighbor's explanation of the events leading up to the present situation, young Frank stood for a while in utter silence, expressing deep reflection over what had been adequately formulated to his strained ears.

His next, decisive step was to sit down and think about it some more. Then, almost forgetting his manners, he proposed that his antique gentleman friend take one also. Again he accepted it benignly, except that he was not hit with the same bleary tonic as his green counterpart.

"Actually, I just moved in a few days ago," Frank declared. "You see, I'm Mr. and Mrs. Harding's son. I used to live here, too, when I was a boy," he referred in evanescent spurts while looking about somewhat pensively.

When the wise old man heard these words, his eyes lit up as if he was coming to some sort of profound, private resolution.

"Of course!" Mr. Thownsend exclaimed with surprise. "I should have known. The resemblance is uncanny," he professed and affirmed while almost jumping from his seat with excitement.

Meanwhile, the young guy, bobbing his head up and down like some crazy yo-yo, beamed with modest pride at seeing the old gent's positive reaction. And furthermore, feeling a little bit better, knowing that they had something in common after all.

"You're the spitting image of your father, Joe. You know that?" he attested, slapping his youthful knee joyfully like a juicy prime cut of veal. Then reexamining his boyish complexion for an advanced verification.

Afterward, the venerable elder grew solemn all of a sudden, and lowered his head to show deep regret.

"I didn't know your father very well, but he was a good fellow, a very good fellow indeed," he stressed with an extra dose of efficacy.

"Yes, he was," Frank replied, confirming his statement unequivocally while effectively controlling his refined emotions, which were becoming a tad undone from this informal eulogy.

"And when my parents passed away recently, I was fortunate enough to be left this wonderful house," he enunciated with his usual indifference (which we all know and love), holding out his arms to express his well-rehearsed, yet meaningful perplexity over the infelicitous circumstances.

Mr. Thownsend then glanced over at him with firm satisfactory accord, nodding his head lethargically in the process in order to properly combine their sorrows on this touchiest of subjects.

"Yet, nothing could ever really replace such splendid persons such as your kind folks were. Nevertheless, it's good to be prepared, even when the most unpredictable accidents occur."

Frank wholeheartedly agreed, and without the use of vocal ratification to prove it either. You could witness it evidently in his blank features. And that, as it was, told the genuine story here.

"What do you plan to do with it now, lad?" he questioned him rather uncompromisingly.

"Well," he responded, nearly choking on his own words, "I don't know really. I thought I might keep it," saying these choice phrases while staring up at the ceiling as if afraid of some unknown wrath from the dearly departed at his crass suggestion. "It's all up in the air right now," he explained, with a wave of his hand and returning his gaze back to the earth-bound mortals once again. Mr. Thownsend, by the way, sat complacent, quietly being heedful while reviewing what was spoken to him, apparently without a care in the world as man's-best-friend was tucked comfortably between his feet, panting in rhythmic resonance. No longer finding this pair of humans interesting, the immature mongrel passed the hour gaping innocently at nothing in particular.

Still, for some reason or another, something impulsively caught our sleuth's direct attention, as the juvenile canine came to the forefront of his brain once more while he struggled to recollect something stored way back in the furthest reaches of his dusty remembrance.

"It's quite an animal, isn't it?" Mr. Thownsend proclaimed, following the young man's visionary tract.

"What!" he cried speculatively, while nearly hopping out of his skin as his mind drifted back from an imaginary abstraction and trance.

"The dog, he's quite a species. Don't you think?" the old gent reiterated with operative niceness.

"Oh, yeah! It is," Frank corresponded receptively.

"You see . . ." Mr. Thownsend began leaning down beside the animal to steady the progressive creature, which had an idea all of a sudden in its small mind of going off snooping, "it's rather a find, if I may say so myself," he remarked while moving in closer in order to inspect its luxurious coat in more detail.

"It must be a crossbreed, see?" he mentioned as he brushed back its smooth, virgin pelt. "It's part German shepherd, but it's not quite right . . . it's fur is way too dark and thick. And its age tells me that it's way too large to be that breed," the perspicacious old man told him while being profoundly involved in the brisk examination.

Frank, meanwhile, was not the least bit interested in the puppy's pedigreed lineage, yet kept his negative views to himself, masked behind an amicable facade of regard.

Just then, the old gent stared up at his young host, glowing with delight over an instant design that had just at that very minute began to materialize in his brain like a flash of dazzling light. Frank whereas was a little taken aback by this, as he expected to hear the worst.

"Listen, Frank, . . ." he started to propose, "why don't you take care of it? It would make an excellent companion for you."

"No! No! I don't think so, Mr. Thownsend," he refuted, stuttering toward a feeble reply. "Look, please don't get me wrong. It's just that . . . I've never had a dog before, not any kind of pet at all, for that matter. I just don't think it's a very good plan or, or fair to this animal if I was to look after it. I don't have the right sort of experience to own such a thing," he protested while pleading his tactless case.

"Come on, my boy!" the old man exclaimed. "I think I can make the presumption that you're all alone here, huh?" raising a moot, uncertain eyebrow while he slowly led himself toward something that Frank had no hard, factual clue to. "So here's the solution to your problem," Mr. Thownsend submitted, filling in his question mark for him. "Think of it as an investment. It would make a splendid guard dog for this big house of yours," finishing his assertion with extended arms.

Frank, on the other hand, didn't know what to say. It actually commenced to make some sense to him as he reconsidered the daft notion.

Later, after a brief pause, Frank spoke up again.

"There's just one minor issue that we haven't addressed," he accented, aiming his forefinger at the ceiling as though attempting to emphasize a major point. "I'm not going to be in the house very often anyway. I have important business to take care of in the city first and won't be spending too much time around here. So until then, until that is all squared away, I can't be two places at once," he declared bluntly, and then he grinned a very clever grin to wrap up where he was installed on this delicate position.

"Frank, my dear lad, look, I don't want to pressure you into anything," Mr. Thownsend resolved understandably, "but I just assumed that, maybe, you would like some company, that's all. I was only saying this for your benefit," he concluded, with a smile of his own while, obviously, on his part, harnessing no ill-will towards his troubled friend.

Hearing this thoughtful sermon, the young man suddenly felt a pang of guilt over his rash objection, which seemed to harbor itself in his gut until it physically hurt.

"Okay, Frank, I'll tell you what. Don't bother yourself with this right away. I can see that I've put you in some horrible hole. Just don't make any final decisions. Just sleep on it for awhile. There's no rush really." Yet, this only made Frank feel worse as he grimaced some more over this petty dilemma.

"All right, Mr. Thownsend, you win. I'll give it a shot," he said, with a sincere radical change of heart.

"Oh! Oh, that's wonderful, Frank," he replied with gladness, totally overjoyed by this ultimate resolution.

"You won't regret this, Frank. I'll even make it easy on you," he added pleasantly. "Seeing how busy you are right now, I could watch it for you. It's still a puppy, so it will be a cinch to train," he chimed finally, telling him all this in one single breath while his mannerisms took on a childlike enthusiasm over this novel project that he was happily developing, which, albeit, was even slightly amusing to his stuffy young friend.

"I'm pretty good at raising dogs, you know?" Mr. Thownsend unraveled with modest pride.

"That's very decent of you, Mr. Thownsend," Frank responded, breaking in a harmless nuance of patronization to reveal his unfeigned appreciation.

"Oh! Think nothing of it. It's my pleasure," he said, with robust sincerity. "It will give me an excuse to have it around my place for a while longer," winking playfully at him with a Cheshire cat smirk to allow his neighbor the advantage of being able to catch a glimpse of his true intentions. Because he was indeed evidently a real lover of such things.

"I was just worried about how I'm going to find a way to talk my wife into accepting another mouth to feed. Yet this shouldn't be too difficult to convince her now, knowing that it's only going to be a temporary predicament," and he laughed sinewily to correctly phrase his authentic sense of humor.

"You know, I have several stray animals running about the house already. It's a kinda weakness of mine," he confessed confidently, making sure his statement was taken with the right gratifying attitude.

The limelighted creature had grown listless, being ignorant of the cordial transaction being organized on its behalf by this dual party of intelligent seniors, as it lay sluggishly on the sterile floor.

But hearing and recognizing the old man's spontaneous guffaw, it became instinctively attentive while they carried on with their important conversation, which was hopelessly beyond the understanding of this simple life form.

"So what sort of occupation do you have?" Mr. Thownsend asked, changing the subject to a more appropriate topic, now that the deal, or deed of, responsibility was sealed and done.

"I'm a lawyer . . . a corporate attorney to be exact, to a very prominent conglomerate," Frank stated distinctively.

"A lawyer, huh?" the old man reaffirmed, sounding redundantly impressed.

"Presently my nephew is in law school," he boasted blithely.

"It can be quite a rewarding profession," Frank added superficially, shifting restlessly in his chair from the circumlocutory inactivity, while his privately calculated perceptions filled in the wide gaps bequeathed by this uselessly garrulous void. He couldn't help but be diverted by these mental files, which he suddenly perceived needed to be resolved on an immediate, future date; and he systematically worked out all the significant agenda, which was building up inside of his workaholic brain and deliberately screened, like a larcenist from this unenlightened layman. Basically, alas, he felt edgy from a lack of knowing what else to say on that circumstantial theme, for the first time in his life, no less.

Subsequently, the truth of the matter was, he really didn't have the balls to tell poor Mr. Thownsend about this urgency, being too afraid to injure the old fella's feelings. Yet, the old gent proved smarter than that, as he instantly picked right up on the politely veiled innuendo. And sensing that he had abused his welcome and this decorous young legal eagle's hospitality, he perspicaciously decided to make his subtle departure.

"Well, I best be going," he announced abruptly while slowly getting up from his seat. The younger man, likewise, did the same, shadowing his elder's actions prudently. Then the vintaged gentleman peered worrisomely around, searching among his feet for the nearly forsaken creature. When he found it where he had originally left it, he fondled it enduringly.

"I believe it's better if I take care of it for now," he declared and advised agreeably while lightly contending to control the frisky puppy's unmanageable licking, which told the current audience that it was clearly grateful for being fussed over by this solicitous old gentleman.

"Sure! If you wish. Whatever you deem to be correct," Frank responded, carefreely unable to grasp the affection that was being expressed between the pair of them. "I really appreciate what you're doing," he uttered with truism of thanks in his shaky tone. "I hope it won't put you out," Frank delved in courteous concern as he bent down beside the duo of doting and fond sentiment and unconsciously patted the dog on its soft crown.

Once he realized what he was doing, though, he quickly removed the sinful, physical evidence, as if he had just touched something that was too hot to handle.

"Nah! My dear boy, don't mention it," Mr. Thownsend argued with satisfied insistence, while secretly intuiting his young friend's queer, embarrassed reaction, but having the discretion to say nothing.

Mr. Thownsend got up once more. His ancient bones creaking in mildly painful unison as he stretched his venerable body after tying a makeshift lead around the mutt's mangy neck from a section of thin rope that he happened to have in his pant's pocket.

"I'll return later when neither one of us is too busy. I have a lot of chores to do myself," he stated after fastening the cord tightly around its tender, immature throat. "Yet, first, I'll have to tell the Mrs. the good news," he grinned with sarcasm.

Afterward, he carefully escorted the dog toward the kitchen door, which Frank obliged by opening for them, admitting the twosome the freedom to leave.

"Thank you again," Frank said as he firmly shook his neighbor's hand farewell."

"Call me John," the old man requested while standing outside the open entrance.

"All right, John," Frank complied in respect.

"I'll try and bring it back tomorrow so it can get used to being around you and this gorgeous place of yours—oh, if it's fine with you of course?" he probed gingerly. Frank merely nodded his sibylline approval, smiling congenially, more for appearance's sake than for anything else.

"Geez, I'm sorry if I'm being a little progressive. I'm not usually like this. I'm just a bit excited for some strange reason."

"Hey, who wouldn't be. Anyway, it's forgotten," Frank commented in a remote drawl, which absolved the babbling, slipper-wearing guardian-temp in tweeds of any wrongdoing.

"Well, take care, Frank!" Mr Thownsend yelled out as he strolled away and with a single available hand waved good-bye. When he reached the end of the pathway, coaxing the pertinaciously frolicsome animal into keeping up with him, which seemed to drastically hinder his already crippled pace, he then ultimately turned westward and headed home.

The young man meanwhile leaned against his back-door arch, watching them with slight amusement while breathing in the refreshing midmorning oxygen like a restoratively invigorating bracer, wondering the whole time how he had gotten himself into this complex mess to begin with.

However, our clever, swarthy character was not without a plan.

Yes, a transcending, traversing text inserted into his etiological temple, which required divined ingenuity and minor input in order to be extracted, decoded, and revealed.

As this appealing sequence was tossed like a salad in his brain, he cooed from the tangy, photogenic results as he tampered with a lobe which tingled with a punctuated throb while an atrocious frothing was evoked from his cerebral receptacle from his widened fatuation over his introductory selection.

When man and beast could no longer be distinguished from environmental ephemera, becoming less than a glance in his accurate vision, Frank turned around and went inside himself. Closing the door behind him, he couldn't exclude the ominous thoughts that did a goose step inside his head as he resumed the challenge of cultivating the revered tasks that would take precedence over the rest of his other daily activities that he may have had.

* * *

The next day, Mr. Thownsend made good on his promise, punctually delivering the pup in the morning. And in time, this routine would become a customary ritual as both master and servant started to grow accustomed to one another's presence. The two friendly adversaries became inseparable consorts in a sort of marriage of convenience. It might not have been fraternal love exactly, but this dubious knot and match of continuance was fastidiously bound together while grazing a razor's edge of unpredictability, which only an unforeseeable term would be able to determine in an inevitable resolution. Also, during the affixed continuance, the aged gentleman became a regular visitor to Frank's posh villa, often advising his young protégé in the proper art of handling his new-found toy.

Therefore, as a far as all parties were concerned, things were running on a relatively smooth course, and in a more platitudinous meaning, as long as the delicate equilibrium was not disturbed.

Furthermore, even though they (Mr. T and Frank) equally had similar intentions in mind, if not in inveigled practice, it was their means of travel that led them onto very diverse terminations of what was taught.

Throughout this duration, the clumsily innocent pet was miraculously, undetectedly (by Frank) transformed into an organic contrivance of disciplined obedience with limited heed. In other words, its new appearance, as it improvingly turned out, pleased and surprised its young master immensely.

So during this short period of time, the weak, feeble animal of the bygone past had matured (somewhat) preeminently into a proportionately large manifestation of trained strength and intimidation. Its once undeveloped muscles and tissues were no more. Instead, it had metamorphosed into sturdy brawn, like a tank which in materiality, took on the shape of a vigorously burly guard dog. A biological machine really, whose sole purpose was to strike fear into any being that had the capacity to be a threat to king and castle. And this is what Frank had envisioned ever since that day he saw that insubstantial creature of meekness leave his property, which, incidentally, he was happy to admit and concede to notify to his conscience of never having to witness it ever forthwith again.

* * *

Over a full year and a half had passed since that initial visit as dandified Frank Harding and his housebroken dog were relaxing in the backyard of his amended, personal Riviera, when Mr. Thownsend made one of his frequent sojourns.

"How goes it, Frank? I got the message that you wanted to see me?" he called from afar.

Frank looked up from behind the financial page when he heard that conversant verse and then produced a smile for his expected neighbor.

"Hello, John! Come on over!" he cried, summoning his ageless friend over while still reclined on his back in a lawn chair. Harking these words, the old fellow made his way toward him.

The dog, meanwhile, sitting quiescently in the grass under a bosky tree, came suddenly alive, wagging its tail excitedly as it caught sight of its elderly pal walking towards him.

"Hi, boy! How are yah!" Mr. Thownsend said soothingly to the mutt.

The dog's eyes lit up and appeared to change temperament, softening in their sockets in heated appreciation while they exchanged their individual greetings. Frank, on the other hand, paid no ordinary regard to this sideshow of affection, pretending instead to be involved in the fluctuation of interest rates and economic trends.

"What do you think, Frank. Max looks really fit and healthy these days?" the old gentleman asserted with subjective honor.

"Huh! What was that, John?" Frank spoke with docile surprise putting down his paper in order to hear him more clearly.

"The dog. The dog's looking better every day, huh?" he repeated himself with a pretense of self-esteem. "What do you think?"

Frank paused for a moment, then stared up at the pair of them.

"Yeah. Sure. I guess so. It eats like a horse; it should be in condition. I imagine it goes with expensive breeding no doubt. Hey! What did you call it?" Frank implied with an insinuation that smacked of light disgust.

"Well, it has to be named something, right? Why, don't you like it?" he responded meekly, questioning its owner for his patented approval while being totally unaware of the derogatory slight.

"Hey, it's okay with me. It's fine really," Frank pacified indifferently as his mind obviously was on something else entirely, and he got to his feet, letting the insignificant pass without another phrase vocalized on its adopted title.

"Excellent, Frank. Besides, I think the name suits him," Mr. Thownsend remarked like a resplendent, responsible donor. "Anyway, I'm sure you didn't ask me to come by to discuss that. Now did you, my boy?"

"Actually no. You know what, Mr. Thownsend, I mean John," Frank corrected himself before recommencing. "There's just this one, slight problem which I am having, but I didn't intend for you to come all the way out here just to discuss my stupid gibberish. We could just as easily have settled this over the telephone, you know," Frank dappled in a reluctantly strangulating grunt.

"Nevertheless, it's nothing to worry about really," he reassured with mollification, yet sounding preposterously equivocal in his neat, palsied, twang.

Then he literally rose to the occasion to address the issue in its decorous context.

"Well, come on, Frank, spit it out. If you don't tell me what's bothering you, how'd you expect us to fix it," Mr. Thownsend spoke up, in jest, not really taking this young fuddy-duddy's distressed, vocal insertion too seriously.

"It's really no big deal actually, now that I think about it," he smirked with a whiff of embarrassment while he attempted to find some amusement for them both to share in in order to downplay the situation a little after creating such a big scene.

"Frank! Please!" Mr. Thownsend exclaimed, needing badly to know what the blazes was causing so much reduction in this youngster's usually melodious speech.

"All right, John, I'll get straight to the point," and then he soughed with alighted quandary as he debuted his bladder-aching concerns. "Anyhow, it's come to my attention that the dog, Max . . ." then hesitating for a microsecond to make sure he had the correctly befitting autograph before moving on with his overdrawn sermon. "Anyhow, it has this terrible habit of taking its naps on my bed when I'm away or when I'm not there to constantly observe and remind it not to. I've tried to keep it off, but it just ignores me. I assume this, because it keeps on doing it time and time again," he complained, releasing this dirndled allegation with an appearance of genuine frustration, which was an evident contradiction to his earlier phraseology.

"Well, that's my story basically," he noted simply while returning once more to his seat from the strenuous, tough exercise that he was forced to partake in. "Otherwise, everything is just great," finishing up by slapping his hands together and gesturing toward an indication of superficial delectation.

"Phish! Is that all! The way you carry on, I thought it was something worse, like it pooping on the Oriental mats or something. Geez, Frank, I was worried for a minute there." Mr. Thownsend reacted with a weird sense of relief. Yet Frank merely glared at his elder friend as if he hadn't quite captured the essential perceptiveness of his indisposition.

"Okay, Frank, I think I understand what you're getting at," the enlightened older man said while comprising a soft, complementary grin.

"You seem to forget that what you've got here is an animal after all. It's not an object that you can program at will to do this and that. You know what I'm saying?" he deciphered while trying gallantly to defend the "defenseless" creature.

"Mr. Thownsend, I understand that. Really I do," Frank refuted with unintentional stringency. "But it acts very strange around me. Like it's . . . uncomfortable or something. I believe it trusts you more than it trusts me," he implied, feeling a little fatuous over his exposed susceptibility.

Mr. Thownsend listened with patient empathy. Then after a brief recess and intermission, he came up with an admissible solution to this minor plight, which he judged in fairness as unobjectionable.

"I think the dog wants to distrust you, Frank. What I mean is, he needs for you to show it some kind of affection. To show that you care. You know what I'm saying?" he expounded with deep regard as ridges began to appear on his forehead from the complexity of the perplexed issue.

"You see, it doesn't know whether its all right for it to express its natural feelings around you. It relies on its instincts for survival, and I presume it must be picking up some sort of hostility from you," he implied, making certain his young friend was grasping the clarity of the complicated case.

"I'm sorry, but that's ridiculous, John. I don't know anything about that kind of stuff. All I know is, that dog is supposed to obey me," he divulged sheepishly while avoiding the old gent's piercing venerable gaze as much as humanly possible.

Yet Mr. Thownsend remained silent a while longer as he attempted to fathom this young man's sequestered personality. He just glared at him in an inadvertently condescending fashion, which disturbed the noble sublime youth very much. Then Mr. Thownsend decided again to speak his mind.

"Look, Frank, I think I can solve this problem very easily for you," he proclaimed, biting his lower lip for the extra incentive he desired. "Why don't you just close the door, pure and simple," he suggested with wide open palms.

"Wait a minute, John. I thought it was supposed to take orders from me, not me from it," he verified with a touch of acrimonious candidness.

"Yes, Frank, but give it some time, that's all," Mr. Thownsend exhorted confidently while patting the stuffy young fellow gently on the shoulder for good measure.

Then Frank's mood seemed to change a bit when he heard these stable, rectifying words.

"You must think I'm acting really foolish over this whole dumb ordeal, huh?" Frank remarked rather glumly as his character became less impervious.

"No, Frank, my boy, not at all, and everything is going to work out fine in the end, you'll see," he reassured. "Anyway, if that's all that is bothering you, Frank, I'll see what I can do," he concluded, with an additional dose of his pleasurable features, which always appeared to be in fresh supply.

"No, I guess that's it John, oh, damn! It almost slipped my idiotic mind. There's another favor that I wanted you to do for me," Frank replied while straining to collect his missing thoughts. "I was wondering if you could do something for me this weekend," he politely asked. "I would really appreciate it a lot if you would watch the house for me while I was gone. I have to go to an important conference, and I'll probably be away for a few days. But I'll contact you if it is prolonged," he stated in an unusually accessible manner.

"Sure, Frank, I can do that for you," Mr. Thownsend responded gladly.

"You can even leave the dog here if you want so it can get used to being in the house alone more often," the young man mentioned with a trace of smugness at coming up with such a suitably magnificent answer.

"Well, it is its job to protect your property anyway, so it seems like a practical idea," Mr. Thownsend informed him while attempting to make silly joke over the younger guy's eloquent formula, which merely brought a meek simper upon Frank's indefatigable face of flawless anonymity.

Mr. Thownsend smiled back in return, as if he had knowledge of some funny secret that he wouldn't and possibly couldn't, reveal to his young friend. He rose to his feet after kneeling before the incipient dignitary.

"If that's all, I'll be on my way. Oh, yes! Have a nice trip, my boy," he concluded as he shook Frank's hand farewell.

Subsequently Mr. Thownsend buttoned up his jacket, already feeling the effects of the elements upon his aged immune system in spite of the prismatic afternoon they were providentially blessed with.

But before he had a chance to leave, he was struck by an instant thought, which curtailed this action.

"So when will you like for me to drop by?" the old man inquired, turning around to confront him with this plausible inquiry.

"Well, tomorrow evening, I suspect. I'll tell you what, though. I'll give you a call over the weekend to let you know what's going on. But I should be returning sometime on Monday. And honestly, I am sincerely in your debt for this one," Frank suggested in a pretentious display of diplomacy.

"Oh! This really must be a big deal, huh?" Mr. Thownsend remarked as he snuggled up to the canine to physically gesture their informal sorrow at departing from each other until further notice, when they would be reunited once again.

"Yes, I hope so. Anyway, wish me luck."

And Mr. Thownsend did just that with sanguine optimism in his ruddy heart of impunity.

When the old gent finally left, Frank gazed pensively over at the adolescent animal still waiting patiently in his assigned corner of the world until its services were required. The creature felt Frank's intolerable eye upon it and fidgeted nervously in its neutral area from this lengthy inspection.

For a brief moment, the young man felt sorry for the infelicitous mutt as it sat in a condition of vulnerability. But that temptation soon waned and eroded away when Frank reviewed the lesson that the elder statesman had tried to instruct and educate him on. And all he could do was quote part of what was enunciated to yours truly; "Huh! Affection and caring, for heavensakes. What the hell am I anyway, fucking Mary Poppins or something."

Consequently, without further adieu on this dubiously hyped subject, he let his enterprising mind shift to more pragmatic affairs, which desired to be addressed presently if he aspired to have a perfect presentation prepared for his "big" meeting on a significant date to come.

"Come on, boy! Let's go in!" he commanded sternly, bowing low to slap his own calf with affirmation. The dog rose automatically on all fours after hearing these orders and dutifully proceeded to follow his master inside.

* * *

Later on, the young man went on his business engagement as planned and was the better for it. It proved to be a highly successful venture. And because of his unequaled dedication and determination to his prestigious firm, which he depended on for his own personal sake and for the corporate detachment, and which worked with him in this helter-skelter company, he was exactly where he wanted to be as he skillfully scaled that slick totem pole of success.

Thus after his accomplished *coup de maître,* he celebrated his good fortune (which to him was justly deserved) with a night out on the town with his fellow associates, who were more than willing to oblige.

Hence when the festivities were happily terminated and the party was officially over and all the good cheer exhaustively exploited, he decided then to perspicaciously say *sayonara* to his fellow, white collar colleagues and call it an evening. And having become the youngest vice-president in his huge corporation's long history at the ripe youthful age of twenty nine, he was a few steps nearer to being a senior partner and joint member of a distinguished establishment as grandiose such as this one was.

And if these rewards weren't enough, to add another feather into his dazzling cap, he had made a very advantageous and beneficial impression on his boss. His boss, by the way, had a very beautiful and lettered daughter (with a bloated dowry to boot!) who he personally introduced to our coltish V.P. and was dying to give away to highest bidder, which luckily happened to be him.

So our super-duper marvel boy certainly was wheelbarrowing away with the motherlode of financial fantasies. Therefore, his goal of being the big kiddo on the block was becoming an authentic reality at more than triple the pace that he had anticipated. He still believed that he had merited all these bonuses and bounties from the crafty, skillful and genteel techniques that he employed with utmost proficiency. Thus he envisioned that there was so much more to gain, and that there was no capable villainous conspiracy in the whole dog-eat-dog universe to destroy that ideal . . . so he naively thought.

* * *

Back on the road once more, the journey homeward was particularly long for him. For it was, after all, three in the morning by his own distorted recollection and account. And feeling extremely tired and worn out, he was barely able to keep his lazy sockets operative in order to focus on where he was heading. Besides, he was also suffering severely from an overbearing hangover from his previous excessive debauchery. He was fighting off this drowsiness that filled his aching skull like a technicolored cyclone.

So it was safe to assume, that he was exorbitantly relieved when he eventually returned to his humble dwelling. Then practically stumblingly from his vehicle, comparable in effect to an extortionist escaping from a very tight spot, he shuffled about in the dark, searching his pockets in anxious frustration for his misplaced keys. Frank then stopped in his tracks, bewildered by being unable to locate them. What he hadn't comprehended was that while placing his careless fingers into his trouser pocket, he had unconsciously dropped them accidentally into the thick, green grass, consequently abandoned to the earth and presumably lost forever without a trace of their former existence.

While pondering wearily for awhile over his ultimate misfortune, he actually expected, in some sordid way, that the tiny, metallic object would just reappear from out of the blue. Nevertheless, his wish was not granted, no matter whether he was promoted a junior partner or not. And so, balanced on his wobbly legs, poised there, in a helplessly pathetic state in his front yard, he peered around the giant place in a fatalistic daze, lamenting over his loss. Subsequently, while pacing the grounds, feeling somewhat disappointedly disheartened for himself, he happened to notice that his second-story window was wide open.

Thus as he stood under it, gaping dumbfoundedly up at the distant sill, his bedroom window, of all things, was practically calling his name, and to anyone else, in fact, if the had bothered to take the trouble to observe this vaunting distress signal.

At first he was terribly upset at the thought of it being unlocked for God knows how long, probably all weekend long, with his luck, and blaming Mr. Thownsend under his breath for his carelessness and absent-minded blunder, while pulling his hair out at their roots for the horrible possibilities that he negatively conjectured awaited him.

But these angry emotions quickly subsided, replaced instead with a more optimistic outlook, which had ironically sliced through his boiling brain pan like a pungent laser. And so, he embodied himself with acute cleverness, which he hadn't really earned, over what he had been given; basically the gift of entry nonetheless from this adventitious benediction. And that's all that really counted at this intense juncture in the initial end.

After realizing the mistake of his providential misfortune, he, in lieu of his petty threat toward the indicted old gentleman, actually felt like blessing the once-condemned person for his remedial negligence now. Moreover, to add to his streak of good tidings, he remembered something that would aid him in entering his house. Something which brought even greater joy to his rejuvenated heart as he hastened to the side of the building that he had deserted earlier.

There, hidden in the bushes, lying sideways in a uniformed heap and leaning against the brick wall for support like some cheap whore was a ladder.

How terrific! his thoughts shrieked in excitement as he yanked it free from its inactive posture. In the beginning though, he had a little bit of a problem releasing it. Yet, he finally found the desperate strength to pull it loose.

He then, with his hindmost drop of energy, dragged it, as if it was a crucifix, toward the front of his beloved home.

Eventually, no doubt, he was able to position it properly on a steady, diagonal surface. As he braced his tedious body to it, he stared apprehensively heavenward at the gaping hole that he urgently desired to reach soon.

After mustering enough courage, he delicately ascended the steep side of the tall structure. While climbing up, he thought about how unusually quiet it was. It was almost similar to the feeling that he had had on the night of his arrival, not so long ago, to this, his new and enduring home.

But alas, our young pal regrettably had not really seen the bold comparison that has been vividly described here. Yet the obscure inklings were powerful within him, even though he hadn't the adeptness to figure it out fully for himself. And because of his distorted reminiscence, he felt rather odd all the same as he continued to move with tender vigilance toward his objective while still bothered about being unable to place his fears.

Thus because of this over-concern, Frank temporarily lost dominance of his concentration, and in the process, he was rudely reminded of his forgetfulness by slipping through one of the rungs of the ladder.

Subsequently he regained his footing, mumbling profanities to himself in an inaudible, semidrunken slur. The jolt apparently sobered him up a bit, bringing him back to his senses somewhat as he resumed his devoted attention to the task unmercifully anointed him.

In mind and body, he was completely in tune now with the drudgery before him while he carefully mounted each slippery step in turn, moving ever closer to the summit. Alas, with all of these obstacles to shoulder, he started to grow slightly dizzy as he moved further and further skyward.

This giddiness that throbbed in his head like a tiny hammer was caused mainly by his overindulgence in the hedonistic frolic and practices of his unprofessional neglect, which he vehemently regretted ever doing, and partially from his being on such a high elevation.

Moreover, to add insult to injury, the pitiless and remorseless wind began to rear its unexpectedly ugly head as it started to act up. Blowing forcibly into his openly flustered features, hampering him constantly as if it was testing his already overexploited stamina, of all things.

Finally though, he came to the very top, after a tough struggle, and placed his trembling hands onto the window ledge for comforting support. He felt a lot better. More like himself again, which made him conceive in advance the foolish notion that the worst was essentially and fundamentally behind him.

The space was just broad enough for him to slip through, because, to tell the truth, he really didn't have the energy to make the effort to open it a wee bit wider. And in his condition, this was greatly appreciated. Anyhow his problems were far from finished while he squirmed and squeezed his tormented bulge through the narrow gap.

Subsequently he was able to get, at the very least, a leg inside, and then he had to virtually hurl himself forward slightly in order to stabilize his permanency. Similarly by establishing this scary position, he caused so much commotion that he could have awakened the dead.

And then it happened, in the wink of an eye. Right before him, was braced a ferocious monster of horrible proportion. Its begrimed sockets glared with fiery malevolency into his own frightened stunned ones. Its sharp fangs glistened in the darkness as they dripped their thirsty muck in a dull ooze around its viciously fresh gums, which, as fate willed it, would be the first and last thing he ever saw in this cruel world before he fell from that window's edge.

Therefore, as he toppled backwards with involuntary despondency, he grabbed at the naked air in a helpless attempt at survival, while suffocating on a scream, which would never be heard. His body then ricocheted off of the ladder, which in brutal reaction cast him aside like an unwanted symbiote, as the disloyal fixture held its ground while stiltedly rocking back and forth for a moment from the rude disturbance.

Ultimately though, he hit the ground with a loud thump, his shape twisted into a contorted lifeless pose, as if there was someone else inside of him fighting to get out.

After awhile, everything grew silent once more, while the corpse blended in refinely with the rest of the scenery in a final act of servitude.

Meanwhile leaning out of the window and peeking down peculiarly from above at the deleted being was man's best friend. It stooped across the sill in motionless innocence, raising its acicular ears in susceptible astonishment at the sight of the deceased form that lay face down in the dirt.

It began to bark repeatedly down at the former life. Yet this frozen caricature of amaranthine agony exhibiting its faded existence on the front lawn, was making no indication toward any response regardless of the dog's inordinate pleading.

The animal meanwhile, propped up attentively on its hind legs, supported by its powerful front paws that hugged the outer ledge, wagged is tail flaccidly, not knowing whether to jump from the high frame or merely wait obediently where it was for instructions, which of course would never come.

But eventually, the devoted creature became restive from this protracted stagnation, moaning and whimpering to itself by this disconcerted disposition.

Then the mutt tilted its head to one side in a decisive attempt to understand the significance of it all, staring futilely down upon its previous master, as it huffed conclusively to itself in deep suspire. Consequently it succumbed to the complexity of the outcome, and with rapid precision, it quietly slipped back into the solace of the bedroom.

Once inside, it impulsively leapt up upon the king-sized mattress and lay its elongated figure vertically across it. Because, quite frankly, it was incapable of any other adequately snug position to satisfy its giant, bulky mass that was produced from its hastily developed growth.

And after making itself cozy, it finally shut its unpretentious eyes to return once again to its inane slumber. Hence, like all of Mother Nature's simple creatures, it immediately forgot about the recently tragic incident, or so it appeared.

If perchance we had the ability to read the animal's mind, we would probably know that it was dreaming about its old buddy returning in the morning, and perhaps retrieving it and taking it way from here forever to a place where it really yearned to be. . . . If we were proficient enough to imagine such speculative fancies.

O let not Time deceive you.
You cannot conquer Time.
In the burrows of the Nightmare.
Where Justice naked is,
Time watches from the shadow. . . .

—*W. H. Auden*

For What It's Worth

The evening snow slowly drifted down while two men in white uniforms carefully descended the stairs of an old, decadent apartment building. In their steady grip they carried a stretcher, which seemed to give them great difficulty as they hoisted it out of the front door.

"I've got it. How are you doing on your end?" the younger of the two men said to his companion.

"Yeah, me too," the other responded, straining with his own side a little.

Once out in the open though, they both felt the cold weather's bite as they quickly heaved the stretcher into the waiting ambulance.

"Man! She was a heavy one," the older guy replied, happy to be rid of the weighty burden. The other fellow just looked at his partner and frowned. "What's the matter with you? You've been in a bad mood all day."

"Man!" the younger guy cried, "Don't you realize this is the third one this week, and it's only Thursday," while sliding the cadaver with ease into its proper compartment and then slamming the twin doors with fury from his equivocal anger.

"So what? What are you getting at anyway, Phil?" the older man asked as he locked up the back tight and secure.

"It's just . . . I don't know. It's the Christmas season, man! All these poor, old people left on their own and dying alone. Shit! It just sucks, that's all," Phil remarked irascibly.

"Hey, dude, relax. It's just a job, remember?" the elder man reminded his sidekick as he tried to cheer him up with this obvious simplicity while they both got into the emergency vehicle.

"I know that, Lenny, but it just ain't right," he complained bitterly while glaring into his friend's face.

Lenny was suddenly overcome by his associate's concern as he studied him extraneously while they pulled away from the curb.

"Come on, don't look at me like that! You know what I mean," Phil said, feeling a bit foolish about speaking his mind with so much unprofessional emotion and care.

Later, as they neared the city morgue, Lenny turned to his distraught partner.

"What you need is a good, stiff drink," slapping his buddy playfully on the shoulder and falling into a short fit of laughter over his pal's odd behavior, which didn't seem to bring much joy to his repressed colleague.

"Yeah, maybe," he commented; only in order to satisfy Lenny's need to give his experienced advice and wise counsel.

They drove through the mixture of slush and compressed snow, which the urban metropolis had ruthlessly condemned and reprobated in moderate silence while the older gentleman kept periodically peering over at his disturbed mate to make sure that he really was quite fine about the whole thing.

"Hey, Phil! Are you okay?" he asked finally, evidently not certain about his buddy's disposition, then having to strike his companion lightly on the knee in order to attract his distracted attention.

"What! Oh, yeah. I'm groovy, dude. I was just thinking about somethin', that's all," he responded cursorily while still gazing blindly ahead with a glassy-eyed stare through his semifrozen windshield.

"Hey, man, we've had worse weeks than this. Remember four months ago when we had triple the amount of work, huh. Remember? So why are you so uptight all of a sudden?" he inquired with total, honest regard toward his troubled, closest friend's exasperatingly extravagant distress.

"I know that I've been acting weird lately. I know it. Maybe it's all getting too much for me now, all this shit. I don't know," he exclaimed while attempting to do two things at once, like concentrating on the road as he drove and trying to explain his odd behavior more clearly to comply with his pal's reasonable questions.

After a brief interlude of soul searching, which amount to nil, they left the subject unresolved, floating in a refuge of limbo where it ultimately belonged evidently.

Thus, in order not to bring it up accidentally, they thought it best to remain mute for the rest of the short journey.

Later, after placing the deceased at the mortuary, they filled out the usual, official forms, and then their hard, working day was eventually final.

To congratulate themselves for a job well done, as was proudly customary, and for surviving another of many strenuous days on duty, they decided to go to a favorite hangout and have a few belts to reflect about things from another perspective. Also to forget their meaningless troubles for the time being, or just to put a couple of cocktails away, merely for the hell of it—whichever it was or whatever happened to tickle their fancy. After all, they felt they deserved a drink just for the sake of it, really. And who could blame them for believing such a tottery and easy prerogative anyway.

After downing a large measure of hard ones, they felt much better, a whole lot better, as a matter of fact.

It was getting extremely late, when the maudlin martyrs drank themselves into a state of absolute oblivion, reaching a summit of ultimate fulfillment (or close to it) in this desperate hour of need.

So on that unavoidably sour note, they called it quits for the evening, being unable to go further on their quest for total detoxification of their sensibilities.

They then left the dense hovel, drolly taunting the miseries of life. But the joker always gets to laugh at you in the grand finale of things when he sees that you have bitten off more than you can chew from the hand that feeds you. And there was no unfeigned, special tonic in the whole universe that could evaporate that utmost fact. But you had to give them credit for trying at least.

Hence, with that Faustian-based concoction to thirst upon, the elixir was sure to exude a perfume of a mendacious quality on them that would only dazzle their minds temporarily.

The younger fellow became quite verbally loud as the shuffled down the street, boasting more than his share (as usual) of suspected glory. And yet, then again, he was very much incapable of actually executing or recreating any of his supposed feats that he spoke of. In truth, he was having a hard enough time just making it home alive.

His well-proportioned elder took it upon himself to oblige in helping to escort his vocal pal, by slinging his friend's loose arm over his steady shoulder when he noticed his friend beginning to falter under the strain of the strong alcohol.

It seemed to take them forever, but eventually they reached Phil's front door, neither one of them knowing why or how they had managed to make it safely without incident.

Standing on his doorstep in subzero temperature, they expressed their complete exhaustion, which it so happened was evidently crystalline by the clear-cut signs of their inebriated lassitude and the strength of their own misty breaths. At the same time, they felt relieved to be there at that familiar spot after such a good time roister, never once caring about the consequences of how they had arrived, or even of how they had ended up at their final terminus without an iota of erratum in their sluggish step with unpremeditated, natural skills of homing pigeons as their guide.

"Hey, Lenny, ole buddy, thanks for taking me home. I think we, I, overdid it this time," he joked while stumbling into the house as the freezing weather began to bring him out of his doped state a little bit.

"No problem, man," he replied with a slight giggle as he found amusement in his intoxicated friend's clumsy entrance.

Lenny followed him inside, shutting the door behind him, while monitoring his pal's movements to make sure that he was properly behind bars, so to speak, also until he felt his helpless (or hopeless) mate was semisecure in his unpredictable actions.

"Wow, I'm really wasted!" he announced, half-saluting himself for his depredated condition, as if the whole thing was a news bulletin to his buddy, while he fell slovenly onto a nearby couch.

"I'd better be going soon. My wife's bound to kill me if I'm late again," Lenny proclaimed with partial seriousness as he aided his invalid friend in taking off his bulky workshoes.

"No, man! Don't go yet! The night is young," he complained, jumping up with great difficulty instantaneously, which caused his head to spin and swirl in a ninety-degree angle of torment and torture, and which he attempted to remedy quickly by easing back onto his pillow.

"Hey, what's wrong with you, Phil, feeling a little tipsy, huh?" he remarked playfully to his dizzy pal while taking the supremely golden opportunity to poke fun at his buddy's comical condition.

"Let's get another bottle. What do you say? I ain't finished yet," Phil replied stubbornly in a semiconscious slur while adjusting the tiny pillow that he cradled like a toddler to meet his awkward requirements for creature comfort.

"You were finished an hour ago," Lenny corrected him, still finding a small enjoyment from his buddy's personal overindulgence.

"Look, I'll tell you what," the perspicacious elder man stated with the absence of jest. "I'll go down to that twenty-four hour deli down at the corner and buy us something to eat. Seeing how you never seem to have anything stocked in this pad of yours worthy to consume," he remarked jeeringly at his host's lack of provisions for a truly laudable bachelor home.

The younger man sprawled out on the couch, made no real acknowledgment of his companion's request and reprehension as he drifted to the shoal of disturbing sleep.

The older man merely grinned at him, as though watching a child dream an innocent dream.

He decided to put the television on. It might ease his troubled slumber some. Furthermore, it appeared too quiet in this lonesome place for the likes of him anyway. He always felt you could relax better if there was some source of sound in the atmosphere to sooth your mood more easily.

He flipped the numerous channels until he found something that resembled intelligent programming.

"All right, Philip, old pal, you just sit tight, and I'll be right back," he mentioned in full understanding of his buddy's comatose deafness.

He left the house with an accidental slamming of the front door, and at that instant, like Pavlov's dog, the dead awoke in a drunken stupor.

Phil noticed immediately that he was alone; he sat up trying to regain his missing memory and composure.

He attempted to rattle the drowsiness from his dusty mind. But it was a losing battle that he fought, not having the strength to compete with such powerful forces.

Then he discovered to his mild amazement that the TV was on.

He glared at its busy screen with strenuous insignificance, in a sort of Cro-Magnon-man-meets-twentieth-century-technology style and depiction type of thing.

He eventually, though, was caught up n the basic, meaningless plot with its fatuous drama on a creative tight rope of genius for his sole pleasure across his shaky attention span.

Inevitably, he would slip and devolve back into his original specification as his eyelids grew heavy while he let himself go relentlessly in a soft Apollo landing on a cushion of deep sleep.

In his ears though, he could still hear the cheap dialogue spoken by the characters inside the twenty-seven-inch box as their synthetic voices trailed farther and farther away on a haze of somnolence.

At the other end of the spectrum though, he appeared, in his wobbly imagination, to being forced to melt and blend within and into the thick living glass of color, which drowned out his very own senses, tempting him completely with an inadvertent form of ecstasy and curiosity, as you will, to venture inward.

Thus, like some special kind of magnet, he was propelled through space and transposed and mutated perfectly into a realistic vision that seemed in his brain to be very clear and strangely familiar.

The stage was set in a tiny apartment not much bigger than the room he had just left behind. He envisioned an old woman in her late eighties nestled comfortably in an armchair, into which she appeared to integrate in odd distinction with, as if they were one and the same.

She had purposely placed herself directly in front of a television set, which was not that much different from his own, as a matter of fact, except that hers was an impeccable replica of her own personality and stature. She was so close to it, that her weak eyes practically bulged in their sockets from the affects of such snug complicity and contact.

Yet, for all practical purposes, it saved her from making too much of an effort or sacrifice to move at all in order to turn the dials to her favorite form of interest, if she ever felt the need, desire, or inclination to do so. Moreover, there was also no chance of her missing something "important" on the entertainment center either, while she was permanently situated and glued to its seducing power.

But for the time being, this didn't seem to pose any major obstacle or primely demanding proposition to be dealt with by her at the moment. For she was utterly engrossed and satisfied in what she saw before her. It was hard to tell, really, which was more alive or who was viewing whom, she or her more active machine, which appeared to have an existence far greater than her own no doubt.

Its sole function it seemed was to fuel her little orbit with substance and meaning, bringing to her true evidence of her very own entity and of that of the outside world.

Her tired, worn-out concentration scanned the frame with vigilant concern, as if starving for nourishment in an imaginary hunt for more rewarding consumption.

She was so absorbed with the artificial characters that whatever emotions or passions they experienced, she also seemed to believe, in a queer fashion, was what she felt, too. Barnacled and parasitical feelings that she needed to imitate, while lacking any genuine ones of her own.

Their pain was equally hers, as was their happiness. When they expressed, she embraced, as though a figurative umbilical cord held them sentiently together somehow. All for one and one for all, as the saying goes.

Every so often, she would intermittently break her own silence by involving herself in the prearranged conversation and confabulation, volunteering her views and reflections every possible chance she got.

"Be careful, Josh. Don't let that harlot fool you again," she would warn the fragments of energized dots that made up one of her favored and recognizable images on her screen.

But evidently, the actor was unaware of her helpful advice, and would do the recited, prearranged opposite, which ended up upsetting her very deeply.

"I told you. I told you not to trust her. She's no good. I told you she was trouble," she would chastise the ignorant vision which was being held prisoner by a planned script that she naively took no heed of.

While she lost herself in the TV drama, she suddenly heard an ulterior noise, which appeared to irritate her very much, revealing to her that she was still a part of this principally universal stage after all. Something would often attempt to dissuade her from her preferred fantasy platform. If she was fortunate enough, this disagreeable distraction could sometimes be totally dissolved with her own specific touch of sheer audacity, while her small group of players in a limited square of their own irregular authenticity would welcome and cajole her back to them, where she conclusively believed she belonged anyway.

She would try on countless occasions to ignore these constant interruptions to her more acceptable illusion. Yet this became too difficult a task at times to dismiss and dispel. Nonetheless, only sometimes would this luxury be possible. In many incidents she was unable to accomplish this though, as we shall inevitably see.

The cause of the annoying disruption appeared to be coming from the apartment above. Subsequently, she unnaturally rose from her chair and yelled up at the ceiling. Yet the thunder continued on regardless of her persistent calls.

Sensing that she had no other alternative, she searched her humble dwelling for her trustworthy walking cane. Once she had it in her arthritic, firm grip, she wielded it with what feeble might she had at the source of the vexatious sound, banging demandingly for a restoration of order and stability.

After a few thrusts, the mysterious thumping from above came to a sudden halt. When she felt satisfied with her stern, objective methods, she placed her tool of affirmative action in its placid corner and returned to her already missed episodes on the precious tube.

When she was comfortably seated once more, she heard a faint rap at the door. For awhile she tried to shun and block this out too, but ultimately, this intrusion just wouldn't go away as easily either.

Instead of getting up to answer it, she sat there and yelled at the disturbance behind the locked barrier.

"Go away! Can't you leave an old woman alone in peace!" she cried in a strong trembling tone.

"Open the door, Mrs. Ryan. It's only me," a kind voice spoke from beyond a dead-bolt security.

When she recognized the intonation, she immediately got up to answer the request without too much fuss this time. Even though she knew who it was, she seemed even more reluctant to open the door, but she knew she would have to eventually.

Thus, as she carefully unfastened a few of the many chains and bolts that adorned her fortress-home with slight caution, which complemented her natural quintessence with the utmost accuracy, she still felt she needed to peek through a crack in the half-closed door. While the offer of ingression was held back momentarily from a state of ineffectual indisposition on her part, if this particular person on the other side had wished or deemed it proper to force their way in, there was really nothing that this insignificantly fanciful and venerable lady could possibly do to stop it, no matter what sort of determination she might have to exhibit.

What she saw didn't really surprise this ancient hermit in the least, seeing that it was probably the only, single visitor that she had these days. It was, after all, the face of an acquainted middle-aged woman smiling back at her. A civil servant or social worker, to be specific, whose valuable services were never appreciated around here, yet greatly required and necessary just the same.

"Hello, Mrs. Ryan. It's just me, Mrs. Simpson. Won't you let me in please," she said gently at her mistrustful sentry's partially concealed, "fearless" features.

The old woman, without speaking a syllable, released the final, flimsy latch and let her in. Yet, she didn't even invite her in actually, but instead, left her standing with deliberate embarrassment in the hallway as she returned to her still warm seat and resumed her habit of glaring at the seductively enticing electronic contraption.

Mrs. Ryan's unwelcome guest didn't seem to be at all fazed by her hostess's eccentric actions, having grown used to this sort of behavior by now.

Mrs. Simpson let herself in and placed a light bag of groceries on the kitchen table.

"I came to see how you are doing today," she mentioned while sorting through the sack of goods to make sure everything was there.

She finally found what she was seeking, pulling out a hand-sized, plastic container and a picayune, imitation pine spruce that was supposed to represent the holiday spirit.

"Here, I brought you your medicine. I hope you have finished using the last prescription that I brought you the last time," she said, holding it out for her to see, like a trophy or something to her inconsiderate patient.

Mrs. Ryan didn't even bother to look at her gift. Moreover, she felt the presence of this solicitous caretaker as an increasing nuisance instead.

This obviously rude benightedness was supposed to have the same affect as on any would-be trespasser, in the form of an objection to her personal invasion of privacy, treating this beneficial offering as a discordant intrusion, like some cold chill breaking into her solitary dwelling from the frigid, cruel world outside.

"And I brought you some soup . . . the kind you like," she announced, keeping her hospitable chin up through it all, accustomed to this kind of acid treatment and reaction of nonverbalization from her obstinate patient.

Cheerfully she put the assortment of medicinal and various foodstuffs on the countertop to proudly display her ample bag of supplies. She then proceeded to place the little, amaranthine evergreen of man-made genius on top of the more important, the almighty, center of entertainment, and on everything else that came remotely close to being in between, which the dowager enchantress dutifully ignored with Queen Victoria snootiness.

Eventually she grew tired of the old lady's detached attitude.

"I think you should switch that set off for a couple of hours and get some rest," she commented, with a defiant, vocal stance, which she emphasized by putting her hands on her solid, maternal hips in added, serious provocation.

When she realized that she wasn't receiving any positive feedback, she moved in a bit closer until she stood right over her.

"Mrs. Ryan, dear, why don't you give this thing a break for a little while, huh?" she stressed, attempting to use a more compassionate approach this time around.

"Don't you dare touch it! I'm watching this! Leave it alone, and leave me alone!" she barked malevolently while making a superhuman sacrifice by pulling her eyes off of the TV for a second or two to make sure her point was properly taken.

"Now, now, Mrs. Ryan, you're not going to give me any problems today, are you? I won't touch it if you don't want me to. But I think you should get some sleep. What do you say? An hour or more isn't going to hurt you now, is it?" she replied, knowing her own limitations full well while assuming that it was in her own best interests to back off from this sticky one for the time being.

"At least let me help you get more comfortable. . . . You see, isn't that a lot better, hhmmm?" she mentioned in a cooing sound in order to be diplomatic with his troublesome case while she fussed over her a little bit.

"Please stop that! Can't you see that you're in the way!" she complained and grumbled and gestured to her to move aside as she tried to fight her off and catch as much of the program as she possibly could, while the band of afternoon thespians inconveniently carried on with their merry play, without her needed assistance of course.

"Mrs. Ryan, I'm only trying to help you. Now please be a good girl and sit still for a minute," she hushed her feisty tribulation.

Ultimately though, the frail, old woman gave in, making no headway with this unreasonable person who refused to stop meddling into her individual, domestic freedom and common, simple affairs. *If I let her have her way for awhile, maybe she will do what she has to do and then go away,* she thought with sly contempt.

After awhile, Mrs. Simpson completed rearranging Mrs. Ryan so that she would be more cozy and acquiescent.

"There, isn't that a lot better," she remarked with soothing satisfaction, smiling in gentle kindness at an expression of devout inconsideration as it showed no inclination toward any sort of gratitude whatsoever.

"Now, Mrs. Ryan, how about lying down for a while, huh?" she asked in a calm, mollified tone, indicating to her covertly to turn off the overly commercialized device laying in depredation before them.

The old woman just leered at her, as she would at someone who she presumed as an intruder that was interfering with her peace of mind.

"I told you before, I'm perfectly capable of looking after myself. So please leave me be!" she hollered in a weak argument, losing her temper a little, which caused her lower lip to quiver nervously from the brief, accidental outburst.

"Well, we both know that, Mrs. Ryan. Yet sometimes I wonder how you get through the day, for heavensake. Now don't get yourself all worked up. You know how that can effect your poor system. After all, I'm only here for your benefit," she stated in her most improved bedside manner.

"Anyway, Mrs. Ryan, dear, it's about time that you got yourself into bed. And to make sure that you do just that, I'm not going to budge from this room until you do. . . . All right then, up you go, and make certain that you take your pills before you fall asleep tonight. Okay, Mrs. Ryan?" she said while switching off the tube with as much discretion as she could exercise at the moment.

Nonetheless, the aging biddy wasn't fooled one bit as she monitored this open disregard of compassion. A deliberate infringement on her fundamentally minimal pleasures, which was packed with hostile regret on her part.

It felt to her as if someone had placed a dagger in her heart, twisting it with a remorseless fist until it took the life force right out of her.

"Well, I'd best be going now. Oh, yes, and be sure to take some of your medicine when you get up, the first thing that you should do, all right, dear? . . . And I'll see you later," Mrs. Simpson told her quite pertinaciously as she tucked her carefully under the covers. "I'll probably be back sometime next Wednesday to check up on you. So get plenty of rest and quit straining your poor vision on that darn television set of yours. All right?" Mrs. Simpson lectured while putting on her coat in order to head directly out the door.

Yet, the widowed Mrs. Ryan no longer heeded her existence as she ogled with transfixed rage over at the blank screen.

The woman who played at being her nurse was about to add something, but then didn't, and she smiled in pale expectation instead. She thought it best to make a swift departure, sensing that she had done her absolute duty. Furthermore, she wanted to flee from here anyway, having had enough of aiding this despairing creature. And that, unfortunately, was the guilt that she had to bear.

When she was gone, the old woman came back to life somewhat, having regained her latitude once again. But the taste was kind of displeasing, to say the least. A mixture of relief and remorse at being left by herself once more, which were very strange bedfellows to nestle with indeed.

"Who does she think she is anyway. Coming into my home as though it was her very own, and then taking over my life," she muttered to herself as she climbed back out of bed in order to reach for the precious button, the knob of potency.

Outside the door, the woman walked on a bed of nails as she descended the long staircase. But before she had a chance to make a clean break, she faintly detected a familiar sound from where she was positioned at the bottom of the stairs.

She waited in the nondescript hallway perfectly motionless, stretching her inner senses to absorb the vibrations filtering down from above; yet it was too dense to fully appreciate actually.

She thought she heard other voices and extraneous laughter coming from Mrs. Ryan's room, but she couldn't be positively accurate on that account.

Thus, even though she was mildly curious, she had more of an urge to run. She always felt as if she couldn't breath properly whenever she was in this morbid place, needing to embody the fresh air outside as quickly as possible once again, for some unexplained reason.

As she escaped through the entranceway, she felt brave enough to grin at her own tomfoolery while she briskly strolled toward another urgent engagement downtown, inferably somewhere very far from here.

From the window above, the pain wearied, feeble eyes feverishly scanned the form of an adult female rushing rapidly down a nameless street.

The window pane was all frozen over with crystallized ice, except for a tiny section of it that the old woman used to peek from.

After watching this sad spectacle, she returned to her popular spot near to the TV set.

Then, like magic, her once rueful images were mysterious, distracted, and disremembered by the more tantalizing ones that she wished to absorb into her brain, all manufactured and fabricated inside that special box of amusement. All for the viewer's enjoyment no less.

In time, she totally forgot about the former contemptuous visitor, and taking with her her more contemptuous world as she gaped like some enthusiastic junky into the bountiful screen.

For awhile everything appeared back to normal, which suited our finicky customer just fine.

Then, out of drastic oblivion, the picture started to flicker about, slowly in the beginning, then at a more violent pitch. At first, she just let this minor scare pass, hoping that it would either go away or repair itself somehow.

But, it grew worse with each passing second, until she was unable to make out anything recognizable. It swirled erratically into a mass of wavy lines of random precision, similar in affect to a beehive swarm of virtual reality. She, alas, couldn't take this much longer, as the tension started to rage inside of her; neither could be controlled at this point, unfortunately.

She cursed at the dysfunctional tube for depriving her of her bargain entertainment, which brought this scarecrow of flesh and bone to her aching feet in a fit of anger and fury. She started banging indiscriminately upon the top of it, wrestling with its stiff antenna until the stem broke off in her clumsy grip, which in turn upset the tiny fake tree that plummeted to the carpet unnoticed.

She was so dithered that she became paralyzed for further judgment. Outside of her bewildered consciousness, she could hear the detraction and deterioration coming through from the television monster while it hissed and spat defiance and provocation at its owner.

This disobedience only made her more infuriated with the unruly contraption. She began to yell at it next, with desperation as her weapon; it took just about all of the strength she could muster at such short notice.

The insane screen became such a jumbled mess of disorganized patterns that it was almost madly hypnotic. A drab gray, fizzled setting was all that remained from her strenuous efforts, leaving both parties, it appeared, to ensue over what could be done to remedy the seemingly fatal results.

At this juncture, she was quite frantic and distraught, and she brought both hands down in fists of mania upon the unprotected television set. Then, like a bad dream, everything went vacuous and vacant in the mind of its electronic brain, and only a brief flash remained for a split second, until it was unavoidably sucked into a fathomless crater of vacuity. A woefully unhappy keepsake and a symbolic reminder of what it had once been was all that she was left with as a farewell valedictory, sunk into unmerciful death within its very own screen, leaving no trace or hope of optimistic renewal.

The old woman watched this intensively, and when it was over, her soul seemed to have been taken along with it. That was when she began to weep in an eruption of deep hysteria, crying to her beloved loss, like a mother losing an only child.

"Come back! Please don't go!" she begged, being unable to accept the fact that this adoration could undoubtedly cause her own demise.

A great agony was breached in her decrepit chest, and she was incapable of sustaining the grief that was feeding it.

Delirious, she fell to her knees as if she was praying to a holy and pious idol that was elevated before her on a table top altar.

"Take me with you. Don't leave me here alone. Please take me with you . . . *plleeaassee!*" she wept over and over and over again.

Just then, everything phased out. And from the depths of a nightmare, a reassuring voice could be heard coming into focus.

"Hey, Phil! Wake up, man! What's wrong with you, dude?" Lenny exclaimed while shaking the lifeless body into some sort of normal function.

Suddenly a pair of eyes opened and concentrated its blurry view on a familiar face that happened to be staring straight back at him, helping reenforce Phil's visionary travail a trifle.

Then our bedazzled utopian sat up abruptly in alert confusion as though ready to meet his maker.

"Hey, Phil, old buddy, it's me, Lenny. Are you all right, kid?" Lenny inquired tenderly.

"I'm fine now, thank you, I think," he responded while still in a semidazed state and being crudely reminded of his disoriented condition by his concerned friend's constantly irritating shaking of his fragile form, which seemed to be more damaging than helpful at the moment as he was cognizant enough to make such a wisecrack, while he attempted to regulate himself to his usual surroundings.

"You frightened me to death there for a moment," Lenny revealed to him with excited humor when he noticed his dormant pal coming out of his deep slumber.

"I had this very weird dream. But it was so real," he stressed out loud as he struggled with his jumbled thoughts.

"I'd say! You said some pretty odd stuff. I thought you'd gone crazy or somethin', man," he added, trying to find some comedy in this otherwise embarrassing situation.

Yet, the younger guy wasn't listening, being too engrossed in his own dark fantasy while attempting to analyze his way through this disturbing maze.

"But it couldn't be a dream. It was much too real, and so vivid too, and so alive," he thought outwards once more.

"Hey, brother, relax. It's all right. You're probably still under the influence of that damn alcohol. That's the last time I take you out drinkin' again," the older gentleman suggested mockingly, while flirting with this individual's tormenting questions and doubts that his friend was forced to deal with presently.

"Yeah, I guess you're probably right. You're always so damn right, aren't you, Lenny?" he replied more soberly while appeasing his friend's skill at understanding it all with a tenuous smirk, allowing his elder to have this insubstantial portion of dignity, yet, on the other hand, not really believing it himself while he sat up erect.

"Damn right, Phil. Here! I made you some coffee while you were snoozing. Careful, it's very hot." Lenny, the wise one, advised while handing him the kitchen mug.

As he drank from the fat cup, he noticed that the television was off and impulsively he raised a dubious eyebrow in ultimate surprise at this new strange development.

He then glanced over at his buddy for some kind of blind reinforcement, who happened to be lounging now in a nearby armchair stuffing his pudgy cheeks with cheap food and such, dying to ask him for his astute, sagacious insight, wanting and itching to tell him something that only he could possibly solve. But then, he decided against it at the hindmost minute, having had enough jolts to last him double lifetimes.

"It wasn't actually that important anyhow," he surmised while he sipped his steaming coffee gratefully.

Then all of a sudden, he chuckled to himself with glee, which was comparable to a mad man happy in his own preposterousness, undoubtedly contemplating how wonderful it was to be alive after all. And he embraced this unique sense of joy, which he felt internally like a welcome, accessible ghost, letting its juices of vitality flow through him where they will.